Breaking the Girl

By

M. C. Webb

Breaking the Girl

This novel contains graphic content. It is suitable for mature readers only.

Breaking the Girl

Dedication

To my aunt Janice.

Thank you for giving me that DoubleDay Romance

Library membership when I was twelve.

Best. Gift. Ever.

And to all the Paytons of the world.

Do what you must,

just survive.

Breaking the Girl

Prologue

-

Axel

Metal security bars obscure my view, but don't completely block out the wandering boy and his dog. Though I avert my gaze, I can still see him in my periphery—dirty bare feet, ragged blue jeans, and faded shirt. His hair is dingy from dirt, but it would probably be dark blond when washed. I have yet to see his eyes clearly but know for certain they are dark and sit slightly sunken while bluish circles surround the lost orbs.

Is he hungry today? Does his heroin addict of a mother know he feeds the mutt his mission food or is she too far gone to care anymore?

Helplessly drawn to the figure, my gaze slowly turns his way to see what's new today. Like the times before, his is head down and his gait slow as he keeps to the shadows of the buildings. It's as if he fears the sun's rays. This nameless boy haunts me for days after I leave the dark confines of Barb's cramped office, and I know with certainty, today will be no different. I'll take the image of the homeless preteen with me when our meeting finally ends. I will attempt to approach him again today, offering money and shoes. He will again run from me.

Tinkling giggles pull me back to the business at hand.

"No, no that's fine with me," the girl says too eagerly.

The boy leads his shaggy dog down an alley and out of sight.

"Axel?"

Barb's masculine voice makes my skin crawl, and I catch a glimpse of my reflection in the window. The image looks mean, cold and I know I've only grown harsher the past couple of years. Funny how being sober can actually make a person worse in some ways. A white hot pain licks up the side of my neck, creeping, crawling slowly to the center of my left eye where it sits and waits to split my skull open at just the right moment.

"We need you to sign," Barb says to my back, not at all hiding her impatience.

Giving the alley one last glance, I turn to finish what will be my last contract this summer.

"Almost done, Candi," Barb tells the girl I've spent the last month training with and I suddenly want to laugh.

Almost done?

Not by a long shot.

Yes, this signing is the end of the road with me, but Candi will undoubtedly be in films, lots of them, and she will never be *done*. This decision will follow her for the rest of her life.

That thought gives me pause and the conversation I tried to tune out of a moment ago becomes much clearer. Taking my seat at the cheap, round table, I ignore the producer, David Magardo, to my left, as well as Barb, the bane of my existence and business partner to my right, focusing straight ahead on Candi. Her bright blue eyes are made even brighter by whatever pill she popped this morning, self-tanning, and platinum blonde hair. Her double-D breasts are on display in her very short, low-cut dress.

The girl would be pretty if not for the heavy makeup and perky role she constantly played. I alone in this room know she's never happy, sometimes drinks way too much, and cries when she calls home. She's young— too young to know what she's doing, yet old enough to choose it all. I've prepared her for everything and now, I let her go in peace.

"Did you stipulate you want a companion of your choice on set with you?"

Candi blinks quickly as if the thought escaped her.

"There will always be an assistant to see to her needs, Axel," Magardo mumbles uncomfortably.

I give the girl a hard stare.

"What he means is his camera guy or *his* assistant," I address Candi, ignoring Dave all together. "I told you to request this be added, otherwise you are their property and will be at the mercy of whoever is on set. At least with a companion, they can look out for you if something goes in a direction you are uncomfortable with."

Like you land in a gangbang with total strangers when you were only expecting girl on girl.

Candi glances uncomfortably at Barb, then Dave.

"Uh, yeah. I need to have someone with me, a friend or someone," she says uncertainly.

I tap the table absently with my forefinger, knowing all Candi wants is the sign-up money with the promise of more. Dave makes a note on the form and lets Barb, then Candi read it.

"This is less money than it was just a few minutes ago?" Candi says, surprised. "Why is it less?"

Her eyes dart from the pages to Dave, to me, then back to Dave.

"The cost involved in shooting changes if you want a *companion* with you while you film. The more terms you add and longer this takes, the less I'm willing to offer," Dave threatens.

Candi's eyes water ever so slightly and I know what's coming. Even though I'm a hypocrite, and even though I was one of those strangers on film for countless girls over the course of my career, I fucking hate what she's about to do.

"I don't need anyone with me if you will honor the amount from before."

"Agreed, now get Axel to sign and I can give you the check."

When the pages are slid to me, I sign, releasing Candi to film at will. I inwardly grimace at the fact I'm most likely the only one in the room who would actually honor a contract. An equally sad and ironic thought, but now I can only eye the door, longing to escape these people and this life for a while.

The boat is ready. The alcohol is stocked, along with the food and my favorite fishing gear. *All that's missing is me.*

I hate all of them, I hate all of *this.* Grinding my teeth, I fight the creeping darkness in my heart.

"Axel?" Barbs pulls me from my musings when the paperwork is complete.

I try to concentrate on the business at hand. Barbara can sense my foul mood and pats her short red hair nervously before smoothing imaginary lines on her black slacks. She attempts to look attractive and professional, and she succeeds to a cheapened degree, but I see her she-devil horns even if no one else does. And just behind her square reading glasses are the coldest, cruelest green eyes I've ever seen. Barb will never be more than a briefcase pimp trying to hold on to her youth to me. What was she now? Had to be close to fifty, maybe more. She was in her mid-thirties when I was a teenager just starting in the business.

The crow's feet around her eyes deepen and my focus sharpens as I realize both she and Dave are staring at me.

"What?" I almost growl.

"We were just wondering if you would consider adding a couple of girls to your schedule. Maybe you could take one with you on your *vacation* and train her on the boat?"

The word *"vacation"* left her pencil thin lips like a curse word. Barbara hates me taking time off and fights me tooth and nail every chance she gets.

I understand what she said, the conniving bitch that she is.

"On the boat?"

A female, on a boat with *me*. That would mean she would have to share my bed and fuck no, that's not happening. I don't want anything to do with the girls other than training them, and that is plenty, *thank you very much*. The very thought of being confined in a small space with one makes my stomach clench with anxiety.

"Uh, no. Again, I have a set schedule, Barb. I'm not changing it. I'm finished working for now."

I glance to Candi and she gives me a sad smile, knowing everyone is talking around her like she's not in the room. Once her check was given to her, she was no longer of importance. I give her a narrowed expression, trying to convey the hard truth that, as of now, she's nothing but a performance act.

Get used to it, sweetheart, it only get worse from here.

One

-

Payton

Oh God, I'm going to puke.

I'm going to throw up right as we land!

Is this plane supposed to rattle? Oh God, here comes those awful flight peanuts I knew I shouldn't have eaten. Shut up Payton, you're making it worse...and now I'm telling myself to shut up. I have clearly lost my mind at this point.

In my defense, I've never flown before, never traveled outside of Mississippi, let alone across the country to Los Angeles. Licking my lips nervously, for what has to be the thousandth time during the flight, I try my best to practice the deep breathing techniques I read about mid-flight only to give up and start talking to myself, internally at least, again. The vibrations of the plane's descent send me further into panic mode.

Oh sweet Jesus, don't let me die in a crash landing, a fiery slide down the runway, or an explosion on touch down. Nobody will ever know I'm dead, not even Ben.

Shaking my head to clear the thoughts, I take deep breaths to calm my nerves. The roar of wind doesn't seem to bother anyone but me as I glance around at the passengers. All are smiling or packing up their various crap while I have a mental break down, picturing the scene from *Lost* in loop in my head—the plane nose-diving, the fire, that God-awful buzzing noise from the fuselage.

Unaware I'm holding my breath, my lungs protest the lack of oxygen and I suck in air repeatedly. An elderly woman to my left touches my arm and I can't stop the jerk of surprise. Her watery eyes set deep in a crinkled face stare at me with pity.

"It'll all be over in a few minutes, dear." The woman's ancient voice matches her weathered face. "Relax and let your mind wander on whatever brings you to the west coast."

Biting back an unforgivable curse, I say nothing, smiling a little in response so not to appear rude. The woman knew this was my first plane ride and tried to soothe me with kind words throughout the flight. It was both comforting and annoying because I really wanted to breakdown without an audience. I try to relax back in my seat and let my mind drift, closing my eyes so as not to encourage more advice from the woman, who probably has two dozen grandchildren on whom she uses the same petting technique.

Nearing hyperventilation levels, I force my mind on something other than my current surroundings. The same image comes to mind more than once. Gripping my armrests, I envision what awaits me in California.

A tight, lean body like a runner's. Defined muscles—not too big, but enough to place him in the hot category.

Yet, it's those incredibly dark brown eyes set against a chiseled face that make my knees weak.

And I get to be with him for an entire month.

That's thirty full days of sleeping in a bed, eating real food, and showering somewhere other than a truck stop. I haven't done that now for months. Living homeless is exactly what everyone thinks it is, wretched and the worst kind of lonely anyone can imagine.

I wake every day and immediately struggle to figure out where to sleep the next night without being raped or robbed. Every night, I sleep maybe two hours at a time before moving on to a different spot under a pier at the beach or a bathroom stall of a rest area. It's a constant battle against panic and hunger, unless it's one of the rare occasions I win a few bucks from a bikini contest or a girl-on-girl Jello fight. That helps, and I'm not ashamed to do it. It at least puts something in my stomach.

One constant thought pushes me forward each day— Ben. I have to survive and believe everything will somehow be all right again. That I can find my way back to him, back to where I left him. That's all that matters, so when I was approached a few days ago by a man from the adult film industry who offered me the opportunity to be "trained" by Axel in the hopes of making real money, I jumped at the chance.

Okay, not really at first. I was grossed out in the beginning, but then I saw him. Even through a computer screen, his animal magnetism called to me. I saw him in all his glory going down on a girl with such passion and ferocity, I jumped at the chance to be in her position. The promise of a place to live and food was only icing on the stud cake.

Flashes of Axel's eyes play on loop in my mind. I can't wait to see them up close…as well as other parts of the man.

I was so intrigued by the idea of staying with Axel, I agreed to everything, abandoning all other questions entirely. Even though both Liz and Randell, the husband and wife recruiters, warned me Axel may not be in the greatest of moods considering I was throwing off his very punctual schedule, I didn't hesitate when I was given a plane ticket and instructions on how to prepare myself.

New clothes and an array of spa treatments were provided, at their expense. Hair, nails, and waxing. *Oh God…the waxing.* I could live the rest of my life without another woman ripping the hair off all my girl parts. If I whined, she only grunted and worked faster. It was a mortifying experience, but it went with the program, I suppose, and the results make me feel like a kitten ready to be petted.

A vibration in the plane's descent shakes me from my thoughts.

Don't puke Payton, do not puke. Almost there.

My body hums with anticipation of seeing the Greek god-like creature I've obsessed over for days. The fact he is the most downloaded, most followed, and most gorgeous porn star *ever* only makes me slightly nervous. Okay, it makes me want to pee my pants, but who better to get the job done than a pro, right?

A jolt and roaring engines tells me we landed safely.

Thank God we didn't crash.

Everyone begins the slow process of exiting to the terminal. Following the line in silence, I walk through the boarding area and off to the side, ducking behind a decorative column I can only assume is supposed to look like something from Rome.

Doing my best to look normal while peering anxiously through the clusters of weary travelers, I search for Axel, hoping I can find him before he sees me. I don't know why, but it's important for me to examine at him without any influence over his actions. I circle around with my one small roller bag, then spot him leaning against his own column, appearing bored and uninterested while taking periodic glances up from his phone.

Axel Stone is magnificent in the flesh, even more so than on camera. Standing with one foot over the other, his weight resting against the pillar, he's oblivious to the looks he gets from both men and woman as they walk past. I can tell by their faces, they think he's famous and stifle a snicker as I watch one woman openly point toward him and giggle to her friend. I can't blame them. The man is a true, magnificent Alpha male and I cannot wait to be under his beautiful body as he does dirty, *dirty* things to me.

Self-consciously, I smooth out my shirt, take several deep breaths to calm my nerves, then stroll casually to where Axel stands waiting for me.

Two

-

Axel

Noise surrounds me. A man and woman off to my left are arguing, a baby is crying somewhere in front, and an elderly woman is pushing a squeaky cart slowly toward the elevator. All this and the constant hum of the lights and meaningless chatter of others milling about wrecks my nerves. I look up and around for the girl, then back down at my phone impatiently before returning my gaze to the crowd of haggard-looking passengers waiting for their bags. I scan each face as they walk mindlessly to the luggage claim.

Why the fuck did I agree to this again?

Oh yeah, the money. I'm getting paid double for this girl, and she'd better damn well deliver. Barbara promised me a ten. Hell, I've seen sixes and sometime sevens but never a ten, which would mean top-dollar signing, high-end bookings. Even so, this shot my vacation to shit, and we were nowhere on schedule. And I'm always on a schedule. Always. Limited times a year, thirty-day training sessions.

Of course, Barbara thought I should be working more. I tried to work less and less and as she constantly reminded me, I was costing her money by not agreeing to more. Now, in the middle of July, I'm adding one? I shake my head in frustration. But I know why I really agreed, and it's not just the extra cash.

"Please, Axel?" Barbara begged. "I know we are contracted out for the rest of the year, but this one is special. She's delicious. A fucking ten, Axel, I swear. Just wait till you see her, you will be thanking me this time in August. You can postpone your vacation. The ocean isn't going anywhere, and we will lose this one for sure if you don't. Liz says she's a doll. Let me send you some photos."

My phone dinged as three pictures came through. I ignored them after a glance of blonde hair and big, hazel eye.

"Your pay will double and it's going to be high as it is. Plus, you will be doing me a favor, Axel. I can reschedule your November arrival. Or we can cancel her all together and you can take your trip then. Trust me, this is not one you will want to pass on."

I sighed, truly annoyed. This was the fourth day of relentless phone calls, voice mails, emails, and texts from Barb. If I were not saving every dollar I had, I'd tell her no—again. But I wanted the money. I wanted to pad my bank account just a little more so I could say fuck you to the entire shit hole that is California. That in mind, I gave in.

"Send me her file," I growled and ended the call.

Barbara is the agent; I'm the trainer. She finds the girls, or has them found, rather; I teach them how to fuck on camera. It's a working partnership, and it's made both of us money. Barb more than me because she has zero boundaries and employs some of the lowest forms of life. I, on the other hand, have class and taste, and there were days I'd been ashamed to be associated with the wretched woman.

I consider what I do as not much different than horse whispering, except the kind of breaking of mares I do is in much higher demand. I can take the roughest gem off the street, spend thirty days with her and, in the end, she becomes the Hope Diamond of the business. At least, she is for a while. In a hundred-billion a year industry, I'm always looking forward to the diamonds in the rough. They are rare, but very profitable.

I close out my web browser and zone back to the airport windows, taking one last longing look at the ocean and the summer I wanted to spend alone on a yacht, swinging on a hammock, drinking cold beer completely naked.

Damn you, Barb.

This trip has been a dream for years and yet, I'm taking on even more work. And yes, it is work. Most men would not find the prospect of training girls how to suck cock or take it in the ass work, but fuck, after twelve years, it most definitely is. When I arrived in this city, I was a high school drop-out with zero money. Porn was all I knew to do, and honestly, I have grown to fucking hate it.

I've completely ruined the possibility of ever having a normal life, whatever the hell normal is. I've been the dominate male so long, I can barely get it up for the average lay. Now, the only time I'm rock hard is when

I'm directing a girl how to hold her tits while I'm drilling them.

I spent seven years in front of the camera, fucking my way to oblivion several times a year, two to four weeks at a time. I was nothing more than a coke addict, blowing my way through any money I made. It was Barbara who approached me with the proposition of training girls for the business when I told her I was done with it all. She wanted me to stay because I was, and remain, her meal ticket.

I only agreed to work with Barb in the preparation of girls in hopes of getting out of this shit eventually. I kicked my coke habit and polished myself into every woman's fantasy. I was already blessed with good looks and a big dick, but possessed zero pedigree. After getting clean and putting on lean muscle, I became not only nice to look at, but the epitome of every girl's wet dream. I've been told on many occasions I look like a movie star, but have the rough exterior of my Liberty, Texas upbringing.

My knowledge of the female anatomy and reputation for making them come on cue is now the stuff of legend, and Barbara wanted to use that to her advantage for major profit. Soon enough, I moved into the trainer role. Not just for internet porn—the absolute apex of the porn industry—but high quality girls who can perform like no other and make the superior videos people actually pay to watch. She picks them, and I teach them. Once trained, the girls sign larger contracts which Barb and I get a percentage.

It didn't take long to see the rewards of my labor. I started out training girls every month, but was soon exhausted. I dropped to six a year and still found sharing my space with someone I had zero liking for, thirty days at a time, grueling. My patience wore thin for the shallow, money-hungry porn starlets. It got to the point I couldn't speak to females because I knew exactly what the next word out of their mouth would be. Although I am not cruel, I could care less about the feelings the girls come with. Teach them to fuck, then get them the fuck out of my house, that pretty much sums it all up.

When you've spent every moment of sex with the thrashing, screaming falsities of the female species, you tend to get a little disengaged from their emotions. And fuck, have I seen it all. The crying, *Christ almighty*, the crying drives me crazy. When I do film, I have to fuck them long enough for the video, but I have to pace myself to get their orgasm captured. If they decide to do some stupid shit, the whole thing is ruined and we have to begin all over again.

They were not all bad, but I haven't looked back once since I got out from the front of the camera. At least now, I have some say over my life. I get fresh girls—fresh meaning they haven't been on camera before. I film a couple times a year with a location I chose, the female of my choosing, and with a profit I demand.

Eventually, I want out of being the lead guy all together. Training girls is at least somewhat enjoyable at times, although it wears my nerves thin. The girls who come to me spend a week going through every kind of physical on planet Earth and receive a birth control treatment—either insertion, ring, or shot because no way do I fuck anyone "on the pill." That's bullshit and girls who suck cock for money can't remember their mom's name half the time, let alone a pill that needs to be taken every day.

"Axel Stone?"

I drag my gaze away from the window and see a young woman eyeing me curiously. She's sweet looking, and I quickly take in the long blonde hair, a pink pouty mouth that could make her rich, and full, not-too-big breasts on an hourglass figure. She's long and lean, but a bit on the thin side. If I were to care, I would say she's stunning, but I no longer consider those things.

They all look the same flat on their backs to me. The only difference is the sounds they make while I fuck them. Still, the girl appears so naïve, *too naïve,* and I have to wonder if maybe she just happened to recognize me. The longer I look, I begin to doubt this is the girl sent to me. There's no way this girl is cut out to enter into the world of pornography. She looks more like a model for a college sorority, and if I'm not mistaken, she's near fainting.

"Yeah?" I ask, a little hesitant because she could very well be a stalker. Would not be my first. I'm caught off guard when odd golden speckled eyes glance at me, then dart quickly away, as if she's shy. The thought of shyness makes me want to growl, but I'm not sure why.

A golden lock of hair falls into her eyes, catching a ray of light spilling in from the window I was just staring out of. As the girl nervously tucks the strand behind a small ear, my stomach gives a clenching spasm. She has the cutest ears I've ever seen and I imagine spending time circling them with my tongue, closing my lips around the lobe, delivering a soft nip with my teeth.

Really? Of all the things to notice, her fucking ears? I stand straighter while masking any interest.

"I'm Payton, I must've made a wrong turn and ended up on the other side of the terminal. I hope I didn't make you wait long."

Again, she looks from me to the floor nervously. Once her eyes return to mine, I get another fist to my stomach. Those beautiful, entrancing gold and hazel eyes make my thoughts hazy and her southern drawl catches me off guard. I have to think hard to remember why I'm standing in an airport.

"Payton Knight?" I clear my throat.

She nods, flashing a brilliant, yet timid smile my way. My interest is truly piqued. This girl is a daisy among the weeds. Not so casually, I let my eyes wander over her body. Her blue jeans and a light pink cotton top with a little blue bird pattern on it look more Suzie-homemaker than Suzie-sucks-a-lot. Of course, I know she hasn't done any professional work, because I do not train girls who have.

"Have you been waiting long?" She frowns and even that is something I take note of. The pucker between her brows is even cute.

Cute?

My dark mood turns slightly darker. No matter the outer package, the girl is work, no matter how attractive I find her, Payton Knight is here for one reason.

"No. Not long. Shall we?" I gestured with my hand for her to walk ahead of me.

She does, then casts a playful look over her shoulder back at me.

"Call me Payton, although I will use the name 'Becca'", she slows slightly, "on film." She whispers "film" as if it were a dirty word. I had to give it to her, the girl had the innocent act down pat. "Is your real name Axel?"

Shit. She's going to be one of *those*. Why can't they just not be so damned predictable? Her type gets doe eyes for me, thinking I'm going to date them or some shit. Suzie-homemaker can shake that sweet ass all she wants, but after thirty days, her and her sweet ass will be hitting the road. But even thinking that, I don't like the way she makes me squirm with foreign uncertainty.

"Yes, Axel is my given name," I reply woodenly.

She smiles and slows her pace to walk beside me. Anxiety hums out of her body along with excitement. I ignore the eagerness I also sense because Payton is about to know me in a not-so-pretty way.

After leading the way to my Audi, I place her bag in the trunk, and notice her waiting by the passenger's door looking around with wide eyes, drinking up the area. There's no come-ons like from most of the girls, there's no suggestive looks as if she's ready to astound me with the best sex ever. Payton just looks to the sky, the buildings, and the other parked cars.

"It's pretty here," she says to no one in particular.

I squint my eyes against the bright light of the sun. The roar of a plane's powerful takeoff echoes across the sky, but I can still hear the thudding of my own heartbeat pounding with some unknown excitement. A soft breeze picks up loose strands of Payton's golden hair, and I watch transfixed as they dance in the wind. She absently tucks them away from her face and that simple movement reveals so much.

With that one delicate move, I know instantly this is not a female I see often. Payton is graceful, soft spoken and I'm willing to bet, mischievous, judging by the glint of interest in her eyes. She looks to me quizzically, and I realize I'm staring. Brushing the thought aside, I proceed to the driver's side door unlocking it with my key fob as I go.

Two men openly stare at Payton as they walk by, yet she remains oblivious to the gawkers and I have a feeling she's not acting with the naiveté shit at all. If she is or isn't, it doesn't matter, because I have a job to do and I could care less what she is. Payton will be gone in no time.

"It's open." She probably thinks I'm going to open her door for her or some gentlemanly shit I don't do.

I fold my large frame behind the wheel and start the car, and the light floral scent of her perfume envelopes me. It's a pleasant fragrance, not at all the bold, almost assaulting smells I'm accustom to with the other females. A very unsettling feeling tightens my chest as unease swims through my gut. The sweet odor assaults me, uncurling the beast that lives just beneath my surface. It also provokes a sadness of something lost to me long ago.

All this moody bullshit from hair and a fucking smell. What is wrong with me?

My dark mood turns into outright hatred for what I am, and resentment for agreeing to teach Payton boils within my chest. No matter how good she smells or how attractive the girl is, I am fucking annoyed as hell I gave in to Barb's insistence against my better judgement. I take the much needed time alone between girls for my sanity, which isn't all that stable to start with. On good days, I'm an outright dick, on a bad day? I can teach Satan a thing or two about cruel.

Gripping the steering wheel until my knuckles turn white, I try to will the car to calm me.

This can't be all that bad, right? Right? Just get it over with and it's one more step toward the fuck you to this businesses.

I have to take several deep breaths before snapping the seatbelt in place, and I can feel the edges of my psyche waver slightly.

"This is nice, Axel." Payton looks around my car.

I don't respond because I know my car is nice. I like nice things and don't need confirmation from anyone that they are nice. Plus, I'm now in a sour mood and don't want to encourage small talk. I just want this to get started so I can hurry the fuck up and end it.

Silently, I navigate through the traffic of the airport. In my periphery, I can see Payton is tense while she keeps her eyes on the landscape. Her small hands are balled in her lap, and her shoulders have yet to relax. Looks like I'm not the only one on edge. Several silent minutes pass before I begin to feel her uncoil slightly in the seat and sense conversation on the tip of her tongue.

"I've never been to California." After a pause, she adds in a soft voice, "I've never been anywhere outside of Mississippi."

I huff out an annoyed breath.

"Really?" I ask in faux interest.

She turns to look at me, and I can actually feel her curious eyes burn as she stares.

Am I attractive to her? Does she feel the same odd vibration between us?

Funny how I never cared if a girl found me pleasing to look at before now, but I find I want Payton's perusals to be satisfying.

I don't look her way, but the more seconds that pass, the more I feel almost compelled to glance at her face. Tension builds and my jaw tightens as my mind wonders what she sees. Unable to resist any longer, I look her way, noting her prominent cheek bones, small nose, and soft pout, the bottom lip slightly fuller than the top. Blush stains her cheeks as she's caught staring, and I realize I am painfully erect. Shifting uncomfortably, I do my best to ease the cut off circulation to my groin.

Whether my brain has caught on or not, my dick has apparently come to the realization it likes Payton. It strikes me as strange I'm not actually annoyed by her presence as much as I am with my decision to have her stay with me so soon after the last girl. And I have to be honest, if it were not for the living status of "homeless" on the initial file I'd received, I don't think I would have agreed to it at all, regardless of Barbara's insistence. But now Payton is here, it won't be so bad as long as she keeps to the schedule and doesn't bother me outside of the training.

Involuntarily, my eyes flash her way again. *Pretty, she is actually pretty.* She'll be beautiful on camera, I'm certain. Maybe it won't be a bad thirty days.

"How far to your house?" she asks and I grin at the shakiness of her voice. Could it be Payton is *nervous*? The girls I get usually want to get started in the car as I drive home, all too eager to get at my cock and try to impress me. It is not all together bad when they come ready. It makes it easier to get started when they are more than willing to learn. Of course, they all know why they're staying with me, so there are no pretenses, no first dates, no flowers or candy. Just carnal fucking for the cameras. But for some reason, I'm getting weird vibes from Payton. Yes, I definitely believe she's attracted to me, if I judge the way her eyes continuously roam my body. She is definitely giving me false confidence or maybe she expected me to jump her the minute we reached my car?

"Just about twenty minutes away, just down from Dana Pointe." I clear my throat against the dryness that's suddenly there.

It's pointless to dwell on the girl's appearance or shy demeanor, but that doesn't stop the almost sad feeling in my chest that I'm about to give her a very rude awakening into the pornography industry. Whatever Payton has been told about her skills as a lover are about to be squashed. Most girls are stuck on the stupid shit their teenage lovers got off on. That does not translate well on camera. People pay a pretty penny to access the best fucking and sucking the eyes can behold. I do not let them down.

"How old are you?" Payton asks and I know without looking, she's studying me once more.

I've spent countless hours naked in front of many strangers through the years. Someone looking me over has never bothered me, yet Payton's examination makes me shift in my seat. And her voice, it reminds me of honey. It's sweet, exotic, and provokes unwanted thoughts of home for the first time in years.

"Wanna guess?" I ask beginning to relax some but still sporting a raging hard on.

"Um, thirty?"

"Not quite," I chuckle slightly.

"How long have you been in this business, Axel?" she asks with timid interest.

Payton really is shy, but completely at ease with me, the sexual deviant capable of the most depraved things, and she's not even old enough to drink a beer? Makes me suddenly feel like the big, bad wolf.

"Since eighteen." I shrug, not sharing that I was actually sixteen and filmed for two years illegally. Women tended to pity that fact, trying to mother me. So, I learned quickly not to share it.

"And you've been in California all that time?"

"Yep."

"But you're not from here. I can hear an accent but can't place it," she says tilting her head to the side.

Shit. Nobody has caught my accent before, or at least, they haven't brought it up.

"Texas." My heart squeezes slightly at the mention of my home.

"Ah. I knew it was southern, at least." I give her a slight smile and watch as she folds impossibly long legs under her round ass. This does nothing to help the pressure pulsing behind the zipper of my jeans.

We drive in comfortable silence for several more minutes. Occasionally, Payton comments about a house as we cruise down Pacific Coast Highway. Oddly, I take pleasure in the interest in what I take for granted. Most of the girls I train are overly confident, unimpressed, and ready to make money. Payton just seems happy to be along for the ride.

I'm not feeling as icy anymore. I hope Payton is as simple to live with as she is a driving companion. Candi drove me fucking crazy talking all the time. She never shut up. She kept trying to have sex outside of the training sessions, and I could not wait to get her out of my space. I shake my head at her memory and feel my neck protest with tension.

"I know we just met," Payton says breaking the silence before she pauses as if searching for words. She sounds nervous again. "And I know what to expect when we reach your place, but you seem really tense. Randell told me you agreed to do this, but didn't really want to. I'm sorry if I've caused you trouble. I do need to work so I won't give you any problems. I'll be a quick learner, okay?"

The pure tone of sincerity and self-consciousness run in her words, both things I've not felt from a female in a very long time. Maybe ever. It doesn't make me feel better, I feel ashamed. I smile stiffly, reminding myself she is new at all of this. I forget sometimes how naïve girls can be, except I don't really see naïve girls, at least not the ones I teach.

"It's fine. I'm just tired is all. It's not you, so don't worry about it."

I haven't had time to recover from Candi before taking Payton on, but she doesn't know that. I suddenly feel bad for being a dick. My personality seems to be in two even pieces at war with one another, and this girl seems to have picked up on it easily.

Before I really think about what I'm doing, I reach over to the delicate hand in her lap. The skin is soft and cool to my touch as I gently squeeze and then quickly return my elbow to the armrest between us. I simply don't do soothing, and I'm more than a little shocked at my actions. I don't do romantic or kind. I wouldn't know how if I tried, yet I feel bad Payton felt unwanted.

"Can I ask a couple of more questions?"

"Ask away." I shrug and try to relax my aching neck.

"I was told you no longer filmed, uh, movies. Or not much anymore. Can I ask why?"

"Well," I take a long, suffering breath. I know I shouldn't be talking about the personal subject, but I can't seem to resist Payton if for no other reason than listening to her sweet voice. "I suppose I had done it long enough. It was just time."

"But aren't you, like, the most popular male star? Randell said you're searched for more and watched more than any other."

Shit. I don't know how to answer that. I think about it a second, then decide to be honest.

"It's true or, at least, I've been told that." The topic makes me slightly squeamish.

"Wasn't the money hard to walk away from?"

I turn my face to Payton to judge her expression, then back to the road. Pity for her floods me.

"I understand the recruiter that spoke with you about this business explained you are paid per shooting or what breaks down to each shoot per day, etcetera?"

"Yes, and by being trained by you, I would receive much more money than trying to do anything on my own," she recited as if she had memorized the sales pitch word for word.

"That's true." I scratch at the back of my head, trying to figure out how much to say this early. The subject is a little personal for my comfort. "The money for me was just okay. I didn't have a backup plan for when I wasn't going to do shoots anymore. It's not like there's a college degree from doing this, and I've never worked anywhere else, so the training thing was a good out. I don't have just one reason I quit filming as much. Like I said, it was just time."

I know I sound annoyed. No one has really ever asked me the whys, and I really don't know how to communicate without sounding defensive. I sure as shit am not about to reveal the steroids, the cocaine, and the pain pills that nearly killed me or the fact I am an empty shell of a human being from living the lifestyle of a porn star year after year. No, I am not going to expose the true causes of my decisions.

"I'm sorry if that was too personal, I just—" Payton's sweet voice trails off in thought.

"It's fine, you're just curious." I shrug, but it wasn't fine. It makes me feel like shit and that's a feeling I am all too familiar with. Feeling like shit is actually my twisted comfort zone. It somehow rights my swaying insides.

Payton unfolds her legs again and turns her gaze back to the ocean, then to my stereo. "Do you mind?" she asks sweetly.

"Not at all." I'm thankful she seems satisfied to listen to music rather than talk more. Payton works the buttons and I watch her slender, elegant hand move across the dials. Her sweet smelling perfume floats my way, causing my mouth to water. I'm suddenly eager to get home. Our initial fucking will at least end the growing tension I'm feeling.

Settling for alternative rock, Payton relaxes back into her seat, her face turned to look out of the window. In the reflection, I can see uncertainty and maybe a little insecurity as we get closer to my house.

Three

-

Axel

We pull into my garage at high tide. The aroma of the ocean breezes through the bay door just before being cut off completely, sealing us inside with a quiet, ominous thud. This part is normally easy. I, along with whatever female is here for the month, enter my house, I lay down the rules of her stay, spending very little time on niceties before moving on to the training schedule. As I pop the trunk to retrieve Payton's small bag, I know this is not going to go as normal.

For one, Payton isn't chatty or overly anxious to impress me. The girls who come here all have one thing in common—I get them work, which equals money. They all want to please me and can't wait to wow me with their "skills." While Payton may have the same goal, she is anything but the usual female I deal with.

Other than the lack of flirting, Payton moves with caution as if she stumbled upon my territory and any movement might set me off. She solidifies this thought when she follows me inside my kitchen at least five steps behind me, all the while not making a sound. This quiet, timid girl has managed to make me feel awkward in my own home.

Turning to shut the door and hang my keys on the designated hook on the wall, I catch her eyeing my Harley Davidson FXR sitting in the second space of the garage. I left the tools scattered around haphazardly, something I never do, but my entire mental state is off with exhaustion and not having the normal time to recover. The sex, I could recover from no problem, but the wear and tear of living with a stranger a month at a time is strenuous.

"Do you ride?" I ask, pausing just before cutting off her view.

She chews at her bottom lip nervously and meets my gaze.

"Motorcycles? Uh, no." She shakes her head, grinning.

Whips of hair spill across her forehead, and I notice she looks really young, like *really young*. An uncertainty creeps in my mind, but it's cut off when the overwhelming desire to lean in and take that puffy bottom lip between my teeth takes over. Not hard, just a little rough so I can truly taste it. Breaking the spell, Payton turns to take in my home before I can act on the thought. Slightly disappointed, I set her bag on the island that separates the living room and kitchen, then straighten my spine to work out the tension at the base. I feel far older than my age.

Payton inspects the near surgically clean area with a look a curiosity and maybe even a little excitement. I've done most of the work in the house myself. My modest, but private, beach home is located on a secluded bend just outside the busy Dana Pointe Beach. The far wall of living room, made entirely of glass, leads out to a pristine deck and my very own beach. Though not a big house, it is one of the few that has true privacy.

It's perfect for me, with three bedrooms I've remodeled to fit my needs, equipped with their own bathrooms, a large living room open floor plan I extended into the dining room, simply because a formal dining area was a waste of space, and an open kitchen with an island. I found I wanted more and more time alone in the house to build something, sand something, create something from nothing—it's the place I'm most content. Sadly, I never seem to have alone time to do those things.

Soon, very soon.

"This is all yours? The beach and all?" Payton asks in wonderment staring longingly out to the surf.

"Yeah. It's not much, but it's mine." I shove my hands in my pockets and watch Payton move around the sofa to the glass doors. A blissful expression takes shape on what I previously thought a *pretty* face. Now, in the natural light of the room, I see she's breathtaking and her body, *Jesus*, she looks like she belongs in the Victoria's Secret Angel lineup. Men could write songs about her curvy ass. And those long, *long* legs, small waist, and perky breasts can't be hidden in that mamaw shirt, although I'm pretty sure that was her original plan.

Fuck me, Barbara was actually right, Payton is a perfect ten. Why the hell is she wanting to do porn? She should be modeling for Ford.

"There are no neighbors?" she asks and I'm pulled out of my lusty thoughts.

"When the home next door became available, I bought it and tore it down to expand the privacy and property line." I wander over to stand next to her.

A feverish desire to take her, to fuck her any which way but sweet begins to urge me on. But first, I have the strangest need to kiss her, to taste her. The heat my body gives off is stifling as I move closer, placing a hand on her small shoulder, and turning her to face me. Inches apart now, I get lost in her hazel eyes.

Licking my lips, I come at her gently, touching my mouth to hers in a lingering, burning kiss, and slowly, I bite that lower lip, dragging my teeth across it softly.

Nectar from the Gods.

A growl escapes me, and, with my hands on either side of her face now, I turn my head slightly to plunge deeper in exploration. My erection throbs with its own heartbeat and I have the idiotic notion of taking her, right here by the glass doors. *The couch? The floor? Who fucking cares?* Lust like I've never known pushes aside any notion this girl is here for anything other than my animalistic pleasure.

Hunger sears through my blood as our tongues touch and retreat to begin again. I drop my hands to unzip my pants when Payton goes still and stiffens. A whimper of what can only be fear escapes her between our dueling lips.

Then, I realize her hands are not on me. I pull my face back and see her fists balled at her sides. An unmistakable look of panic sits on her face. I feel like an idiot standing here with my hands poised at the fly of my jeans.

Gritting my jaw, I quickly remind myself the harsh reality that this girl, this beautiful, sweet, naïve girl is only here for *work*. Pleasure of any kind coming from me will be given under the glaring lights of the studio room. She doesn't want me in the sense of *wanting* me, she's only here to learn to perform.

Stepping back, I grin to mask the disappointment clawing in my chest before I realize how very stupid it is to think just because I find someone attractive, they would find me the same. Truth be told, I wouldn't like me either. I'm a piece of shit degenerate who has ruined many lives. I can't forget I'm about to ruin another for money, although she's ignorant of that fact.

"Let me show you around." I turn my back to her and return to the business at hand.

I show Payton her room—on the opposite end of the house from mine on purpose, separated by the living room and kitchen so we have some space between us, at least. Next, I take her to the room where we will be spending most of our time. The "training" room is simply a small studio, much like she will be filming in. I'm not in to BDSM, so its dominant furniture is the bed along with an ottoman, and a couch. A Tantra Chair sits tauntingly unused in the far corner as it's designed for pleasure and there's not much pleasing in this room.

There's only acting and a whole lot of tears from the girls. The cameras I use for the sessions sit on their tripods just under the stage lighting on the back wall.

As Payton walks through the room looking around, I flip on the overhead lights, drowning the space in a perfect glow for recording. The pale blue walls complement the filming nicely. The smell of the sterile cleaners used in both this room and the girl's bedroom two days previous still linger in the air. I'm a bit OCD about germs, though you'd never know it from the shit I've done on camera.

Payton touches things lightly with her fingertips, as if trying to memorize the feel—the arm of the couch, the down comforter on the bed, one leg of a tripod, then the sheer over the window. Every move is fluid and calculated as if she were in a trance or lost in a faraway thought. I stand still and watch, noting the slight tilt of her head when something catches her interest. She pauses at the window, opens the privacy blinds, and then looks out on the beach. A vacant expression overtakes her face as I watch her profile lit by the sun.

Helpless to stop, I study her. I know Payton is not the typical female I train. She's quiet and soaks up every detail of her environment, and every word I say as if it were the sustenance of her survival. She's not confident, though she has every reason to be. She isn't attention-hungry or eager, like the girls I've trained before. I get none of those things from Payton, and I find it intriguing, only adding to the longing I already feel for her.

Christ, she looks like Brigitte Bardot and has no fucking idea.

My fingers twitch to touch her, to wrap that hair around my hand and tug. Clearing my throat and adjusting the cramped confines of my jeans, I say the first thing I think of.

"I hope you'll like it here."

Whoa, what? Where the fuck did that come from? I never care if the girls are comfortable. They're here to learn, that's it. That sounds too close to giving a shit.

Payton brings a hand to her face. I can't see what she's doing but her deep, slow breaths suggest she's trying to calm down. I let my eyes drift along her body twice, landing on her ass both times while I wait for some kind of response.

"Do we just get to it or what?" She glances over a shoulder to where I stand, then back to the window.

My throbbing cock is screaming *yes!* But I hesitate with Payton. Everything she's shown me says to take it easy. That's not something I normally do, but Payton is not the normal hot-to-trot female I'm used to. There's no harm in giving her a few minutes.

"Do you want to go to your room and relax a while or watch TV? You have to be jet-lagged. We can become acquainted later."

Straightening her shoulders, she turns to face me fully. Her sad eyes are slightly damp. I hadn't noticed the scattered freckles across her nose until she steps close to me. Now that I can look her over fully, I can appreciate the front of her is just as beautiful as the back.

"Sure, unless you want to get started. I'm fine either way."

I give a slight shrug to indicate whatever but as I study her face, I'm conscious of the uncertainty in her eyes. Payton seems strong-willed, but her shyness catches me off-guard. It makes me uncomfortable, unprepared, and slightly unsure of my skills. Yet, I'm still ready to pounce.

"You relax first. Get settled in. Are you hungry?" I frown at the concern in my voice. Normal me did not care if the female was hungry.

Where is this shit coming from? Next, I'll ask if she wants to cuddle after I pound her from behind.

"No, thank you," Payton replied, walking past me.

I follow her to the kitchen and watch her pause to retrieve her bags, then proceed to her room, closing the door behind her. I want to follow and watch as she changes or just simply walk around the room some more.

Then, it hits me. Before this moment, I'd completely forgotten what attraction feels like when it's not associated with sex. Every interaction I have with a girl revolves around banging. All be it staged, but still, that's what I know best. I find myself a little too comfortable just watching Payton's pretty mouth move, or her fingers slide along something as she walks.

I widen my eyes to stretch the tired muscles, then wander to the fridge for a beer. I gulp the first one down while standing in the open door, then reach for another before settling on the couch, lost in thought. More than once, I look to the door of Payton's room.

Come out already.

The waiting only intensifies my impatience. I'm uneasy, on edge, and my skin crawls with the want of her. The same skin that's comfortable being unaffected by females. I'm looking forward to fucking that uneasiness right out.

Giving up on willing the girl from her room, I settle deeper into the couch and flip through the channels until deciding on baseball highlights of the previous night's game. I finish my beer and close my eyes, drifting into a comatose-like nap.

Four

-

Axel

Dragging my lids open, I find an Angel's game in the fourth inning. I frown because it hadn't even started just moments before when I'd closed my eyes. I bring my hands to my tired eyes to rub them, and I have to squint at the digital clock on my cable box.

That can't be right.

4:14 p.m.

"No fucking way."

A giggle comes from behind me and I turn to see Payton sitting on one of the bar stools at the kitchen island, one foot curled underneath her. Her damp, long blonde hair hangs past her shoulders in delicate waves and she's makeup free. The tiniest bit of denim encases her hips, leaving her long legs and feet bare. The Mississippi Rebels t-shirt she's wearing makes me grin.

She has to be the cutest thing I've ever seen. No, not cute, fucking gorgeous.

Most of the women who came wouldn't leave their room without being camera-ready with heavy makeup.

Payton cocks an eyebrow playfully and matches my grin with her own.

"I amuse you?" I ask playfully while standing and stretching, thankful I'm finally in a good mood. Sleep is so under-rated. I smile slyly at the way Payton's eyes roam over my body.

Look your fill, sweet girl.

Payton's eyes gleam with interest. She wants me and I certainly want her.

"You do, amuse me, that is." She smiles sheepishly and bites into a sandwich.

When did it get so hot in here?

I pull off my shirt and walk to where Payton sits assessing every move I make. I place a hand cautiously, lightly, on each thigh, leaning down so our eyes meet.

In my line of work, there are no presumptions or foreplay that don't involve fingers or tongues. Everybody who came to my home knew they were here to fuck or be fucked, but I have an irresistible urge to play with Payton, not just physically, but tease her.

Her eyes light up as I lean down to steal a bite of her sandwich. The peanut butter and jelly tastes better than any high priced meal I could have ordered in. I watch a delicious pink tongue dart out of her mouth, wet her lips, then dive back inside nervously. That one simple movement has me hard instantly.

Payton is a seductress, that explains it. She's just been acting this whole time?

"You have," she stops to clear her throat. She's nervous and that knowledge makes me want to beat my chest like Tarzan. "You have jelly on your—" Again, she wets her lips as she studies my face, settling her eyes on my mouth. She leans in to me, freezing me in place, and licks my lower lip slowly, agonizingly sinfully.

Fuck. Definitely acting. Or not? I can't fucking think with her tongue lapping at me.

I feel the lick all the way to my toes. That tongue, that mouth, I can't wait to taste it all. My knees go weak and my dick jumps painfully, pressing against the zipper. I push my tongue out to my lips as she draws her face back to look me in the eyes. I'm on the verge of saying fuck training and just take her in the kitchen, but I don't want her to shut down again. I need her willing. I swallow back the surge of lust, remembering who and what I am. I can't do anything outside of the training room, no matter how hot she is. If I do, then it will cross the line from work to pleasure.

No, I am a pro, my job is to teach her how to become a pro. Even inwardly reminding myself of that doesn't calm the storm raging inside my head in this moment or the desire to just fuck her for the fun of it.

"You ready to get started?" I almost growl.

The tiniest bit of fear flashes across her face. Uneasiness creeps over me again. *Damn it.* I hope she isn't thinking I would take her on dates and other romantic crap before we get down to business.

"That's why you're here, remember?" I raise my eyebrows in question, trying to correct the out of bounds flirting and redirect back to the business at hand. Her full mouth turns up at the corners.

"Of course, I remember."

She reaches to finish a glass of wine I hadn't noticed before. I have the strangest urge to take it from her. She isn't old enough to drink. Obviously, the wine is at the ready for my female company, and her drinking is no big deal, yet for some reason, I want to keep her away from things she shouldn't have. Placing my shirt around my neck, I watch as she swallows. My mouth waters at the movements her throat makes when tilted back. I lick my lips again in anticipation.

"I'll meet you in the studio. I'm just going to clean up." I wince at the shaky way my words came out.

Payton nods and pours another glass of wine. I walk to my room and into the bathroom slightly dazed.

Should I shower? Should I jerk off first?

I'm so worked up from just Payton's presence, I'm slightly afraid how I'll react to sex with her.

Me, afraid of coming prematurely? Yeah, right. That's ridiculous. I'm a fucking animal.

I shake my head and use the bathroom before I wash my face and brush my teeth. Five minutes later, I stand bare chested and looking at my body in the mirror. I appear no different than I did earlier this morning, yet I feel weaker for some reason.

Maybe I'm sick?

No, not sick. I get a complete physical twice a year and blood work draw one week after I finish each training session. I take every precaution imaginable to protect both myself and the females I train. People don't like watching a condom-wrapped cock in action—that is a fact—so I stick to the regimen even if I'm not filming.

Inhaling deeply, I dry my face and give jerking off one more quick thought before dismissing it. I'm a fucking machine, and I simply don't have problems with premature ejaculation.

But then again, I haven't been this turned on for a girl in years, maybe ever.

After scowling at my reflection one last time, I make my way to the studio, a little too eager to get started.

Music seeps through the partially opened door, and I nudge it wider to find Payton with her back to me. Leaning against the door frame, I cross my arms as Payton sways slightly to Ed Sheeran's "Thinking Out Loud." I figure the wine must be kicking in because her shoulders aren't nearly as stiff now.

Lithe body moving side to side, Payton is oblivious to me and just how damned beautiful she looks. My heart hammers with anticipation to touch her, while my mouth waters to taste every inch of her silky skin. But before I do anything, I want to start recording her, just like this—sultry curves swaying with the skin at her back playing peek-a-boo at the waistline of her shorts. I have no idea why, but she's just simply breathtaking.

I push off the frame into the room and touch the record button on the camera, signaling them all to begin, then resume my watching. This lovely, innocent, quiet beauty has me twisted up on the inside so much, I can feel my body tremble with need and nerves.

Payton turns, still swaying, lost in the music, eyes closed, and head slightly back with lips parted. My breath catches in my chest.

Fuck, she's sexy.

And she still has her clothes on. That alone should warn me I'm heading down an unknown road. I don't admire women, not like the average male. Sure, I'm attracted to some more than others, I'm a guy, but not this staring and drooling kind of guy Payton seems to be turning me into. I see girls weakened, weepy, fucked within an inch of unconsciousness, so the appeal of just watching a woman is not within me. But shit if it isn't there with Payton. I could just watch her all night.

Just watch her?

I give my head a good shake.

You're losing it, Stone.

Payton opens her eyes slowly, then focuses on me. Instantly, pink blushes her cheeks at having an audience.

"Hey." She stops, breathless.

"Hey."

Christ, that was stupid.

She places her wine glass on the bedside table, then walks toward me holding her hands out. I straighten, suddenly nervous, which is fucking unsettling because I don't get nervous.

"Dance with me?" Her voice is just loud enough for me to hear it. I shake my head. I don't dance. Not ever. I'm a sex machine, wouldn't know how to dance. "Please? I'm really nervous. It'll help loosen me up."

That makes two of us, at least.

But I'm helpless as Payton places her hands in mine, tugging me to the middle of the room. Excitement dances in her eyes that now appear slightly green against the light blue backdrop of the room. She wraps her arms around my neck and places her head on my chest, as easily as if we've done this every day for the last twenty years. My mind screams for me to stop and get things back on the real reason we are in this room, but my hands wrap automatically around her waist as if my body operated without needing my brain's permission.

My heart beats wildly against my ribs, doing its damnedest to escape the confines of my chest as Payton gently rocks side to side. I just kind of stand there, as she moves against me, feeling awkward as hell. Her hair smells divine and I catch myself running my lips along the smoothness of her forehead. Pushing back silky strands away from her neck, I bend my head to kiss lightly at the bottom of her ear. I'm rewarded with her tremble.

I remember the same effect on a girl I dated as a freshman in high school. The situation was similar, and I realize that was the last time I danced with anyone. That makes me sad, and I don't like the feeling. I want to fuck those memories back into their box. Pushing Payton back slightly, I take her mouth in a desperate frenzy, placing my hands on either side of her face to gain total control. A soft moan escapes her lips as I push my tongue inside.

Playtime is over.

Or just beginning. Either way, I am not going to dance. I'm not going to *feel.* I release Payton long enough to turn the music down low and slip back in control. She needs to see and hear herself on camera so she will know what areas to improve on. I eye her body before landing back on those mesmerizing eyes.

Before becoming entranced by the green, I reach the bottom of her shirt and pull it quickly over her head. Payton says nothing as I reach around to her back, unclasp her bra, letting it fall to the floor. I waste no time unbuttoning, unzipping, and then pushing the shorts and panties over her ass down to join the bra. When I finally have her fully naked, I take a step back to admire her body. Payton is a mixture of shyness and sin, and the sight of her pale flesh scattered with goose bumps does something unnatural to me.

Dusty rose nipples jutting out, begging to be sucked and that small, bare cleft between those luscious thighs? I want to fall to my knees and worship every inch of this woman.

"Fuck, Payton, you're beautiful," I hiss. "Lie down," I order, finally deciding on tongue-fucking her first. I can't wait any longer to taste her sweet heat.

Payton does as I command, and I grin wickedly when she keeps her legs closed, resting on her elbows like she has no clue what to do. Her wide eyes suggest she's slightly scared. I grin wider down at her, reassuringly.

"You're ready to get started?"

A nervous chuckle comes from her throat. "I thought we already started?"

"Not hardly," I growl and slowly descend, parting her legs as I go, stopping long enough to suckle her nipples. Abandoning my own rules and punctual filming schedule, I groan once I have a perfect hard crest in my mouth. I don't care how professional I'm being because, fuck, I *want* her.

Payton moans low as I softly tug each throbbing peak with my teeth, actually grabbing hold of my hair. Her hips undulate with the need so I lower my mouth, trailing nips along her stomach and hips until I can't hold back any longer. I rub my thumb gently down the slick crease between her legs, and she bucks her hips until begin pushing slowly inside. She stills at my probing.

"Christ, you're tight."

She whimpers when I begin kissing closer and closer to her wet core, all the while I continue the slow movements in and out with my thumb. Her ragged breath indicates she's already close to coming.

"Oh, baby"

What the fuck did I just say? Baby? This is business, you dumbass.

But why not enjoy this?

Because she will think it means something.

Spreading her thighs further apart, my thoughts go quiet as I replace my thumb with my mouth.

Oh, the honey.

She tastes divine, like ambrosia, just like I knew she would. I lap at her, building her body to a slow burn. Payton's hands grab hunks of my hair again, and she gives sounds of surprise and absolute pleasure as she grinds my face against her. I'm having a hard time keeping my professional control in the madness. Rotating my tongue in hard circles, she cries out, so close to climax.

I give an encouraging growl against her flesh, then add my forefinger to the mix. She tenses before crumbling in pieces. Payton's body shatters, shaking almost violently with her orgasm. She releases my hair, and I watch in ecstasy as she tugs on her nipples and cries out my name.

"Axel! Oh God, Axel!"

The sound leaving her lips calls forth something from deep in my soul, and I don't think I ever want this to stop. I want Payton to say my name over and over before the night is through. I lick her until her aftershocks subside, and she begins to squirm and back away from the sensitivity at her swollen nub.

Standing, I make quick work of pulling off my jeans, grabbing my throbbing cock to keep it from bouncing as I climb between those goddess-like thighs now glistening with a slight sheen of sweat. Once I nestle in between, my eyes close at the feel of her heat.

So fucking hot. Don't come before you get inside. Keep it together.

My body hums, almost vibrates with the need to enter her body. I have to take a deep breath before I look down. Payton's eyes widen fractionally when she drops her gaze from my face to my dick at her core. It gives me pleasure watching the excitement and fear reemerge.

Guiding the throbbing head to her slick entrance, a hiss escapes between my teeth. My breaths come hard and ragged. Pure, carnal need pulses through my body. Bracing myself to move forward, I slowly exhale and begin the slide home. My eyes close in ecstasy, and in this moment, I am so fucking glad I didn't bother with the Caverject.

I feel everything. Every fucking thing.

"Axel?"

No. No. No. Fuck, don't start talking.

"Shhh," I breathe, trying to concentrate on the sensations and knowing I am not going to last long with her. The first time doesn't matter, not really. It's a watch and learn filming, what we look like and all that basic shit. I don't need to last long in the first filming.

Keeping my eyes at half-mast, I lower my mouth to hers, hoping that will keep her quiet. Payton wraps her arms around my middle, responding to my kiss as her body begins to shake with more than anticipation. She shivers beneath me, and I can feel the frown slide across my face.

Ending the kiss, I pull back to search her eyes.

"Just relax," I sooth.

Glowing hazel eyes meets mine, and for the first time ever, I have to ask if she really wants to do this.

Don't you dare say no, I'll die if I have to stop this now.

Payton nods slightly, giving me a shy grin then raises her hips to mine while simultaneously wrapping her legs around me. I push further, just inside her sweet heat, completely unprepared for the grip. My breath leaves me, and I become light-headed.

"Christ, you're tight," I growl and don't recognize my own voice.

A little *too* tight, almost painfully so. I press forward slowly, gently, as Payton begins clawing at my back, holding on as if she were drowning. She whimpers and shakes as I inch forward, only making it a third of the way inside before having to pull back to ease the tension.

"Shhh. Relax. Just relax," I encourage soothingly before pressing my mouth back to hers.

I'm at a loss how to respond to the trembling—lost in lust, but at the same time, I am very aware of the vise-like grip around my cock. I know I'm bigger than average, not huge, but damn, I can barely get inside Payton. It's almost like an invasion.

Again, I push forward, making some progress, reaching halfway this time. It's like I'm tearing through her tender flesh. Payton pulls her face away to arch her back and whine.

"Just do it Axel, please?"

I move my mouth to her breast, unable to stand the sensations. It's making me crazy, and I have to resist thrusting. I pull back, then push forward, sinking inside further, but still not able to make it all the way. Payton pants hard underneath me, so I wrap my arms around her waist, trying to keep her from bucking me out entirely. Then finally, I push inside to the hilt.

"Christ," I groan and almost come as Payton lets out a scream mixed with relief and pain.

I growl like an animal and command my body to still for a minute, giving us a both a much-needed moment to adjust. Pressing my mouth back to Payton's, I taste the salt from our mingled sweat. Even with the full entrance, she continues to tremble and whimper in pain. With my body stilled, it's evident Payton's shaking is almost as if in shock from trauma. It's not normal, and I have no recollection of any female having violent trembles before. Not ever. I try to sift through my many sexual encounters but can think of none that comes close to this with Payton.

She's gripping me so tight.

Need to thrust.

Don't thrust yet, give her a second.

With something close to madness, I fight to control the situation. An inconceivable thought forms, just as I begin to pull back once more. I frown, trying to get a hold of my senses as reality hits me so hard, I feel as if I've been kicked in the chest. I look down, *really* look, searching Payton's face. Her eyes are shut tight, and she's breathing shallowly through her clenched teeth as if in agony. The sides of her face are wet with tears.

Fucking *tears,* for Christ's sake.

A dread floods my body as the truth stomps over me in combat boots. I can't move. I'm literally frozen, still buried inside her unbelievable tight sheath.

"You're a virgin," I breathe, my voice thick with gravel.

It is a statement, not a question. I back my cock painfully out as Payton opens her eyes wide with...what?

Fear? Desire? What?

"Holy shit, Payton. What. The. Fuck?"

The movement of dislodging my dick from that grip is the hardest thing I've ever done in my life, but I couldn't do it fast enough. Had I had any alcohol in me, I wouldn't have had the strength to do it. I look down at her, then at my throbbing dick, and find a thin streak of bright red blood from my forced entrance. Stumbling backward from the bed, my stomach roils at the sight.

I'm going to throw up.

"Axel, please, don't stop."

Steading myself, I reach to turn the camera off. Bile rises up my chest, invading my throat. I have to swallow several times so I truly don't throw up.

Chest heaving, icy anger takes hold as my thoughts realign.

"Why the fuck did you not tell me?" I all but scream.

Payton sits up, looking very much like the victim.

"This is not happening." I run my hands through my hair, yanking at it. Trying to get ahold of myself, I reach for my jeans. "This is not fucking happening."

"I don't understand." Payton's voice catches, and I jerk my head up to search her face. Tears spill down her cheeks as shame joins the anger taking a strong hold of me.

Crying? She's fucking crying!

"Why did you come here?" My voice does not mask my anger and comes out harsh, unmoved by her confusion.

Payton's tears flow and she curls her legs protectively to her chest, encasing them in her arms. A sob leaves her throat, and my gut clenches from guilt. The girl is breaking right in front of me.

You piece of shit, Axel, you sorry piece of shit. Look at your handy work! Take pride in what you have done.

But how the fuck was I supposed to know?

I'm livid—my insides stretched tight in disgust as a thousand thoughts swim in my head.

"Payton! Why are you here?" This time, she jumps as I raise my voice. "Un-fucking-believable. Are you even of age? And don't fucking lie!"

Her chin juts out defiantly.

"I'm not fucking lying! Yes, yes, I'm twenty, and you know why I'm here," she says a little stronger but in a rush with what sounds like wrecked nerves.

All your fault.

I push my protesting erection down in my jeans, not bothering to button them. I'm now covered in cold sweat my body is not thanking me for not finishing.

"Axel, please, let's keep going. I don't understand," Payton pleads.

I can't look at her, just the sound of her voice is ripping me apart. Pushing my hair off my forehead, I groan as I let a bit of anger go.

Fix it, I have to fix all of this.

"Get dressed. Get your shit and be ready to leave in fifteen minutes," I say in a dead voice.

I'm ice cold, and fucking pissed. I don't look back before storming out of the room and into mine, slamming the doors as I go.

Five

-

Payton

My body quivers from head to foot. I fall back and stare at the ceiling. The look on Axel's face was murderous as he left me rejected on the bed. I want to be angry, but confusion rules and dominates all other emotions. It was all just humiliating.

Just awful.

I jump when a door slams shut and there is no stopping my tears. I feel rotten like a piece of fruit left to ripen only to be forgotten completely. To make things worse, I'm not only suffering from the physical trauma between my legs, but my chest is so tight, I have to fight to keep breathing.

Curling into a protective ball seems the most natural thing to do at this point. Realization creeps through my mind as I tuck my knees tight to my chest. I had finally given up my virginity, and I'm not sure it could've gone any worse.

What the hell was wrong with Axel that my being a virgin would cause him to run? I thought men were supposed to gloat at taking someone's virginity?

I add that to the long list of shit I don't understand. I rub my tired eyes then freeze when another door opens then closes. Standing a little unsteadily, I peak through the blinds to see Axel stomping through sand toward a solo lounge chair by the water. The sight of his tense, broad back walking away from me causes sadness to well deeper in my chest. New tears come forth.

He's really going to make me leave, and then I will never see Ben again.

Wiping my eyes, my heart sinks further with the knowledge. I'm a very long way from home. Not just home in Mississippi, but *home*, as in I hadn't been anywhere comfortable in years. I'm so incredibly lonely and, at this moment, I feel a sorrow I had never allowed into my heart grip tight.

I dress numbly, pausing every few seconds to wipe at my eyes. Axel wanted me ready to leave in fifteen minutes, but where the hell am I supposed to go? He's so mad, I halfway expect to be tossed out of the car the minute we reach the airport. I have very little money, and that was forced on me by Randell as I boarded my flight in Mississippi.

Randell. He recruited me to be here, so surely he can help?

I sprint to my bedroom and pray he answers the phone. Maybe he could help me. It's not as if I have anything to lose at this point.

I have the number pressed and ready to send when I pause to think. I can't call and confess Axel's reaction. My situation is embarrassing enough without bringing anyone else into it. Exiting the screen before hitting send, I decide to stiffen up my spine and confront Axel. There was zero reason for his reaction, and I will demand he teach me how to act for film or take me to Travis' place, just like Randell told me to.

Travis. Randell had warned to only go to him if I was desperate and had no other options. Travis is another trainer, and one Axel apparently has a bad history with. The thought of him makes my skin crawl, but I don't have an alternative.

You're doing this for a reason. This is all for Ben, so just suck it up already.

"I can do this," I say when I catch a glimpse of my reddened eyes in the mirror. "If Axel refuses me, then I will do what I need to."

Axel's angry yell filters through to my bedroom, and I freeze to listen. I can't make out the words he's saying, but when I walk to the back glass door, I can see his fury in his posture as he paces the beach, talking on the phone. I feel so ugly, hideous, and unworthy of him.

First, Axel had to be talked into taking me, then I end up being what I could only describe as grotesque with my virgin abnormality. No wonder he's disgusted with me. It is abnormal to be a virgin at my age. Then I remember, there's nothing about me that's normal anyway.

I need more wine.

I'll wait until Axel hopefully calms down a bit. I drink and watch Axel for a while, sitting on the couch, growing stronger with every sip. He's overreacting, and it's not as if I'm fifteen and as pure as the driven snow or something. I wanted Axel to break me in. Who better to pop my overly ripe cherry than a man who knew just how to make it memorable?

I throw my head back and laugh out loud. It was definitely memorable. I don't think I will ever forget the burn of his entrance, the look of pure lust that faded quickly into uncertainty and ended with a crash of rage on his beautiful face. I sigh at the mental pictures of Axel and his skilled movements that set my body off like fireworks.

I want more, damn it. I want to complete our union until I can feel his release inside me. I want Axel. I may have signed up for thirty days of training, and that was all good for my end goal and need of quick money, but it's Axel I want like I'd never wanted anything in my life. More than food, or shelter, I *want* that man.

The wine loosens my tightly wound muscles while soothing the sting between my thighs. I sink further back into the couch and drink from the bottle, still watching Axel through the windows, and I decide I will just have to convince him to let me stay. One way or another, I'm not going anywhere. I drink my wine and continue to observe him fuming in the sand. I wish I knew who he is talking to, or screaming at more accurately, but whoever it is, they're receiving a tongue-lashing the likes I've never seen before.

"Shit," I mutter another rare cuss word.

I would almost feel sorry for Axel had my sexual history, or lack thereof, not been duly noted in the ten-page health report I endured poking and prodding for prior to my flight. The longer I sit and watch Axel, the angrier I become. Unable to remain still, I pace. When that does no good, I sit again, pausing the drinking long enough to press my fingers to my throbbing temple.

How did this go so wrong?

Casting a killing look out to the raging man on the beach, I have the uncontrollable desire to break something. Looking around for a vase or a picture, I quickly realized there's none. Actually, there's absolutely nothing that decorative. The walls are pristine and blank. The only thing hung there is the TV. Even the tables by the couch are empty. Everything in the house is void of personality. Standing and really looking at everything, I realize I'm in a very lonesome and cold place.

My anger evaporates at the thought that the house, as lovely as it is, represents a hollow person. There's no evidence of pride or love in this place. I might as well be standing in a hospital room. It's clinical and I get the impression Axel is attached to nothing and no one.

The kitchen is spotless and the only thing out of place is the napkin I used for the sandwich earlier. The plain cabinets, appliances, and living room furniture look more like a showroom display than a home. Shouldn't there be something that looks used?

Hasn't anyone ever cooked for him? Or cuddled under a blanket and watched a movie on the couch?

A new emotion forms with my ebbing ire and embarrassment—pity. But I can't exactly say why. All I know is I have had warmer places to stay on the streets. Even homeless have things they cherish. The blankness of Axel's home appears as if love has never lived here at all.

Six

-

Axel

"What the fuck is wrong with me?" I whisper to my shaking hands. "I'm a piece of shit, always have been."

How could I not know? And much, much sooner?

Reaching down, I adjust my still hard cock and curse the sky for the blue balls I will have when it finally decides to go down. I'm so worked up, so angry, and I don't trust myself to not fuck Payton into tomorrow if I see her naked right now. Shaking my head, I realize this is the first time since I lost my own virginity to a prostitute at thirteen, that I associate shame with sex, and fuck if it doesn't make me feel like absolute shit.

Taking a swig of my Jack Daniels, I watch as the lights change on the water, still trying to calm down. Only after my dick is semi-deflated do I look at the files on Payton on my phone. I skip the shit I'd already read through to focus on her medical file. Just skimming through most, I read the narration from the doctor more closely. I'm looking for three sentences down in some long, boring notation. In almost unreadable scroll sits the words:

Patient hymen is intact.

It's buried in other meaningless shit, and it looks like Japanese to me.

How the fuck did I not see that?

No sooner does that thought form than rage takes over again. I don't think anymore. I touch my contacts, then jab a finger at Barb's number as I walk through the sand and water, pacing like a crazy person hyped up on meth, a look I'm very familiar with in others. Barb answers on the fourth ring.

"Axel," she coos, causing my skin to crawl.

"You would think it an important detail to tell a man that he was about to stick his dick into a virgin!" I spat without preamble.

Barb laughs, actually *laughs* at me. I would strangle the bitch if she were in front of me.

"I would think you would be *thanking* me. What's the problem, Axel?" Her snake-like venom slithers through the phone.

"What's the problem?" I hiss and take a long swig.

What was the problem? Oh, yeah.

"The fucking problem is I don't do shit like this, and you fucking know it. I'm the last person to pop some girl's cherry!" I scream, utterly consumed with fury.

Barb remains silent while I drink, cuss, and stomp back and forth on the beach. It's quiet so long, I actually think she may have hung up on me.

"Axel, what difference does it make whether she's been with one or one hundred? Just teach her how to act, that's why she's here—"

"None! Fucking none," I scream back. "She's been with fucking no one, Barb. I can't teach her how to do anything. You need to call a cab and have her sent back to Missi-fucking-ssippi."

My body warms in response to the whiskey. My rage is now slightly detached from my body. I turn back to my house, unable to stay in one place long.

"I'm not sending her back. You have thirty days to get her ready. We have a contract and she can fetch a good price."

"Do you even hear yourself? *Fetch a good price*?"

"Axel, we have a contract, this is what we do. A good price is what we're after, or have you forgotten that fact?"

"A contract I can end any fucking time I want," I snarl, choosing not to agree with the *we* shit.

I have the absolute power to terminate any contract of any female I feel necessary.

"You would renege on a contract because she's a virgin? That's just stupid. What the hell is wrong with you, Axel? This is what you get paid for. It's business."

I close my eyes in disgust.

"Did you know in some cultures the act of taking a woman's virginity is sacred?" I ask through gritted teeth. "Sacred, Barb. This girl hasn't even lived yet, and I'm supposed to prepare her to be savagely fucked on camera by multiple men a day? In what world does that seem right to you?"

"Axel," Barb purrs and I'd never wanted to harm a woman before this moment. "I didn't know you had become so *soft*."

"Mock me all you want. I probably just fucking ruined that girl for life."

At this point, I'm aware I need to hang up the damn phone before I become weepy, but I also know I need Payton away from me. I rub alcohol off my lips with the back of my hand and catch the smell of Payton's release. My body responds as if doused in lust.

"Aww, fuck!" I groan to the bulge in my jeans. It had finally calmed down, but now it's standing at full attention.

"I don't know what to tell you, Axel, she's an adult and obviously wants this, otherwise she would have told you. I'm not going to help you take her innocence then get rid of her. Besides, it was in her medical file. I tried to tell you she was special, but you just brushed me off. It's your mess, you go clean it up."

"Fucking bitch," I say before ending the call.

Barb is a cold-hearted snake and I'm just now realizing she'd sell her first born if it meant more money in the bank.

After several steading breaths, I trudge heavily through the sand, knowing I'm both buzzing and on my way to being adrift in unknown waters. My dick aches with each step, and once I walk inside the house, my eyes immediately go to Payton where she sits on the couch watching me. I can't look directly at her for long as guilt rips at me. Instead, I move into the kitchen and beeline for the refrigerator and the magnet with a cab's name and number.

"I don't see your bags, go get them. A cab will be here in a few minutes. I'd prefer you wait outside on it."

Yep, I'm being a dick.

Payton is standing beside me before I have the number dialed.

"This is bullshit, Axel! What's so wrong with me? Does my being a virgin make me repulsive?"

I actually wince at that last question.

"Repulsive? Don't be such a child," I respond mockingly while taking a step back.

Payton raises her hands to my chest and pushes me. Hard. Caught off guard, I stumble backward into the kitchen wall. Her delicate face is screwed into a murderous glare.

"I'm not a child! I am a grown woman. I made the choice to enter into this agreement, you are a fucking asshole for failing to uphold your end of the deal!"

I shove my phone in my pocket, abandoning the cab.

"If you were a man, I'd bloody your lip," I growl down at her. Payton's face sobers slightly with fear. "That's right, sweetheart, don't think for a second I'm some honorable guy that will be pussy whipped into marriage or some shit. Do you know who I am?" I step into her and almost falter at the heat and electricity sizzling between us.

This isn't normal.

I don't feel body heat, and I don't get lost in hazel eyes or tongues that sweep across pink lips nervously. I'm a thin edge from ripping her clothes off when realization dawns with what she just said.

Repulsive? Is that how I made her feel?

Tears threaten to fall as she searches my face for something.

"I'm sorry," she begins, ripping my chest open anew. "I just don't understand why you don't want me. I have gone through every humiliating process that was thrown at me from the waxing to invasive pictures, to doctor visits. I just don't understand. I was accepted. They said you agreed to teach me."

That crease between her brows, I don't like it.

I put it there. She's hurting, and it's my fault. Maybe I should go through with this...

No, that's ludicrous.

I take a step back to put some space between us and ignore the lovely southern accent that only seems more pronounced with her anger. The retreat doesn't help so I turn my back on her, heading toward my room and away from Payton and her piercing accusatory stare. I can't think straight around her. If I were an honest man, I would just admit I really don't understand my hesitation except everything in me screams to get her the fuck out of my place and away from Barbara.

Payton will be thrown in the pit with a pack of dogs the minute I sign off on it. I suddenly realize my lawyer knew what he was doing when he demanded I have the final say on all the females I train. The thought of reneging never occurred to me until this moment with Payton.

"Axel? Can I stay?" Payton's voice breaks with desperation as she follows me down the hall. "Please? I don't know where else to go. I have nothing. That's why I'm here." I abruptly stop and turn back to face her.

Tears run, but she quickly wipes them away as if they would offend me. I have to harden my heart for her sake. "You asked me why I was here. That's why. I don't have anything to lose, and I need the money."

I give Payton a disgusted look as she is very near breaking down completely. In spite of being irritated, and regardless of my rage, I feel pity for the briefest of moments.

"You have no idea what you're entering into, Payton, but stay until I can arrange for you to go back home," I say coldly before entering my room and slamming the door behind me.

"I don't have a home," she says so low I'm not certain I heard her correctly.

Either way, I don't respond. Every nerve in my body tingles. The muscles in my shoulders are stretched tight with tension, and I have to wash my hands, my face, and my body because I can feel Payton everywhere.

I knew she was homeless from the information sent to me. But, how's that my problem?

Still boiling, I strip out of my clothes and shower. My frustration stays at the maximum limit as I dry off, put on my oldest jeans, and sit mindlessly in front of my computer.

I jab my fingers at the keyboard and locate Payton's file so I can read it thoroughly, internally kicking myself for half way looking it over before she arrived. This whole damn set up had my normal routine completely fucked up, and I neglected to do my usual pristine job of pre-work. This is all Barb's fault for pressuring me. God, I hate that woman.

I scan through medical files and questionnaires. There is very little social insight.

Payton Andria Knight, known as Payton, is a twenty-year-old white female, blonde, height − 5'9, weight 135lbs, measurements 34-26-36. Born in Hancock County, Mississippi. Parents—both deceased. One unknown sibling. Location found—local bikini contest, Biloxi. Subject has agreed to meet and discuss our consideration of her relocating for possible Legacy work. Suggestion for subject to remain with Axel. Not a good candidate for Travis.

I scroll through the procurer's notes, despising how he called the girls "subjects," then again, he did what he did, and so far, he was decent at it. There isn't much by way of personal information, but I do see Payton attended one year of schooling at Ole Miss University. Less than two years later, she's with me.

Why would she leave college to come to California in hopes of being a porn star?

I shut off the computer, only slightly less pissed now, then wander back to the kitchen for a beer. Payton is sitting on my couch again, watching TV, when she hears me approach. She sits up straighter and watches me intently. I say nothing as I reach for a bottle, twist the cap off, and toss it in the trash. The effects of the Jack are dulling, and I don't want to sink into drunkenness tonight, but I have to try and relax. I drink my beer and watch Payton for a long moment then notice the sandwich she made earlier sitting on the bar. I grab it, eating it in three bites.

I don't even remember the last time I ate.

Still chewing, I sit on the couch opposite Payton. Her stare back at me is full of uncertainty. It's almost dark outside and the only light comes from the kitchen, casting half of her face in shadow. It's enough I can clearly see confusion, and what I believe to be fear, in her eyes while she watches me quietly watch her.

Fuck, she's so pretty, soft in all the right places. And her taste is intoxicating.

I have to shake my head and sip my beer before I get lost in those deep eyes, high cheek bones, and perfectly shaped jaw hidden only slightly by the mess of silky blonde hair.

Utterly beautiful.

She stares back at me almost challengingly. My dick strains against my pants, knowing what she feels like underneath me, but I think the thing that turns me on most is the fact Payton is oblivious to what she looks like or what she does to me.

She has no idea how much I want her.

Clearing my throat, I wipe my mouth with the back of my hand, and summon kindness with all of my strength before finally speaking.

"Why are you here, Payton?"

Before she answers, she picks up her wine, then curls her legs up under her bottom. I want to gouge my eyes out at the sight.

Virgin, I remind myself.

"I was offered the opportunity to make some money, and I was intrigued." She shrugs a shoulder, and her eyes dart to the floor then back to mine. "I want to be here. I was told you were the best, and being trained by you would get me filming much faster."

"So, the adult film industry *intrigued* you?" I ask, trying not to sound sardonic but failing miserably.

Payton nods. "And the money," she adds, sounding ashamed.

"Aww, now that, I understand. That is the sole reason why all women come here, but before you believe everything Barb told you, allow me enlighten you."

I stand and slowly walk to Payton where I bend down, placing a hand on her thigh. Ignoring the tensing of her shoulders, I retrieve the remote beside her butt. She sits perfectly still except for the shiver from my breath on her neck. I can't seem to help it. I want desperately to be away from this woman, and at the same time, I want to play with her.

Remote in hand, I return to my seat across from her. I don't know what the fuck I'm doing. I'm supposed to be preparing this girl to make money for me ultimately, but I've never met anyone so innocent and naïve before. It just seems wrong for her to be here. I need to show her exactly what this pursuit of money could entail.

Pressing the controls, I access my private files from my computer through the digital storage of my TV and type in my password. Scrolling through dozens of files, I find the one I update almost monthly on the girls I have either worked with, or trained, through the years. I've never shared the information with anyone. It's my own personal file, one I am not at all proud of. Stopping at a particular face, I pause before speaking to give Payton a moment to understand what she's seeing.

"Lizzy Martin, 28," I glance to make sure Payton is looking at the redhead on screen then return to look myself. "She died from a heroin overdose eight months ago. She had twenty-eight dollars in her pocket."

I click on the next file of Lizzy's autopsy photo, letting it stay on display as I remain silent so Payton can really see the bruised body, the infected track marks up and down thin arms and legs before moving to the next girl, then the next, showing smiling faces, then their dead bodies.

"Olivia Stallings, 24. Suicide. Terri 22, Makenzie 34, Kylie 19..." On and on, their faces flash across the screen. All either dead or in jail. There was no happy ending for any of them, and I carry that in my soul daily. I suppose that's what makes me such a cold bastard.

"Heather—"

"Okay! I fucking get it." I look back at Payton. She's breathing hard and scowling at me. Unfazed, I scowl right back.

"No, you don't, Payton. Out of the sixty-plus women that have been trained by me, half are dead. Maybe fifteen total actually make a little money. Now, imagine the number of those I actually filmed with either diseased or dead because they end up filming shit for pennies to support whatever habit they've picked up. Either way, I got paid, so the odds of you making money in the long run are very slim."

I click on a different folder, this one for instructional purposes during training, but for a different reason now.

"Lily and Ari." I glance to Payton to make sure she's still paying attention. "This girl-on-girl scene was watched online more than two million times in a month. They each made five thousand dollars to film it, the producers made hundreds of thousands, as well as their agents. I made a nice percentage of the overall profit. Call it finder's fee or training, I still produce well-behaved females, and they do not continue to make anything after the initial filming."

Payton turns her face from the screen to look at me.

"I know what you're trying to do. It's not working."

Ignoring her, I click on a different folder.

"This is Kelsey." I nod toward the dark-haired beauty on display surrounded by several men, all jerking off while waiting their turn to come in her mouth. "She is giving stellar blowjobs. I know they're stellar because I taught her how to give them for the cameras. Sad thing is, this shoot took more than eight hours, so the guys just end up fucking her throat while she takes it. Kelsey has received more downloads than any other adult film star in history. Her pay for that year was roughly sixty thousand dollars. She will regret filming this until her dying day, as they most all do. The ones that live long enough to regret it, anyway."

Payton stands, placing her hands on her hips. I look up at her, hoping I've made my point. She narrows her eyes on me.

"Are you a sadist?"

"What the fuck kind of question is that?" I growl, standing to tower over her, yet she looks utterly unintimidated.

"It seems like you're turned on by these girls' death and misfortune." I snort and exit out of the files. "Do you show this stuff to everyone or just the *virgins*?"

She said the word "virgin" as if to slap me with it. Now, I narrow my eyes at her.

"You know when the last time any porn star actual enjoyed sex was? They don't, trust me, sweetheart, most days I filmed, I don't even remember and the others I wish I could fucking forget. So yeah, I suppose I am a sadist. None of that changes the fact that you don't belong here. You need to go back home."

Anger clouds that beautiful face as she folds her arms and tilts her chin up in defiance. "All the more reason I should be here, Axel, and if you don't teach me what to do," she takes a threatening step toward me, "I will let Travis teach me. That is where I'll go the minute I leave here, and isn't he, like, your competition or something?" She shrugs, tossing her hair back off her shoulder. "It's your choice."

I let out a disgusted sound. "Go ahead. That snatch of yours will be pounded to hamburger once he has you tied and donkey fucked for his little web series. I don't care either way."

The lie is bitter in my mouth, and I have to take a step back from her, almost falling on the couch. The close proximity to her body makes me very uncomfortable.

And why the fuck is she not afraid?

"Oh yes, you do, Axel! You do care. Don't believe me? Then go look at the film, at your face when you realized I was not as loose as your other girls. A guy that didn't care would have finished and would certainly not have gone ape shit at the idea of fucking a virgin. You couldn't get away from me fast enough."

She had me there, but I keep my poker face in place.

"You need to leave. Go back home." It's all I can think to say.

Payton uncrosses her arms and eyes me for a long moment before throwing her hands up in defeat.

"Fine! I'll go, you brutish asshole! I'll call Travis to come get me. Happy now?"

The bile rises once more from my gut and instinctively, I grab her arm just as she pushes past me. I'm furious once more, not to mention confused at the war going on in my head and at Payton being so eager to trade me for Travis so easily. I place a hand on either side of her face and bend, nearly touching her lips with mine. Her scent is enough to make me weak, and I have to remind myself what it was I was saying.

Oh, yeah...

"You will regret that if you do."

She places her hands on my chest and pushes. I retreat only inches.

"If you don't want me, then I'll go to Travis. It's that simple. Either way, next month, I'll be working, and if I end up in your stock of dead girl or junkies, it will be you that has to live with that reality for not honoring our agreement and giving me no other choice."

There's no hesitation, just dead-serious words. I drop my hands and feel my jaw protest at the pressure I'm putting on it. On one hand, I feel obligated to save the girl from the brutality of Travis Beckner, who is nothing more than a two-bit pimp and the lowest form of scum in the adult film industry. The last girl I knew who went to Travis, he talked her into filming a gang bang for a thousand dollars. She was thrown from man to man and raped repeatedly on screen, fucked every way imaginable. She hasn't been heard from since, and her photo still sits in a pile of missing persons.

I know enough, and have been told enough to know, girls simply disappear into the underworld when they get away from Travis. The thought of Payton actually being done that way makes me physically ill.

Is she bluffing? I can't tell.

I see determination in her eyes, and in this moment, I don't want to take the chance of her actually going.

Payton watches me, waiting for me to decide. My entire body hums like a tuning fork this close to her, not to mention the throbbing heartbeat in my pants.

Your move, Axel.

"Fuck." I inhale deeply, then take her wrist, pulling her through the living room and outside onto the dark beach.

"Where are we going?"

I keep moving, pulling her along. My bare feet sink in the sand with every step, and the cool night air raises goose bumps across my chest.

"Axel?"

I don't answer, *can't* answer as I let her go, flipping the padding of my singular wooden beach lounge to dislodge any sand, and then turn back to Payton. The glow of the moon, the sound of the waves, only feet from where we stand, give a calming effect to my pent-up nerves.

"What are you doing?"

"I'm fucking you, Payton. For the first time. Off camera, off schedule, I'm fucking you because that's why you're here, right?"

And I'm going to really go ape shit if I don't. Oh God, I want this woman...damn me to hell, I want her.

I stand hesitant, adrift, feeling shit I'm clueless about and helpless to fight. Towering over her as excitement and testosterone flow through me, I feel the slight trembling rolling off her in waves. Absorbing it, I bend my face to her, our noses nearly touching,

"You do want me to fuck you, right?"

She shivers, causing me to grin wickedly.

"Yes," she whispers.

"Then, shut up," I growl and give one chaste kiss before pulling her shirt off. Slowly, I move to her shorts, running my knuckles down the soft curve at her sides, roughly grabbing her hips while pressing my erection into her stomach. I stealthily take my time unbuttoning and pushing the denim over her hips, revealing skin that glows in the moonlight. Small hands hold on to my shoulders as I remove one foot, then the other. Eye level once more, I pause to give her one more chance to say no.

"Last chance." I trail my lips down the side of her neck like I've done it a million times before when, in reality, I have no fucking idea what I'm doing. "Say the word because I'm almost at a point of no return."

"Don't stop, oh God, Axel, I'm on fire." Payton pushes her hands through my hair, pulling at it desperately wanting more, then stills. "But shouldn't we do this on camera so you can see what I look like?"

Pressing my mouth to hers, crushing it, silences her. Wrapping an arm around Payton's waist, I move my mouth down to the pink crests of her nipples, suckling and biting without regard to the pressure.

Payton throws her head back and moans while running her fingers through my hair, pressing me harder into her flesh. I slide a finger between her legs, and she jerks at my touch. I sit on the lounge chair, and place one of her long legs over my shoulder. Without hesitation, I bury my face between her legs, skipping any introductions, rubbing my nose in circles over her most secret place as my hands squeeze her ass before moving my fingers to probe at her opening.

So wet and yes, on fire.

Holding most of her weight with my arm wrapped tightly around a thigh, she balances herself with hands in my hair, on my shoulders, scratching at my back, and I begin to rock her gently against my tongue, slowly entering one finger inside her heat. The groan that vibrates against her mound doesn't sound remotely human, and I make the mistake of looking up, into that face.

The pure pleasure of being on the brink of orgasm has Payton's features clenched and breathtakingly gorgeous. I know, in this moment, she is the most beautiful creature I've ever seen. In the glow of the moon, I watch the globes of her breasts shake with the pleasure coursing throughout her body.

Just before she comes, I reduce my probing tongue to soft kisses, placing a second finger slowly inside. No matter that my body is screaming to pounce and do it hard, I have to prepare her. The blunt entrance from earlier was just wrong, but I had no way of knowing what I was doing at the time.

Now, I let my instinct go and massage her tender flesh for a moment, stretching her to the limit, then I push a third inside, moving in and out, trying to ease the tension. Payton gasps and shakes with a mixture of pain and desire for more. Pressing my tongue back to her nub, it takes only seconds before she begins breaking apart with orgasm. I watch her face contort and her breasts tremble under the raging force. If she were to merely touch my dick, I would blow from this sight alone.

"Perfect," I breathe, completely out of my depths.

Once only aftershocks remain, I guide Payton to the lounge, laying her back. The moon illuminates her pale skin, and for the briefest of moments, as I pull off my jeans, I can only think of angels.

Payton is an absolute angel. Maybe that's why I felt so much guilt earlier?

Yeah, guilt was what I'm still feeling. Not something I've felt often, but it is definitely there. She deserves better than me, she deserves some nice guy to give her a nice house and babies, not some piece of shit porn freak show.

As if sensing my hesitation, Payton opens her legs and reaches for me with both hands. Piece of shit or not, Payton wants me, that much is obvious. Swallowing the guilt, letting it drain away, I crawl between her legs and lay half my weight on top of her body, holding the other half on my elbows.

Softly, I press my lips to hers and slowly kiss them, suckle and lick them. Desire for this woman is making me crazy, but I want, *no need*, to do right by her. I have to go slow even though my cock is screaming, "Go! GO! Go!" I take my time to relax Payton further, as much as possible.

With agonizing force, I end the kiss and wrap a hand around my dick to guide it inside her body. Watching closely for discomfort or pain, I press forward. Her eyes lock with mine, encouraging me silently. I release a shaky breath as I make progress.

"Deep breath, baby girl, tell me if you need to stop," I whisper.

Christ, I have no idea what I'm doing, what I'm saying.

But Payton nods, biting her lower lip as I sink further inside. Everything slows at the penetration, and I'm suddenly aware I've sobered up yet on the high of my life. My pulse rushes through my body while our middles lock tight and lips join in unison.

Heaven. It's fucking Heaven.

Tongues sweep across lips, every exhale and inhale taking us somewhere foreign, unknown, yet blissful. We're strangers but familiar with each deepening stroke. Opening my eyes while moving within her body, I find Payton staring back at me, perhaps mirroring my look of fascination and wonder as we kiss. Our eyes stay locked, and I allow myself to feel...*everything*. It's transcendental. Those penetrating hazel eyes make me slip in concentration, and as it becomes too much, I lower my face to her ear.

"Fuck, I'm not going to last long. This feels too fucking good." I growl against her shoulder, then bite down as, thrust by thrust, I press deeper.

She moans, and I move faster, still trying to keep a slower pace but aware of her throbbing need. I want to rejoice she's about to come again, but I try to keep from ruining it with my own release. Moving to frantically kiss her jaw and neck, I whisper for Payton to let go with me. After slow thrusts that burn, igniting us both, I pull back and shove forward quicker, deeper. Crying out and arching her back, she whimpers and her nails claw at my shoulders. Deep breathes, slow, slow, then repeat the action, I'm drawing out every quiver and moan Payton will give me.

"Axel," she whines and tilts her hips, grinding against me.

The sights and sounds are so intense, I have trouble processing it all. Pure, carnal need consumes me, and my body burns torturously from holding back. Once I can feel her inner muscles contract, I quicken my pace, wrapping my arms around her waist, crushing her body to mine. I descend on her nipples, unmercifully chewing at them as her orgasm builds with each thrust.

Absolute euphoria takes hold, Payton comes and I'm not prepared for the intensity of it. My orgasm slams into me, knocking me off-guard, and I actually let loose a primal howl to the sky. I jerk violently, raising to grip the lounge, the wood splintering under my hand at the pressure. My entire body seizes with the release and relief that seems to have no end and no mercy.

Then, finally, *Jesus Christ*, fucking *finally*, I come down from the surreal orgasmic high, placing my forehead on hers, and for a long moment, we simply breathe each other in. I inhale the sweet smell of old wine and the salty sea along with the clean scent of her shampoo. Our chests press together, and our heartbeats mingle. It's the single strangest sensation I've ever experienced, and if I have to identify the feeling, I'd say it terrifies me.

Seven

-

Payton

Axel is a sex god.

No wait, Axel is a *fucking* sex god. In the silence, even as our breathing calms and the cool air of the night makes me shiver, I'm as relaxed as a cat in a pool of sunshine. Even though I know I'll probably be sore from the intrusion, I can't help but wonder when we will do this again.

Soon, I hope. And often.

As the haze of great sex fades, I sense a change in Axel. It's not very noticeable at first, but when I touch my fingertips to his broad back, it's obvious he's very uncomfortable. Withdrawing from my body, he backs off of the lounge. I can't see his face in the dim lighting but his body language is screaming tension, possibly even anger.

I reach for my discarded shirt and quickly shove my arms through, watching the unpredictable and frustrating man before me as he pulls on his jeans. I sit and wait as a thousand different feelings roll through me.

Did I do something wrong? Was this a one-time thing and now I really do have to go? Oh God, it was awful for him. I must really, really suck at sex.

Awkward.

This is so fucking awkward.

Not talking, not looking at each other is making me jittery. I just had this man in my body, experiencing something I know in my gut will never be repeated as long as I live, and all I can do is wish I were in bed, curled under a blanket, hiding from the world. I'm mortified because it's blatantly clear he regrets what we just did.

God, I have to be horrible.

Axel just stands there, hands on hips, head tilted down to the sand, breathing. I sit like a church mouse waiting to be kicked out of the house for being so *virginal*.

What will I do now?

What can I do? I'll do what I have to in order to make it back to Ben, that is a promise I will keep.

Unable to take any more of the silence, I stand to say something, anything. Maybe apologize for being a brat or for being a shitty lover, anything to break the weirdness of the moment. I open my mouth to speak but Axel beats me to it.

"You hungry?"

His face is turned toward me but is shadowed. I can't measure his mood but the question makes me think that maybe, if only for tonight, I can eat.

"Um, sure." My voice sounds like it came from a stranger.

"Good, I'm starving."

Axel walks past, back toward the house, not sparing me a glance or a fuck you or anything. I have this overwhelming need to touch him but I know it's crazy. This wasn't a love match, and he obviously isn't into cuddling.

But to be held by him, just for a few minutes, would be bliss.

Exhaling deeply, it takes me a full minute to locate my panties. Abandoning my shorts all together, I hurry after the brooding, sulking, beautiful man while fighting back my girlie wants and needs. I enter the backdoor he leaves open and slide it closed behind me.

"I'll fix us something while you clean up," Axel says with his head in the fridge.

It's said as an order, and while I want to say something to let Axel know I don't like orders, I become aware of the feeling between my legs. Dismissing being dismissed, I quietly enter my room and retrieve the small toiletry bag from my suitcase and proceed to clean up.

Twenty minutes later, I reenter the kitchen and close my eyes at the smell that greets me. My mouth waters the moment tacos are recognized, then I pause to take in the view. Axel's tattooed back is to me, his big arms bunching and releasing as he grates cheese in a bowl. He must've cleaned up too because his hair is wet, and there are tiny beads of water visible on the golden skin of his shoulders.

I want to touch him so badly, run my hands up and bury them in his hair while pressing my body against his.

The lust is so strong, I could almost float to where he stands, but the moment he turns his face and sees me, it vanishes. His tense posture returns, darkening Axel's features, and, once again, I'm struck with the reality that I'm in a place I'm not wanted, no matter what we just did.

Am I that displeasing that he scowls at me?

You'd think getting laid would brighten his mood but, oh no, not my porn star. Getting laid looks to have made him meaner.

Suck it up, Payton, think of Ben. You can handle this guy's dislike for a little while. But it would've been so nice to have been wanted.

I can't help it, it affects me, and I wilt like a scorched flower under the glare of Axel's dark eyes. I fake a small smile, and Axel grimaces then tosses whatever he's holding away where it clatters to the floor.

"Fuck!"

Now what did I do?

Understanding dawns when blood runs thick from his forefinger. I reach to turn on the kitchen faucet and take hold of his thick wrist, pulling at it to wash off the cut. Even though I'm in rescue mode, I can't help but notice the resistance Axel gives as I try to help.

He can't stand me touching him.

Ignoring I must actually repulse the guy, I hold his hand under the cold stream.

"Here, just hold it under the water for a moment, and let me get the Band-Aids. Do you have a first aid kit?"

He doesn't respond, so I pull my eyes away from the emergency at hand and see Axel is looking at me, like *looking* at me. His eyes rake down my hair and eyes, landing solidly on my lips.

Why is he acting so strange?

Then, I get it. I have zero makeup on.

I must really be hideous now.

"First aid kit?" I raise my brows in question.

He stands there staring as if I'm speaking Japanese. Chocolate brown eyes narrow. He pulls away from my grip, turning so I can no longer see his face while yanking a paper towel out of the holder and wadding the thing around the cut.

"It's fine. It'll stop in a minute," he grumbles.

I let out a frustrated sigh and turn off the faucet.

"Let me finish the food, okay?" God knows I can make myself useful somehow, and maybe if I feed the guy, he won't be so grumpy. Then again, getting laid didn't really help so food most likely won't either.

Quietly, Axel sits and holds the injured finger. I clean the mess of the cheese up and busy myself with the meat, onions, sauce, and tomatoes while he broods in silence. All in all, when I finally set the island with tortillas and fixings, Axel's shoulders are little more relaxed. I silently pray a full belly will warm him to me.

"Want me to make you a plate?" I ask politely as blood wells anew when the paper towel comes off and a fresh one replaces it.

"No, I can do it."

Not waiting on him, I pile my plate, starved and even though my company is a reserved grouch, I eat happily.

More than once, I have to stifle a snicker watching Axel roll a taco only to have the innards fall out while he brings it to his mouth. This gains me new glares, but I am quickly adapting to them.

"Why won't you let me help?" I ask curiously.

I know the answer, but I also know he will never admit to being a prideful caveman who doesn't need a woman to take care of him.

Before he responds, I hop off my stool and stand between his parted knees.

"Stop being a brat and let me help."

"A brat?"

"Yeah, a stubborn brat, at that."

I reach to make the taco properly then bring it to the most beautiful lips I've ever seen on a man. I lick my own involuntarily and blink away dirty thoughts as Axel bites down.

I could kiss you all night, handsome man.

"All night and not only on the mouth."

"What did you say?"

Oh shit! I said that out loud.

"Nothing, just now you can get it in your mouth, at least, you know, without it falling apart."

His eyes never leave my face. Folding the tortilla to fit better in that glorious mouth, I chance another glance at him. Brown orbs watch me questioningly, maybe even coldly, like he's preparing for me to either strike like a snake or explode at any moment. My stomach clenches at the intensity of the gaze.

"What?" I ask and feel my playful mood diminish. "I'm just trying to help."

Axel takes the taco from me and nearly inhales it. I sit on the stool beside him and make another. We're quiet while he eats, and I drink more wine. It seems I can't get enough, and the longer I sit with Axel watching me, the drunker I want to be.

A grueling ten minutes later, I begin to clean up. When I reach to load the last dish into the washer, I hear Axel get down from the stool and walk to lean against the wall next to me. I toss in the detergent, then shut and start the cycle before acknowledging him. Arms crossed over his broad chest, eyes piercing and jaw set, Axel looks like a dark, delicious piece of candy I really, *really* want to lick.

At least, I do until he says, "You need to go home."

"Why?" My spine stiffens, and I cross my own arms protectively.

"Because you need to, that's why."

"Just because you think I need to go doesn't mean I need to go."

Molars grinding, a bit of anger flares across his features as he pushes off the wall and rest his hands on the kitchen island.

"I don't want you here, isn't that enough of a reason?"

Pain slices through me.

"But I thought since—"

"Thought since I fucked you that I would somehow be on board with teaching you to do the same to others on film?"

I have to fight back tears.

"That wasn't exactly what I was thinking but that's why I'm here, isn't it?"

A deep inhale in and Axel drops his head.

"Look, I am a douche bag and should have never done," his eyes search the counter top for words before returning to my face, "I shouldn't have done anything with you, to you, I mean."

"I asked you to."

He shakes his head and closes his eyes, looking exhausted. "It doesn't matter, I shouldn't have." I remain quiet, standing opposite him at the kitchen island. Axel opens his eyes and is wearing the look of pure conviction when he says, "I'll make some kind of arrangement for you until you can get back home, but I think it would be best if you leave in the morning."

Too hurt to respond, I just stupidly watch as he walks to his bedroom and shuts the door.

I stand and stare at the place where Axel stood for several minutes, and I don't even realize I'm crying until I taste the salty tears on my lips. It takes several more to start moving toward my room. I mechanically brush my teeth and climb into bed, knowing I'm not wanted, not even by a guy who, according to his porn's bio, has made over 1500 movies and is ranked in the top ten of male porn stars of all time.

To think I am the one not wanted crushes my heart, though for the life of me, I can't understand why. I'm here to learn what I can to break into the industry and make good money and damn it, come morning, I'm going to put up a fight to do just that. I've got too much shit to do not to get that contract. That money will help me tremendously.

And Ben.

Oh God, Ben.

Axel is going to have to have me physically removed. I don't have time for a traditional pathway to film. I would have to do amateur for months before a pro producer would even consider me, and I'm not doing webcam shows. I'm entirely too awkward to do that. Axel has to help me, or my only hope of getting paid is over. There won't be anything for me back home. Minimum wage will not help me and certainly won't help Ben.

But then, there's Travis?

I could go to him, Randell told me I can use that name to get Axel to cooperate. But laying here, I don't have hope Axel will do anything other than exactly what he said. I'll have to leave in the morning. This is his home, and I'll be damned if I beg.

My last thought is of Ben before I drift away. That lazy smile, those beautiful baby blue eyes.

Oh Ben, I am so sorry.

Eight

-

Axel

You're doing it wrong.
Don't push all the way in.
You came too soon.
You need to hold her ass cheeks apart.
You need to prop her leg this way.
Don't look toward the camera.
Don't do it softly.
Don't stick your ass up.
Hold her like this.
Put this cream on your dick, it will help you last longer.
You want a little blow to get you going?
I don't give a shit if it's your third filming today, we are on a schedule. Take this pill, you will feel better.

The commands dance around my head, taunting me. Have I been ruined by the business? I suppose at sixteen, I was ruined, most likely before I ever filmed the first scene. I didn't know a different way of doing things then. I had been properly trained like a dog for so long, I only knew the clinical way of performance with zero aftermath or emotion. The females were all cold, empty, and money hungry whores. That's the only type of woman I've ever known—from my mother to Barbara and every female costar I've ever worked with.

Not one of them had any kind of need or want for me. None. I'm the douche who fucks them with a numb dick for hours to get that five minute clip of film-worthy orgasm. Most of the females can't get away from me fast enough, and the feeling is mutual. It was fun at first, especially when I got to film with Reece. My best friend and I would party between filming, but even that got old after a while.

And him leaving the underbelly of society to become an officer of the law? That took the only fun out of working all together. I've spent the past few years drugged out and asleep. My entire world has been routine, neatly on a schedule without any kind of disturbance. My success at sobriety requires that, my heart will only allow that but, I recognize there's something way off with Payton.

Way fucking off.

That realization makes me uneasy. There's not shit I can do about her choices, but I know I want nothing to do with helping her out with them. The act of taking her for the first time is one I will regret for the rest of my life. I'll burn in hell for that alone if not all the other awful, unforgivable shit I've done. The thought makes me want to rip my flesh from my bones.

Glancing over, I see it's six a.m. and I'm not even sleepy. Dead tired, but not sleepy. Sitting up and forgetting about sleep entirely, I rest my elbows on my knees and push my fingers through my hair, yanking hard.

What the fuck am I going to do with this girl?
Girl?
Not a girl, but still, a *virgin*?
"Not anymore thanks to you, you piece of shit," I whisper to the dark.

Thoughts of the act make me want to hunt and destroy something, and, at the same time, I want to do it again. And again. And again.

Fuck, I'm going to Hell.

No sooner had the words left my lips than a strangled cry rings out from somewhere in the house. Instinct takes over and I'm instantly on alert, body tense, hands balled into fists, ready to kill. Leaping from the bed, I grasp for the knob, nearly tearing the door from its hinges as I burst from my room. I storm past the glass doors to the beach and to the spare bedroom, looking for the threat.

Nothing. I got absolutely nothing.

Maybe I'm dreaming and will wake up in the boat drifting across the Atlantic?

But no. I'm still very keyed up from Payton's presence in my home. Every nerve in my body vibrates.

All is quiet, nothing out of place. It had to have come from Payton's closed door but damned if I'm going in there right now. I stand perfectly still and wait, hoping a little the noise came from outside, but the beach is private. Very few people ever venture down this far and the cry sounded too soft to be Reece. He's too far up the beach to be heard anyway.

"Ben." The name comes on a hoarse moan, and now I know for certain, it's coming from Payton's room.

The need to fight to defend my home, or worse, a girl, is instantly replaced with rage, and I absently wonder why I'm angry at the mention of another man's name. I don't bother to knock, just twist the knob and slowly open the door with as little noise as possible. Soft light spills onto the bed from the hall. Payton is asleep, but not peacefully. She's thrashing all over—her feet kicking and her face bunched up in agony.

Tightness grips my gut and the breath leaves me as I watch her chest rise and fall rapidly with the dream or nightmare she's lost to. I want to wake her, but I just stand and observe, weirdly ready to fight if something tries to attack.

Just when she goes still and I am convinced it's over, Payton rises straight up in the bed and screams bloody murder. The sound is so shocking, I stumble backward, caught off-guard. After a few unsteady seconds to find my footing, and launch myself in the room, grabbing hold of Payton's arms, shaking her hard.

"Wake up! It's just a dream!"

Sobs, a whole fucking lot of sobs, burst free and she grabs at me, wrapping her arms around my neck and squeezing.

"Axel!"

Payton buries her face in my neck, and I sit like a statue.

What the fuck is going on? And why does she smell so good?

I do what seems to be most natural and rub awkwardly at her back. That's when I realize she's naked.

Oh, fuck me, Payton is completely naked.

There's nothing between me and her perfect skin. Tight nipples brush my chest, and I'm instantly ready to pounce.

"Oh God, it was awful." Payton sobs and I'm yanked back from the thought.

"You were dreaming." I nudge her away and hold her at arm's length.

She grinds small fists at her eyes to rid them of tears and sleep. Her breasts sway with the movement, and I have to look away.

She's really fucking naked.

"I'm sorry, I didn't mean to wake you."

"You didn't," my voice comes out thick.

A hand lands on my shoulder, and I stand, adjusting myself so my erection doesn't show through my boxers.

"You should go back to sleep, get some rest."

Lame, so fucking lame.

But my head is screaming to *get out. Now.*

"Wait, don't go yet. Please?"

Payton's voice is broken, and I fight the need to comfort her. If I do, it will only make it harder to get rid of her tomorrow. Or today, rather.

"Stay with me, please? Just for a few minutes. I don't want to be alone just yet."

Like a rigid, reluctant robot, I sit back down, unable to leave while she begs. Placing my elbows to my knees,

I look at the dim light on the floor and wait. Payton doesn't lie back, and I can feel her eyes on me, all over me. My skin pricks at her perusal and the sexual tension in the air is palpable.

"You said Ben."

Glancing to the side, I see her go completely still. Another moment passes, and she shuts down completely.

"Is that your boyfriend?"

Payton shakes her head and closes her eyes.

"A boy I knew, back home," she whispers almost painfully.

I nod, knowing that's all I'm getting. And like a switch flipping, Payton leans closer, seeking comfort. I fight the two things I want to do more than anything: running from the room and pulling her closer.

"Can I touch you, Axel? Just a little?"

A puff of air leaves my lips, and I can see a fire behind Payton's hazel eyes. There's also what I can only think is caution, skepticism, or maybe insecurity? Her blonde hair is tousled, and just as before, I'm drawn to the beauty of her clean, makeup free face.

Sitting up straight, I place my hands on my thighs.

"Touch me how?" I croak out.

Real smooth, Axel. You sound like a scared teenager.

"Any way, every way you will let me."

She wets her lips, and my heartrate picks up at the sight of her tongue. My eyes drop to the puff of lips then back to the hypnotic eyes.

"I'm going to hell," I whisper.

Not out loud, stupid.

Payton tilts her pretty head to the side and frowns. "Why would you say that?"

I shake my head and close my eyes.

"Nothing."

"Keep your eyes closed and think of whatever girl you want, but just let me touch you. Please?"

I frown.

Whatever girl I want?

Such an odd thing to say, but because it's what she wants, I close my eyes. The sensations are instantly heightened. Warm hands come to my chest then slide slowly to my shoulders. Weight shifts, and Payton straddles my lap. I fight against the need to open my eyes once her breasts brush my chest, and my breaths come faster, louder, and yeah, she's completely naked. This is abundantly clear when I feel her hot core through the thin material separating us.

I'm tense, so fucking tense, my muscles protest and yet my guilt is forgotten for the moment. I slowly drag my hands up her slender thighs.

"Yes, touch me, Axel, you set me on fire."

Wet lips touch mine, and I surge up to deepen the kiss. Tongues dueling, we hungrily kiss, nip, and suck at each other. Desire for this woman reaches new highs, and as tendrils of fire lick across my skin, pausing only to breathe, I know I want her to burn me down, leave nothing but ashes when she's finished using me.

A hand slides down my chest, over my abdomen, and grips my erection. I drop my head back and a hiss escapes through my teeth.

"I want to forget, just for tonight. Can I do that with you?" Her voice is low and sultry, nothing shy about her now.

"Oh fuck, use me, Payton. Whatever you want." I groan.

I have a brief moment of sanity at the sound of my voice, and I question why I spoke, but quickly, it's gone, when my lips meet hers once more. Just as I begin kneading her ass, she pushes me back on the bed. Opening my eyes, I watch my erection spring free when my boxers are yanked off. The sight of Payton climbing on top of my body sends me to the moon, but when she holds my erection up and slides down, locking our pelvises tight, I'm in orbit.

"Fuck. Me." I growl, not meaning it literally, but that's exactly what Payton does.

Not waiting a second and just as crazed as me, she begins an unmerciful ride. Her gorgeous body rising and falling hard, she is fucking away the dream while driving me insane. Payton whimpers and moans, but if there's discomfort, she's ignoring it.

Head tilted slightly to the sky, her long neck is exposed and a completely foreign feeling comes over me. It's completely ludicrous, but I'm feeling it all the same. For the first time in my life, I'm falling. My inner fucked-up barriers drop away and I'm exposed.

I am lost.

Helpless.

Raw and utterly shattered by this woman, this beautiful stranger.

Reaching up, I cup the sides of her face and tenderly rub, then slide down to her breasts, coming to rest on the curve of her hips. The feel of her skin, the sight of her pleasure, and the sound of my name leaving her lips makes my heart actually ache.

"You are so beautiful," I whisper.

Payton slows and searches my eyes. What she sees, I can't say, but in almost slow motion, we move as countless unspoken words pass between us.

"Axel?" Payton says my name in a breathless huff.

"Hmm?" is the only reply I can muster because my mouth is busy, and my hands are consumed.

"Am I doing it right?"

I go absolutely still at the question.

How many women ask me that?

Countless, faceless women. Payton asking it turns my heart to stone. Trying to mask my idiotic emotions, I turn my attentions to the sex and most importantly, getting her off. Teasing her delicate skin, suckling her breasts—one then other—I take control, and just like that, my shields are firmly back in place.

"Axel?" She's unsure now. Good. "Is this okay? Does this feel good?"

We are not on camera. We are not being filmed and she just wants to know if it feels good.

Right?

"Feels great," I say thickly without removing my mouth from a nipple.

Is this good, baby? Is it good for you?

Long, chipped red nails on my body.

I shake my head as unwanted memories begin to take hold, and I desperately need them out of my fucking mind. Needing to turn everything around, I decide Payton could use some dirty and I could use the control. I lick my middle finger, then reach around her hip and slowly glide the first knuckle into her ass. Tight resistance greets my invasion and Payton's head falls and a grunt of shock leaves her lips. I have to grin because at this point, she's at my mercy.

Delicately, I tease at her puckered entrance, playing more with her mind than her body while erotic curiosity reigns. The result is exactly what I'm after as she squirms, unsure if fear or pleasure should rule in this moment.

Payton falters in her pace so I wrap my free arm around her waist and begin thrusting my hips. Seconds later, she shouts a wicked curse to the heavens and I let go a massive orgasm of my own. I crush Payton to me while she holds onto my neck for dear life. I'm willing to bet she's forgotten whatever it was she wanted to forget in the first place. Sadly for me, she's awakened things I'd long forgotten.

Nine

-

Axel

"Let's try the thirty days? Please, Axel? If it works out, then okay. If not, no hard feelings and we go our separate ways."

The silence is broken and reality is restored with Payton's words.

Post-coital peace evaporates, and what's left is sweat-sheened raw skin and rapid heartbeats. I'm not given a moment of relaxation and the fact Payton has no idea what just happened inside my cold, damned to hell heart makes me want to tear the walls down with my bare hands.

I lie on my back with Payton beside me, her face turned to mine while I stare blankly up at the ceiling, revealing nothing. I wouldn't give her the satisfaction of knowing what war raged in my head.

She'd probably get off on it.

An annoyed sigh slices through the space between us.

"Axel?"

Gritting my teeth, I turn my face to hers. I want to scream at her, be cruel in some way because she has no clue she's ripping me clean apart.

"I understand you have a choice and I was completely off your usual schedule, but Randell said Travis wasn't an ideal fit for me and I can make more money learning from you."

The sound of fucking Travis' name leaving her lips makes me want to growl like an animal, the thought of him fucking her, or having her fucked for his live freak shows? Murder comes to mind.

I have three options. One, I can pack Payton up and send her back to the boonies where she really belongs. Two, I can teach her the ins and outs of porn and get paid. Three, I can let her leave, knowing she will go straight to Barbara—the devil herself—and sign her soul away to Travis.

Fury and resentment rise. I know I am fucked no matter what I do because none of these options are appealing in the least.

Exhausted, I give up. I stand and shove my legs into my boxers, not bothering to take the time to see they're actually backward before I leave the room without a word. My skin crawls like tiny insects are nesting, and my skull is stretched so tight, I have to feel if it's coming apart at the seams.

Soft padding of feet across the wood floors follows me, and I know Payton is on my heels, anticipating a response. The sun is rising so I can forget about getting any sleep. Movement at the back door brings me to a stop, then I recognize who is pressed comically against the glass, hands over eyes peering in like some peeping tom.

Glancing to see if Payton is naked, I'm struck with the fact a sheet wrapped around her body is just as appealing as her being unclothed...and fuck if her lips aren't red and swollen. I want to hate her so badly, I really, *really* do.

"Do you know him?"

"Unfortunately," I say, rolling my eyes dramatically and walking over to let in the stalker. I motion for Reece to come inside. His wide, 6'3", body-builder frame squeezes through the door and his size fourteen, wide boots thud on the hardwood. Dark, messy hair shines with slight perspiration and I imagine he may have jogged here.

"What the fuck you doin', Axel? I thought squatters had taken over while you were out or one of those crazy-ass fans of yours broke in to masturbate in your bed again."

The policeman, and sometimes security man, who is also my only friend, walks closer to examine me with suspicious hawk-gray blue eyes, and I halfway expect him to shine his light in my face to better inspect me. He squints comically, then offers me a deep frown before leaning in closer to smell me, inhaling deeply.

"Jesus Christ, you smell like pussy and whiskey, not that it don't make my mouth fucking water but not on you at fucking six o'clock in the morning. Whata' you doin' here? You said you was leaving," Reece grumbles in his barely noticeable southern Louisiana accent.

"You're fucking crowding me, Reece, do you mind?" I step to the side to shut the glass door before walking to refrigerator for water. I don't have to see the moment he spots Payton to know when he does. Reece clears his throat, and, in my periphery, I watch her straightening and self-consciously gripping the sheet tighter.

"Well now, who might you be?"

Twisting the lid off my water bottle, I turn to watch the two. Payton's hazel eyes quickly look to me then back at Reece, and I don't blame her for being instantly on-guard. Reece is a lot to take in at first. The full-sleeve tattoos on display are enough to make a person pause, but it's the beautiful face that takes you by surprise. His tanned Cajun skin tone, and big, rough exterior is in complete contrast with the sharp jawline and high cheek bones male models dream of. Those things for sure have not escaped Payton's notice.

I have to get out of here, I have to get away from this house, this girl.

"Hello? Cat got your tongue, motherfucker?"

"What do you want, Reece? I got shit to do."

Reece looks from me to Payton, trying to figure out what in all hell is going on. Payton looks at me with a similar expression only laced slightly with hurt? Confusion? Fuck if I know, but I turn and leave them to figure it out.

"Wait just a damn minute—"

Ignoring them, I walk to my room, tossing my half-empty bottle in the trash as I go, and just as I swing my bedroom door shut, Reece pushes it open, then shuts it behind him. I don't bother looking at him, I just pull clothes from my closet and start dressing—running shorts, t-shirt, socks.

"What's going on, Axel?"

"What? Same shit, different day." I side-step him when he tries to make eye contact.

"Why are you here? Who's the female?"

Shoving one foot, then the other in my Nikes, I stand only to be met with Reece's face inches from mine.

"Talk."

"There's nothing to say. Barb had this girl come. Like I said, same shit, different day. I gotta go, I'd say make yourself at home but that's kind of moronic statement considering you always do. I'll catch you later."

"Axel, God damn it."

I exit my room before he can argue, grabbing my keys and ignoring the call of my name. Just as I back the bike out of the garage, I see Reece at the garage door flipping me the bird. I give it right back and peel from the driveway like my ass is on fire.

What am I running from?

Fuck if I know, but every bone in my body is screaming to get the hell away from Payton.

Ten

-

Payton

Watching the man slam the garage door shut, my stomach roils with fear. Right now, watching the big guy turn and unbutton his uniform shirt, I'm terrified. I inch backward on my tiptoes. The man watches me with a wicked grin.

"Relax, honey, I'm just getting comfortable. I'm the last person that's gonna mess with you."

Feeling minimally comforted be his words, I pull my sheet tighter to my chest.

"I'm Reece LeDoux, and as you can see," a meaty hand gestures down his body and gun, "I'm a cop, which isn't a declaration of not being a complete douche, but in my case, it is. You got nothing to worry about. What's your name, sweetheart?"

Tossing the discarded shirt on the couch and untucking the t-shirt from the waist band of his pants, Reece cracks his neck from one side to the other.

"LeDoux? That's a French name."

"My family was Cajun, so yeah, it's origin is French."

Reece smiles, and my God the man is beautiful. His crystal blue eyes and perfect white teeth are panty melting. Too bad I can only appreciate his good looks, and not actually want him. At the moment, I seem to crave brooding darkness in the shape of Axel.

"I'm Payton."

Reece inclines his head to me, then bends to untie his boots, one after the other, then props his feet on the coffee table and gives me his best cop stare.

"Why don't you go get cleaned up, then you and I can talk? You like eggs?" He stands and walks to rummage in the fridge.

I don't answer, I just back into my room, shutting and locking the door behind me.

I can't believe Axel left me in his home with a total stranger.

A laugh bubbles up and I have to cover my mouth when I remember Axel himself is a total stranger—a stranger I willing gave my body to, over and over.

"Oh God," I whisper and search the ceiling for answers.

After several long moments of internally kicking my stupid self, I finally shower, shave my legs, brush my teeth, and dress in one of the outfits Randell bought me. I'm not comfortable and decide on wearing my denim shorts. Still not at all comfortable, I leave my room and walk to Axel's. Reece glances up from the kitchen island and watches me pass without a word.

I don't hesitate to enter the bedroom. Dark mahogany furniture fit for a king fills the space and an enormous bed takes up most of the suite. I ignore the rumpled covers, and head to the chest of drawers. I find socks and boxers in the first one. I grab a fresh pair of both. I also take a Motley Crue t-shirt from the closet. I don't bother shutting or locking the door, just strip and pull on the pilfered clothes.

That's better.

I'm more at home in baggy sleep attire and oversized socks than the pretty girl outfit.

Not bothering with looking in the mirror, I walk in the kitchen braver than I feel. Still on the stool at the island, Reece is sporting a cocky grin when he sees what I'm wearing. Eyeing me head to foot with an amused expression, he whistles low.

"That suits you mighty fine, Payton."

"Thanks," I mumble and tuck my damp hair behind my ears.

"Plate's in the microwave."

Suddenly starved, I retrieve the plate and almost gasp at the size of the omelet. Having to use two hands, I carry it to the island where I sit opposite Reece. He waits to speak when my mouth is full with the first bite.

"Wanna tell me what you're doing here?"

I chew and swallow. "I could ask you the same thing."

A bark of laughter brightens his blue eyes.

"I'm here four, maybe five times a week when Axel doesn't have anyone here, so I'm kinda always here."

Chew. Swallow.

I don't want to pause to talk because the omelet is that good. I only stop to sip the coffee the cop poured before I begin again and shrug absently.

"I'm visiting."

"Visiting." Reece eyes me suspiciously.

I nod, my mouth full.

"That's bullshit and we both know it. Right now, Axel is supposed to be off, on vacation, but I find him very much here and with you. This vacation, mind you, is all he's talked about since New Year's. A month alone. That was a gift to himself for reaching two years without his drug of choice. Nothing would make him cancel that, so I ask again, why is he here with you?"

He said "you" like it is a dirty word. I take my last bite of omelet, surprised I got half down and return to my coffee. Just when it's at my lips, I glace over at Reece and say, "I guess he changed his mind."

The guy smirks and crosses his arms.

"Why don't we cut the shit? I'll tell you who I am, then you tell me who you are."

I shrug and set my cup down.

"There's not much to tell."

"Um-hmm, right."

I cross my arms and return the incredulous expression. I like Reece. He's like a big, playful dog, but I can sense he is protective of Axel and wouldn't hesitate to turn on me if the time came.

"Okay, go ahead. I've got your name, so we can skip that part."

Reece grins and wipes his hands on his pants, then leans forward to rest his arms on top of the counter. His overwhelming size is hard to ignore, but once I get past the bulging tattoos on his arms, I see his skin is rich mocha and his azure colored eyes are deep set with dark, long lashes. Reece LeDoux is clean-cut with tidy hairlines and a neatly shaved face. There's nothing overly done and he has just the right amount of swagger to tell me he gets laid, and often.

"Bypassing my name, I am an officer of the law, as well as friend to Axel. I am single, hate the beach, and can't stomach the smell of jasmine."

"Family?"

"No," he says without hesitation before interlocking his fingers and studying me closer. "Your turn, Payton Knight from Hancock, Mississippi."

I frown.

"I read your file on Axel's computer while you were in the shower. Yes, I have access, and I'm a cop, Payton. I'm not *not* going to check on you."

Placing my hands in my lap and lowering my eyes, I have to wonder how much checking he did.

"There's nothing to tell and since you're friends with Axel, I'm betting you know why I'm here."

"Sure, but can I trust you're not a reporter wanting an inside scoop of my buddy? Or any ulterior motives, maybe infiltrating the competition for that piece of shit Travis?"

"I don't know Travis, and I wouldn't waste my time or body for a 'scoop' as you put it." I meet his gaze and know my cheeks are burning.

Reece chuckles and holds his hands in the air.

"Okay, okay. Keep your hair on. I had to ask for no other reason but to get that type of reaction. Now, tell me why you're here."

"You know why."

"Okay then, why is Axel here? Why'd he agree to this?"

Reaching for my coffee, I shrug and realize I'm doing it because I'm uncomfortable. Shrugging is something I haven't done since I was a teenager and my mother hated it. She made me break the habit by making me hold my arms in the air for hours on end. My shoulders burn from the memory.

"Cut the shit, I know you're homeless and that, more than anything, would cause Axel to let you in, it's the running just now that has me wondering."

My cheeks burn with embarrassment at my homeless status.

"I don't know what you want me to say." I nervously tuck a strand of escaped hair behind my ear. "But I know he doesn't want me here. He's expressed he wishes me to leave."

Reece recoils, and an ugly frown darkens his handsome face.

"Why the fuck did he say he wants you gone?" he asks harshly.

"I have no idea." I hold my hands out by way of demonstrating my state of ignorance.

"You need to back up and tell me everything. I'll find out one way or another, but you can save us both some time. Start with when you got here."

My shoulders sag in defeat. "He got me from the airport yesterday."

"And he has already told you to leave?"

Reece looks me up and down, searching for some kind of alien presence. I don't know why, but I wanted to tell him all of it.

"It was fine at first but then we," I shrug again then want to kick myself. "You know."

"And?" Reece waves a hand at me to continue, "You have sex and then what? Wait, you don't have a penis, do you?"

I burst out laughing in spite of feeling so wretched.

"No, I don't have a penis."

I stand and put our plates in the sink, then return to lean against the counter, keeping my eyes down.

"I kind of didn't tell him I hadn't been with anyone and he sort of went berserk."

Glancing up, I see Reece is concentrating on my words.

"What the fuck does that mean?" He blinks rapidly then clarity widens his eyes. "Not been with anyone, *how*?"

I stay silent and bow my head with shame. I'm a freak all the way around.

"Okay, so you're not that experienced. What's the big deal?"

"I didn't tell him before we did anything, and I guess he figured it out during. He just leapt off of me and has been like a wet hornet since."

Reece's mouth actually falls open, and his eyes go blank like someone just hit him on the head. Several silent moments tick by, and I wait for some kind of input. Clearing his throat, Reece stands up and begins to slowly pace.

"So, you told the man nothing and just let him keep going?"

"I didn't think it was that big a deal, I'm not completely ignorant to sex, I just never—" I let the proclamation hang in the air and cross my arms protectively.

Reece runs a hand through his hair and rubs the back of his neck.

"He feels guilty," Reece announces more to himself than to me.

I stay quiet because I need the insight. He glances at me, then turns to look out of the glass door at the ocean.

"Axel is a complicated person. You have probably guessed that already."

"Yeah."

"He hasn't had the same kind of nurturing most people grow up with. Hell, the only love he's ever been shown is by the women he's fucked and that ain't healthy at all."

The image of Axel going rigid and pulling away quickly last night on the beach comes to mind.

"If he wants you to leave, you will need to. He'll ask me to remove you if it comes to that." Reece turns to look at me, and I blanch at the thought.

"Has that happened before? You making someone leave here, I mean?"

Reece tilts his head to the side and gives me an incredulous look.

"Females get their feelings confused and Axel wants no part of that, so yeah, I've taken a few away from him over the years. Hell, I even married one of his stalkers."

I recoil.

"Yeah, I did the porn thing for a few years. That's where Axel and I met and became buddies. One of the girls that thought he loved her showed up one night out of the blue and I came and picked her up and took her back home. We ended up in bed together, then that moved to filming together. It was a crazy few years for all of us. Lots of drugs being used, and no one around to tell us we were stupid."

I sit at the island and watch an array of emotions come and go in Reece. A tender look at the memory molds into sadness.

"I loved her. The only one I ever gave a shit about."

Swallowing hard, I watch as Reece looks back at the water. I want him to finish the story, I want to know everything and just as I'm about to ask, Reece walks to the couch and drops down.

"She died from AIDS two years and four months ago. I picked up the pieces of my life, got sober, and joined the force. Haven't looked back since."

A single tear slides from my eye listening to the broken voice explain his heartbreak as simply as one would their grocery list. Reece is so detached yet so affected. He glances at me when I wipe my eyes.

"It's okay, I'm okay, and God knows Wavy is okay now. The diagnosis and treatment sucked but I never got it and she never got better. I buried her in a church cemetery and me and Axel was there for her until the last bit of dirt covered her grave. The way I see it was maybe I was meant to come get her, maybe she was meant to be crazy and wild. Who fucking knows why anything happens?"

"I'm sorry, Reece, I don't have the words to say how sad that is to me."

"Are you going to tell me why you're really here?"

My spine stiffens at the abrupt change of subject.

"What do you mean?" I ask defensively.

"Call it a cop's instinct or just a nosey asshole looking out for his friend, but nothing about you says you're here for the acting job."

"I can't talk about it."

Shit, I may as well have just admitted to a crime!

Reece surprisingly doesn't press further. He just stands and grabs his uniform shirt and boots.

"Figure it out and don't fuck with Axel's head. He's got demons of his own to live with."

Before I can respond, Reece leaves the way he came in. I race to the sink, throwing up all I ate. Gasping and crying, my head bowed, I have to wonder if I will ever see an end to this whole fucking nightmare.

Eleven

-

Axel

Legs tired, lungs screaming for me to stop, I slow my pace and rake an arm over my grit-covered face. Once the sweat is wiped from my eyes, I realize I'm in front of an all too familiar church. Soft singing carries out to where I stand in front of big, dark, mahogany doors. I stare at the entrance and listen to the song. Something dark in my heart stirs, and I have to bend at the waist, bracing my hands on my knees.

Spasms clench my stomach, and I dry heave. Several moments pass, and my legs decide sitting would be best and buckle beneath my weight. I have enough foresight to turn and plop my ass on a step. Resting my elbows on my knees, I sit with my head down, listening to a soft song of praise for a God I've long forgotten. An odd calm takes hold of me and I relax.

"Hello."

I jerk my head up to see a middle-aged man in what looks like the garb of a priest.

"May I help you?"

My arms are too drained to push my dead weight off the church step.

"Um, no thanks. I'm just catching my breath."

The priest smiles politely, and I realize I'm covered in sweat and wearing only my shorts and running shoes. Leaving my bike at a strip mall to run, I only meant to go a couple of miles, but it appears I ran several more than planned without realizing it.

"Would you like to come in?"

My too-long hair is stuck to my forehead, and it takes a couple of swipes to push it away. Sweat stings my eyes as I shake my head no. I drop it down once more and hope the priest walks away. He doesn't and must take my silence for invitation because he sits a couple of feet from me on the same step.

"Sometimes, it helps to talk," he says quietly, "Sometimes, it's just sitting quietly with a stranger that brings peace."

Surprisingly, after a few moments, peace does sweep over me. I take a deep breath and slowly exhale.

"I am Father Ezeal. This is my parish."

"I won't give you the impression I'm a religious man. I did not stop for absolution."

"Yet, you stopped all the same. What troubles you, friend?"

I rub my face then scratch my growing beard.

Fuck it, what's there to lose.

"I have corrupted and damaged many souls because my own is lost, broken, ruined."

I glance at the priest and see he's not looking at me but at the tattoo shop on the corner where a couple walk arm and arm.

"Funny how stains on the skin stick, isn't it? Get a permanent reminder of a split-second decision. Sometimes, it results in a work of art, other times, the skin is so distorted, there's no way of knowing what's on it."

I look to the shop, then the priest. He slowly turns his head to look back at me, and I see his eyes are clouded-over, white, milky glass orbs look straight through me. He's blind.

"You can't see me?" I blurt out in surprise.

"Oh, but I can."

My skin tightens under his scrutiny.

"Whatever you have done, you need only ask forgiveness."

"I am the devil. There's no forgiving me."

"No, you are not the devil, or you would not say you were. If you were damned, you would merely go about your life damned and none the wiser."

I shake my head, unable to believe him.

"You run past here three times a week, and I say to you now, what it is you run from can be your salvation."

"That's impossible because I run from the shit-storm of my life."

"I ran from the law for six years. I was wanted for manslaughter and could've ran all the way to Mexico. The minute I stopped running and told God I was through, I went to prison for twelve years. It was the greatest thing that could have ever happened to me. I lost my sight but saw clearer than I had my entire life."

"What if someone asks you to give them the means to kill themselves, and they come to you for help in carrying it out?"

Because that's what you would be doing, killing Payton.

No way I'm coming out and saying exactly what Payton came to me for, not to a priest, but death seems a fitting stand in for porn, and I am a better alternative for Payton than the likes of Travis. I suppose, in a way, I would be a clean 9mm to his double-barrel shotgun.

"To that, I do not know. You can't be responsible for another's life or their choices. If you can help them, then by all means, help, but from there, it's not on you is my stance."

We sit in comfortable silence, watching others walk up and down the street, going about their day having no idea I'm splintering apart as I think over the priest's words. After what seems like hours, I bid the man goodnight and walk back to my bike. I ride aimlessly, stopping only for food at the pier where I sit to watch the sunset.

Am I doing it right?

Does it feel good to you?

Long, red talons scrape my skin.

Dead, sightless eyes and dirty needles scattered across the floor.

Thoughts of the years gone by rattle around in my head, the girls I've known and never loved, Reece and Waverly, Barbara, my mother. None I saved, and none returned to me. I feel like a curse upon them all.

Abandoning my half-eaten sandwich to the birds, I ride my bike back to the house. It's dark, and I squirm at the thought maybe Payton is gone. Silently, I enter the kitchen, and I see no signs of life. The living room is vacant and the guest room is open. As quietly as I can, I walk and look inside, expecting Payton to be asleep or in the shower. The room is empty, the bed neatly made, and the only sign of her being there at all is the lingering scent of her shampoo.

She's gone? Did Reece actually take her? Oh, hell no, what if she's in his bed right fucking now?

The sudden thought causes bile to rise. Fighting the pocket of my running shorts for my phone, I stab in the number while I pace in the empty room. There's no answer. I end the call and dial it again. This time, a sleepy grunt greets me.

"What?"

"Did you take her with you?"

"What the fuck, Axel? You know I worked sixteen last night," Reece growls and the phone thumps as if it's been dropped then picked up again.

"Did you take Payton with you today?"

"Why are you asking me that?"

I think a moment because, technically, I have zero reason, and it's not as if Payton isn't an adult. I use the only logical explanation.

"She's under contract with me and you know the rules."

Reece can fuck them all he wants once they get their deal signed and I get paid.

Fuck, I feel like a pimp all of a sudden.

Sitting on the bed, I drop my forehead in my hand.

"She was in the kitchen when I left. I made her an omelet, and we talked. That is it. And fuck you for asking."

Exhaling loudly, I lie back on the bed.

"I think I'm losing my mind, Reece."

"Have you done anything stupid?"

"That is the million dollar question, isn't it?"

"Well, have you?"

"I haven't used anything, and I don't want to." I lie.

I want to fill my body with as much morphine as I can and sleep for days.

"Good, now where would she go?"

I leave the room so I can get away from her scent and think, mindlessly stripping out of my clothes on my way to my room.

"She doesn't have much money, and I don't think she would go home. She was dead against it when I brought it—"

It doesn't register at first, but once I'm fully inside my bedroom, I stop dead before getting to my bathroom and turn toward the bed. Curled in the center, almost hidden under the mess of covers, is Payton. Her mouth is slightly open, and her eyes are dancing behind her lids—no doubt dreaming again. She takes my breath away, and I back out of the room before I wake her.

"You still there? What the fuck are you doing, Axel?"

I don't answer until the light is off and I'm back in the kitchen.

"Never mind, I found her."

"Where?"

"My bed, asleep," I answer, trying to sound nonchalant, but probably failing miserably.

I can almost hear Reece thinking. No way any of the girls sleep in my room, *ever*, and he knows it because I have to have my space or I would go insane. It would be like speed-dating every thirty days, and I have no desire to do that.

"Let me get this straight because none of this is adding up for me." Sarcasm drips with every word, and I hear ice tinkle around in a glass. I can picture his big body sitting up in bed drinking Jack on the rocks. "This girl shows up and you say fuck it to your long overdue date with fucking King Triton and his mighty fish. You fuck her once—"

"Twice."

"—and lose your damn mind? That must be some potent pussy."

"She was a virgin. I kinda lost my shit, but I'm better now, I think."

"And you're good with her getting in the business."

"No. I want her to go home."

I glance to the bedroom to make sure Payton is still in there.

"There was a time I wanted Wavy to quit, you know that, right?"

"Yeah, I know." I shut my eyes and see the beauty. I'd never seen Reece happier.

"I had to let her make her own decisions, you hear me? We decided to do our own thing cause I wasn't about to share her. In the end, it worked out. If you can't

126

handle that then maybe it's best you let her go or give her the tools to survive the business. Either way, it's not your call to make."

"You're the second person tonight to tell me that."

"Thought that shit was original as fuck. I need to stop watching Lifetime movies."

"I'll talk to you later."

"Walk softly, my brother."

I end the call still conflicted.

Why the hell does Payton affect me like this? The mere fact she's in my bed and I have every intention of sleeping there with her should have me worried. But it doesn't. At all.

Finally saying fuck it, I go to bed.

Twelve

-

Axel

Few things in life smell better than bacon. None I can think of as I drag my lids open. My clock tells me it's early but my body is rested. Following the smell, stopping only to brush my teeth and use the bathroom, I enter the kitchen in the best mood I've had in days. It's because I have a plan.

Lying next to Payton in the night, I decided I would make her think I'm teaching her the tricks of the trade, but, in reality, I will be doing no such thing. It's an undermining, selfish, controlling thing to do, but it's the only thing I can think of to make all this right somehow. With that at peace in my mind, I sit at the kitchen island and watch Payton move around in my boxers and t-shirt. I'm surprised I'm not pissed off that she helped herself to my things.

She's far too cute to be mad at.

Her blonde hair was a mess yesterday. This morning, it looks like it barely survived a tornado. It's piled in this messy bun thing on her head, and I have to grin. Payton looks like a tomboy ready for a fight rather than the beauty I picked up from the airport two day ago. I clear my throat to announce my arrival. Payton turns her face and gives me a shy smile.

"Hey."

"Hey."

She transfers food to plates and sits beside me at the island.

"Will you let me stay? Please?" she asks, not wasting time.

I chew my bacon, purposely avoiding any eye contact. If I go with my plan, I can keep her to myself for a bit. If she figures out what I'm doing, she'll hate me. I turn to look at her.

"Let's talk about it later, okay?"

And the sleeping arrangements. I secretly hope she does it again tonight.

Payton nods and chews, her eyes darting from her fork to her plate nervously.

"Can I ask you a question?" she asks cautiously.

"Sure."

"How did you start doing this? Porn and training girls and stuff?"

I get up and pour coffee, letting the question hang in the air. Once we both have cups, I decide I probably will have to answer, or she'll just ask me again.

"By accident, mostly. I did some photos, then film when I was young. I continued to do it to support my drug habit for several years, then got tired of it."

"You got tired of the drugs or the filming?"

"Both things. Don't get me wrong, it was nice to be in demand. I was worshipped by females, fought over by agents, and never went without work. But the schedules and shit took its toll on my body and soul. I reached a point where I could no longer keep up. The more I filmed, the heavier I got into drugs. Barb knew I was a money-maker and approached me with this alternative." I wave a hand to indicate our situation and shrug. "I was glad to get clean and get out from the front of the camera, even though I continue with a couple of films a year."

"How long have you been training girls?" she asks, tilting her head in curiosity.

"Feels like a lifetime," I answer, not hiding the exhaustion in my voice.

Payton smiles sadly at me then reaches to touch my cheek. It catches me off guard, and I jerk away out of her reach.

"What are you doing?"

Frowning, her hand retreats.

"I just wanted to touch you. I'm sorry if it made you uncomfortable."

I shake my head.

"No, its fine. I just didn't know what you were doing." I chuckle, embarrassed. "Go ahead." I reach to place her hand on my face but it stays limp, unresponsive.

"Did none of the girls ever touch you, Axel?"

I frown at the pitying tone in her voice and let her hand go to rest on her lap.

"Of course, Payton, just not on the face." I stand and place our dishes in the sink, extremely uncomfortable with topic. Payton watches me silently. Once I finish with the plates, I reach to get more coffee, glance over my shoulder to ask if she wants more and catch her scanning my back.

"You want some more?"

"Not yet." She stands and walks to examine my back closer. "Can I touch this?"

Her fingers meet my skin before I respond, and I'm surprised it doesn't cause me to burst into flames. Placing my arms on the bar to give her a clear view of the image on my back, I brace for the probing.

"This is amazing, Axel."

I smile to myself then tense as her fingers glide smoothly around the outline of my tattoo. The ink is relatively new. I suppose she hasn't seen it up close, and coming from Payton, the touch is somehow deep, penetrating to my soul. Her fingers move to the wings of the angel spread wide from shoulder to shoulder. In her arms, she struggles to carry a dying demon with equally massive wings, the demon is bathed in a reddish hue against the soft grey of the angel's body. The demon is limp and the angel wraps one arm around him and uses the other to grasp his neck. His head is tilted back with her lips pressed to his.

I never knew if the angel was kissing him goodbye to let him drift dying back to Hell or if she were trying to save him to enter Heaven with her. Either way, it is a work of art covering the entire span of my back down to an inch above my waist line.

"Did you design it?"

"No, Waverly did, before she died. She was Reece's girl. She put a lot of hours into it."

"Reece called her Wavy."

"Yeah, we all did," I explain sadly.

I'm self-conscious under Payton's touch and examination. I've spent my life in the most intrusive profession possible, yet this woman makes me feel exposed. Her fingers leave me, I straighten and return to my seat. Payton follows, ignoring the chair, opting instead to hop up on the bar top, placing her feet on the empty stool. Her toes are painted a pretty pale pink, and I have to fight the urge to worship them with my tongue.

I sip my coffee, sifting around my head for questions.

"My turn with a question."

Payton gives me a sheepish grin.

"Okay."

"How is it a pretty girl like you is still a virgin at twenty?"

She sips from her cup then grins wickedly.

"Oh, didn't you know? I lost my virginity." She smiles, and I see her teeth are perfect. "But really, I didn't wait on purpose, I assure you."

"Are you religious? Were you saving yourself for marriage?"

"No." She shrugs. "I had a boyfriend that tried and just before I went through with it, I found him in the dugout of the baseball field. My best friend was on her knees quite literally sucking him off. After that, I kind of shied away from boys, and girls for that matter."

"Ouch."

"Your turn," she says, and I squirm at having to answer a personal question.

"You know, I don't really do deep discussions. This kind of thing," I gesture from my chest to her general direction, "is not something I usually allow, and by not usually, I mean never."

Instead of deterring her from further examination of me, she smiles and seems to consider it a challenge.

"So, we are both having firsts? It's a bit adventurous, isn't it?"

Her eyes light up mischief, and I have to chuckle.

"It appears so."

"Okay, we can take turns. I'll ask a question then you ask one of me?" When she crosses her legs, I catch a peak of her pink skin between her legs and my mouth waters.

"Okay," I agree, thinking I'd just about agree to anything with her.

"Okay, have you ever been married?"

"No," I say instantly, amused at her lack of knowledge where I'm concerned. "Have you?" I ask, playing along.

She shakes her head and giggles. Several messy golden strands fall in her face, and I reach to tuck them behind her ear, surprising Payton and myself in the process. It's so out of character for me, and I know she has to be aware of that fact. To mask my actions as normal, I reach for her feet, placing her legs closed and settling them in between my thighs on my chair. I rub her calves and ankles, trying to distract her from talking.

"What's been your longest relationship?" she asks.

I pause, looking down to her legs then back in her eyes.

"You mean like dating?" She nods, and I notice lust stir in her eyes at my touch. "I don't do relationships, Payton."

I bend my head to kiss her knees—one then the other. She places a foot on my chest and pushes me back to look her in the eyes. Disappointment floods my groin when I see shock on her face. My tactics of distraction are not working.

"You have never been in a relationship?" she asks incredulously.

"Is that so shocking?

"Well, yeah." Payton pulls her feet free, crossing them in front of her again. "I mean, I get your profession and the possibility of a jealous girlfriend, etcetera, but never? Like never ever? What about dates? You do go on dates, right?"

I shake my head, thoroughly amused.

"I'm a sex god. Heavy is the crown and all that shit. I have women if I want, but for the most part, I just train girls for film. It's much less complicated than dating."

Instead of laughing, I watch Payton's face fall in pity. I seize the opportunity to drive my earlier point home.

"This business will hollow you out, Payton, both physically and spiritually. You will be fucked into a shell of a person. No matter how many times you tell yourself that it's just sex, and you will stop as soon as you get enough money, you are forever changed. You don't see people as people anymore because you're only surrounded by machines driven to seek the possibility of fame and fortune that never happens, only I am aware it will never happen. Never. It's worse for females. Males only have to stay hard through the hours of filming. Females have to endure tons of shit you can't even imagine."

She swallows and casts her eyes around the room, avoiding my gaze. Deciding to end on that point for the morning, I attempt to return to a lighter mood.

"My turn. So, you have only ever had the one boyfriend?"

Payton shrugs.

"I haven't had the opportunity to date much."

"Not even at Ole Miss?"

Pain dances in her eyes at the mention of her school. "No."

"How come? I thought college was where most people explore their sexuality."

I can tell she could crack open if I press a little harder, so I reach for her legs again, tucking her feet between mine and rubbing her calves in a soothing motion. I may not understand relationships, but with a woman's body, I am an expert.

"Let's save some time, shall we? Start at the beginning. Where you grew up, did you have a dog and so on," I instruct, prodding her to keep her from thinking too hard.

Payton picks at a hang nail, not meeting my eyes. Her body is relaxing under my massaging hands, and I can see she wants to talk about her life. I have to wonder if she ever has before.

"Let's see," she begins in acquiescence. "I had a simple childhood. My dad worked on an oil rig in the gulf. My mom got to stay home and took care of me. It was great until hurricane Katrina happened. My dad got swept out to sea during the storm."

My hands stop at the sudden announcement of what I knew to be a devastating admission, but I quickly continue to knead the muscles of her legs so she will continue. Other than the reminiscence in her eyes, her face is absent of emotion.

"My mom and I did the best we could after the storm. My dad's life insurance helped, but it wasn't enough to help for long and my mom struggled to find work. I received a partial scholarship to attend Ole Miss University, and I worked part-time to help pay. I was on the cusp of finishing my freshman semester when my mom was diagnosed with aggressive cancer. She died last spring. In less than a year, we lost the house, we lost everything and to add to my losses, my scholarship was given to someone else. So, to cover all of your questions about my still being a virgin? I haven't really had the chance to explore before now."

There's sadness in her voice, but when she averts her eyes, I get the distinct impression she's not telling me everything.

"So, you have lived alone all this time?" I ask, keeping a straight face.

"Yes." She averts her eyes again.

Not a lie, but not the whole truth. Or possibly shame for her homeless status?

"Was there no one you could have stayed with, family? Friends?"

Chewing her bottom lip nervously, Payton shakes her head.

Something about these particular questions are making her very uncomfortable.

"What about you? Any family?" Payton asks, eyes crinkling in the corners with playful interest.

Well, shit. I hate talking about myself.

"My dad is dead, and haven't seen my mom since I left Texas when I was fifteen, and I'm perfectly fine with that," I deadpan to show I am unaffected by being an orphan. "What family I knew then are long dead to me. The only family I have is Reece, though he's a pain in my ass most of the time."

My fingers slow to sensual strokes, the tips coasting along her long taut calf muscles. The feel of her skin is intoxicating and oddly soothing.

Everything about Payton in soothing to my soul.

"What about friends? Surely, after knowing so many people through the years, you have some friends that remain."

Clearing my throat, I sit up straighter.

"I have acquaintances, but none I would call friends. For the most part, I end up being a part of a girl's sordid past, a time in her life she wants to forget."

Payton blanches at that, and the pity that fills her eyes makes me want to end the probing.

Too far. You revealed too much, and now she knows nobody has ever wanted you. Nice job, Axel.

Before she can ask more questions, I decide it's time to change the subject. Payton's breath hitches as I glide my hands up the inside of her luscious thighs, tracing circles with my thumbs very close to her wet spot. Head falling back, her long neck is bared, inviting my lips to taste. Rising from my chair, I oblige, cupping her nape to hold her in place while dragging my lips along delicate skin leading to the shell of her ear. I nip the lobe.

All sadness leaves the room in one long sigh of pleasure. Puckered nipples rub against my chest as I kiss, lick, and nip my way to them. I caress one peak then the other through the fabric of the t-shirt and Payton arches her back, thrusting her chest out to me. Pulling back to watch as I play, Payton lets her legs fall open completely, wantonly.

Responsive...she is maddeningly responsive to me.

But I don't touch between her legs, not yet. I need to make her crazed for my touch.

I want to be wanted.

No, I need to be wanted even though I don't deserve it.

Pulling the shirt up high enough to expose her breasts, I teasingly cup both globes, running my thumbs over the hard peaks. My cock throbs to take her, but my instincts say *slow down*.

"Axel," she says breathlessly, tilting her hips higher.

"Shhh, I'm going to take care of you. Just relax."

Hazel eyes burn with desire as I expose her glistening sex. For a split second, I lose my train of thought when I see how swollen with arousal it is. With Superman-like restraint, I pace myself, slowly revealing her soft pink inner flesh.

My pent up breath leaves in a gust.

"Axel?" Payton questions my perusal and tries to close her legs self-consciously.

Holding her thighs apart, I meet her eyes and shake my head.

"No you don't. Just let me see you."

She casts one last look of uncertainty, then she relaxes her legs once more.

"Touch your breasts for me," I instruct.

She looks unsure at first, but acquiesces when I give a nod of encouragement.

"Tug on your nipples, Payton. Do what feels good."

Relaxing further back on the island, Payton traces her breasts tentatively. I watch while lazily caressing between her legs with my knuckles.

"That's it, Payton, stoke the flames, feel the burn of my touch."

Lips parting, eyes closing, she begins to pet both breasts, pinching her nipples in turn.

"Yes, Payton," I growl lazily, parting her flesh once more.

She lets out a cry of frustration as I bypass her swollen nub to tease her core, spreading moisture as I go.

"Axel, please?"

With my free hand, I release my cock, touching the head gently against her heat. Payton undulates her hips, trying to work herself down on it.

"Please, please." She pants wildly.

"Please what, Payton?" I tease her clit in wide circles.

"Fuck me, Axel! Please? This is, ah, killing me."

Positioning her ass off the bar, I slide home, nearly coming in the process. Payton grinds her hips against me, and I groan from the agony.

"Hold still, Payton. Give me a second."

Gritting my teeth, I retreat then advance once more.

"Fucking hell. This is too good, feels too fucking good. *Never* ever felt this good."

"Yes, so good," Payton moans an agreement.

Inhaling deep, I realize I spoke out loud. My initial need to drive her crazy has backfired, and I am the one mad with desire. I thrust furiously, needing to make Payton come, making her moan harder, louder.

"So good, Payton, feels so fucking good," I groan, gripping her hips, driving deep.

My voice doesn't even sound right anymore.

What's the hell is happening to me? This is not me, it's not real.

Yeah, buddy, it is.

Payton's body tightens under my grip, and in the next moment, she breaks apart, trembling uncontrollably with her orgasm.

Am I doing it right?

Does this look good?

Voices from the girls I've trained try to invade my thoughts, causing me to falter slightly, disrupting the unbelievable pleasure I'm feeling. As if sensing a change, Payton rises up to pull me close, searing my lips with a kiss.

Deep and long, it's the kind of kiss that you never want to end. It is a means to an end. But Payton kisses as if it's the very sustenance needed for her soul.

She wraps her arms around my neck, and I circle her waist, pulling her off the bar to straddle my waist as I stand. My stool falls to the floor with a crash, but I ignore it, completely consumed with Payton—her smell, her taste, her moans of pleasure. Still feverishly kissing, and pumping into her, I carry her out of the kitchen and to my bedroom.

Bedroom? Wait, Bedroom? Too much, way, way too much.

Need to stop, need to turn this around, but I can't.

Shutting off my thoughts, I lay Payton back on my bed, taking a much-needed reprieve. Crawling on top of her soft body, my heart beats wildly at the sensations flowing through me while I further explore her mouth, ears, and neck. Her hand reaches between our bodies to stroke me, but I hold her still and shake my head.

"Don't. I want to come inside you," I breathe against her neck.

"Can I be on top then?"

Groaning in response, I let her push against my chest to lie on my back.

Once we're in the correct alignment, I wrap a hand in her hair, pulling her face to mine to continue the mind-blowing kissing while I guide her hips down on my length. Once I place my thumb to her sensitive nub, Payton bucks wildly.

"Oh God," she cries against my lips, arching her back.

Pulling my mouth free, I rise up to suck a nipple while she grinds her hips with abandon. When I thrust up hard, she lets loose a scream of pleasure.

"There it is, that's what I'm after," I say, repeating the thrust.

She rises and falls harder, driving me closer and closer to insanity, becoming lost in the sensations. I try helplessly to slow her pace, but Payton resists for a split second before finally giving control back to me. I lie back and place my hands lower on her hips to rock her back and forth in a steady rhythm, buying myself only moments more.

Resting her hands on my chest to steady the grind, Payton begins that delicious whimper I will never get enough of. With every few rocks, I pull her body up and slam deep inside. Her muscles contract around me, and it takes every ounce of restraint I have to hold back until she shatters apart once more.

But she does something that shocks me to my core. Payton places her hands on my face and gently kisses me—slowly, agonizingly slow. It's raw intimacy like I've never experienced, and it momentarily takes my breath away. I increase our rhythm, and we deepen the kiss further. I want more yet my body is reaching a high peak, threatening to violently crash from the emotions boiling under Payton's touch.

"Come on, baby. Come on, Payton," I coax, almost pleading against her lips.

I rock her harder, and the instant I feel the pulling throb within her sheath, I'm gone. Pushing my hips up, holding on for dear life, I let my orgasm go while Payton continues to grind, riding her own to completion. I yell something vile, feeling my entire body tense and release from the roller coaster ride. I come harder than ever before in my life.

Payton says my name along with something I can't make out, mostly because my hearing is gone, then she collapses on top of me, still trembling with pleasure. I lie still, breathing heavy as my body tries to return to Earth. It takes several long minutes, but finally, our breathing begins to steady.

Do I hold her?

I don't know what to do with my hands.

Awkwardly, I do what feels good, wrapping my arms around Payton's warm body, squeezing her to me even tighter. Closing my eyes at the odd feeling of satisfaction, I sigh with contentment.

This feels right.

The moment she falls asleep against me, I gently push her head to the pillow and cover her with a blanket, leaving the bed long enough to use the bathroom, lock up the house, and turn the lights off. It may be daylight out, but being in bed all day in my darkened room sounds like Heaven.

As I climb back in bed ten minutes later, I feel the slightest tug on my conscience that I have so far broken almost all of my own rules. Sharing my bed with Payton is the biggest of them all.

I don't fall asleep instantly. I lie a long time watching Payton by the soft glow coming from the bathroom. There is no doubt the girl is different to me, even without the virgin status, Payton is just *different*. She's beyond beautiful, but I swear, when we talked in the kitchen earlier, I could see part of her soul, and it was pure.

True, she doesn't belong here. I have no right to her, yet she invites me into her body without hesitation. Through raw emotions, I'm able to make her feel better, but I wonder if I have changed her mind at all about joining the black hole of adult movies.

Thirteen

—

Payton

Warm.

I'm so warm, and my bones have liquefied during the long sessions of sex and sleep over the last day? *Day and a half?* Every inch of my body feels loose and well used. I'm just a little sore, but that's a small price to pay for total satiation. Axel gave me pleasure beyond anything I've ever known. Many times, I caught myself praying it would never end, only to be reminded of my very transient situation. Still, I wanted him like nothing else.

Rubbing sleep from my eyes, I turn slightly to focus on the object of my desires.

Appearing like a Greek God with an arm over his eyes, bicep bulging and hairless chest on full display, Axel looks just as well-used. Scratches from my nails crisscross his torso, and his lips are rosy from our endless kissing. I want to soothe them with my tongue, and I regret nothing. If anything, I want him more now.

There was no satisfying the hunger I feel, and more than once, I woke up reaching for him, or he reaching for me. It seems even in slumber, we cannot get enough of each other.

Sitting up, I stretch much like a lazy cat rising from a nap. As much as I hate to vacate the comfort of Axel's bed, a twenty-four hour sex session has left me needing a shower in the worst way. I sigh, reluctant to leave him.

I want to make him mine.

If only I had such powers. Other than the absurdity of thinking that about a complete stranger, Axel has made it abundantly clear he does not do relationships. I'll have to keep reminding myself how I came to be with him.

Ben. Ben. I am here because of Ben.

I will chant it the next time I feel like I could stay cocooned in Axel forever. I certainly can't waste the opportunity to learn, knowing it means actual money—money I desperately need. If I can do well, I can make a decent amount just signing on to film the first couple of times. Maybe that would be enough, and I will be able to take care of things.

Ben. I can make things right again.

The house is gone, so I will never correct that, but the rest, I have to deal with. I have no clue why I lied to Axel, but at the time, a cancer death seemed more acceptable than how my mother really died. In reality, she had the worst kind of disease, and it infected us all.

But I can't think about it, let alone talk about what really happened with a man I just met—a man who has very meticulously deflowered me, so very precisely seduced me. My body quivers in response to memories of Axel's hands, mouth, and the weapon between his legs that he uses in the most meticulous ways to kill me again and again. Of course, I can't really judge a comparison to other men, but I can't imagine anything could ever be better than Axel Stone.

Lost in thought, I watch him sleep with sorrow, knowing I can never have him all to myself. I am one of many, and though I might be agreeing to have sex on camera, I have good reasons. I can only pray I won't get sucked into the bottomless pit Axel tried so hard to show me exists. The images of the dead girls gutted me, and more than once, I dreamed I was looking down at my body on a steel autopsy table.

Shivering at the memory, I force my mind to dismiss it and turn my attention back to the sleeping Axel. He has the rough exterior of a working man. By the looks of his home, he spends a lot of time fixing it up. The house is immaculately kept, with fine details to the organization, yet it's comfortable. This place is nice, and I can't say I would mind living here beyond the thirty-day mark.

But that's the naïve thought of a little girl. No man is going to save me, I have to save myself.

And Ben.

With a heavy heart, I exit the bed to do my morning duties. I wonder for only a second if Axel minds if I use his bathroom. Not knowing all the rules yet, I've so-far opted to use mine in case it's too personal to him. But once I see Axel's shower, I abandon the idea of returning to my own entirely.

Having rinsed my mouth with mouth wash, I turn my attention to the walk-in and my mouth parts in awe. Positioned slightly out of view from the room's entrance, the shower takes up a chunk of space along the back wall.

Feeling slightly giddy, I step inside and turn on the three shower heads, testing the water until it reaches hot perfection. Pushing a couple of buttons on the wall, my heart leaps with excitement when warm mist rises, instantly coating my skin in silk. No clue what the stuff is, I close my eyes in balmy bliss.

After a few seconds of Heaven, I pull my eyes open to see the previously fogged glass is crystal clear, revealing a giant window that gives the most excellent panoramic of the beach. It's like showering outside on the sand, and the thrill makes me feel oddly foolish that something so simple can make me so happy. I stand under the soothing jets and watch the waves roll onto the shore, not even caring if someone can look in and see me naked while I gawk like an idiot. I just take it all in.

Lost in the water, both outside and in, I don't hear Axel join me. It's only when he traces my arm with the back of his fingers that I realize he's behind me.

"You are breaking all the rules," he says in a low, gravelly voice.

Was that a disapproving tone or one of praise?

Unable to hide the fact that this shower, as perfect as it is, just got a hundred times hotter, I watch as Axel steps back to wet his hair. Beach view forgotten, I step under my own stream and stare, transfixed as water runs down his hard chest, through the peaks and valleys of his stomach, ending in a steady stream around his cock.

"Is that a bad thing?" I ask, my voice cracking.

He looks down at me with delicious, dark eyes, peering deep into mine. Blood rushes to my core just from that look alone. Axel slowly rakes his eyes down my body before returning to my mouth where he stares at my lips as if assessing how to best attack them.

"It's not very professional," he replies, sounding slightly hoarse himself.

"I don't know the difference, so it doesn't matter to me."

I hold his gaze for a long, quiet moment and watch the storm brew behind his eyes. He seems to analyze me, or maybe it's just the "unprofessional" situation he's referring to.

The girls don't touch him.

The girls don't sleep with him.

The girls don't shower with him.

It's very unprofessional.

What *do* they do? The question makes me suddenly feel guilty.

Maybe using his shower crossed a line?

Looking at him now, I would swear he's enjoying my perusal of his body. Axel's eyes grow hooded as my cheeks most likely flush pink with embarrassment. I can't imagine his attraction to me can come close to mine for him. He makes me weak in the knees, and more than a little breathless. We're inches apart but the heat between us is palpable.

Water mists around us, creating tiny droplets around Axel's mouth. Placing my fingertips to his lips, I rub gently then trace his jawline with both hands, coming to rest at either side of his beautiful face.

How can he have never experienced the feel of a woman's touch?

How can a female stand being near this man and abstain?

Touching him is all I want to do, yet I hesitate when I feel Axel tense, resisting the intimacy. Slowing my fingers, I watch his face as I stroke. It's a precise yet delicate movement on my part because Axel gives me the feeling he's on the verge of pulling away.

Maybe it's because it's new to him and not like his normal touching that's reserved for onscreen?

Either way, I don't want to cause him to jerk away again. Pressing my body into his, I wind my fingers into his hair, lightly pulling until his face reaches mine. I'm rewarded with his strong arms around my waist, his erection hardening between us and his mouth, *oh God that mouth,* crushing against mine. I control the slow, growing burn, not allowing him to go too fast.

His response is stiff, as if he's unsure of what to do. After a long minute, his resistance diminishes and Axel seems to want to go as slow as I do. I'm sore but feel incredibly relaxed in his arms as water gently massages us. After a moment of kissing so good my toes curl, I pull back to examine him—the need to memorize his face and body in the light of day overtaking the lust.

Axel's eyes, dark whiskey in the light from the window, show conflict, maybe even discomfort at the intimacy. He cups my nape, pulling my face back to his, kissing me with hunger. Strong hands cup my ass, and I moan in his mouth when a finger slides teasingly between my legs.

The only sounds, other than my constant whimper, are our lips softly separating then meeting deliciously while our hands roam each other's bodies. It's tender and ignites a wild fire within me. When I can no longer stand it, I reach to caress him, wrapping my fingers around his hard length.

Axel ends our kissing to graze at my jawline and ear. My breath is ragged with anticipation, wanting him inside me. Moving my hips to better align our bodies, Axel catches me off guard by picking me up and backing me to the widow. My butt comes to rest right at the bottom lip so I know if anyone could see us, they will know for sure we were having sex. Beyond caring, I wrap my legs around his hips, and Axel places my hands on the back of his neck.

"Hold on," he warns and excitement floods me head to foot as I lace my fingers together.

Water drips, trailing down his lean, broad chest, pooling between us. In this moment, I can't imagine anything more beautiful than Axel. Ecstasy overtakes his face as he enters my body. Inch by glorious inch, he sinks inside, making me moan while stilling me instantly. Axel watches our joining, then glances to my face. Once he realizes I'm watching him so intently, he grins sheepishly.

"What?" he asks, sounding self-conscious.

The bright light of morning spills through the window. His dark eyes glint with mischief, making him almost look like a boy and not the sex God he's known to be.

"Nothing, I'm good," I say rolling my hips. "Better than good. You are amazing."

Axel's grin widens, and he leans back to plunge deep inside me. He moves a hand to my lower abdomen, keeping the other on my bottom pressed against the window. When his thumb begins circling my sensitive center, I lean my head back against the glass and cry out, rotating my hips against his, grinding him deeper as his thumb works its magic.

"So fucking beautiful," he growls.

No sooner have the words left his mouth than I'm shattering apart in waves. There is no break after I begin to come down from that orgasm before Axel slams his body against me, driving in deeper. I cry out again as he plunges long and hard, and my orgasm picks back up, bursting from within.

Axel backs his hips up, letting me ride this one, but just as it begins to dissipate, he slams into me again, causing the orgasm to deepen and begin anew. I claw at him, shaking uncontrollably, then bury my face into his shoulder and bite down as the aftershocks continue to rip through me.

"Fuck." Axel groans, and within two thrusts, he's coming, gripping my ass so hard, it hurts and feels incredible all at the same time.

Returning my hands back to the sides of his face, I rub the stubble there as we take a moment for our breathing to return to normal. He doesn't resist my kiss or touch, but responds in kind while lowering me to my feet. There's a tug at my heart string while Axel holds my waist until I get my balance. Turning my back to his front, I pull his arms around me, desperate to feel safe with him.

But I'm not safe, or cherished. I'm merely here for a few days.

We stay like that for a long time, just holding each other under the water while the waves roll onto the shore outside. I want to cry, grieve over something I didn't know I had lost until now. Maybe it's the knowledge I will never know pleasure like this again in my life, or maybe it's Axel's admission he himself has never experienced intimacy, and I'm his first as much as he is mine.

Most likely though, it's the reality of my situation and the fact that it is not going to change. My time with Axel is incredible but it's a fleeting moment in time. It will be gone and just a memory soon.

He kisses my neck softly, and the sadness deepens when I realize he's saving me, and he has no idea he's even doing it. He has no clue that I'm alive for the first time in years, *in ever*, and I know if I'm not careful, he can surely break my heart.

I have to clear my throat before speaking.

"Do we start filming today?"

Axel stiffens and doesn't reply.

"Axel? Do we?"

"Sure, if you want," he mutters dismissively.

What the hell?

I don't know what I expected, but a hole burns through my heart. Steadying my breaths, I blink away tears and pull out from his embrace. I don't look back as I wash my hair and body, then quietly leave the shower without him. The sex is beyond anything I could have ever imagined, and being a twenty-year-old virgin, I have imagined a lot.

But Axel unravels me and puts everything where it's supposed to be, but it's tainted with the truth of why I'm with him at all. This is not a love story and Axel is not going to be my white knight. I have to save myself... somehow. I have to get everything back on track and shut my heart away for good because I cannot handle the heartbreak I know Axel will give me once the thirty days are over.

Returning to my room, I haphazardly rummage through the small bag of clothes Randell and Liz had so generously bought me. Choosing a pair of khaki shorts with a thin blue blouse and a matching set of pale blue lace underwear, I dress without looking in the mirror.

I've wasted precious time playing hide and seek in Axel's bed. What the hell was I thinking? One thing is for sure, I haven't been thinking of Ben.

I'm forced to stop and take deep breaths to mentally prepare myself for the business I need to be trained for. I brush my hair and apply light lip gloss and mascara using my small compact. Leaving my hair damp, I exit the room with my spine straight and proud, ready to take on the world.

Axel's in the kitchen, dressed in jeans, biker boots, and jacket over an AC/DC t-shirt. His wet hair hangs long around his ears, making him look extra sinful. Unaware I'm watching him, he takes quick bites of something then hurries to dump protein powder in his orange juice. He catches sight of me standing quietly as he turns away from the sink.

"Hey," he says with his lopsided grin, then quickly busies himself with drinking and eating.

"Hey," I reply weakly. "You look like you're in a hurry to get somewhere."

Resentful I haven't hurried about a damn thing since arriving, I walk to the refrigerator and notice Axel watching me with uncertainty. Deciding on a bagel and orange juice, I only slightly wish he had included me in his breakfast plans, then I have to inwardly kick myself.

Stupid, whiny girl

"Yeah, I had it on the schedule—" He breaks off and his eyes wander down my body then back up to my face. "I have a standing appointment and probably won't be back until later this evening. It's on the schedule," he says again, as if this *schedule* explains it all.

"Okay, I'll see you later then." I fake a sweet smile though I'm dying to know what a *standing* appointment is for a guy who does porn.

What if he is filming? Then he'd be with other girls.

The thought sickens me, and again I realize just how out of hand I've let things get.

Ben. Ben. Ben. The only reason I'm here.

Axel doesn't owe me an explanation, and by the confused expression he's wearing, I gather he isn't exactly accustomed to explaining himself. Still inwardly chanting why I'm here, I pick at my bagel as he finishes his drink.

The beach sounds good, and I need to find this damned schedule he keeps talking about.

"Okay, I'll see you later then?"

I smile. "Bye."

He disappears through the kitchen door into the garage. Just as the door shuts, I walk quickly to my room to retrieve the papers on my dresser, guessing they hold the schedule. A quick glance tells me it's here, among the others, and I return to my breakfast to read while eating. Sex must've worked up my appetite because I end up adding both cheese and salmon to my bagel before finally sitting back on the island stool.

Looking down to the papers as I chew, I almost choke when I see the last page of suggestions for anal sex. It takes me several deep breaths and the entire contents of my glass to get myself under control again. I actual cough for a good minute. Once my eyes clear, I decide to start with the front page so not to be overwhelmed by what started the whole choking episode.

The top sheet states the days and what to expect on each. That's not surprising, so I move on to the second sheet. It's mostly suggestions for soreness, muscle cramps, dietary needs to stay hydrated along with a variety of things to consider while being trained by Axel. The third page is a list of don'ts. Glancing over that list, which consists of a whole bunch of "don't approach Axel at certain times" and "do be on time for training sections," I return to the fourth and final page where a list of lubes are approved, and the anal sex precautions are listed.

"Dear God," I breathe, clamping a hand to my mouth while my eyes probably bug out of my head reading about the enemas.

Ways to prepare your body for anal sex.

The best time to use any enema, including fleet...

Once the fluid is clear, use a butt plug in preparation of your scene...

I suddenly feel idiotic for not researching all the stuff prior to reading it so casually over breakfast. Enemas for day seventeen. I'm to do them that morning in preparation for that afternoon, and a lesson in anal sex. The idea of having sex with Axel had me so excited, I never once thought about actually learning any of the other things I was going to be exposed to.

Anal Sex with Axel?

Maybe.

Anal sex with strangers?

My stomach does several summersaults.

Can I really do this? Enemas, lubricants, and butt plugs?

After reading the papers, I have a whole new image of what I'm going to be doing.

Jesus, what have I gotten myself into?

Although I trust Axel not to hurt me, I can't imagine doing these things. Not when I just finally had *regular* sex. I want lots more of that before moving on to the other stuff.

I'm still daydreaming when the kitchen door opens, revealing a big male frame holding a motorcycle helmet. I jump as if I'd been caught masturbating.

"Oh, my God!" I grab my chest, nearly falling off my stool. Time slows as I flail like a fish to get my balance. I clutch the counter, breathing heavily while Axel bursts out in laughter. "You nearly gave me a heart attack!" I scream.

"I'm sorry," he wheezes and actually doubles over, his butt resting against the wall as he holds his stomach. "The look on your face was priceless."

I narrow my eyes and stand to trash the remainder of my breakfast.

"I'm glad I amuse you," I reply acidly. "I thought that helmet was a weapon, and I forget what you looked like with clothes on."

My smirk shuts him up, and to his credit, Axel looks slightly disconcerted. Standing up straight, he pushes his broad shoulders back with something akin to pride. I mimic his posture.

"I came back to ask you if you wanted to go with me."
He glances down at the floor before returning his gaze
to mine.

*Is he self-conscious? Axel is asking me to go
somewhere with him?*

"Like a date?" I ask a little too eagerly.

Axel frowns and shakes his head.

"No, not a date. Just something I do." Looking
regretful he brought it up at all, Axel stares at his shoes
and scratches his neck. "You can do whatever you like,
of course, but I thought I'd ask."

"Uh, sure," I respond automatically.

His head jerks up to gauge my expression wearily,
then I look down to the page I had been reading. Axel
follows my eyes but gives the schedule no attention.

"You need to dress a little more casual, though. I
mean, you look great, but I'm taking the bike and you
really need jeans on. I wouldn't want to scuff up those
pretty legs." He gives me a grin.

Axel is flirting with me?

"Can I borrow a t-shirt? I have jeans but I only have
shirts like this." I indicate to my silk blouse.

"Take your pick." Axel gestures with a hand and
follows me into his room.

I find a Harley Davidson t-shirt that looks almost
ancient and begin undressing. When I see Axel leaning
against the door jamb staring at me, womanly pride
consumes me. Heat sizzles when our eyes meet.

"That's pretty," he says and nods to my bra just
before he lunges for me.

One second, I'm holding a t-shirt, the next, I'm lifted off my feet and pressed to the wall. I open my mouth to his, simultaneously encircling his neck, pressing hard into his firm body.

"Damn it," he growls into my mouth, "I'm already late and—"

But his words die away once my hand caresses the bulge in his jeans.

"We can make it quick," I say when his hands slide down to squeeze my ass.

"Turn around," he hisses.

I obey, ready for anything. Axel reaches a hand around my chest, cupping a breast, stroking the nipple with his thumb as the other hand slides between my legs, finding a sweet spot to play with. I let my head fall back against his chest as he strokes me to insanity.

He bites lightly up and down my neck as if starving. "Axel," I moan, reaching back to stroke him.

"Fuck. Stay still." Leaving my body long enough to pull my panties down and lower his jeans, I feel the heat of his body and realize his shirt is also gone. Unrecognizable noises fall from my mouth as Axel presses my chest against the wall and pulls my ass back toward him. He strikes quick and hard, causing me to cry out with searing pleasure. He fills me so deeply, I feel like weeping.

"God yes," I breathe against the wall.

This is what I want, primal need, and total possession.

"So fucking good, feels so good," he growls as he pounds unmercifully into me. When he returns his fingers to my front, my body tightens instantly.

"Axel!" I squeal just before I ignite into white hot flames.

Strong hands grip my hips, and Axel hammers into me, pushing screams of ecstasy from my lips. His body tenses, and I know he's holding back in fear of hurting me.

"You feel so good, don't hold back, Axel."

"I'll hurt you."

"No, you won't, please," I beg.

No sooner do the words leave my mouth than my breath catches. He plunges, a striking force that shatters my body from the inside out. He is unmerciful—in and out—sending me over an edge I hadn't realized I was standing on. I come apart as Axel comes undone behind me.

"Payton," he growls, pulling me against him as the full length of his thickness pulses deep inside.

It takes my breath away and causes my body to momentarily go still with shock. It hurts, but the pleasure far outweighs the pain. After giving me one last light thrust, Axel begins slowly backing out.

"You okay?" he asks into the hair at my neck, holding onto my waist.

"More than okay."

On shaky legs, I turn, holding onto his strong arms for balance, laying my forehead on his heaving chest. I wrap my arms around Axel's torso and pull him with me as I lean against the wall. In all our coupling, Axel never truly held me after, didn't lie still long enough to feel the powerful exchange of energy our bodies experience in the aftermath of immeasurable pleasure. Right now, I need his warmth. I need his strength.

He's tense, so I pull my face back to look into his eyes.

"Just stand here a moment?"

Looking down at my face, he nods stiffly. I rest a cheek to his chest, then I feel him tilt his face, leaning it against my hair in a move that cannot be mistaken as pure contentment. A sigh of what I hope is satisfaction breezes through my hair, and I have to close my eyes and agree.

Fourteen

-

Payton

"So, it's another first for you?" I tease as Axel shoves things aside in a cabinet, digging for an old helmet.

"Uh, yeah, I suppose it is," he tosses back over his shoulder.

I can't help but smile because with every movement Axel makes, the muscles of his arms bulge against the sleeves of his black t-shirt. The two-sizes-too-big borrowed Harley Davidson t-shirt I'm wearing is tied in a knot in the back, and I'm also rocking the new jeans Randell bought me back in Mississippi. After our incredible sexcapade, Axel began hurrying me to get cleaned up and dressed as he was already late for something. What, he refused to say.

"You're still not going to tell me where we are going?"

"Nope," Axel says to the innards of the cabinet. "Finally."

He produces a scratched-up full-faced motorcycle helmet very much like the one I'm holding. After brushing his hand around the inside, Axel places it on his head and snaps the strap. He already carefully adjusted the straps to mine but he rechecks them before climbing on the bike and waiting for me to join him.

Rebellion and excitement cause butterflies in my stomach as I slip on behind Axel, wrapping my arms around him.

"Ready?"

He glances back over his shoulder and I nod. After guiding us out of the garage, stopping only the push a button to close it, we proceed out onto the highway. I giggle and grip harder as we speed up and wind crawls through my shirt sleeves, bathing me in the dry California air. Strands of hair fly out from my braid, scattering wildly. As we pick up more speed, I cast my eyes to the ocean. The sun glimmers across its surface— little widely-scattered diamonds. The sight takes my breath away.

It has to be a dream. I'll wake up under a pier, watch the sun rise, then try to find food and work for the day. I'm still homeless, friendless, and no Ben.

Tears flood my eyes as I think of his blue eyes. The bike jolts as we decrease speed in traffic.

Not a dream.

Moments later, we pick up speed once more. Resting my head against Axel's broad back, I allow the feelings of uncertainty to disappear. For the thirty minute ride, I'm free of nightmares, and though I'm lost, I at least have a plan.

Twice, we stopped at traffic lights and soon turn away from the water and toward the towering buildings of the city. Massive structures loom over us on the left and right. It's congested and industrial. The few tall industrial-type buildings with faded gray fronts and truckless trailers backed into the bay doors appear abandoned, barely standing as if a good wind would make them cave in. More than once, I think of "The Walking Dead" as we pass the street people scattered throughout the area.

We leave the larger buildings, following a road into an area filled with smaller warehouses before coming to a stop just outside a loading dock to one of the metal buildings. Axel squeezes my hand while he places the kickstand against the ground and turns off the engine.

He pulls off his helmet, shakes his hair out wolf like and glances back at me.

"Careful climbing off, the exhaust pipe is hot."

I carefully climb from my seat and unclasp my helmet, taking it off as Axel climbs off and waits with his hand held out. I pass it to him and check out our surroundings. Trash litters the empty lots, the buildings appear abandoned, and every now and then, I catch a glimpse of someone scurrying from tree to tree in the distance. It gives me an uneasy feeling.

"Where are we?" I tear my gaze away from the ragged fringes of our surroundings and hurry to catch up to Axel. He's already several yards away. "Wait up."

Axel hurriedly pushes through two sets of swinging doors before we reach the inside of a large kitchen. There isn't much by way of appliances, but it's bright and clean. In the center of the room, at one of the three large tables, a beefy bald man viciously slices at a ham. His caramel-colored skin and dark eyes contrast against the white apron he wears over his denim overalls.

"I'm sorry I'm late, I got held up," Axel announces without preamble.

"Fucking 'eh, you're late, the crowd's gonna be busting the doors in and why the fu—"

The man stops mid-word and mid-slice when he catches sight of me—his mouth hanging open and his beady eyes narrowing comically.

"Lenny, this is Payton. Payton, this is Lenny." Axel tosses a hand between us but offers no other explanation.

"I'll be a baboon's ass." Lenny wipes his hands on his apron as he approaches me and immediately wraps huge arms around me in a bear hug. My feet actually leave the ground. "Hello, Payton. It's a pleasure to meet you."

My feet return to the floor. All I can do is laugh and mumble, "You too."

Glancing at Axel, I find him wearing an apron identical to Lenny's and holding one out for me. Lenny looks from Axel to me while I don the apron. When Axel offers no further explanation, Lenny gestures wildly for us to move to the table to work.

"I still don't know where we are," I mention to Axel, but it's Lenny who responds.

"Of course the ass didn't explain. Come with me, darling."

Axel grins while Lenny practically drags me through a set of interior doors. I'm not sure what I expect, but it's not a dining hall full of maybe two hundred people. Lenny leads me behind a serving line where three servers hand out bread, meat, potatoes, green beans, and pudding.

"That way is Orange County," Lenny gestures to the right, then to the left, "Laguna Beach down there. Two of the wealthiest places in these parts and these," he gestures to the room of various races and genders crowding around for food, "are the forgotten wives, the tossed-out husbands or the vets coming home after their service, except they don't have a home no more. Twice a week, we give them something to eat and a place to rest their heads. I'd do more if I could, but we operate on a skeleton crew and food is limited."

The burn of tears stings my eyes as I take in the lost expressions, the hollowed eyes, and cheeks.

I am one of them.

For many months now, I've shared in their desperation. Casting my eyes from one to another, I see my own hungry face looking back at me.

Are they as determined as me to make a wrong right?

Do they have someone waiting on them somewhere too?

My vision goes dark and my lungs burn as I fight to breathe.

"Easy now. Sue, get this girl some water." Lenny's large hands guide me to a chair.

"What the hell did you do?" A tiny, black woman comes into focus. "Will you go back to the kitchen for the love of Pete and his wretched dragon?" she barks at Lenny. He obeys, leaving me with the pint-sized lady I can only assume is Sue.

She fans me with a towel and hysterical giggles burst from my lips at the same time tears stream from the corners of my eyes.

What is wrong with me?

"Good God almighty, what the hell are you on, girl?" Her face wrinkles with concern while her huge black eyes examine me skeptically.

"I'm sorry, I'm not on anything, I promise. I think I'm just *shocked?*"

Yeah, I'm shocked, shaking with a room full of people just like me.

Grinding the heal of my palms into my eyes, I look up to thank the woman. To my horror, Axel stands over me, searching my face.

I stand slowly. "I'm fine, really," I say way too fast.

Axel narrows his eyes, but before he can say anything, the woman begins waving her towel at him to leave.

"Y'all go on back to the kitchen, now. Good Lord, have mercy on me," she grumbles before returning to the serving line.

"That's Sue, by the way," Axel says while motioning for me to enter the kitchen. "You sure you're okay?"

"I'm sure. What can I do?"

Lenny pokes his head out of a walk-in cooler, looks me over, then darts back inside.

"You can finish the ham, if you want?" Axel nods to where Lenny was when we came in.

"Sure, anything. I'll do whatever." Determined to show I'm not a complete basket case, I retrieve the knife and begin slicing.

Don't press me, please don't press me to talk.

When Axel doesn't move for a long moment, I chance a glance to see him watching me, a look of uncertainty in his eyes. Afraid he will regret bringing me with him, I smile reassuringly.

"I think the bike ride and the excitement got to me." I shrug.

Say okay and walk away.

After watching me for a moment, Axel walks to the cooler where he and Lenny discuss what's needed.

"Thank you, God," I whisper as the pair busy themselves with metal containers and paper plates and take them out to the food line. I cut happily for several minutes before a teenage Mexican girl approaches me holding an empty tray.

"Hi," I say but she just looks at me expectantly.

Axel passes by on his way back to the cooler.

"She doesn't speak English, she wants you to give her what meat you have."

"Oh, I'm sorry." I begin filling her tray. She gives me a smile and returns to the dining hall.

"What do I need to do once I'm done here?" I ask Axel before he can disappear through the doors again.

"You want to refill cups? It's just tea and water, but it helps keep everyone from crowding the line."

"Absolutely. I'll be right there."

He smiles that crocked smile that makes me weak in the knees, then pushes through the serving doors, and I think my heart gives way slightly.

Trying to ignore the ramming beats against my rib cage each time I look at Axel, I happily pour water and tea, speaking to everyone with interest. Most eat and leave, others stay inside, taking a break from the heat. Every now and then, I catch Axel watching me from where he hands out towels or blankets.

More than once, I get lost looking his way, thinking about the roller coaster ride I'm currently on. When the crowd starts to die down so only a handful remain, I help pack up left overs for Lenny and Axel to deliver to the ones who live on the streets further down from the warehouse and couldn't make the trip.

"We won't be long and Reece hangs out until we get gone in case someone gets out of line," Axel nods to his friend who I have successfully avoided since his arrival earlier. I feel slightly embarrassed with the way things ended with our initial meeting. "You good?"

"I'm good," I say weakly because I've been holding back tears off and on all day.

Though I smiled like nothing was wrong, I kept picturing Axel handing me a plate of food on the streets where I'd spent most of the time since my mom died. More than once, I had to shake off the knowledge of just how lonely a life these people are living.

Where do they eat when they're not at the warehouse?

Do they sleep with some kind of weapon in case someone tries to rob or rape them like I do?

Or like I did before Axel?

Making a vow to never be in that situation again, I stiffen my spine and know that the money I will make from adult films can keep me off the streets and get me back to Ben. Nothing else matters.

After Axel and Lenny leave to hand out the food, I return inside to help Sue and the non-English-speaking girl clean up. I'm a little scared of the tiny black lady. She rules with an iron fist as I observed many times over the hours. She speaks in Spanish to the girl, then turns tired eyes to me. The girl returns to the dining room with a broom, and just before the door swings shut, I catch Reece winking at me.

"She's a good girl. She's not legal and won't tell a one of us just how in Hades she crossed the Rio Grande and made it all the way up here. Only the good Lord knows."

Sue shakes her head as if the girl were more than she could comprehend. I smile and return to washing the metal serving trays, but feel her eyes on me, studying me.

"Tell me, girl, how come I've never seen Axel with a girlfriend, in the nearly fifteen years I've known the boy, then in you come, pretty as you please?"

Why indeed.

Swallowing self-consciously, I can't think of a response. How am I supposed to explain I'm not on Axel's normal "schedule" and, therefore, not a part of his usual plans?

That he felt sorry for me, and offered to bring me along?

As I process what Sue asked, her words sink in. I frown at her.

"*Nearly* fifteen years? You have known Axel almost half his life?"

"Of course, I have." She swats a hand in the air dismissively, as it were common knowledge. "He stayed right out there on them steps for many months. I fed him and clothed him. He got some work and grew up, now he's paying it back like they all should be doing, but they don't all feel the need to give back like my Axel does."

Her face showed the first signs of emotion as she spoke of Axel.

Axel was homeless, too?

He and I actually have something in common?

Somehow, I doubt I will ever get him to talk about it though. I muse and dry trays, waiting for more. Sue just wipes and mutters about random things that need to be done.

"It's good he comes back to help," I say, trying to start up more talk about Axel.

"Help? Hell, girl, if it wasn't for that boy, none of these people would've eaten today. This is Axel's place."

"Oh, I just assumed you or Lenny—" I trail off trying to wrap my head around everything.

Axel's place?

Whoa, no way. Axel feeds all these people?

Why am I so affected by this?

Because it could be me he is feeding.

It is me.

Sue makes a tsking noise, and I realize I missed some of what she said.

"Lenny used to be a pimp, and I use to be a prostitute. I married the fat bastard not long after Axel come out here. He's been helping ever since. Axel ain't told you none of this?"

Um, no. I doubt he talks to any of the girls about anything.

Plus, all we do is screw.

I stay quiet, sensing she isn't really asking the question.

"We been doing this awhile now. You're the first girl he's ever brought here, matter of fact, you're the only person, other than Reece, that's come with him at all."

Fifteen years?

"When you said he got a job, what kind of a job, do you know?" I ask before she drifts off topic.

Sue doesn't hear the dread in my voice, but I'm starting to piece the puzzle of Axel together.

"I don't know what he was doing. I do know a red-haired woman, Brenda, or something, was with him a lot."

"Barbara," I whisper, but Sue is already walking away from me, speaking in rapid Spanish to the girl again. I hadn't even noticed she'd come back in the kitchen.

Finishing up with the trays and serving utensils, I joined Sue for coffee at the table I sliced ham from earlier. After pulling together two wooden stools that barely support our weight, I sip and try to think how best to bring Axel up again.

Just ask, the worst she can do is bite your head off.

"So, you and Lenny are like foster parents to Axel?"

Sue sips her coffee and pulls a discarded sales ad closer to look over. I wait for a response as she pulls a small pair of glasses from her apron pocket and perches them on her nose. She appears old when she looks my way once more.

"I suppose I'm a lot of things to that boy, hell not just him, a lot of them."

Sue glances around and I suspect she's looking for the Mexican girl before returning her dark eyes to mine. "Where are you from? Not here, I can hear the accent."

"Mississippi."

Sue nods and returns to her ads.

"How long you been homeless?"

My cheeks warm.

"Is it that obvious?"

"We all have a look, like we know things others won't ever understand." Sue narrows stern eyes on me. "And the way you broke down out there in the dining room. Ain't no shame in empathy. Keep that with you always, no matter where you go in this life."

"For a while now. My mom died and I didn't have anywhere to go."

Among other things.

Averting my eyes, I have to rub the dampness there before it runs down my face. The scraping of the stool catches me off guard, and as I look to see if Sue fell, I realize she had climb down and is reaching out to me for a hug. My head falls automatically to her shoulder, and I weep for the first time in months. We stay like that a long time, her hand running soothingly up and down my back, and before I know what I'm doing, I'm telling her everything.

Even about Ben.

Surprising myself, I let it all out and Sue sits quietly as I purge. By the time I finish, Axel is back with Lenny. After a few minutes of polite goodbyes, I follow Axel to the bike as Lenny locks up. Twice, Axel asks if I am feeling all right, and I respond a simple, "Yes, fine."

But I'm not fine.

I'm overwhelmed with the day and my unplanned confessions to Sue. Plus, talking about Ben only reopened wounds that were barely together in the first place.

I haven't been thinking of why I'm here.

Ben.

After some advice, Sue and I spoke more about Axel. The knowledge I learned only made me ask more questions. Sue was either unknowing, or unwilling to admit what I was piecing together. We ended our coffee and our talk with her giving me a slip of paper with her phone number and address in neat scrawl.

"You call me anytime. You don't have to be alone anymore."

This brought on a new batch of tears, and now, I feel guilty for some reason.

Maybe I shouldn't have asked so many questions about Axel.

And I have a suspicion Axel isn't being one hundred percent honest with me. We pull in the garage just as the air begins to chill with the night. Axel holds the bike steady, and I climb off, removing my helmet as he follows quietly.

"I think I want to take a shower and go to bed," I say through numb lips.

"Okay." By the time he responds, I'm already in the house, heading toward my room, stripping as I walk.

He's letting me do whatever I want.

Even sleep with him, eat with him, and shower with him.

Why, when that's against the rules?

Feeling odd and completely out of sorts while I shower the day away, my thoughts turn to the rules once more and why exactly I'm not being treated like the others. A thought I'd dismissed earlier comes to mind, and I have to bite back my anger.

Once I'm dry, I'm convinced whatever is happening with Axel and me needs to be reset. I don't know why he took me to the warehouse today, but it's left me feeling lost more than ever. At first, I thought it was a kind gesture to share something with me, but as I brush my hair, I wonder if he wanted me to see the faces of the lost souls to make me consider that I might be one of them after agreeing to adult films.

Why else would he show me the dead girls' pictures?

For the same reason he wanted me to see the homeless. To shock me into going back home.

"Well, fuck that. He has no idea," I say to the mirror.

Axel is trying to get out of teaching me anything so I will fall flat on my face. I swear by all things holy, I'm not going to be the stupid virgin he obviously thinks I am. He didn't want me to begin with, then when I get here, he repeatedly tries to get me to go home. Now, I'm furious and vow I will go through with the thirty days. Then, I will make a nice chunk of money just to spite him.

"Asshole," I mutter, now fuming.

There has to be a way to show Axel his homeless visit didn't have the effect he had hoped. Mind made up, I drop my towel and walk naked into the living room.

Axel's sitting back with his eyes half-closed watching Sportscenter. The only way I know he sees me is the tilt of his mouth at the corners as he takes in my lack of clothing. Ignoring his look of desire, I say nothing as I make my way to him, determination blazing.

Show him you are not a sweet innocent.

When I reach him, I drop to my knees and pull off his jeans with very little effort. His cock stands at attention, but I ignore it. Also ignoring the look of both confusion and lust on his handsome face, I rise to straddle him, tugging off his shirt. Axel's hands cup my breasts so tenderly, it takes my breath away.

Damn him and his magic hands.

Grabbing a handful of his hair, I wiggle against his crotch until we are aligned. Arms circle my waist and his mouth kisses, licks, sucks, and bites at me. Pressing on, willing my brain to stick with the plan, I don't bother being gentle, can't if I tried right now.

Once deeply seated, I move against him, anger almost slipping when he growls against my breasts. Breaking away when I pull on his hair, Axel tilts his face up.

Expecting me to kiss him?

"Am I doing it right?"

Instantly, his body turns rigid, his hands fall to my thighs and he stops to search my face. Fisting a handful of my hair to look in my eyes, he searches. Whatever he sees, it doesn't please him.

Okay, maybe I should have waited until after my orgasm to ask the question.

No regretting it.

I squirm, wanting his hands back on me, and I try to ignore the sudden chill between our bodies.

"No, you're not," he says icily.

Axel picks me up easily, laying me on the couch and pressing deeper inside my body, hard.

Too hard.

Crying out in pain, in lust, in anger, I bite down on Axel's shoulder. A roar echoes through the room and he thrusts even harder. I whimper with frustration because it feels good.

Feels so good.

No sooner does the thought cross my mind, I tense, growing angry once more. And damn him, Axel begins to slow and kiss me. Unable to resist, I part my lips.

"Shhh. Relax, Payton. Just relax." Axel lifts his body from mine, then places his thumb at my center, pressing down and rubbing. "Whatever you're thinking about, let it go."

He presses harder and my legs spread wide in response. He drives into me, and the moment I let go and just enjoy it, my orgasm begins to build.

"There you go, Payton, come for me."

With those words, I come undone, and just as I peak, Axel places both hands on my hips, pulls my body off the couch, and slams into me harder. The intensity rocks me to my bones, and I begin to claw at his shoulders. Thrusting deeply, Axel hooks my legs in the crook of his elbows, bending me nearly in half and pushes harder, quickening his pace, now chasing his own orgasm.

A deep rumble resonates from his chest, and I get lost in his heat. Axel throws his head back, and every muscle in his neck tightens as he comes. In this moment, I can't recall why I was mad at first, I can only think *I did this to him.* I don't care he's using me then will be done with me only to toss me out.

I'll let him use me, and later, I'm going to use him.

M.C. Webb

Fifteen

-

Axel

"Like this?" Payton looks up at me while practicing her oral skills.

I grin, enjoying both watching her clumsily sucking while looking at the mirror and the reflection of her bare ass in the air. It's day five, and she wants to explore. Explore *more*, rather. My stamina has been thoroughly tested the last few days and so far, I surprised even myself.

As fun as it is for both of us, judging by the multiple orgasms I'm supplying Payton, she is constantly reminding me I'm not a good teacher, and I constantly distract her from learning anything to use on camera. I'm not in the teaching mood and had, so far, done great in *not* teaching Payton anything. I'm just enjoying her not knowing much as she discovers things on her own.

"Axel," she whines, making my grin widen.

Tilting my head to the side as if thinking over her question, she becomes frustrated with me once more. When she begins backing away, I cup her nape.

"Payton, you couldn't give a bad blow job if a gun was held to your head."

"You're not showing me anything, Axel. And you're doing it on purpose."

Grinning, I lie against the pillows propped up on the headboard of my bed, enjoying the attention a little too much. Payton gives me a sardonic look, pushes my hand away, and begins backing off the bed. I throw my hands up in defeat.

"Okay, come on, Payton, I'll help you."

And a sudden rush of nausea courses through me at the thought of *helping* her and that leading to her sucking off another guy.

She can't, I can't teach her to do that.

It's impossible, and I've known that since day one.

But what if I don't?

Travis, that's what.

Having to swallow back bile at the thought, I again dismiss the idea. Payton smiles, and I glance at the mirror as she crawls back up to put her mouth on me again.

"So, what do I do?" she asks seriously.

I take a deep breath and let it out slowly. I have, so far, avoided giving instruction but Payton has apparently reached the limit of her patience or figured out I'm purposefully sabotaging her learning.

"Wrap your hand around the shaft," I instruct, annoyed at the loss of fun sex with her.

We're transitioning into teacher/student situation and I don't like it.

Fucking hate it, actually.

Payton wraps her fingers around me, and then waits. I give instructions that are not at all my usual teachings and have to inwardly cuss as she expectantly waits on directions.

Directors will love her.

Male leads will fight to be with her, and you will have led her to Hell.

Payton obeys my every command, and it rips my insides apart. And the fact that she is nowhere near film-worthy only pleases me more. I don't have it in me to teach her how to relax and try to stay calm after two hours of trying to suck and look good. The male always ends up fucking the female's throat, scrapping her teeth in the process because her mouth will be swollen and sore to the point she couldn't suck a Popsicle, let alone a dick. No, I won't tell her that part.

I hope like hell she never figures it out either.

"Now what?" she asks, dragging me out of my thoughts.

"You're doing it. That's it." I rest my head against the wall trying to not feel what I'm feeling.

Possessive.

But no right to be.

Grinding my teeth until they protest, I grasp Peyton by both arms and drag her body up against mine.

Possession.

She squeaks out a feeble protest before I shut her down with a kiss.

"Fuck, Payton you drive me crazy." I break free from her mouth, trailing kisses down her neck and up to her mouth again. "Turn around, and you can do whatever you want to me. There's no instructions needed because it doesn't matter what you do. It doesn't matter."

I scoot down on my back and watch her turn and place a knee on either side of my face.

"Yes, that's it, now just lower yourself down." I try to sound like I'm not enjoying every second of her compliance while also trying to sound like I'm instructing.

Once comfortable, Payton lowers herself to my lips. I'm drowning in wetness within seconds, thinking there is no better way to die. Letting her do whatever feels good, I just rock her body until she's breaking apart as I lap at her. Before the aftershocks end, I push her sideways onto her stomach, wrapping my hands around to squeeze her breasts as I enter her from behind in one swift thrust.

Yes, possession.

But it's a lie.

Payton screams into the mattress as pure, carnal need grips me. Releasing a nipple, I wet the tip of my thumb, placing it at the opening of her back door. She immediately tightens at the sensation, and I hiss in a breath, loving the grip.

"Axel?"

Grinning at the fear in her voice, I push my thumb inside, just a fraction of an inch and Payton comes instantly. Her orgasm fuels mine, and I clutch at her hips, thrusting deep two times before following her over the edge. I come in hard waves, and I swear, for a split second, I leave my body.

Yes, possession.

But am I possessing her, or is she possessing me?

Crashing down, I fall to the bed, pulling Payton against me. We lie silent, breathing heavily for a long time. I have no idea what time it is and really don't care. We have days in my bed, on the couch, on the beach, or taking showers only stopping to eat. We've had no concept of time and never once did we turn the TV on. If we were not fucking, we were talking and with each passing hour, I grew more comfortable with the closeness I'd never had before.

Truth be known, I never really wanted it, didn't know I could actually *crave* it. Not until that day I took her to the warehouse with me, before we left and she ask me to just hold her a minute. Something in me shifted in place in that instant, and now, I can't seem to stop myself.

The extent of my interactions with females was maybe sharing a meal in between filming. I'm not a complete idiot and recognized when a woman wanted more than on film, and occasionally, I gave it to her but I'd never abandoned my rules. If I relaxed them even the slightest, I regretted it instantly and couldn't wait for them to move on.

But with Payton, I don't want the falsities of sex on film. Not that any sex was not pleasurable, because it was, but it is nothing like the heat-filled passion I feel with Payton. I've caught myself several times trying to steer her away from wanting to return to the training room. I know as soon as I give in to her requests of teaching her, she will no longer look at me with the piercing hazel eyes adoringly.

Besides, I'm not sure I can *just* train Payton anymore, and know we can't have both the training and the passion. One would smother the other because intimacy does not translate to film, even though that is what I sell. It's all staged on camera.

Payton brings up my teaching her to be in front of a camera more than a couple of times each day, but so far, I've been able to distract her. I'm going to keep distracting her as much as possible, hoping to squash that desire out entirely.

When I think she's fallen asleep, I press my front to her back, burying my face in her hair, sinking into my new favorite position.

"Axel?"

"Hmmm?"

"Are you ever going to teach me anything I can actually use when I leave here?"

I slgh heavily. Apparently, I'm not fooling her.

"Of course," I lie into the flowery scent of her golden hair.

Payton is quiet a minute, and when I'm on the verge of sleep, she wiggles out from under my embrace.

"Where you going?" I ask sleepily.

I've spent years not allowing a woman to sleep with me, and it only took a few days of Payton for me to feel like I need it. I know this is a Payton thing, and that doesn't seem to bother me.

"I'm going to take a shower," she says with a hint of annoyance.

"Want me to join you?" I ask, hoping she'll say no because I don't know if I can stand up at the moment.

The pause she gives is just long enough to be uncomfortable. I pick up on a different feeling and pull my head away from the pillow to look at her.

Payton stands by the bed looking down at me. The bathroom light is on and her naked form is...tense...maybe even angry.

Here we go.

"What?" I ask, slightly annoyed myself.

She chews at her bottom lip, and I roll to my back leaning up on my elbows.

"What's wrong?"

"You know what's wrong. You are purposely not teaching me anything, Axel." It was a statement, not a question. "You're having fun, and though I am enjoying this maybe too much, I still have to learn something before the thirty days are up. I need to land that contract. I have to be able to make money, Axel, that's why I'm here, even though you seem to have forgotten that fact."

Her words wound, and I just look at her stupidly. The foreign feeling of resenting her actually *wanting* to film burns like a branding iron, and I realize for the first time, Peyton really does want to film. She's after the contract, and it hits me hard she's not any different from the others who have come before her.

Fool. You're a damned fool, Axel, to ever do this with her.

186

"I just don't want to get things confused. You're supposed to help me so I can get decent work, otherwise I'll be forced to be in snuff films, right?" She says looking slightly on the verge of hysteria.

I've got to somehow distract her from these thoughts.

Tensing with a familiar disgust, my jaw clenches at thought of her in that type of porn. I'm sickened because the desperation in her voice tells me she will do the worst of them if it came to it.

"Come on, Payton, you can't be serious," I say in an attempt at lightening the mood.

She stares down at me, the hard lines of her face forming with outrage. And yeah, it's anger that shows through her eyes. I haven't seen this side yet. All the other sides, yes, but angry Payton, though beautiful, is a little intimidating. Just as soon as the emotion shows, it disappears.

"What are we doing, Axel?" she pleads, sounding utterly exhausted, and I make the mistake of chuckling.

"Is it not obvious?"

The anger returns in a rush and she swings her shirt at me. It lands with a crack across my chest.

"Fuck you! You think because I sleep in the same bed with you that you can treat me like a cute puppy then when the clock runs out, I'll go back to Mississippi? Return to what? A minimum wage waitress job at the truck stop? Have six kids and live off the government? Or maybe you thought I would stay here and live off your dick from time to time." Her voices rises to a desperate shrill. "I'm not Axel! I'm going through with this whether you help me or not. I have to!"

"Treat you like a cute puppy? Live off my dick?" I repeat in a deadly whisper. My anger is beginning to bubble for the first time in days. Rage and misery, my old friends, surfacing, rising up to turn my heart to ice. "Fine, fuck Payton! You're a little enthusiastic about spreading your legs for men to jerk off to you, aren't you?"

"You asshole!" she screams, swinging her shirt again.

The snap enrages me further, and I shoot off the bed, standing opposite her, a slew of words on the tip of my tongue but I remain silent, not sure which to toss out first.

This feels an awful lot like disappointment and if I'm not mistaken, loss.

"I can do this," Payton gestures to the bed then back to me with a hand, "anywhere and with any man, Axel."

I'm not going to lie, that fucking hurt and the steel plates of my interior slam back in place.

"Fine!" Just like that, I snap back to my senses. "You should go sleep in your room. We can get started tomorrow," I sneer in one cold breath.

Payton eyes me cautiously at the sudden change of my tone. I know I look menacing, I know I'm cold—ice cold—and I feel like a fool for ever abandoning that with her.

"Axel? I didn't mean...I just need..." She makes a move toward me but I point toward my bedroom door.

"Get the fuck out, Payton."

She flinches with pain or shock; I neither know, nor care. I make a mental note she will need to work on facial control for the camera. Before she can make it out of my bedroom, I walk to the bathroom and slam the door before saying something unforgivable. Placing my palms on the counter, I stare down in the sink, my breathing heavy as rage claws at me.

What the fuck is wrong with me?

I look at my naked reflection and almost laugh when I see I'm shaking, fucking *shaking*. It feels like my mind has been on vacation for days and decided just now to show back up, but now it's injured, rearranged.

Who was I fucking kidding?

Myself, apparently.

Payton is here for one reason and one reason only, so that's exactly what I will give her. After dressing in jeans and a hoodie, I walk with purpose to the kitchen. Payton's door is shut. The light is on, and I can see her shadow from the crack at the bottom Absently, I open a cabinet, grab a bottle of old, dark rum, and retrieve my flashlight from the utility drawer, then walk to the solitary wooden lounge chair on the beach. I snort, remembering fucking Payton there just days before.

That was your first mistake.

Sitting on the edge, I drink fast and hard, wanting to be drunk as quickly as possible, so I can become numb in disbelief at how I'd given in so easily to Payton.

And I took her to the fucking warehouse.

Now that I think about it, that seems to be the day things changed and she became more eager to be trained. I shake my head at my own stupidity.

After several minutes, I begin to calm slightly and turn on my green lit flashlight to watch the crabs run across the sand while waves roll by, sweeping them to and fro. The creatures never stop moving, even when they're dragged backward. They fight to gain control, then get swept away. Some bury themselves after making some progress, others dig in, trying to escape the undertow.

Watching the crabs is something I do when I don't want to think or feel. After Payton pretty much said I was wasting her time, and she could be with any random dick, I really don't want to think and feeling is too confusing. I really don't know what the fuck I'm doing with her.

Obviously, she doesn't give a shit about me breaking my own rules, allowing her to sleep in my bed, or showering with me.

That means absolutely nothing to her.

Fuck it, I'm done being nice. I'll teach her more than she can handle.

Making up my mind, I pull the hood of my shirt over my head and slide up on the lounge to sit for hours, drinking and watching crabs until I finally fall asleep.

Sixteen

-

Axel

Somebody shakes my shoulder, hard, and if I could feel my arm, I would punch the
motherfucker for touching me.

"Axel?"

I squint at the morning sun and try to cover my eyes. My arms feel heavy and I realize I'm lying awkwardly on top of both my hands. They're both numb as I try to sit up.

"Fuck, Reece, what time is it?"

"It's half-past seven. I thought you were dead. Shit, Axel, you'll fry if you don't get out of the sun. Good thing I spotted you before I headed home."

I pull my hood over my face then curl up on my side.

"Axel, get the fuck up, man. You'll be blistered if you don't. It's July. In Cal-ifor-nia. This is skin cancer season."

I suck in a heavy breath, then exhale just as hard.

"Shit, all right. Why are you down here, anyway?"

"Because I saw you laying here and thought you were dead. Did you not hear me the first time?"

Groaning, I struggle to sit up. It's low tide and my head swims as I look out at sea.

"Well, clearly I'm not dead, so you can go back up the beach, you annoying bastard."

I swing an arm in the general direction. Reece just shakes his head and stalks off muttering something incoherent but sounding something like, "crabby bastard." Standing unsteadily and stretching, I feel like shit and wish I hadn't drank so much. With heavy footsteps, I make my way through the sand, then my kitchen and bedroom, not looking up until I reach to turn the hot water on in my shower.

Keeping my eyes closed, I step inside, letting water soothe me, but it does nothing for the images of Payton pressed against the glass as I fucked her.

No, not fuck, something else.

Something more happened between us, or so I thought at the time. Now, it's a foolish memory because apparently, it's just my warped sense of *more,* and those images of Payton staring hungrily back into my eyes as I buried myself inside her body will haunt me for the rest of my life.

Not just the shower, but *all.*

Bitterly, I know that feeling is gone and there isn't a damn thing I can do about it. She's going to do what she wants to. Payton came to me for a reason, so I will give her what she wants, though with me, it's a grudging obligation.

It takes me another thirty minutes to really wake up, and by that time, I'm thoroughly pissed off, near boiling with anger but also determined. Fuck feelings, I've never allowed them to cloud my judgement before

Payton, then in she walks with her virgin pussy and I'm unmanned.

Never again. Not ever.

I say this to myself several times as I dry and shear off the week-old scruff around my face and neck.

The doorbell rings and glancing at the clock, I know it's the grocery delivery. Opening the front door in just my towel, I wave at Reggie, the forty-something Asian man who delivers food and mail from my post office box almost weekly. I pour orange juice and watch him place two heavy bags of groceries on the counter, taking out the more fragile items.

The kitchen is spotless and I realize Payton must've cleaned. We raided the cabinets, eating whatever we found completely naked, taking time out to kiss or touch. We were in constant contact with one another. For a brief second, I feel regret that those moments are over, gone, replaced by something I no longer want to do.

Not with anyone, especially not with Payton.

But I will do what she wants for the simple reason of saving her from the slimy hands of Travis, but then I have to wonder why I would try to keep her from Travis at all. That is where she will eventually end up anyway. They all end up with pimps one way or another the majority of the time.

I pinch the bridge of my nose, listening to Reggie ramble on about shit I couldn't care less about.

"And there's mail for both you and your um—," Reggie glances around the living room and toward the bedroom door, hoping to catch a glimpse of a woman, "guest," he finishes dryly.

"Thank you," I take the mail and hand him his usual tip. "See you next week, Reggie."

"Sure thing, Axel." Reggie leaves, apparently understanding today is not a shoot the shit kind of day for me.

I busy myself with tossing stuff in the fridge and pantry, pausing only to take bites of a bagel and drink more juice. Once I have something in my stomach, I take eight hundred milligrams of Ibuprofen in hopes my head will stop throbbing. Payton walks into the kitchen a few minutes later, and I do my best to ignore her completely.

Still fuming from her words, I search through world news on my phone without actually reading a single word. Bored with that option, I switch to sifting through email, and messages. Not bothering with the rest, I take a moment to answer Barb's.

Barbara:

Still mad at me?

At least let me know if the girl is being trained?

Axel, you have got to stop ignoring me. This is no way to run a business.

If I don't hear from you by Friday at the latest I will come by. We both know how much you like that.

Glancing at the calendar, I inwardly curse Barb and send a response.

Fuck off Barb, you will have your properly trained mutt soon enough.

Using the word "mutt" felt wrong, but it's what Barbara refers to the girls as and it will get her off my back for now. I can just picture her lips smacking in anticipation of getting Payton to work immediately. Fresh meat always sells fast, and Payton would fetch a pretty penny.

Pausing only a second to note I fucking hate Barb, I brace myself before looking toward Payton. She's still in only a t-shirt, long blonde hair swept up in a messy bun and bare legs on display. Her eyes have the glint of gold I find myself drowning in, willingly so, at least until last night. Now, they stir an uncomfortable mix of resentment and pain.

"Good morning," Payton says, pouring coffee.

There's none of her usual cheer in her voice, and I'm wondering if she's just as conflicted.

She said she could be doing this with any guy, so no.

Why would she be conflicted? I'm the only one here that got side-tracked.

I'm going to train her and get her out of my house.

"Hey," I reply dryly then return to my phone for somewhere to look other than her. When she takes a seat at the bar in front of me, I reach behind my back for the schedule, only making a quick change with the time frame, and lay it on the counter, sliding it to Payton.

"What's this?" She sounds sweet and curious.

I'm unaffected.

"It's the schedule. I run on a schedule and rules as I explained before. You will see I have crossed out the first few days so we will start on today."

Setting my phone down, I look at her fully, folding my arms across my bare torso. My chest gives a slight squeeze, but I shut that shit down fast. Payton's red-rimmed eyes make it look as if she were the one who drank all the rum last night. She's wearing a weary expression as she looks at the paper, but that turns instantly to uncertainty when she look at me and takes in my frigid exterior. I fight the urge to introduce myself for the first time considering she's never once met the real me. Who I've been with her the past few days was a joke.

"You have mail," I nod at the small stack by the last of the grocery bags, "I'll meet you in the studio in forty-five minutes."

Don't look at the confusion in her eyes, don't feel sorry for her, just fucking leave.

I turn to leave the kitchen and head back to my room, away from Payton and her goddamned beautiful fucking face. I get half way before she calls out to me. Pausing, I turn my head in that general direction while refraining from looking straight at her.

"Axel? Are you mad at me?" She sounds desperate, maybe even hurt.

Turning just enough to look at her over my shoulder, I give her a wicked grin.

"That would require feelings, Payton. Don't flatter yourself in thinking I have those." I stride away quickly so I don't have to see her reaction. For some reason, I know I won't like it.

Trading my towel for jeans, I turn my attention to the cameras, focusing in, all business mode. There had been no recordings since day one and cursing myself for becoming distracted, I sent that file to my computer, knowing it would never be seen.

After preparing the digital files for new recordings, I look over the schedule. The first two weeks of training are primarily getting comfortable with the camera and learning the positions and the fact there will be people around, holding microphones or lighting, but that's only if she got decent work.

If she didn't get decent work, then there is usually a room of maybe two, sound and film, which results in cheesy work that is offered up on free sites. Those videos make very little if anything based on how many clicks it receives. Most of the time, a girl is paid a few hundred dollars, tossed in a room to be fucked in every hole then be tossed away with the trash. Quick money for cheap fucks.

Payton doesn't deserve that. None of them do, but especially not Payton.

She's not ready for any of this.

She will be dead within a year, or worse, on skid row with a heroin addiction and a baby she can't feed.

Just like the boy.

I drop down into the chair. If I didn't sit, I would have thrown up at the thought. I watch the water outside the studio's window. It helps, but the raw knowing of what's to come for Payton still sickens me.

Exactly forty-five minutes later, Payton enters the room, and I know there's absolutely nothing I can do to stop what's been set in motion. This is what she wants. I'm no one to her to say she can't proceed, she made that abundantly clear last night.

Purposely not looking her way, I busy myself with nothing in particular. I pull the covers off the bed, leaving only the fitted sheet and pillows. Once the covers are tossed to a corner, I then check the cameras, the sound, and lighting, deciding to open the blinds, drenching the room in sunlight instead of the harsh fluorescents. Payton stands quietly, her hands clasped together, waiting to be told what to do.

"Take your clothes off and get on the bed," I instruct.

She hesitates only a moment before discarding her clothes and crawling to the middle of the bed. Sitting, I adjust a camera angle to focus in on just Payton.

"You can begin. If you need lube, it's in the night stand to your right, but use it sparingly. That shit gets everywhere and I'd prefer it not end up all over the house."

I sit back in my chair, stretching my legs out wide in front of me. Payton glances to her right where I indicated, then back to me.

"I don't understand."

I don't hide my deep sigh of impatience; I make a point to sound as annoyed as possible. Payton has to get used to it from me, or a director who will replace her just to simplify things.

"You are going to spread your legs and get yourself off. You did read over the schedule?" I raise my eyebrows and give her a look that asks: *are you stupid or something?*

"I am supposed to masturbate? And you—"

"Teach. I am here to train you. You may begin anytime."

I make a point to check my watch, then fold my hands across my stomach waiting.

"So, I just what? Start touching myself?"

Closing my eyes with faux exhaustion, I open them and nod slowly.

"Pretend you're alone in your room, it's just you. You have masturbated before, correct?"

A red flush creeps up Payton's neck and across her cheeks, and I fight a snort at what a silly girl she is.

"Well, go ahead. Begin."

"But—"

"Okay," I hold out my hands for her to stop talking then lean forward in my seat to appear as intimidating as possible, "this is the first thing you need to store in that head of yours for later—time equals money. Never forget that. You are on a schedule, and while you question everything, time is ticking by so that's more money that has to be paid out to the crew, and trust me, honey, you will need to come on cue or you will never work in this business. And when I say on cue, I don't mean actual climax. You will be lucky to have one of those ever again, but I'm referring to exactly the way the director tells you to. If it's in pain, you sell it, if it's two hours of someone performing on you and your legs hurt so bad they shake? You sell it. You show up, do as you're told and that's a wrap. Understand? You will not be given a time for Q and A's, get it? If it's a rape scene, you do it, if it's an anal fucking, you will receive it, girl on girl, and so on. You will know what you're going to film beforehand, just as I have given you a schedule of what to do here. You are expected to show up, do what you're told, then go where ever the fuck after. Probably into the next film because like I said, time is money, so you will most likely be filming three to four films in a day."

Payton licks her lips nervously, eyeing me as if deciding on something to say. I lean to my left, placing my hand on my temple while my chin rests on my thumb, and I try to look bored. I remain unaffected by Payton.

She is just another girl I'm training.

After a short pause, that stubborn girl who's capable of cleaving my chest in two like she did last night, shows up and timid Payton disappears. She lies back, propped on pillows and spreads her long legs wide. My lips part involuntarily, and I bite the inside of my cheek to keep focused at the business at hand.

Payton touches her breasts, tugging on each nipple then trails fingers down to juncture between her thighs. Wetness glistens, and I have to swallow a few times when my mouth waters knowing what she tasted like.

"Like this?" Payton asks, looking directly at me, hunger burning in hooded eyes.

I nod, just a fraction.

"Like that," I say, then check the camera to make sure she's in alignment.

Payton dips a finger and begins to grind her hips while watching me the entire time. I remain unaffected.

This is just work.

Then, why am I having a hard time breathing?

Watching her face as she moves, never looking at her body, I sit perfectly still. Just like normal, except this *isn't* normal. My sanity is slipping, and I fight the need to rip the room to shreds. Everything in my soul is screaming *WRONG, this is all wrong!*

This is no different than assisted suicide, you bastard.

No, this is what she wants.

But what do I want?

Payton begins undulating, nearing orgasm. I remain perfectly still and watch as her eyes stay locked on mine until she throws her head back to cry out with the release.

As much as it is a turn-on, it also makes me physically ill. I close my eyes until it's over, feeling something rollover and die inside my chest.

Once her hand relaxes, Payton lies waiting for me to comment. For a fleeting moment, I think she expects me to fuck her. I fight back pity and know for certain she just doesn't know me very well.

Standing before it gets too awkward and something shows in my face, I turn my back to finish transferring the recording.

"Get dressed. Meet me in the living room," I command coldly, not turning around.

Don't turn around, you wouldn't if it were anyone else so just don't look at her.

Don't want her, don't need her.

Keeping my eyes forward on the camera so I don't have to see Payton's body longer than necessary, I force myself to revert back to Axel Stone and all business, yet the turbulence Payton causes in me remains.

Busying myself with nothing, I listen for Payton to dress and leave. As soon as she's gone, I run my fingers through my hair, trying to ease the tension before joining her on the couch. I want to yank out strands as I rub, but end up taken several deep breaths to calm the raging war in my chest.

Business. This is business.

I can't look at her, nor do I speak as I make my way to sit on the sofa facing the screen. Payton sits rigid on the sofa to my left, knees curled protectively to her chest. Ignoring her, I begin pushing buttons on the remote, bringing the Payton file up then playing the video.

Only then do I watch Payton to my left as she watches herself on the screen. She squints, bites her lip, and then closes her eyes partially as she watches herself orgasm. The sound of her moans are so familiar to me now, I can pin point the second she starts coming. When the recording stops, I exit out of the file. Payton turns to me, red in the face.

"How do you think you looked?" I ask, remaining cold.

"I'm not sure." She shrugs.

"Would you pay to watch that?"

She pulls her lower lip between her teeth, clearly uncomfortable.

"I don't know."

She frowns, as if the thought never occurred to her.

"I have addressed timing and while we may be in the beginning stages of your training, you need to remember that first and foremost. As far as any masturbation scene goes, it was okay, but *just* okay. You would be lucky to get it on a free site. I don't think it would make it on a webcam sell, but that's hard to say with you not having a following."

I run my hand through my hair, very aware of Payton's eyes on me while looking injured by my words.

Business.

"No one really knows what they look like until they see themselves. You did better than some. Your climax needs work, but the main thing is you're not considering the people that want to jerk off to you. You are a salesman. You have to sell yourself within a few seconds or people get bored, and you have to sell the climax. You come, your subscribers come."

"I was doing it for you, I didn't consider—"

"Well, that was a waste of both of our time if you were performing for me," I snap.

A second after the words leave my lips, I watch Payton's eyes fill with tears.

"I'm not your audience, Payton. I don't even watch porn. As ironic as that may seem, to me, it's no different than any other job. I clock in, then clock out. It is you that has to lure people in and convince them to subscribe to your channels, webcams, or become a member of the site. This all has to do with selling yourself to those willing to pay. That's the cold hard facts. On average, masturbation scenes last about five minutes. You will have about forty-five seconds to lure someone in, then keep them watching as you deliver the climax. Do that, and you make money. Give them a show, and they will seek out your other videos."

Payton sits up straighter and tries to blink away tears. I close my eyes and rub the bridge of my nose, feeling just like I slept in a lounge chair all night. She touches my knee, and I jerk away instantly.

"You don't touch me unless I tell you to," I practically yell, nearing a violent outburst.

Business Axel, keep it together.

This is why I did drugs in the first place.

Do I want to go back to that?

Unable to finish the thought, I make an effort to calm down. Payton sits back looking stunned.

"Why are you so mean? So *cold*?" she asks weakly.

This makes me laugh without an ounce of humor.

"I am who I've always been. It's not my problem you thought otherwise. This," I gesture to the image on the screen then to where she sits on the couch, "is just a job. *You* are just a job. My evil old man taught me that fact a long time ago, at thirteen actually, when he pushed me in a motel room, and patted me on the back telling me to 'have fun' with a prostitute he paid twenty bucks to turn me into a man for my birthday. Not much has changed. You all want to be paid to make somebody a man, doesn't matter if it's on your knees or through a camera lens."

Standing, I glare down at her, vindicated that she's feeling an ounce of what I did last night, judging by the anguished expression she gives me.

Unaffected.

Having to look away, I check my watch, ever aware I just shared something I had never told anyone but Reece. "We are behind. Let's go." I proceed back to the studio more than a little embarrassed and pissed off that Payton has weakened me so thoroughly.

After a long minute, Payton follows. I set the camera as she begins to undress, unable to look at her

"Put your clothes back on, Payton," I order with disdain. "I will undress you. And I expect you to follow the schedule I gave you earlier to save me from having to remind you every time you come in here of what to expect."

After finishing with the files, I look to see Payton standing, her hands clasped in front and still clothed.

"Get on the bed."

She does as instructed without question. Once she's settled, I move to lean a knee on the side of the bed, then reach down to pull her shirt up over her breasts and suck on her nipples. Sorrow for what is about to happen churns through me while hatred for my position burns in my gut.

Payton has no clue I'm filming her reactions, her body language, and response to my movements. She's looking at me with dreamy eyes while I easily fall into my alter ego, knowing how to stand, tilt my face for both close views and long angles of the camera. I ignore the tremors Payton is having as I run a hand up her inner thigh, then press it against her mound through the cotton fabric of her shorts, all the while keeping my mouth on her nipples in turn.

She moans and places a hand in my hair lovingly. I reach for it and place it back to her side roughly. Once I'm satisfied enough time has been spent on her breasts, I remove her shirt then shorts, skillfully taking my time staring into her eyes. I'm in character as the guy with the big dick preparing to fuck a silly blonde, she is just being naïve Payton, looking at me as if we are rehearsing for a melodrama full of love stories and rainbows. I'm not sure I've ever felt more pity for any one person before.

Removing only my shirt, I lay her back sideways on the bed, pushing and pulling her body in the right angle for viewing while pushing her legs open with the one closest to the camera slightly higher. Slowly and meticulously, I lick Payton to the brink of orgasm then stop just before she comes.

Hiking her ass in the air, I pull my jeans off and then back her up so I can remain standing as I fuck her from behind. When she raises and arches ready for me, I put a hand on the back of her neck and press down so her face is in the mattress, shifting her leg closest to the camera so my cock can be seen drilling only partially at her. It is not a pleasurable position for the female, but she never matters during filming. The girls only need to sell their imaginary pleasure.

Gripping my cock, I guide it to her wet entrance then push inside without warning. Payton cries out but I don't give her any time to adjust to my size before I'm pounding away unmercifully, keeping the steady, unrelenting pace. I know she's nowhere near being pleased when I stop thrusting only half-way so nothing is obscured from the camera.

I'm completely numb from the benzocaine, ensuring I can go for at least an hour. But Payton feels all as she clutches at the sheet, moaning and panting with each thrust I deliver, trying to shift for me to plunge deeper and gain a release of her own, but I hold her easily at the angle best suited for camera, knowing her back would be aching in the morning.

It is all very clinical, as usual, and goes on for more than an hour—almost boring and most definitely mechanical. It doesn't take full penetration for a man to orgasm but, sadly, Payton doesn't know that. She's still under the impression all sex is pleasurable. I clench my teeth, knowing she's about to get a rude awakening.

Without any kind of warning, I pull out and come across her ass, not making a sound. But Payton sounds as if she's crying at the sudden stop of what I assume she thought should be her orgasm. Once I finish, I pull my pants on and walk to the camera, keeping my back to her.

"Get cleaned up and meet me in the living room in ten minutes."

There's a small sob and I look up long enough to catch a glimpse of Payton's naked bottom as she carries her clothes out of the room.

Yep, she's crying.

Can I do this to her every day?

Can I break her repeatedly?

The better question would be—will this break me in the process, because I don't feel far from it now?

Pausing, I inhale heavy and exhale with no relief for the shitty way I feel about the whole fucking thing.

Business. And no one is going to show that girl an ounce of kindness, it's my job to prepare her for that.

Ten minutes later, I pull up the video and watch it with Payton. Again, I sit at an angle so I can see her face as she watches me fuck her. I know she didn't orgasm and that doesn't concern me in the slightest. In fact, it gives me satisfaction knowing she's at least experiencing some of what to expect later with strangers. The time for false orgasms will come later in the training, but we're still in the learning camera positions stage.

When the video finishes, I turn it off and wait for a reaction. Payton simply turns her body slightly toward me and waits for me to speak. Her eyes are dry and look menacing.

Good.

"What did you think?" I ask after several minutes of silence.

"I think you're a cold-hearted bastard."

I tilt the corner of my mouth in amusement but know even that's a cold look.

"I am not the one trying to sell anything, Payton. I did exactly what was expected of the male role. I'm only here to act and teach you how to sell yourself. Now, how do you think *you* looked?"

"I think I looked fucking miserable."

I nod.

"Yes, you did."

She frowns in confusion.

"You sold nothing, and if I paid to watch you get fucked from behind, I would want my money back." I close my eyes, trying to summon more patience. "Nobody gives a shit if you come, if you hurt, if you're tired. Nobody cares, Payton. You are simply a hole for some guy to make a deposit, but while he's doing that, you need to act as if you're having the time of your life. Do you understand?"

Payton stares at me blankly. I wait. She stands with determination then walks into her room and just as quickly returns to the sofa with her iPhone. I look at my watch, checking to make sure we're still on schedule as Payton thumbs her phone.

"This is what I want to do," she says holding the phone close to my face. "*I want this.*"

Leaning back to better see, I give her a sardonic expression. The film she's selected is me with a pretty redhead on the screen. The girl is arched with her head back on a bed wearing a look of ecstasy on her face. She's having the time of her life. If I recall, I got her off twice in less than ten minutes.

"I filmed that two years ago. The girl's name is Skylar and she's a junkie that lives on skid row. She was a junkie before we filmed that, but still." I shrug and look at Payton's face which looks like I'd just let the air out of her balloon. "She made six thousand with the one-time contract for three films, I make thirty-five percent of each download. Intimacy filming is not in high demand. Very few do them. I chose to, knowing I had the fan base to make money with them, but make no mistake in understanding it is still acting Payton. Smoke and mirrors. That shoot took almost all day for a twelve minute film and we were sick of each other by the time it ended. It might seem more like a pleasurable coupling, but we still had to act. *You* will not be in intimacy films. *You* will be in average porn for years, and then, maybe, you will get a following, then again, maybe not. You will fuck men that repulse you with body odor and bad breath. That's the reality. The females come and go. They decide they want to marry or have kids or get fat or they the develop holes in their face from digging at imaginary coke bugs under their skin. The females do not last long. You're young and will flood the prime sites, but it will be very difficult to keep you exposed to gain followers and eventually, you will just be another video among thousands. You will not make money per click. You will be paid for the day of filming and that's all."

Pausing to give Payton a minute to absorb what I'm saying, I watch a thousand different questions dance around in her eyes.

"What about the contract I get after we are through here?"

"Ah, yes, the first is always the largest. Depending on how many films you agree on, and let's make up numbers. Let's say you sign a twenty-thousand dollar contract. The fine print states you must, in-turn, bring double that in profit. Then, let's say you don't bring that profit in the time frame, you will then need to film more in effort to cover cost. Some girls can bring that kind of profit fairly quick, others do not. Those that do not are bound to their contracts and will not be able to work with anyone until their obligation is fulfilled."

"And you think I can't bring that kind of profit?"

Inhaling deeply, I decide to be honest.

"With the right director, sure." I shrug, not caring, but in reality, my stomach is bubbling with acid.

Payton gives me a small smile I don't return.

"Why are you so mad at me, Axel?" she asks, flipping her mood at lightning speed.

I shake my head in disgust.

"I don't know what you're talking about." I stand to get a protein juice premade by the grocer. Payton follows, and by the look she's wearing now, she's on the verge of violence.

"What happened in twenty-four hours? You were fine yesterday, now you're just *mean*. You're purposefully trying to sabotage me before I even get started."

Payton lays her phone on the bar. Her chest is rising and falling hard with building anger. Drinking down the mix in three gulps, unaffected by her words, I decide it's not too early for beer.

"Don't get it confused, sweetheart. I'm being paid to do what I do, and you willingly signed up for it. You should be thanking me."

Hurt flashes in her hazel eyes. I twist the cap off my beer and toss it toward to trash can.

"So, you fucking me the last few days was a part of this bargain?"

No, not even close.

"Yes, Payton, it was." I lie easily. "If you took it as something more than that, I can't help you. I explained the sleeping together and all the other shit was not what I normally allow, but you wanted to, so I let you."

"You *let* me?" she repeats the words in disbelief. "Like a fucking stray dog, you *let* me sleep with you."

Fury dances in her eyes as she searches my face for the smallest hint of a lie. She finds none. Instead of talking, Payton turns to look at the schedule I gave her earlier then looks to the clock on the stove.

"We have one more session today, I'd like to get it out of the way, if you don't mind. That is, if you're up for it," she sneers as if implying my dick couldn't handle another round so soon.

I roll my eyes and snort.

"You have no clue who you're fucking with, Payton. I'll finish my beer then meet you on the bed."

She storms off without giving me another glance. As soon as I'm alone, I allow my shoulders to relax and feel nothing but grief so deep, I have to rest my hands on the counter to steady myself. Looking down in the trashcan, as if it holds answers to how the fuck to get Payton to just go home, I see the mail she received earlier. I pick up the letter from Ole Miss University and shake it out to read. It's a letter of denial for a scholarship she had reapplied for just weeks ago. Although it's an apology letter, it also states she should apply again. I toss it back in the trash, feeling like shit.

Seventeen

-

Payton

"No, fuck Payton, no!" Axel growls and pulls away from my mouth which is sore, raw, and trembling from the stretching.

I've forgotten what day we are on, losing track the minute I walk inside the training room.

I did as I was instructed, and anytime I tried to reconnect with Axel, he resists. He remains so frigid cold, I can't reach him. Not with a kiss, a touch, nothing warms him to me. We have fallen into separate routines and only come together in front of the camera.

At first, I cried about it for a few days. Then, I became determined to learn whatever he taught me if for nothing else than to spite him. But in the back of my mind, I also tried to get back what we had shared those first few days.

But it was gone. Just gone.

After two weeks of trying, I deadened my heart against it. I had to learn what to do so I could make money, because I *had* to make money. That's the bottom line, but every time I came in contact with Axel's touch, I melted as he hardened into marble.

"What did I do now?" I ask, sounding like a true bitch.

I'm so sore and tired, I don't think there's a muscle left in my body that doesn't ache. Axel runs both hands through his hair in a gesture I know to be irritation brought on by yours truly. He's so beautiful to look at naked—his broad chest, his long muscular legs, and his tapered stomach with its hills and valleys.

Realizing Axel had spoken, I sit up straighter.

"What?"

He turns to the camera and ends the recording. I stand and retrieve a towel to wipe off of my face and chest.

"I need a break. Go do something," he announces, sounding as tired as I am but still shooing me away like an annoying fly. "We'll meet again later this evening."

And just like that, I'm dismissed for the day. Axel hasn't budged from his icy demeanor toward me. If anything, he may have gotten a little colder. He kept the same monotone, the same distance. We had not eaten together, slept together, or come together since he kicked me out of his room.

Most sessions, I don't orgasm at all, and when Axel does, it's so mechanical, absent of all emotions, it actually hurts to watch. When I first saw Axel on that computer screen, I thought him a fascinating creature. Now that I've shared something much deeper those first few days, I just can't accept the ice cold heartless man who is teaching me.

I physically ache to touch him in a way that isn't sexual. But, it's impossible now, and I have tried, many times. Experiencing *that* man from the day in the shower, when I could see straight to his soul, then experiencing the man in training sessions, I'd swear they were different people.

But I had set myself up, knowing I would fall. I got too attached and forgot why I'd come to Axel in the first place. If I didn't know better, I would think he forgot as well, or at least tried to, in the beginning. I saw a bit of remorse the day he let slip the story of his dad hiring a prostitute to rape him, because what else would a grown woman do to a thirteen-year-old boy? It was rape, but I'm not so sure Axel knows that.

Quickly dressing, I leave Axel as fast as I can because he acts as if the sight of me makes him sick. This does nothing for my confidence and I'm losing weight as a result. That's another thing he chastises me about, I'm too thin and on camera it doesn't look sexy, it looks like I'm anorexic.

Asshole.

With that thought, I walk to the fridge, trying to find anything to just swallow and not have to think about. After several minutes of just staring, I decide on a cheese tortilla, cold with a glass of wine.

"No, fuck that, I'm taking the whole bottle," I hiss at no one.

Deciding on a beach day, I walk to the lounge chair and flop down, miserable, pissed off, and sexually frustrated. I'm also hoping when I get up, I'll be drunk.

I'll drink the entire bottle just to piss him off.

Axel told me there's nothing's worse than a drunk girl on camera when I was just that earlier in the week. I don't really have anything to lose at this point because he criticizes everything I do, even going as far as blaming my inexperience to not behaving properly.

Properly.

Growling in frustration, I drink and chew on the cold tortilla, not at all wanting either. Anger and confusion threaten to pull me under, but hurt trumps them both as I hear Axel start his motorcycle and drive away. There's no stopping the tears now, not as the anger and hurt war to rule me.

He's going to the warehouse without me this time.

He hates me now.

What exactly did I do to cause all this?

And to make matters worse, I can't sleep without dreaming of Ben, waking up in cold sweats, screaming at the top of my lungs., I can sense Axel on the other side of the door listening. He never comes in my room to comfort me like he did that first night, and I so desperately want him to.

Watching the water roll onto the shore, I know I'm more lost now than ever before—something I once thought impossible. Wiping my eyes, I'm not entirely sure which loss I mourn for more. I have so many to choose from, and Axel is just one more on top of an already large pile.

"Hey, pretty lady. What's got you so sad looking?"

Holding my hand up to block the sun, I'm greeted with the silhouette of a giant.

"Oh, hey Reece." I wipe my eyes again.

Reece and I had spoken a few times when I'd seen him on the beach as I walked aimlessly when Axel left the house, or I wanted a break away from him. The cop is sweet and seems harmless enough. Turning my face back to the water, try several times to dry my tears, but they seem to come stronger now. To my horror, I actually hiccup like a child.

Reece sits down beside my feet, adjusting his gun belt and looking out at the horizon. His badge glints in the light like a beacon sending Morse code across the water. His presence is oddly comforting, even though I don't not know him well.

"You okay, darling?" He turns serious eyes on me. His face is handsome, kind, a stark contrast to the tattoos creeping up his collar.

"Sure," I nod as he looks me over.

"Axel's not mistreating you, is he?"

He's probably asked that particular question before to the others in the house who have come and gone. I realize Reece must've walked down here to check on me.

"No, but it depends on what you mean by 'mistreat' because if you mean is he starving me, or hitting me then no, but if you mean he's a heartless bastard that never fails to tell me I'm wrong and silly, then yes, but I don't think that's grounds for an arrest."

Reece chuckles and I laugh a little.

"Yeah, well, Axel is different. Of course, when you grew up like he did, then you're bound to be a little odd."

I perk up in interest.

"He's told me some. Not all," I explain evasively because now I really want to know how he got to be so damned mean.

Reece chews on a hang nail.

"Yeah, well, I can't be telling his story. It wouldn't be right."

"It's okay. I just wish I knew everything that happened with his dad." I poke the one thing I do know which is his dad had paid someone to abuse his child.

Reece eyes me cautiously.

"He told you about it, then?"

"Not everything." I squirm with the lie. Axel hasn't told me anything. "Tell me what happened?"

"I shouldn't, Axel would probably kill me, but, seeing you're so upset, I'll give you the worst of it. Maybe after, you'll understand better. I've learned over the years that understanding can calm the worst of heartbreaks."

I sit up, crossing my legs and see the seriousness in Reece's eyes.

"I won't say a word, I swear."

Reece smiles sadly at me.

"He was drunk as shit when he told me this stuff then I researched the details after but when Axel was fifteen, wait let me back up." Reece puts a hand over his mouth and rubs in thought before continuing. "Axel's dad would beat him and his mom. It sounded like a daily occurrence the way Axel told me. It must've been pretty bad, too, because when Axel came home from being God knows where at fifteen, his daddy had his momma down on the kitchen floor slapping at her, then choking her. Axel said he tried to break it up, but it took him swinging a Louisville slugger at his dad's head to get him to stop strangling his mom. Killed the fucker instantly."

Reece points two thick fingers at his temple dramatically and all I can do is stare in disbelief.

"You mean Axel hit him with a baseball bat and *killed* him? Actually *killed* his father?" I ask through numb lips once I find my voice.

Reece puckers his lips and nods heavily.

"To make the whole thing even worse, he was charged with his murder. Axel was released, and the charges were dropped after his mom explained that she would have died had Axel not done it. But it gets a little worse."

I brace myself because I can't imagine worse.

"The day Axel was released, his momma took him to a bus station, handed him a ticket to Hollywood, told him he had killed the only thing she'd ever loved in her life and there's no way she could live with him after that. Told him he was a handsome guy and to do his best in Hollywood. Then, she pushed him out of the car at the Greyhound station and drove away. He ain't seen hide nor hair of that woman since."

"Shit," I breathe because there are no words. "So, that was when he was fifteen?"

"Yep," Reece says standing.

"So, he has been doing adult movies since?"

"Yep." Reece looks at the water and not at me.

"So, that's why he's never been in a relationship, or doesn't know how to act when someone touches him in a loving gesture," I say more to myself.

Reece turns back to me and smiles sadly.

"Axel is what he is. He is feral, doesn't know any different. Honestly, he's done the best he could with what he was handed. He told me that stuff drunker than shit and has never spoke of it again. I'm not sure he remembers telling me so don't you go telling him I told you. I don't want him mad at me."

I giggle because Reece wears a police uniform and a 9mm strapped to his side, yet he's afraid of Axel.

"I won't, I swear. Thanks for trusting me."

"I didn't tell you so you could feel sorry for him. Hell, he's alive, which is more than a lot of people in his shoes can say."

"Why'd you tell me at all?"

Reece straightens his tie and pulls his pants up, ready to return to his security post. He looks down at me, serious again, brows drawn together in thought.

"I think you should know you have more in common than not. Maybe now you know, you won't be so quick to cry."

I watch Reece walk away before I can respond.

<><><>

I'm watching the screen but don't really see what Axel and I are doing. Feeling him watching my reactions while I watch our latest porn episode is making me slightly crazed, and I can also see what Axel is going to criticize me about. It's perfectly clear to me I will never make it as an actress. I simply can't hide the longing in my face or the discomfort.

A sharp pain jabs my right hip as if in agreeance and I rub at it absently. Right now, I'm exhausted, and sadly, still very sexually frustrated. The orgasm denial I get, to an extent, because Axel is trying to show me there's not going to be release every time I'm on film.

But why can't he just be with me?

To show me incredible pleasure for days and then nothing? No, not *nothing*, I'm screwed raw most of the time and my hormones are making me insane. Not to mention the constant lust I have for this broken, cruel, very beautiful man.

An animal-like sound coming from me tunes out my thoughts, and I'm embarrassed for the hundredth time today. My facial features and the noises I make are nothing like the stuff I'd seen online. They're ugly and sound tragically like a pig, maybe a llama?

I'm a lost cause.

My hopes of making things right for Ben are fading fast, and I'm not sure I can keep this up much longer. Shame and anger wash over me because I can't help but think Axel has planned all of this from day one. The screen goes black, and I turn to meet his tired gaze. We are both spent, but I stubbornly hold onto the shred of hope I can at least get the one contract if nothing else.

"So—" he begins, but I cut him off.

"I didn't sell it, I was too noisy, I moved causing the view to be obstructed many times, I touched your face and I never once looked as if I were enjoying myself," I say in a bored voice.

Axel's mouth twitches, and I think, for a second, he's going to laugh. But no, he's gritting his teeth.

"I know. Is there more, or did I cover everything?"

"I think you have the gist of your issues," he says, standing to toss his empty beer bottle into the trash then retrieve another one from the refrigerator. I try not to notice, but he is drinking more than he was when I first arrived.

We are driving each other crazy.

But I came here for a reason.

Anger rushes through me, and I suddenly want to strike out, to hurt or embarrass Axel like he does me routinely.

"Did Barbara get you off the streets and make you do porn as a teenager?" I blurt.

Too bad for Axel, he's mid-swallow and once the words leave my mouth, he starts choking, slamming his bottle down on the island to strangle through my question.

"Where the fuck did that come from?" he croaks but his face tells me I've struck gold.

Catching him off guard, I can see the truth just before he frowns it away.

"Did she? Is she the reason you are like this?"

My voice is bitter cold. Axel wipes his mouth on the back of his hand, narrowing his eyes at me.

"Who told you that?"

Shrugging innocently, I say nothing. No way in hell would I squeal on Sue, although she was just talking random things, she told me more than enough to put the pieces together. Reece just confirmed what I'd already figured out.

Axel glares at me, and I begin to feel about an inch tall. Seeking respite from his anger, I look outside but eventually return my gaze to his. His brows are drawn together in deep—*what*? Not embarrassment, but maybe *disappointment*? There's something is in his dark eyes, I can't quite figure it out, but it makes him look even meaner.

For the first time, I'm afraid of Axel. True fear tingles up my spine and my situation is crystal clear.

No one knows or cares where I am. I could be killed and disposed of and nobody would ever look for me.

Of course, I have thought this very thing before, but it was a passing thought, a naïve girl's dismissal. Swallowing hard, I try to smooth things over.

"I'm sorry, I was curious is all," I stammer.

Silence. Several moments I hold my breath, waiting, but Axel doesn't speak, he just stands there with that hard expression, drinking his beer. After a moment longer, he walks to his room and slams the door shut. The sound echoes through the living room bringing my heart to a new low. I lashed out and hurt him. It had to hurt for his tragedy of a childhood to be thrown up like that.

What is wrong with me?

I would never want to hurt Axel, I'm just so sick and tired of the criticisms. But that doesn't make what I did okay.

With a heavy heart and a sore back, I walk to my room. My body aches with want of Axel, and I now really, really *want* him. I haven't had an orgasm in days, and that has left my body oddly suspended and raw. I look over the next day's schedule. Axel had marked through a couple of things, telling me I wasn't ready for most of it and thankfully, anal sex was pushed back.

Abandoning a bath, I swallow four sleeping pills and crawl into my cold, empty bed. Just before turning off my lamp, I realize I took a medication without needing it. I would've fallen asleep on my own and the pain was not bad enough I needed to take something for it.

I just took it to be taking it because I want the assurance I'm going to sleep. Also, I don't want to dream of Ben.

With a sinking feeling, I realize Axel is right about me. I will be numbing myself with drugs in no time. Darkness takes me just as I picture my body on a steel slab—pale, waxy skin with blue, grotesque marks up and down my arms.

Eighteen

-

Axel

"Stop, Payton," I growl as she grinds on top of me. "Fucking stop!"

It's day eighteen and we're just as fucked up as we were on day one of this shit. Payton avoids me now. I avoid Payton. We only meet for sessions just like all the girls who came before her. It's a reality I wake up and go to sleep resenting because unlike the girls before, I long to be with her. My body aches for it, my mind crazed with the wanting.

But, it's like she's said before, she can do this with any guy, so I drink and sleep to keep from losing it and to not make a damned fool out of myself again. I'm just taking it one day at a time, and then she will be gone and I will go back to being normal.

Normal? Have I ever been normal?

Not just no, but fuck no, I don't even know what the word means.

Shaking my head to rid myself of thoughts, I try to concentrate. For hours, I've tried to guide Payton through positions and scenes, and so far, it has gone very badly. There is simply nothing even remotely *normal* about having sex on film, that's why it's important to act the part. Payton has failed, no matter my teaching, to grasp that on film, it's necessary to act like she's going to come any second for as long as a guy does his thing.

Payton moves again, slowly, taking her time, rubbing my chest. My body wants to respond, to get her off, but I remain in character, not slipping once, knowing it will only give her a false impression of what the reality of making porn is. But I close my eyes in a moment of weakness and sigh at her touch—the warmth of her hands on my skin, breath fanning across my neck, and those lips as they graze my collar bone. My eyes open, and I'm brought back to Earth, pushing Payton up and giving her a hard shake. Hair spills over her eyes, and she covers her breasts with an arm protectively.

"Damn it, Payton, just fucking stop!"

Pushing back her hair, Payton looks hurt.

She doesn't get it. She doesn't fucking get it.

And she never will, because Payton is not the kind of girl who can fuck and separate her feelings. She wants to feel, needs to be felt. She wants something she will never find in this business.

Body straight as pride takes hold, I see the anger in her hazel eyes. The eyes that appear glassy from being tired or maybe hungover?

So it begins.

"What?" Peyton yells back, now just as pissed off as I am.

My erection deflating, I begin moving to stand, but Payton doesn't budge.

"Tell me what it is now I'm supposed to stop?" she demands.

"Stop trying to make love to me. This is just fucking. Get it straight in your head!"

Payton narrows her eyes at me, then raises her hands in disgust or defeat, I'm not sure.

"Fine!" She moves off me in a fury. "Let's just move on to something else, then."

Rolling my sore eyes, I grind my palms to them, truly exhausted from being under the same roof with Payton. When we're not fucking, we're fighting about fucking. The fight that's brewing this time is the same one we've had for the past two weeks.

I haven't budged, simply because I know exactly what's going to happen to Payton when she leaves my house and if she thinks her co-stars will be any kinder, she's a fool. I have said this many times, but Payton is under the impression she can wiggle her cute ass and a man will respect her.

Payton doesn't understand she's just one flavor among dozens. The guy with the big dick doesn't matter because he's just the guy with the big dick.

I should know that better than anyone.

"You think you can act like a girlfriend or something, but it doesn't work, Payton." I repeat the same thing I said the day before. "You're not going to be paid to make the guy *feel* good and you might as well know now that you're there to be fucked, to show your body. Grinding on top for pleasure comes across on film as lame. That's the shit on home movies these fucktards with their kid's recorders do. If you want to be in that shit, you can do that anywhere with anyone."

Standing, I feel exhaustion with everything down to my soul, but until this moment, I've been too proud to admit defeat. One of us is going to have to give. Pulling my jeans on, I let my shoulders slump and try to be gentle.

"This is not working," I say with absolute conviction. "This will never work with *us*."

And once I say it, I realize I've been holding that knowledge back, even from myself. Maybe a part of me hoped Payton would wake up one morning and say this was no longer what she wanted, and she really never did. Pain comes, and I welcome it like an old friend.

Misery will be along soon.

Let her go, it'll be better than doing this one more day.

With sadness, I look a Payton. She stands naked with her arms folded under her breasts. Dark circles show through the makeup she uses to try and conceal them, her ribs are visible and hipbones protrude. Those beautiful hazel eyes are glassy, and I have to wonder if she is taking something or just drinking too much. I know I don't look much better.

We are literally killing one another.

As usual, she's mad. I see the beautiful girl, but feel the beginnings of my rigid outer layers form in defense against her. I have to do this or nothing is going to change.

Except *she* will change.

Payton is still just as naïve as day one, but not as sweet. She has already changed. Of course she has changed, I warned her she would. The knowledge I'm causing those changes makes self-hatred boil over inside me.

"We're done, Payton," I say without any emotion.

"So, what now? Where's your damned schedule?"

She looks around, but my next words break that train of thought.

"*I'm* done, Payton. I have tried, and you're just not getting it." I don't bother to hide the defeat in my voice.

She snaps her eyes to mine.

"What do you mean *you're* done?"

Trying in vain to relax, I take a long, deep breath. Some kind of emotion claws from within me, splitting me at the seams. I don't understand, nor recognize it but whatever it is, it makes me want to fucking cry.

"You are either unwilling, or rather unable, to make the transition. I suspect the latter."

She shifts uncomfortably foot to foot, biting down on her lower lip.

"Why can't you just treat me like you did when I first got here?"

I sit on the bed, and I run my hands through my hair, trying to think of how to say what needs to be said.

"I've already said why. That was a mistake." I raise my eyes back to meet Payton's, needing to watch as I end this thing. "This is the reality of what you're going to be doing. You will not be comfortable, you will not be considered as a person, you will always be a show dog there to perform. Don't you get that? I'm trying to help you, but you can't separate the two in your mind. I don't know if you have feelings involved and expect me to act on that, but it's not the reality of what you are going to be paid to do."

Stick to the subject.

Bringing up feelings wasn't a part of it, so I try to guide the conversation back to my point but the words die as Payton sniffs.

"You just act like you have nothing for me. You don't care if I feel good. You're just rotten to me. You're cold." I snort at that because it's certainly not the first time I've heard it. "Now I amuse you? Fuck you, Axel."

Anger back at the surface in an instant, I shoot to my feet, towering over her.

"Don't you fucking get it? This isn't some stupid fucking love story, Payton. There are no fairy tales here! Nobody is going to come to your rescue. They are not going to give a shit about you. There's no emotion involved in this. This is a fucking job! Your heart and your mind mean shit to the guys that will fuck you bloody and the producers that let it go on. You will be numbing that feeling with drugs in days. You want me to hide that reality? Well, I'm not!" I try to convince her of this one more time, then I see that she's quivering with an unmistakable look of fear.

Of me?

Enough is enough.

"This whole fucking thing was a mistake from the beginning, and I'm not doing it anymore. This is over, Payton. Get your shit packed. You need to leave."

Nearly knocking her down, I can't get away fast enough.

"Axel, please."

Payton follows me into the hallway. I turn in the confined space almost to my room holding my hands up in a stopping gesture as she reaches for me.

"Please, Axel," she says in a desperate plea.

Don't give in, or you will add her to the body count.

"Just fucking go, Payton. I'm tired and I'm not doing this with you another day." She reaches a hand to touch my face. I pull back out of reach. "Don't fucking touch me."

My voice sounds more like a growl and tears run down Payton's hollow cheek. The sight of her breaking apart rips at my already raw nerves.

She's what? Hurt? Sick? Sorry? Rejected?

Against my brain screaming to retreat, I put a hand to the back of her head and press my forehead to hers, closing my eyes.

The scent of her hair, the feel of her skin, I'm lost to it.

But I am breaking this girl.

No, I *have* broken her. Warring between wanting to push her out of my house to save her, I also want to soothe the hurt I'm causing in the process.

Payton's ragged breath feathers against my lips then her hands are in my hair, tugging my face to hers. It stirs me. In a moment of pure and raw weakness, my resolve vanishes.

One last time, one last kiss...

Bending to touch my lips to hers gently, my chest gives a squeeze in warning. Ignoring it, I part my mouth and the instant our tongues touch, we both ignite, bursting in flames of desire. Frantic need takes over as my hands land on her bare ass, and I pull her body up to align with mine. Payton responds by wrapping her legs around my waist.

We kiss with a desperate hunger to feel something, anything other than what we were just minutes before. I press my body into hers, slamming us both against the wall, unable to kiss hard enough or deep enough. She moans in my mouth and it's a pleasured sound that fuels me further. Clawing at my back, she breaks the kiss to speak.

"Axel, please. Please. Please. Don't stop, I want you so bad."

Too weak to resist, I buckle, knowing what she craves so desperately. Every instinct in me is screaming to provide. Without further thought to what I'm doing, I give in. Jerking my jeans down, I push inside of her in one hard thrust. Primal need consumes us both. Like an animal, I thrust hard, unmercifully, urging her to come, knowing I have cruelly denied her that for days.

"Come on, Payton." I slam inside harder, deeper, surprised the wall doesn't cave.

The sounds of need coming from her throat, warm, damp flesh slapping against mine, rock hard nipple rubbing my chest while those long legs squeeze my waist—it's all too much.

"Fuck," I growl at the sensory overload, biting her shoulder then neck. "That's it, baby."

Pressing her harder into the wall, I can feel the beginning of pressure build within her body.

"Oh God, Axel!" she screams to the ceiling when I quicken my pace.

Inner muscles spasm in one long, pulsing orgasm that clenches me, sending me higher and higher.

"Fuck!" I yell, bracing one hand on the wall while the other locks Payton in place. My entire body tightens at the release. "Fuck," I repeat as I go blind with the intensity.

My body stills at the ecstasy, the only sounds are our mingled pleasure, and for just a moment, everything is right.

Perfect.

Neck, arms, shoulders, legs. One by one, they slowly relax, and with it returns the crippling sorrow.

Setting Payton on her feet, I look down into those big hazel eyes I can so easily get lost in. As I pull up my jeans, understanding clearly what has to be done, I harden my heart, preparing for the beating it's about to receive.

"Go pack, Payton," I say without emotion. "There is nothing here for you."

Not waiting for her to respond, I walk to my room and shut the door softly. I'm aware of my cruelty, but I know no other way to end this. If we continue, no way could I live with the results. I'd rather eat a bullet than sign Payton over to the industry.

The only sensible thing to do is get her away from me and this business before she's sucked into the dark oblivion. No, I would rather her get away from me than take that chance. She *has* to go.

After throwing on a t-shirt and boots, I exit through the kitchen into the garage, start my bike, and drive away, hoping to never see Payton Knight again. I don't stop until I reach my destination and pull my phone from my pocket. Dialing a number I hoped not to use for this purpose, I hold my breath until she finally picks up.

"Axel?" a sweet voice I'm quite fond of answers on the second ring.

"Hey, Beth, I have a favor to ask," I say without preamble.

My nerves are shot and the urgency in my voice can't be masked.

After a brief pause, Beth responds, "Name it, hon."

Her willingness to help me is due to the fact that I pulled her from the grips of Travis Beckner, thus starting a long-standing mutual hatred for one another. After bumping into Beth with Travis by her side at a director's New Year's party three years ago, I assumed the black bruise along her pretty jaw, which was heavily covered with makeup, was due to the bastard who clung to her arm possessively.

It took me all of five minutes to get her to crack and begin sobbing. She wanted out, but Travis controlled her with blackmail and drugs and she provided profit in return via sexual favors, better known as prostitution, to his business partners. Her story was too familiar to

235

me, and though I trained girls myself, I do it only if it's their personal desire to learn. I only hope they could maintain some control over their lives with the knowledge I provide. Travis takes girls and prostitutes them for favors or profit before sending them to Barb for work.

The man is a cockroach, so when I saw the bruises, I took Beth home with me, got her in rehab, then helped her once she was out. Of course, this created further friction between myself and Travis, but fuck him. I'd always hated the bastard. Three years later, Beth oversees a five-star hotel just thirty minutes from my house. The connection had come in handy more than a few times.

"I have a friend that needs a ride from my place, a place to stay, and food. I'm not sure how long, but just charge me by the month for now."

"Okay, sure." Beth repeated what I said as if writing it down. "I'm texting my driver now. Does she need medical attention?"

I smile sadly, knowing her driver would remove Payton willing or unwillingly from my house. Beth and I have done this dance before and she never questioned me.

"No, she does not need a doctor." Then, I consider saying Payton might need a shrink.

Maybe I've messed her mind up so bad there's no coming back?

Glancing around the hotel bar, I take a corner booth, ordering a Scotch neat but not drinking it yet. I become aware of a frisky pair of brunettes eyeing me like cat nip from their high top table two seats away. I keep my eyes averted so not to give them hope. Beth tells me a car is on the way to collect Payton now and a room will be waiting for her.

"Is there anything else?"

Smiling sadly at Beth's kindness and willingness to help, I relax slightly knowing at least Payton will be safe. Beth is a rare friend. Even though I don't have the traditional friends, I know I can count on her for most anything.

"That's it, except you could have my contact information left in her room just in case she needs to reach me. She is unfamiliar with the area, and I'm hoping she will return home. An airline ticket will be delivered in the morning with cash to travel with, but I don't know how long she will stay before deciding to leave. She's a bit stubborn."

Beth chuckles. "Give me a call if you need anything else. I'll make sure she's taken care of."

"Thanks, Beth. How's the baby and Riley?"

With that question, Beth enters into a long story about her eight-month old daughter, Penny, and her executive husband, Riley Cummings. I can't help but grin and occasionally chuckle at how Beth's life has turned out. It was worth the hell Travis always tries to sling my way just to hear that not all who follow the dark path end up lost.

"Oh, my gosh, I'm rambling." Beth pauses ten minutes later to take a breath. "You didn't need to hear about breast milk!" She laughs, and I find it easier to do the same. "We need to have dinner soon. I'll take good care of your girl, Axel. Let me know if you need anything else."

"Thanks, Beth."

Ending the call, I take an occasional drink in between checking the time. Twenty minutes later, I sit watching the hotel entrance waiting when the two females approach. Giving them both a pained smile, I inwardly cringe wanting to only be left alone. They're attractive brunettes, with similar brown eyes, might even be sisters. Both are clearly on the prowl with their short dresses, sky high heels, and low, plunging necklines with breasts on display.

Does this shit actual attract males?

"Hi" they say in unison.

"Hello," I reply politely.

They share a look I want to roll my eyes at. Seriously, it is too easy to get laid in this town.

"Are you an actor?" the taller one asks, almost giddy with excited energy.

Oh shit, here we go.

"Not anymore," I say with a wry expression.

"We were wondering if you would like some company?" the shorter one asks.

I hesitate because I don't want company, but reconsider since they show no signs of moving from blocking my view of the hotel lobby just outside the bar.

"Aww, well, sure." Maybe I can buy them a drink while I watch for Payton to arrive.

Holding out my hand, I gesture toward to opposite side of the booth and glance to the lobby as they shift.

The pair of girls giggle conspiratorially. Instead of taking the opposite seat, they both slide in beside me in my bench which was made for two, yet somehow, fits all three of us. The girl closest to me actually rises off the seat, sits astride me, then moves to my other side so I'm positioned in between the pair, all the while, I'm leaning back to give them room to get comfortable.

While this would have most men lost in the ideas of a ménage, I, who have partaken in countless three-ways, am no longer affected by two drunk girls looking for attention. On the contrary, they irk the shit out of me. I've seen too many one-night stands turn into a lifetime of diseases, so the prospect of sticking my dick into random snatch isn't for me anymore, and these two are not at all thinking of having safe sex. I don't even need to buy them drinks.

"So, are you waiting for someone?" the one on the right asks, following my gaze to the lobby doors while the one on the left places a hand on my thigh.

"Um, yeah, sort of."

The hand moves up my leg. I snort, half-way enjoying the attention, half-way repulsed by it.

"Oh my," the girl with her hand trying to stroke me says.

I wrap my hand her wrist, stopping the assault and try to see past the girl on my right into the lobby, but now she's in on the discovery of my cock as well. The girl on my left actually moves her head down to my chest, purring softly while the one on my right slides her fingers in a circle over my nipple through my shirt. The

239

sensation causes me to jump involuntarily, and I take my eyes away from the lobby to assess just how the fuck I'm supposed to get out of the situation.

"Okay, time out," I say, holding the universal time out signal. "Let's order something to drink, shall we?"

Gingerly, I brace the woman closest to my crotch into a sitting position. Her eyes are hazy in a drunken lust. My hands on that one only seems to invite the other girl in to take her friend's place and I jerk as she squeezes my crotch.

"Whoa, now, hang on just a minute." And suddenly, I'm trying desperately to get ahold of the situation. Right in the midst of the girl on my left descending again on my dick like it holds all things holy, I hear a voice that causes my eyes to close and my body to turn rigid.

"Axel?"

Payton stands not ten feet from where I'm being mauled by two ferocious felines in plain view of the public while no one bothers to help. The girl on my left straightens as Payton approaches the table. The girl on the right scurries away, sensing all is no longer fun. Payton watches the girl retreat then turns her gaze to the more aggressive of the two. She smiles sweetly, looking the girl directly in the eyes.

"He likes to be fucked in the ass with a strap-on while you call him Tony and pull his hair," Payton says, not even blinking. "And be careful, he just got rid of a nasty case of crabs."

A groan of mortification bubbles up my throat, and I'm silently praying to God nobody around us heard that. Payton turns on her heel and stalks off with her blonde ponytail swinging. I look at the girl beside me and grin.

"She's just joking."

But the girl is eyeing me skeptically. Although I had no plans to be with her, the idea of what she thought of me kind of bothers me. I don't waste any time trying to explain, I scoot out of the booth and almost run to catch up with Payton.

I follow until she stops at the concierge counter. Without looking directly at Payton, I place my hands in my pockets and nod at the receptionist. She's aware of who I am through Beth, known as "an important business man" to the area. Payton turns to look in my direction, sees me, scowls, and then turns back to the desk. After a short exchange, we're shown to the elevator.

"Thanks, I'll take it from here." I hold out a tip for the bellman and take Payton's bag following her in the elevator. She folds her arms under her breasts in an angry huff as I lean back into the wall watching her. A strange thought crosses my mind as I look her over.

"You ever think how odd it is just how mad I can make you in just a little over a couple of weeks' time?" I ask. She doesn't respond, just keeps her eyes on the changing number of the floors on display. "That doesn't strike you as strange at all? Because it confuses the shit out of me," I say honestly.

Payton inhales deeply but says nothing, still refusing to look my way. We reach the seventh floor, and I wait while she exits the elevator and walks to find her room.

Once she opens the door with her key card, she turns to me with a determined look, and I wonder if she's been mentally preparing to say something the entire elevator ride.

"You know, when I saw you at the airport, I thought you were gorgeous," she places a hand over her heart and looks dreamy eyed while I grin a cocky grin but feel anything but flattered. "Then, I thought when you had sex with me on the beach, you were wonderful, and I would worship you." My face falls because I can sense where this is headed. "But you have crushed any and all pleasant thoughts I could ever think of you, Axel, because you are cruel, you are cold, and I think you were thinking I could just be your plaything to do whatever with then send me back home. As if I would travel across country to do just that? I came here with one clear understanding, to learn from you, but all you have done is complicate my life further, not to mention cost me more than you can ever imagine."

Payton fights the tears that begin to fill her eyes and swipes them away furiously.

"I trusted you! I trusted you to help me so I could get the money I need! Now, I can't make anything right and Ben—" Payton stops mid-thought.

"Ben what?" I press, but she's shutting down, anger ebbing away. "Ben what, Payton? Are you running from someone? Are you being threatened? Tell me."

She just shakes her head, refusing to explain why she says that name in her sleep.

"You're a bitter disappointment, Axel. I came here under the pretense you were the best to get me where

I need to be. You have wasted days I could've been learning, to get decent work, at least, but you wanted to drive me away. Well, congratulations. You have succeeded in crushing any desire I had in knowing you."

She jerks her bags from my hands, but I don't go. Wounded by her words, I still need to see she's safe and will not try and stay here.

"You can leave now. I'd appreciate it if you don't come back and just leave me to live my life in peace."

The muscles in my jaw protest when I finally unclamp my lips.

"You will go back home, then?"

Payton casts her eyes down then back to mine.

"Don't concern yourself with what I do, that would require feelings, and I would never presume you had those." She places a hand on my chest for me to step back then shuts the door in my face. I stand motionless, not sure of what to do.

Demand an answer? Pound on the door and tell her that yes, I'm a bitter disappointment to life in general and not to just her? Or do I explain I'm hurting her to save her from a far worse fate?

I stare at the numbers on the door.

Yeah, this hurts.

But she will be better off hurting now, than later if she continued this Godforsaken path. Payton can go home and not pursue this fucked up way of life.

If this is the right thing to do, then why does it feels so bad? Like something is dying in my chest, hollowing me out further. Soon enough, there's going to be nothing left.

This is just business. Like anything else, it just isn't for Payton.

Even knowing that is true, it does nothing to ease the guilt that tears through me as I make my way out of the hotel in a daze. Feeling truly lost, I decide to head back home, but first, I need to take care of one more thing.

And it's long overdue.

Mind made up, I make my way across the parking lot and back to my bike, trying not to think of the puffy eyes Payton had or the sag in her shoulders. She's not the same young woman I picked up from the airport just over two weeks prior. If mere days with me did that to her, then I really did do the right thing in sparing her the brutal industry she set out to join. I know, without question, she would get work, but it would be low budget, maybe fifteen hundred a filming and maybe three shoots a day.

It would take her a week to recover from the physical issues of being used in every way available, probably by two men at once for many hours. It would take a lifetime to recover mentally so she would seek something to numb the pain and get her through the next day of filming, only her body would soon tire and become flabby from poor eating habits and drugs or alcohol. This would send her further down the pipe and, eventually, she would prostitute to support her habits.

The thought of Payton selling herself for a fix literally makes me sick. I have to swallow bile rising more than once, and I need to get her out of here, away from this mess and overwhelming guilt at what I've done to so many women.

Tugging on my helmet, I let determination rule me. Now I know Payton is safe, I can address another burning issue I've tried to ignore, but like an abscess, Barbara infected me, making me sick from the inside out.

Nineteen

-

Axel

First, I drive to her home, finding it dark and empty. Bike idling in the driveway, I call her assistant. It's only after I throw around a few threats that she gives me the name of a restaurant where Barb is meeting with a producer.

Ten minutes later, I walk into a black tie only French restaurant, not bothering to remove my jacket or gloves, carrying my helmet under my arm. I forget I even have it until I set it on the table in front of Barb, a middle-aged man, and very young female. The trio are seated in a candle-lit round booth and were deep in serious discussions before I interrupted judging by the expression on the man's face. He shrinks back slightly in his seat as he takes in my appearance.

"Axel, what are you doing?" Barb looks from my helmet to my face, brows drown together in question and shock. Maybe it's the hate that radiates off of me that causes the look to change to one of skepticism.

"Barb." I nod in greeting while sliding in the booth next to the girl, positioning her and her companion in between me and Barbara in the circle.

I pause to examine the girl and guess her barely eighteen. The guy is probably closer to fifty.

Fucking pimp.

Resting my arms on the table, I lean into the girl's space as if I want our conversation to stay private.

"How old are you, sweetheart?"

The bleach-blonde bats her heavily coated lashes at me. Knowing I affect women this way, I do nothing to encourage it. The girl leans toward me, giving me a full view of large breasts.

"I'm eighteen. *Barely* eighteen, how old are you, handsome man?"

She places a hand on my upper thigh, inching it up. Just before she reaches gold, I gently take her hand and place it on her lap.

"Old enough to know that pretty, *barely* legal girls are turned in to ugly, washed-up hags by twenty-five. Do yourself a favor and go get an education," I say without the slightest bit humor.

Turning my attentions to Barb, I see she's gritting her teeth while holding a butter knife. If this were at all funny, I would laugh. The humor is gone now that drugs don't numb me from these types of situations.

"How dare you come in here and interrupt our meeting," Barb hisses at me then looks around for a waiter, or someone to physically remove me from the restaurant more likely.

"Do it, Barb, and I will make your life one of misery, behind bars at that."

She turns narrowed eyes back to me, but the threat has my desired effect. Her cheeks pale, and a snarl forms at her thin lips.

"What do you want?" she asks through clenched teeth.

"Is that the best you can do?"

Barb's perfectly set red hair unravels slightly. The crow's feet around her eyes give her an ancient appearance. Understanding that I loathe the woman, a moment passes where I also feel sorry for her. She, like me, knows no other way of life. But unlike me, she's a lost cause. I'm redeemable, or hope I am. Before she can start up again, I sit up, placing my helmet in my lap and resting my hands on it.

"I'll make this quick and you all can return to your dinner." I glance at the pair then back to Barb. "It's good you sent Payton, but she did not work out. I won't be signing off on her so the contract is void without my approval. And it's also good you canceled November because I won't be available."

Barb watches my face with distaste. What I'm doing is costing her money, and there is nothing more important to her. Lots of money in the long run because I produce quality women. Where they go after the initial agreement with me and the agent is out of my control but for the first few films, the girls produce excellent work, *profitable work*. Barb, being the one who sets all the preliminary work and contracts, receives a large cut plus a pinch of what the girls make on down the line until the contract is fulfilled.

How have I not seen Barb clearer before now? Done this very thing sooner?

But it took Payton to snap something in me, causing me to think, causing me to *feel*.

Not wanting to get too distracted, I dismiss the thoughts, but not before I understand Barb's continued work with Travis is, in fact, what started the crumbling of our business relationship long before Payton. I've always refused to be associated with the man and refused to share any of my knowledge of the business with him based solely on the fact that he is a piece of shit who leaves discarded women all over the state. I've never shared as much as a drink concoction with him, and Barbara has always resented that. Hates it, actually.

"And where will you be, Axel?" Barb asks icily.

I shrug, not caring what happens next now I have Payton tucked away.

"Just not available. I won't be available the next calendar year, either." Pausing to cock my head sideways for dramatic effect, I add, "As a matter of fact, this is our last meeting."

Barb smiles wickedly.

"And what exactly are you going to do, Axel? You're a tool, what are you going to do for money? You have no education, zero talent in any other fields, so what will you do? Nobody in this business even particularly likes you since you have pretty much pissed them all off in one way or another through the years, *dick* that you are." Barb smirks, but her words no longer affect me.

At one time, I would have thought I couldn't do anything else. No more. I smirk right back at her and stand to leave.

"Don't worry about me, I'll be fine. Just know I'm not doing anything else. Don't send anyone my way, don't even call me because, frankly, I don't think you're a very good person Barb, so yeah, fuck off."

Tucking my helmet under my arm, I look once more to the pathetic girl. She watches me hungrily, chewing at her bottom lip, big brown eyes wide.

"Whatever she tells you," I point a finger in Barb's direction, "is a lie. You need to run."

"You sorry sack of shit, I can't believe you just said that. You will be begging to come back to me and I will be the one telling you to fuck off—"

Just as Barb begins a new round of insults, I turn my back and stride out of the restaurant. It feels good to leave her even though I know Barb will most likely try to entice me to continue to work, but I no longer care about anything after Payton. It may be only days after meeting her, but my entire outlook on my life has changed. I will no longer keep to a schedule because I don't care what time it is. I'm not due to be anywhere, and thank God, nobody is due to be at my house anymore.

Strapping my helmet on, I walk my bike out of the parking space and start the engine. Wasting no time getting home, I speed through the night. There's shit to be done, it can't wait any longer.

As I drive down PCH, my life runs in a loop in my mind. I arrive at the same conclusion more than once. If

I were to be honest with myself—I am remarkably good at being honest with everyone else but myself—I would have to admit I've never been happy.

And further examining that truth, I realize I have been slowly disengaging from the business for several months. Not just with Barb, but the whole fucking thing. It's not new that I don't return emails, or calls and I've cancelled more than two filmings I had scheduled earlier in the year. All this was prior to Payton's arriving. She seems to be the straw that broke the camel's back, finally.

Guilt still plays with my heart when I park my bike in the garage thirty minutes later. After pulling off my helmet, gloves, shirt, and boots, I know I will always feel guilty when it comes to Payton.

Unable to glance at her bedroom when I enter the house, I continue on to my room but the emptiness from her absence hangs thick in the air. Without thinking about what I'm doing, I turn to the kitchen, grab several trash bags, walk to the training room, and begin tossing videos, files, pictures, anything and everything that has to do with what I've done the last twelve years in the bags. Even the sheets and comforter aren't spared. I empty every drawer, shelf, and the contents of the closet.

Several full trash bags later, I grab a six pack of beer from the fridge, matches, and lighter fluid, then make my way to the solitary wooden lounge on the beach. Picking a spot not too far from my chair so I can sit and toss the evidence of my adult life into the flames, I dig a semi-decent hole, placing the sheets at the bottom and pour the lighter fluid inside. Once the fire gets going, I open my first beer and begin tossing away every bit of remorse I have from my life as a porn star, followed by bits and pieces of my life as a teacher.

My identity drifts away with the smoke, and I feel liberated in an odd way. Even though the lifestyle left me hollow, I know this is not all I will amount to.

It just can't be all I'm worth.

Somewhere in the flames, a spark of hope ignites that I can learn something, anything other than all I've ever known.

I want more, I need something else.

But do I really deserve it?

Half-way through the pile of burning shit and three beers later, Reece shows up. I've always found his cop uniform funny, no idea why, but being dressed in official uniform, gun on hip and all, reminds me of Bay Watch and a possible spin off for Dana Pointe Police Department or Orange County Harbor Patrol.

"Hey, Reece, want a beer?"

"Hell yes, but I'm on duty, so I'll pass."

I chuckle. "You ever going to get off this security shit?"

Reece shines a flashlight into the bags and bends to sift through pictures, DVDs, and a variety of porn paraphernalia. He may have filmed some, but his time in porn looks like child's play compared to mine. He just did it for the experience; I made it a lifestyle. He stops to look closer at a photo of me and his eyes widen. I chuckle watching his reaction to the different contents of the bag.

"You've lived some kind of life, Axel."

"You know probably better than anyone else." I relax back in my chair, raising a knee to rest my beer on. "You left me, you fucker, you got out and I hung around, fucking up more and more any chance at a normal life. I'm not at all proud of it," I admit.

Reece moves to another bag, shining the light inside. There's nothing more to be ashamed of in the bags, and really, I couldn't summon shame if Reece held his gun to my head. I am officially depleted of all emotions and sit raw from them as he moves from bag to bag, curiosity taking hold of him.

"In answer to your question, it doesn't look like I'll be going anywhere any time soon," he says, again widening his eyes at something I can't see.

Reece works for the police department but oversees the security for a construction company a quarter-mile up the beach. It's more like he keeps an eye on the millions of dollars of equipment the company stores there.

I reach and pull a handful of unknown papers from a bag and wad them up one by one before tossing them in the fire.

"You're not going to give me a ticket for burning shit on the beach, are you?" I ask but not seriously.

"Looks like it's some form of therapy, so I think it best to let you continue." He pauses, turns off the flashlight and watches the flames. "What's eating you, Axel?"

I toss more paper at the inferno.

"I gotta get the fuck out of here, Reece."

"Oh yeah? You rob a bank or something?"

I snort.

"Not this week," I say, sitting back to drink my beer and think.

"This wouldn't have anything to do with Payton, would it?"

I watch the fire for a moment, analyzing the question.

Everything, it has everything to do with her.

But does it? She was only here for a short while.

Apparently, that was long enough.

"So, does it have anything to do with her?" By the light of the fire, I see Reece turn his head toward me then back to the flames, a look a concern in his eyes. "Is she why you're all tense and burning shit in *California* in the dog days of summer when flipping the ashes off a cigarette could spark a forest fire that could last for months?

Feeling conflicted, I press my lips together in thought before speaking.

"Maybe a little...hell, I don't know. I'll admit, I've seen females in every kind of situation you could imagine and then some. Most are pains in the ass, a lot are whiny bitches, few are pleasant to work with, but Payton, she did something to me I didn't think possible."

A deep ache forms in the middle of my chest at the admission and I have to rub at it.

"Do I wanna know what it was?" Reece asks with caution.

Shaking my head at him, I chuckle.

"She made me *feel* things, I mean actually *feel* like worry and shit. She infected my brain or put a spell on me. Whatever the fuck it was, no woman ever did before."

"That doesn't sound all that unpleasant."

"It isn't, but I don't know who I am anymore," I admit, wincing at the despair in my voice.

"Why ain't she out here with you? You know, making you feel and shit?" Reece questions with humor.

Asshole is trying to make me feel better.

"I made her leave."

"Why would you do that?"

"She needed to get away from me. She doesn't belong here, and she certainly doesn't belong in this business."

"Holy shit. Axel Stone, pussy whipped?" Reece puts a big hand to his chest as he fakes shock. "I never thought I'd see the day. Wonders never fucking cease."

"Yeah, not whipped, Reece."

"I don't know, you seem kinda whipped to me. Only a couple of reasons a man gets rid of a woman and nothing you said sounded as if she annoyed you. Sounds more like you care enough about what happens to her and want to protect her."

I jerk my head away from the fire to look at him.

Was that what I was doing?

Reece was quiet a long time as I search my conflicting thoughts.

Can't be. I know nothing of caring for another, and hadn't I done everything in my power to hurt and humiliate Payton? Even as ignorant as I am about feelings, that is not something people do to the ones they care for.

"You know," Reece says, not hiding the humor in his voice, "you could sell this shit and make a tons of cash."

He kicks at a trash bag.

"This shit is not for sale and don't even think of taking any of it, you fucking perv."

He chuckles, and I'm glad to get away from the Payton talk. It's too confusing to think about too deeply right now.

"I could put some of it on eBay? We could split the profit," he teases. "No? Well, I better get back. You'll be okay?"

"Of course."

"All right, I'll check on you after a while, you know to make sure you're not dead or anything."

"Sure thing, buddy." I give him a salute and watch him walk back to his post.

It takes most of the night and the remainder of the beer to get everything burned. The fire does nothing to help me better understand what happened with Payton, or what I want to do next in my life.

Once the last flame flickers out, I stumble to kick sand over the charred remains. Entering the house with a great buzz, I walk to Payton's bedroom and stand a long time just staring and rubbing at the center of my chest. When my blinking lasts long enough for me to sway, I step forward and fall face-first on the bed. Her flowery scent envelops me. I bury my face in it and fall hard asleep to dream about a virgin girl I wish I'd never met.

Twenty

-

Payton

"Well, shit," I tell my reflection in disgust.

After my mother died, I was down to one hundred and twenty pounds. On my five-nine frame, that was literally skin and bones. I never wanted to go back to that but looking at my body now, I know I'm dangerously close. I look and feel like shit. My hair needs to be washed, my eyes are puffy, and my nail polish is chipped.

Your fault for pushing Axel. You let your feelings get involved.

But I did try to correct everything, didn't I?

"Fixing it was impossible because he was mad from the start, Payton." I growl in frustration trying to figure out what I have done so wrong.

But it was always wrong. From the moment Axel found out I hadn't been with a man before, it all went to Hell in a handbasket. The shock on his face told me more than I was willing to bet he would ever acknowledge. Now that I know his father ripped his childhood away so thoroughly with brute force, I kind of understand why he reacted the way he did.

Maybe it triggered something he'd long buried. Either way, nothing excuses the cold reality of his training sessions. That was just awful. Knowing him the way I did those first few days, then him distorting into almost a monster in front of me overnight...was shocking.

Adding insult to injury, I must've been really stupid to think I could have stayed detached from emotions while with Axel. Never once did I fool him, and I certainly wasn't fooling myself. He's right, I have feelings for him I can't separate, regardless of his treatment, but what could've angered him so much he just kicked me out?

Unless all that in the beginning was him just having a good time?

Was I supposed to just pretend I didn't need the money or the work? Just go back to being homeless and leave Ben to strangers? Those two things fuel me when my heart wants me to curl up and die, end this worthless existence all together.

No, I'm not going down this easy, I can't.

Eyeing my iPhone, I sigh, depressed by the fact I have no one to call—no girlfriend to vent to or mother to ask for advice. No soul would miss me if I were gone.

Not even Ben.

Tears threaten to surface and I rub away the wetness and self-pity.

"Okay, Payton, suck it up."

A note sits on my bedside table and I pick it up for the tenth time today.

Stay as long as you need to. Call if you need anything.

Like the first nine times, I roll my eyes. What could I *need* from Axel? Nothing, not a damn thing, and I know as sure as shittin' I am not about to call him. He threw me out. Sure, I had no claims to stay, but still, he could've at least kept me for the remainder of the month.

A knock sounds at my door. My belly flips at the thought that maybe, after three days of silence, Axel has come to apologize. One glance in the peep hole tells me no, not Axel, and the knowledge further cements the fact that I am, in fact, stupid.

"Yes?" I say through the locked door.

"Payton, darling, it's Barbara, I have come to discuss business."

Business?

Shit!

Glancing around nervously, my eyes land on the mirror. I look awful, my room is a mess.

"Just a minute," I say hurriedly, rushing to the bathroom and vigorously brushing the knots out my hair. My clothes are all stained so I quickly decide to wrap myself in a robe, hoping I look like I was about to take a shower. As a last thought, I kick my dirty clothes and shoes behind the bed and when things are at least presentable, I open the door.

"Hello." I smile, probably too wide with nerves.

The woman who brought me to Axel stands shorter than me by several inches, with flame-red hair, blood-red lips, and green eyes that could pierce iron. I have not yet met Barbara face to face and have had very few phone conversations with her before arriving in

California, having signed all the paperwork with Randell, but she looks like I had imagined.

"Hello Payton, *dear*," Barbara says with faux affection.

Not waiting on me to invite her in, Barbara brushes past me, nose in the air.

Nice to meet you, too. Come on in.

Instant dislike for this woman consumes me, and I begin an internal sarcastic miming at her back. Just as I begin shutting the door, a man steps from the side, previously unseen from my vantage point. He smiles slyly, causing my skin to crawl as he undresses me with his eyes, head to foot. His tall, thin frame and greasy dark brown hair give me the creeps, but it's the way his watery blue eyes examine me that has me instantly on-guard.

"Hi, sugar," he winks and smiles, flashing big teeth that are severely crooked on the bottom.

Bile rises in my throat, and I want to recoil, but I'm aware that if Barbara is here, then something is definitely up. I don't need to show displeasure when I don't know what prompted the visit. Only half-way returning a smile, my face is wiped clean as soon as I get a whiff of his foul cologne that fails to mask the unpleasant smell of his body odor.

Oh, barf. He smells like cat piss and Axe.

I shut the door as the pair make their way to the only two seats at a small table by the window, forcing me to sit on the bed in front of them. They both eye me as if examining me under a microscope.

"I'm glad we can finally talk. I normally do not talk with the girls until they're ready, but considering your time with Axel was cut short…" Barbara speaks in a nasally voice, and I know instantly she looks down on everyone. Keeping a perfectly straight back, she tilts her head, peering at me with her pointed chin in the air as if she were her royal highness and I the lowly peasant girl lucky to have attentions.

"Why do you wait until they're ready?" I ask when her announcement dies away.

She looks amused as she swats a hand my way dismissively.

"Oh dear, Payton, some of these girls can be rather," she looks to the man for the right word then back to me, "*expectant* of my time. I can't babysit their feelings or fulfill their every need. I have a business to run."

I bet you have a mirror and ask it "who the fairest of them all" is every day, too.

Inwardly grimacing but keeping my expressions natural, I glance at the man. His face reminds me of a rat with his small eyes, pointed nose, and chin.

He looks as bad as he smells.

"This is Travis," Barbara explains dismissively, following my gaze. "He has agreed to take you on considering Axel thinks you're not good enough for him."

That statement cuts too close to the bone, and I look for any signs it's a lie in Barbara's snide face. Finding nothing, I swallow down the hurt.

So, that's what it is? I'm not good enough?

Now, I'm struggling to keep my face straight, but thankfully, Barbara begins picking at a piece of imaginary lint on her pants, completely oblivious to me. Travis just bites his nails with vigor.

"I'm sorry, what do you mean?" I ask, trying to mask a cracking voice with a cough.

Barbara looks at me as if I were a child. A bored frown mars her overly made-up face.

"To help get you ready for film, darling, that is why I paid to bring you here."

Her words bring the ugly truth into the light, and I'm momentarily stunned.

Travis is going to take me on?

I have a debt to pay.

Fuck. Shit. Fuck!

I cringe at the thought of Travis' hands on me.

No way, just no fucking way.

"Um, Barbara, I am uh," I search for a word, casting my eyes around the room in panic, "decided not to pursue this further. I am grateful for your interest in me but I don't think—"

"Ah, but Payton, dear, we have a contract. Before you make the mistake in thinking you can accept my hospitality then scurry back to that mud hole in Mississippi without honoring the contract, I would advise you to think wisely."

There is no mistaking the warning in her voice.

"Whether you want to continue or not, we have a contract." Travis finally speaks and his voice is as unpleasant as his face. "We can tie you up and have you dog-fucked and we have a contract saying you okayed it, so don't play coy with us, sugar. If you resist, we will throw you to the wolves, if you cooperate, you get me." He says it as if that were the best option.

I struggle, trying to muster up a response, *any response.*

I'd prefer the dogs.

When I signed that contract, it was to work with Axel.

Not in a million years did I think I would be pushed out and thrown to this animal. My heart hurts at the thought.

Damn you, Axel, how could you do this to me?

Barbara removes a piece of paper from her oversized purse and holds it for my examination.

"Is this not your signature, sweet Payton?"

With a shaky hand, I take the paper, which does have my signature at the bottom.

"You signed it, and it was witnessed by two others. It clearly states if you for any reason are dismissed from Axel Stone that your agreement will be transferred over to me," Travis explains silkily, and I mentally picture a spider weaving a trap for the moth. "Like I said, cooperate and you get me, either way, you are now my property."

"Let's not get too hasty, Travis," Barbara purrs. "Let's give her until tomorrow to honor her agreement."

My pride diminishes, and my shoulders slump as Barbara pulls the paper from my hands.

"Of course, everything you have learned from Axel, you can keep but starting tomorrow, you will learn from Travis. Rest assure, he can give *great* guidance."

Great guidance? Oh, my God, what do I do?

Internally, I begin panicking all over but stay perfectly still.

Travis stands, making his way to the door. "I look forward to picking you up tomorrow, so I'll see you then."

Barbara follows, and I'm too stunned to say anything as I walk to the door behind them. My knees shake with every step I take.

"How did you know I was here?" I ask them as they step over the threshold.

I have no idea why that's important, but I need to know. Barbara turns back to look at me but Travis keeps walking, uninterested.

"Axel came to see me, said you were not what he would consider good enough. Travis was, of course, sure he could shape you into something profitable. I assumed you were here considering Axel's pet runs the place, plus the room is in his name."

There's no warmth in her voice or eyes. I just nod, agreeing with her as she gives a time to be picked up and ready or not, I was going. Once the door is shut and I'm again alone, I sink to the floor and cry.

How many times did Axel warn me of this kind of behavior?

Before Barbara's visit, it only seemed a vague thought, but I'm now seeing first-hand this is an ugly place to be.

To my credit, I only give my phone and the note a brief glance before dismissing the idea of calling him.

He thinks I'm not good enough for him, so really, why bother?

The depth to which that cut should kill me.

Twenty- One

-

Axel

There's a theory that a human needs at least twenty-one days to break a habit. Longer if there are deeper connections to the habit. This is the reason I place so much importance on day twenty-one when training a female to be in adult film industry. It's the day we discuss finances and planning for her future. It's the day I make a decision about her wellbeing—whether that be continuing to work in front of a camera or convince her to do something else with her life.

Either way, by day twenty-one, I know if she will work out or not and she has been given enough training to at least survive what she's about to do. It also gives her a break in routine to think. If she continues, then we spend the following days perfecting her orgasm face or sucking techniques. Whatever she needs to work on, that's where the focus lies.

So, when day twenty-one for Payton comes around, I do some self-inventory. Proud of the fact I haven't spoken to Payton, nor have I called Beth to check on her since seeing her safely to the hotel, I feel slightly hopeful that in my absence she will see things clearer. It had become abundantly apparent I had to stop thinking about her after only a day or two. But not thinking about Payton only made me think more about her when my thoughts return to her. Obsessively so.

Twice in the days since her arrival at the hotel, I had to stop myself from going to see her. When I realized what a terrible mistake that was, I turned my bike around and drove in the opposite direction, then finally returned home to drink, sleep, and think.

What good would've come from me going to see her? I've known her for less than a month.

I have no right to inquire about her well-being and I know it would only confuse her more. Hell, it would confuse me more, but I just can't seem to get her out of my head.

Then, day twenty-one comes, and I know the habit of Payton has taken root and I'm not sure I can handle it much longer. I'm a man who has never known intimacy. Not ever, before Payton, anyway. I didn't even recognize it at first with her. There were subtle ways she touched me or stood against me that caused odd, foreign feelings in my chest, like I couldn't catch my breath, but instead of killing me, the feelings breathed life into me. It's as if I've been asleep forever, then she came along, and I'm finally awake. I both hate and love it all at once.

While deep in thought lying in bed going over day twenty-one, the doorbell rings. I ignore it. Then, the knock comes followed by Reggie calling my name. Grudgingly, I trudge to the door in just my boxers and let him inside.

"Did I wake you up?" he asks without preamble. "Or interrupt anything?"

He gives me a sheepish grin I ignore while I pour myself milk and wait for him to set the grocery bags down. Once he is relieved of the burden, he passes me the mail.

"Here's your mail, and here's Payton's mail."

I reached for it, frowning.

"I sent you a message to deliver hers to her hotel room," I say with irritation, looking through the contents.

"I did, Axel, but they said she checked out a couple of days ago."

I jerk my head up.

"What?"

"Yeah, she's not there, and I didn't have anywhere else to take it so I brought it here. Figured you would have her forwarding address or something to send it to."

Hope leaps in my chest.

Payton decided to go home?

"Did they say where she had gone?"

Reggie shrugs, and shakes his head. "They wouldn't tell me, anyway."

I turn my attention back to the mail as Reggie chats about nothing, oblivious, as usual, to me completely ignoring him.

"Anyway, that's how my whole week went."

"It'll get better," I say without a clue what I'm referring to. My attention is on the Texas A&M

University letter. Before breaking federal law and opening Payton's mail, I hand Reggie his tip and said goodbye. Grabbing an apple from one of the bags, I sit at the bar, contemplating opening the official-looking envelope.

It's too late for Payton to attend fall semester at Ole Miss. She stated more than once she did not want to return, but I took it upon myself to inquire on her behalf to Texas A&M before our disastrous training sessions. Like Beth, I had helped someone else out of the business several years ago. Kelly Maclea ended up a junior Dean of Psychology at Texas A&M. After I called to inquire about Payton possibly coming there, Kelly requested all of Payton's transcripts and scholarship papers from Ole Miss, which was easy enough to request with Payton's signature on a half-dozen digital files in my possession. I simply copied it to the request forms and all but forgot about it. Since I hadn't heard from her, I just thought it might be beyond her powers to help Payton.

Holding the envelope up in the light, I strain to see what it says. But no amount of light reveals its contents. Not knowing where Payton has gone, I decide to call her cell in the off chance she will want to speak to me. I do have her mail, after all, so I have a reason to call.

Without thinking too much about it, lest I talk myself out of it, I dial her number. A robotic voice mail prompt tells me she's not available. I end that call then log onto the airport website to see if the ticket voucher I sent to Payton has been used yet.

It hasn't.

A creeping sensation starts at the base of spine and works its way up my back. Payton knows no one in this wretched state but me. Considering what options she has, logic begins to take ugly shape.

Without a second thought, I call Barbara.

"Let me speak to that red-headed hell hound," I growl when the receptionist answers the phone.

"Axel?"

"Yes, Libby, now put me through."

There's silence for a long moment. Thoughts of murder run through my mind.

Strangulation? No, too clean.

Nine millimeter to the back of the head? No, too quick.

Drowning? Yes, and in toilet water.

"She's not here, Axel, you want me to forward you to her voice mail?"

Not responding, I end the call, yanking a shirt over my head, and shove my legs through jeans and shoes in one quick motion. Deciding on the car, I tear out of my garage seconds later, making the twenty minute drive to Barb's office in twelve minutes flat. Ignoring Libby's protests as I cross through the office in a venomous rage, I turn the knob to Barb's inner office. The door doesn't budge. I raise my booted foot and kick it in, sending wood flying through the air.

Unprepared for what is just beyond the threshold, I momentarily freeze. A teenage boy no older than I was when I first started this business is hurriedly trying to pull on his pants. Barbara is buttoning her blouse.

My vison turns red as I look from the Barbara to the boy.

"Get the fuck out of here. Come back, and I will beat the shit out of you."

The boy's face shows no signs of shaving yet and for some reason, that enrages me further. He grabs his shoes and shirt, nearly tripping over his feet trying to get away from me. Once he's gone, I turn my lethal glare to Barb.

"Where is Payton?"

"I'm calling the police. This is the last time you have interrupted my—"

Crossing the room in three strides, I wrap my hand around her throat and shove her into the wall. Terror tears through her eyes. Libby is behind me shouting, but I silence her with one look back.

"Shut the fuck up, Libby." I turn my face to Barb, inching so close, I can smell the mint of her breath. "One more time, where is Payton?"

A blood vessel pops in her right eye and a moment of pleasure courses through me at the sight. Barbara claws at my arm and struggles to breathe. Easing the pressure slightly, I try to calm my desire for murder just enough for her to speak. She gulps in air.

"Fuck you," she says, then spits in my face.

Unfazed, I move my hand to her perfectly kept red mane and yank, dropping her easily to the floor as I rub the spit off with the sleeve of my t-shirt. Dragging Barb by her hair across the office, Libby tries to block my way out. She turns to reach for her phone, but I take her arm, jerking her back to face me. She squeezes her eyes shut as if I'd strike her.

"Look at me, Libby." I gently shake the arm I hold while Barbara claws at the one gripping her hair tightly. Libby's eyes meet mine. "Payton Knight, where is she?"

Libby winces and I let go of her arm to show I'm not going to hurt her. All the while, I hold on to a fist full of Barbara's flame red locks. She kicks and screams at me but I'm unmoved.

"I don't know, Axel, really, I don't know," Libby whispers.

"Travis, give me the address of where he is." I know Travis doesn't own any property and often moves from rental to rental, leaving a path of destruction in his wake.

The last place I knew of him occupying had to be fumigated for weeks due to a bed bug infestation. The thought of Payton being in something like that terrifies me, and I want to kill him for it. I follow Libby back to her desk, dragging Barbara along. After a few clicks of the keyboard, Libby shows me an IPhone tracker.

"It's where his phone is, at least, but he normally doesn't go anywhere without it."

Peering closer at the monitor, I recognize the location and kiss Libby on the cheek.

"Don't call the cops, okay? Take what you want and get away from here. Apply somewhere nice. Use me and Beth for references. You deserve better than this shithole, Libby."

An eerie calm replaces my anger as make my way to my car with a thrashing woman screaming every obscenity imaginable at me. I shove her inside the trunk and twice shut the lid on her before she finally understands I'm not stopping. The tires squeal when I tear out of the office parking lot and pull onto the highway. It's a good fifteen minutes before I pull to a secluded area, parking just shy of the sand. I pop the trunk, and Barb lunges at me, trying her damnedest to claw my eyes out. I catch her and shove her backward into the sand where she stumbles and falls to her knees.

"Listen to me, Barb, or you're getting back in the trunk, only this time, you won't be breathing." I stand over her, ready to grab her hair again. She seems to wilt now she's in the sun.

"What the fuck is wrong with you, Axel?" she screams.

"If you try to cause me any trouble at all, you will have the feds on you so fast, you will not have time to blink. The boy today was your last underage, do you understand me?"

"Fuck you, Axel. You don't tell me what to do and besides, he was eighteen!" She sinks further in the sand, knocking her off-balance.

Vehicles whiz by on the highway in a hurry to get wherever the fuck normal people go, none pay us any attention.

"Do not tempt me, Barb. I'm giving you one and only one warning. If I so much as hear of anyone underage, I will provide damning evidence to put you away for years. You know I can, too. There's another fifteen years until we reach the statute of limitation on me. Hopefully, by then, you'll be dead if we are all lucky."

"I never forced you to do anything!"

"No, you didn't, I just couldn't eat until I did what you wanted!" I scream back.

My chest heaves and something inside rips open, revealing a nasty, infected wound. All this time, I thought I'm this way because of my parents, but that's not true. It's Barbara. It always has been.

Did Barbara get you off the streets and make you do porn as a teenager?

Payton knew, because she cared enough to pay attention.

Pushing my fingers through my hair, I yank and roar at the realization.

"You did this to me!" I snarl at Barb, very close to snapping her neck. "You fucked me up so bad, I pushed away the only thing I ever wanted for myself."

The vile, twisted things this woman has done to me and had me do to others all because I never thought I deserved better race through my head.

Why would I when my own mother didn't want me?

How do I still feel this when I'm a grown man and she has no hold over me?

Hitting my chest with my fist, I try to get control of my rage. With effort, I slow my breathing.

Barbara climbs to her feet and tries to run at me, only to fall again.

"If I see you again, I will kill you, Barbara," I warn with absolute certainty.

Sliding behind the wheel, I drive away, seeing flame-red hair in my rearview. The woman I thought helped me, was a surrogate mother when mine didn't want me, and for many years was my lover, faded away in the distance. The sight left me sickened with newfound understanding. I feel nothing but disgust I had allowed such a creature in my life as long as I had.

It took Payton to peel back the ugly knowledge of what I had to live with, exposing the raw reality of a sick, twisted woman taking advantage of a lost kid.

Just get to Payton, you can figure all this out later.

If she will still have me, that is.

I try to calm down as I drive the remainder of the way to where Travis is. Over and over, I try to mentally prepare for what I'm not only about to see, but also what I am about to do.

"Premeditation, Axel, remember what that means," I warn myself.

When I pull into the driveway of the many rows of seaside condos, my heart sinks. I have no idea which unit Travis occupies. Taking another chance, I dial Payton's cell again.

"Hello?" a girl who is definitely not Payton says in a sleepy voice.

I glance at my watch.

11:45 a.m.

"I'm sorry, I was trying to reach Payton."

"You have the wrong number," she says and hangs up.

Disappointment floods. I sit back further in my seat to contemplate how to find her.

The wrong number.

No, it's not the wrong number, so why would the girl say that?

Unless Payton is using another name?

The thought comes to mind and dread follows as I again dial Payton's number. The same female voice answers.

"Hello?" she says, now with a hint of annoyance.

"Is *Becca* there?"

Until now, I'd forgotten the name Payton told me she would use on film the day I picked her up at the airport.

"She's in the bathroom puking," the girl explains, still half-asleep. "Hang on."

Rumpled sounds come through the phone then I hear a knock on a door followed by muffled voices.

"You've been in here all morning, what the fuck are you doing?" someone asks.

Gripping the phone so hard it squeaks, I strain to hear what being said, but I can't make out anything. After a long pause, the girl returns to me.

"Becca can't talk, she's sick."

"Where is she?" I demand.

"She's in the bathroom, I already said that." She lets out a whine and I imagine she's fallen back in her bed.

"No, I mean *where* as in the location of the place you are now."

"Oh, we're at Travis'. Becca got a little banged up and isn't feeling great but I'll have her call you back."

"No, I know which apartment building but which *unit* is she in?" I ask desperately.

God save me from drunk females.

If this girl hangs up on me, I might not ever find Payton.

"Oh, hell, I don't know. Let's see, I think we're in apartment ten, no twelve. Yeah, we're in twelve."

Spotting the unit, I end the call, pulling to a stop sideways at the front door. In a newly ignited blaze of fury, I climb from the car and storm through the unlocked front door. The apartment is a large two-story, with no Payton in the main floor rooms. I climb the steps two at a time and check the bedrooms on the second, ignoring the questions from females in various stages of sleep or undress as I run from room to room. I barge through each door scanning.

"Payton, where is she?"

The girls take turns looking to each other then back to me.

"No idea."

I slam the door and move to the next room to find it empty. In my haste to move to the next, I trip over a tool box in the hallway, scattering hammers, screwdrivers, and nails across the landing. A tarp hangs on a banister and I nearly fall to the floor below, only catching hold of a loose railing at the last second. Growling with rage, I launch myself toward the next bedroom. It's empty as well but I notice the bathroom door open with the light on.

"What the fuck are you doing, Axel?" Travis shouts from behind me but I ignore him, heading toward the bathroom.

My breath leaves in one gust as I take in the scene. A girl with jet black hair sits on the lip of the tub, completely naked, stroking the back of another girl on the floor, who is equally naked. My heart picks up when I recognize the blonde hair that covers the face on the floor.

In two strides, I'm looking down at Payton. Her side is bruised as if someone has punched her there, her long legs are semi open, and a deep, bloody welt on the inside of her thigh stands out against her pale skin.

"I said what the fuck are you doing, Axel?" Travis growls at me and, again, I ignore him and look toward the girl on the tub.

"What happened?" I demand, reaching down to push Payton's hair away from her face. My breath freezes in my chest as I take in the beaten, bloodied face I know, without a doubt, I love even though the concept of that is unbelievable to me.

Seeing red, my vision blurs and my rage takes hold. When I'm sure Payton is breathing, I stand slowly and face Travis.

"Is this your handy work?" I gesture to Payton.

My body vibrates with anger, and I know I can kill him so easily in this moment. I need to get Payton out of here, so I fight the urge with all of my strength.

"Bitch wouldn't bend, we have to teach them, don't we?" he says in a conspiratorial whisper as if we were on a team about to take turns.

As I cock my head sideways, something must register because Travis takes a step back into the bedroom. His pale blue eyes swim with fear.

"Why are you here, Axel? She said you didn't want her, do you want her back? For the right price, we can make it happen. I've already got offers for her."

Frowning with faux concern, I take a step toward him, closing the distance within striking range.

"You have something on your face, Travis." I lean in as if trying to get a better look. He walks backward and I move forward, matching his steps. "Yeah, right there." I rear back and slam my fist against his nose. The sound of bone breaking only encourages me to do it again, this time making contact with his ugly teeth.

Travis stumbles backward out onto the hall landing.

"Aww fuck, Axel, you fucking psycho!"

His face is contorted with pain, and he looks like he's about to pass out. I step out of the room as Travis hit his knees, holding his face with one hand while the other lays flat against the floor supporting his weight. I spot a ball-peen hammer among the scattered tools and pick it up.

Travis spits blood out of his mouth, and before he can raise his head to look at me, I swing the hammer down hard on his hand. Travis crumples and screams. Girls come flying from their bedrooms, but I have one purpose and there's nothing and no one that's going to stop it.

"Motherfucker!" I scream down in his face. Travis curls his hand out of my reach, howling. I knock my knee to the side of his face with such force, the wall rattles as he falls against it. "You will never beat on anyone again!"

It takes all my strength to not place the hammer through his skull. Instead, I opt for the next best thing, pushing a foot on Travis' chest as he rolls on to his back in agony. I reach to get his uninjured hand. He fights me but I have the superior strength and am fueled with too much hate to stop. I work his hand free to lay on the floor, moving my foot on top to hold it down. Travis keeps it closed and he tries to work it out from under my boot. I slam the hammer down on the fist and once it opens, I crush each finger in turn.

One of the girls screams at what I'm doing, but I have no mercy. I return my attention to the previous hand and take turns on the fingers there. One by one, I smash them. Splattered in Travis' blood, I stare down at him while he screams like a wounded animal. I aim a kick to the side of his head and he immediately goes still. Tossing the hammer to the floor, I nudge Travis to roll to his side so he doesn't inhale blood and drown. I would be pleased if he died, but with a house full of witnesses, I'm not too keen on going to jail.

Returning to the bathroom, I carefully maneuver Payton to where I can lift her. She doesn't stir as I wrap her in a sheet from the bed and carry her down the steps. One of the girls opens the front door for me and another walks to my car and opens the passenger's side so I can lay Payton inside. Once she's situated, I stand and thank the girls.

"Don't worry, we're not going to mention you to the cops. He had that coming."

She gives me an appreciative smile.

"What happened?" I nod toward Payton. I'm in a hurry but I also want to know. If she's overdosed, I need to tell the doctors what drugs.

"We did some girl-on-girl stuff but then Travis tried to mess with her. She refused and he beat her, once for insulting him by refusing and again for calling him a pencil-dicked motherfucker."

"How long has she been here?" I ask, opening my car door.

She shrugs. "Couple of days."

"Do you know if she took anything or what was given to her?"

"I think just ecstasy but could've been Molly cocktails, too. I'm not sure but we did drink a lot."

I nod. "Thanks."

"No problem, hope she feels better."

I sink in my car and flee the scene just as I hear sirens in the distance. I know I'm probably going to jail, but my concern is only for Payton. Reaching out, I rub her arm and the side of her face, trying to wake her.

"Payton, if you can hear me try to open your eyes, or moan or something."

No response.

We reach the emergency room entrance and I lift Payton's lifeless body as gently as I can and carry her inside. After a slight commotion with the staff, I place her on a hospital gurney and watch helplessly as she is wheeled away.

"You will have to stay here. An officer will be here to take your statement," a nurse explains. I look down at my hand then the splatters of blood across my shirt and realize they must think I'm responsible for Payton's injuries. "If you'll come with me, we can get you patched up while we wait."

"I'm fine," I say, a little in shock now that my rage is turning into fear.

"You're bleeding on my ER floor, so no, you are most certainly not fine."

"Just take care of Payton," I reply, shoving my bloody hand in my pocket.

The nurse looks at me like I'm an idiot.

"Do you have any idea how many germs you just introduced into your blood stream?" I look to see down the hallway through a thin strip of windows, ignoring the nurse. "Come with me, please."

I let out a frustrated sigh and follow the nurse obediently to a room down the same hallway Payton was taken. I perk up when I realize she's leading me to a curtained area across from her.

"Have a seat." The nurse gestures to a bed.

I listen to a different nurse try to wake Payton.

"You didn't ask me if I did it," I tell my nurse.

I look at her name badge.

Kallie James NPRN.

Her dark blue scrubs and her dark blonde hair pulled back tightly make her look much younger than I suspect she is. When she looks me in the eyes, I'm met with a dark shade of blue. She pulls a table in front of me then sits opposite, reaching a gloved hand to my cuts.

"Because her injuries are at least several hours old, and your wounds just happened."

"Oh," I say a little impressed at the observation.

"I'm the city's forensic practitioner, so I notice things like that."

Payton finally responds to her doctor. She sounds drugged.

"Where am I? How did I get here?" she groans hoarsely.

"A man brought you in."

"A man?" I know Payton well enough to hear the fear in her voice. "Who?"

"I'm not sure. I'll ask one of the other nurses. Just lie back. Someone will get you in just a moment to take you for a CT scan. Let the IV do its job and relax."

My nurse cleans my hand but stays silent, letting me hear what is going on with Payton.

"A CT scan?" I whisper to nurse Kallie.

She nods

"Make sure there's no brain swelling or bleeding and they will assess her facial bruising as well, then they'll get an x-ray of her ribs."

All your fault for making her leave.

Closing my eyes, I swallow the rising bile.

"I hope to hell you kicked his ass," an all too familiar voice says behind me.

Jerking around in disbelief, I see Reece stepping inside the curtain. Relief washes over me, and I give him a genuine smile.

"Remember you said that when you see what I did," I say seriously.

As if on cue, a bed rolls by with a howling man on top. I can barely see him, but he's holding his hands away from his body and his face is covered in blood. My nurse gives me a sardonic smile.

"All right, Axel, start talking."

Reece pulls a chair up to sit beside the nurse and I watch as she rubs something foul over my cuts. After giving me a minute to think, Reece again presses me to talk.

"Can we *not* talk?" I ask him, really not wanting to go to jail.

"No. You can just be arrested then talk in an interview room."

I scowl at him.

"You're my best friend," I protest.

"I'm your only friend," he counters.

"Even worse, would you really arrest your only friend?"

"You're not my only friend."

"I am your best friend, you're my only friend."

"Axel, you're confusing the hell out of me, will you stop wasting time and just tell me what happened?"

"Fuck, I'd really like to not go to jail."

"Then, start talking, we will go from there."

After a few deep breaths, I relay the story, leaving out Barb entirely. More than once, the nurse nods in approval at what I'd done. Reece rests a foot on a knee and just listens without expression.

"Aren't you supposed to be writing this down or something?" I ask him after finishing.

"Why? I'm not here for a statement."

My face falls in disbelief, "Then, why the fuck are you here?"

"I came to eat lunch with her."

And to my utter surprise, Reece reaches a hand over to my nurse and pats her leg.

"Nurse Kallie is your *girlfriend*?"

I look from Reece to Kallie, then back to Reece.

"Don't look so surprised, Axel, she wants me for my money."

"And your big, beautiful penis," she says, throwing him a flirtatious wink.

That statement shuts my mouth and makes me a little queasy. Before the silence can get awkward, a nurse opens the curtain to Payton's area. I can see her lying propped on her side with her head resting on a pillow. My gut is in knots and I'm at a loss for what exactly I can do to make this better.

"This is my fault," I whisper.

As if sensing me, Payton looks to where I sit. A deep blue, crescent-shaped bruise covers her cheek bone. There are bruises also along her jaw and neck. Gritting my teeth, I wish I'd killed the fucker.

"Axel?"

I look at my hand and ask Kallie to just tape it. She spreads something like glue across the top followed by gauze. Before I leave him, I turn to Reece for help.

"Can you go do what you did to me and not get a statement from Travis? I'd like to know if he wants to

286

press charges. If he does, then let him know Payton does, too."

It is a bluff because I know Payton enough to know she would rather not deal with pressing charges, but I want Travis to think that. As much as I want to see Travis go to jail, I certainly do not want to join him.

Reece nods and punches my shoulder in a good ol' boy gesture.

"I owe you one," I say then turn to Payton.

She watches me from her bed as if I'm there to hurt her further. My chest constricts and million razor blades attack my throat. I don't want to speak, don't think I can, so I just let the silence settle us both down as I pull up a chair and sit beside her bed.

"We can talk later, okay?"

She gives a slight nod. And in an action so foreign to me, yet so very natural, I place my hand at her jaw then rub my thumb over her bottom lip. Instantly, she relaxes under my touch.

We sit silently until a nurse comes to take her for scans. I wait in the chair unnoticed by others as they walk up and down the hall. An hour later, Payton is returned to the room just as Reece sticks his head around the curtain to see if we are alone.

Satisfied we are, he moves toward me.

"Strangest thing happened earlier," he says, wearing an unmistakable mask of humor. "So, this dipshit comes in the hospital and says he was robbed earlier. When he approached the guy robbing him, the guy kicks his ass and breaks all ten of his fingers."

"The fucker must've deserved it then," I say with conviction.

Reece nods, then winks at me.

"Anyway, you two have a good night. Be more careful on that bike of yours, Axel. You all could have really gotten hurt."

Reece winks at me again, then pats Payton's foot awkwardly.

After much whispering back and forth, Payton wants to go with having a motorcycle accident, so we work to get our stories straight. We conspire together then relay our story to the doctor, telling him the accident did not happen on the highway, but in my driveway. The fact Payton was naked when I brought her in is never brought up and I suspect nurse Kallie covered for us.

Payton is released just as night falls.

She's prescribed rest for a few days for her bruising, mild concussion, and sprained ankle. I promise the doctor that's exactly what she will receive. But then, I consider I don't know if Payton will even want to go home with me.

"Payton?" I meet her eyes.

"Hmmm?"

"Will you come home with me? Let me take care of you?"

And try my damnedest to make all this up to you, maybe explain things better.

I wouldn't if I were her. I'm the reason she was hurt to begin with, but she nods.

"I don't have anywhere else to go," she whispers, allowing a solitary tear to leak from her eye. I brush it away with the back of my uninjured hand. A small part of me wants her to say she would come because she wants to be with me, but I dismiss that idea because it's silly to even think.

After getting released, I drive Payton back to my house and pull into the garage under very different circumstances than the last time we entered together. I turn off the car and we sit in silence while the garage door closes behind us. Payton turns to look at me and waits for me to say something. I turn to meet her gaze, trying to say a million different things with my eyes alone.

"What?" she asks finally.

"I was just thinking about that theory of breaking or starting a habit in twenty-one days." I lean my head back against the head rest. "I've known you for twenty-one days and I think you are a habit to me now."

"Don't be silly, Axel, I'm not anything special."

There are a great many things I want to say in response, but they die in my throat. I neither know how to act or feel, but know I'm drowning in guilt and I want to try to make everything up to Payton.

After insisting she let me carry her to my room, she flat refuses to get in bed until she takes a shower. Reluctantly, I agree, knowing after being at Travis' she probably needs one.

I help her to my bathroom where she brushes her teeth and stares in the mirror at her injuries while I get the water just right. I untie and remove her hospital gown, tossing it in the trash and gently wrap my arms around her torso. I stand with her back pressed against my chest, looking at our reflections. Bending my head to her ear, I'm on the verge of saying something, but I don't have the words. Instead, I nuzzle her ear, letting the moment pass and help her to the small, tiled seat of my shower.

Payton is weak and her legs tremble slightly when she puts weight on the sprain. After getting her seated, I start to shut the door when she calls to me.

"Stay with me?"

Payton looks up at me with pleading eyes. Water drops sparkle across her cheeks and red lips. I want nothing more than to stay, yet I want to run at the same time.

The wanting to stay wins.

Awkwardly, I hold her too-thin frame while she washes her hair and body. When I help her move fully under the water, she presses her bottom against me playfully.

"None of that, Payton," I growl.

She turns to face me, pushing her breasts into my chest and weakening my knees.

"I didn't do anything with anyone, I swear. One of the girls touched me but I couldn't even do that long."

I frown at her.

"I'm glad, but that's not why. I'm just mean not until you're better."

"Oh," her face falls. "But it's just some bruising, I'm not broken."

I gently push her hair back.

"Answer me something?" Payton raises her big eyes back to mine. "I'm clueless when it comes to feelings. You know how I've lived my life for years. I want to know, *need* to know, what you thought when I wanted you to leave."

"Is that a question?" she teases, wincing slightly when her injured cheek moves as she smiles.

"Tell me," I urge.

"Well," she casts her eyes to watch the condensation run down the shower door, "I understood you didn't want me, not as someone to teach, or to do anything with."

I nod, gathering that much.

"That's not at all why, Payton." I can't mask the regret in my voice.

She looks up at me and waits for an explanation.

"You were hell-bent on leaving anyway and how I was to you, during the training? That was the legit deal, Payton. I'm actually more considerate than most men in this business, but make no mistake, that's how it is for the females. I treated you no different than any other woman that's been here for the same reason. The only difference is you and I spent nearly a week in a different place, so going to just training would never have worked. I'm not sure it ever would have with you. I feel different with you."

"It's the whole virgin thing, right? Barb says you didn't like that about me."

I make a disgusted sound and turn the water off. Grabbing a towel, I begin drying Payton gently.

"Trust me, the virgin thing? It was shocking, but that's not why."

"I don't understand. Why did you make me leave if it's not because you didn't want me?"

I rub her hair, trying to figure out how best to answer that.

"Because I wanted you away from *me*."

She doesn't respond, but I can tell the words confuse her. I step around to face her again.

"I don't have the words, Payton, I don't mean I didn't want you here with me, I meant I have nothing to offer you."

She studies my face for a long minute, then frowns.

"You mean...what do you mean?"

Growling in frustration, I carry her to my bed. Once she's in place, I walk to my chest and put on a pair of boxers. She ignores the t-shirt I hand her, opting to stay naked and torture me further. I lean my butt on the dresser and cross my arms.

"Just say what you mean, Axel. You don't owe me anything. You don't have to pity me if that's what it is. I'll figure something out, and I'll make sure it's before you have more guests, okay?"

Now, it was my turn to frown.

"I'm not having more guests, Payton. I meant what I said when I told you I was done. Not just with the sessions with you, I mean I am done with this business entirely."

Payton wraps her arms around her knees and studies me.

"Did I mess things up?"

"What do you mean?"

"I asked Barbara, when she and Travis picked me up, about the two girls from the hotel bar. She said you were scheduled to have them stay soon."

I huff out a breath I'm sure contains smoke.

"And let me guess, once you heard that, you were more willing to go to Travis?"

"Well, I didn't really have a choice. They told me they could have me bound and dog-fucked and there was nothing I could do about it because I signed a contract agreeing to it."

Closing my eyes, I pinch the bridge of my nose, trying to fight off the beginning of a headache. I can almost hear Travis' threat.

"They lied. They both lie to everyone, Payton."

Her cheeks flush with embarrassment.

"So, the girls were not—"

"No. I didn't know them. They were just two drunk girls in a bar. Haven't seen them since." I find it strange her mind would go to that and not the lying about being dog-fucked.

Was my being with someone else more hurtful an idea than being raped by animals?

My head is foggy at the thought, and I'm beginning to understand I know absolutely nothing about females, or at least the one in my bed.

Payton tosses her head back and looks at the ceiling.

"You thought I made you leave so someone else could be here? Another girl?"

She returns her gaze to me.

"Axel, you were so distant and cold. Why would I think anything different? I thought you hated me. And Barbara said you came to her and told her I wasn't good enough for you."

I put my hands up in a stop gesture.

"Okay, let me back up, I'm going to try and explain why I am so emotionally moronic, something I've known for a while now but only recently realized I don't have to stay that way." Payton watches me, waiting patiently. "Something happened with my parents I think somehow damaged me. Fuck, I need a drink, but I don't really want to, so I'm just going to say it and maybe it'll help you understand why I'm such a damned fool."

Just as I open my mouth to tell Payton everything, she holds up a hand for me to stop.

"Reece told me, Axel. I don't want you to relive that for me unless you want to. I want to know *this* you, more, but I thought you should know Reece told me. Please don't be mad at him. I don't know what happened after you left Texas, though."

Taking a long inhale in, then out, I rub my neck and let it go. Right now, after everything that's happened today, I don't have it in me to get pissed off at Reece. In fact, I feel kind of grateful I don't need to explain the death blow I'd delivered to my own father. No matter the circumstances and no matter what a wicked bastard he was, he was still my dad.

"I didn't know I'd killed him, I just thought I'd knocked him out. I called an ambulance for my mom and while there, the paramedics told us he was dead." I pause to run a hand down my face at the memory. I feel raw but nothing can stop this purging. "Once my mom sent me here, I drifted from place to place for a while, working odd jobs, sleeping where ever I could safely. Barb found me by the warehouses and I started filming a few days after my sixteenth birthday, though nobody will ever admit that. I had a fake birth certificate, and my mom was right, people paid to see me, it just wasn't Hollywood films."

With difficulty, I remain detached from the story, having never told a soul except Reece in a drunken state, but even he doesn't know everything.

"She used you, didn't she? Barbara, she groomed you for this life?" Payton whispers.

Shame washes through me, and I have to cast my eyes to the floor. All I can do is nod. Barb's long red fingernails on my young pale skin still haunts me. That woman controlled my every move for years.

Why could I never understand it was wrong before?

Crossing my arms over my chest, I look back to Payton, determined to finish this broken, dark piece of my history. For some reason, I feel compelled to lay it all out and have no secrets with her.

"My last name was changed from Stein to Stone, and every experience I've ever had with a woman has been detached, void of all emotion, knowing how they can lie, and fuck for anything they want, even while a man beats on them. The drugs helped for a while, even though I overdosed twice. Barbara did not help my image of women in the least, then you show up." I gesture to all of her. "And you destroy me in the best way possible."

And it scares me to death.

Letting out a long, deep breath, I watch Payton closely as she absently rubs her fingers back and forth over a stitch on the duvet. She looks beautiful, even with the darkening bruise on her cheek.

"So," I say when she is silent too long, "I wanted you to leave because I didn't know what to do with you. You wanted me to teach you, and all I wanted to do was stay in bed with you. Giving you what you wanted was killing me because it pulled me back under to feeling nothing, and it caused you pain in the process. It made me crazy, and I couldn't stand causing you pain, but I was also giving you what you wanted."

Payton sits still, not speaking, not moving. Only occasionally, she'll look to the bed then return her gaze to me.

She's disgusted by me? I said too much.

"Say something," I beg.

Payton chews her bottom lip while watching her roaming fingers before turning sad eyes on me. My heart stutters, afraid of what she'll say.

"I don't know what to say, Axel. I'm shocked." She shrugs, tucking damp hair behind an ear. "I'm sorry."

"Why are you sorry? I'm the asshole that caused all of this."

"No," she shakes her head, scattering golden strands around her shoulders. "I should have listened to you. If I had trusted you, then it would've saved us both a lot of trouble."

"You had no reason to trust me. I should have talked to you, confided in you. My only defense is I was ignorant to all this, and you kind of threw me with the feelings."

Payton giggles, and I grin at the sound.

"So, it's not the virgin thing?" she asks, teasing me.

I chuckle and shake my head.

"I'm not going to lie, that was shocking but no, Payton, it's not the virgin thing. It's just you."

She gives me a blinding smile, then slowly holds out her arms, much like the night on the beach, she reaches for me, inviting me in.

My breath catches and all I want to do is fall into her warm body.

But, I can't. Wincing, I shake my head.

"You have had a rough few days. If I come over there now, I'll hurt you, so just close those pretty legs and lay down and *rest*. I'll join you when you fall asleep."

Payton frowns, and even that is beautiful to me.

"Axel, please? I want you."

Narrowing my eyes, I shake my head, this time with less conviction.

"Please? You will make me feel better and I need that more than anything right now. Make me forget the last few days, Axel, please? You won't hurt me, and we can stop if you do."

God, I want her more than my next breath.

"I just told you some pretty fucked up shit about my life. Maybe you should take a while and think about it."

"I will, but in all that you just shared, you also told me you cared about me, more than a little from what I understand," she says with a grin. "Come *show* me what you meant in case I got it wrong?"

I push off the dresser, not having the strength to argue more. In quick succession, I pull off my boxers and careful not to touch anything hurt, I push Payton's legs further apart, making room for my face. I touch the red welt mark on her inner thigh lightly with my fingertips.

"What did this?"

Payton looks down to where I'm touching and giggles.

"I wrapped my legs around a banister and Travis tried to pull me off. I think I broke like four of them but got that in the process. That's how I got the bruises on my side too."

I scowl, remembering the tools and the tarp, picturing Payton holding on for dear life.

What if she'd falling to the floor below? She could've died.

That image sends me crawling up her body to cradle her face. For a long moment, all I can do is stare down into the golden depths of her eyes and thank God she's alive and with me. Stroking her hair, I begin a slow soul-searing kiss, trying to convey my want, my *need* of her. Payton responds in kind, then when I move to rub feather-light kisses to her eyes, along her forehead, temple, down to her neck, she begins purring like a kitten.

"I could do just this all night," I whisper against her skin.

She digs nails into my shoulders, pushes her hips up to encourage my possession, but I continue the assault with my tongue on her breast, licking and sucking.

"I will kill you if that's all you do, but don't stop doing it." She pants, pressing my head harder into a breast.

It's only when Payton begins to grow impatient, clawing at my back, and only because I fear paining her further making her thrash against me that I push between her legs.

Mindful of her ribs, I hold all of my weight off of her body as I rock slowly, grinding into her heat, letting the pressure build with each passing minute. But this doesn't last long because Payton keeps pulling me down by my hair until my mouth is crushed to hers once more. I thrust harder involuntarily as she arches her back, breaking free from my mouth.

"Don't hold back on me, please Axel."

"Christ, Payton, I *can't*. I'll hurt you," I grumble, trying to hold on to my sanity.

"No. You won't," she pleads.

Torn between trying not to hurt her and making her say my name louder, I drive deeper, quickening my pace.

"Mmmm, that's more like it."

Within seconds, she begins trembling with her approaching orgasm.

"Fuck." I groan, reaching to the headboard as Payton thrusts her hips to meet mine in perfect alignment to reach deeper penetration, and I swear, I actually hit something in her body.

She cries out, fracturing beneath me, and it takes all my strength to hold on. Giving one last hard thrust, I let out a loud moan of ecstasy as we both come undone.

Seconds of suspension, loud, thundering heartbeats, and heavy breathing subside in a long exhale of satisfaction.

My body trembles as I try to keep my weight from crushing Payton, and I hold still, hoping I haven't hurt her worse.

"Twenty-one day habit, huh?" She giggles and I collapse beside her on the bed, struggling to catch my breath.

Twenty-Two

-

Payton

Happy.

I'm truly happy for the first time in maybe my entire life. It's all so very simple, yet I feel like royalty with Axel. Who would have ever guessed I would be so thoroughly cared for? Not me, and I fight pinching myself as we share the beach lounge watching the tide roll in. I'm wearing my little yellow bikini even with my bruises an ugly greenish gray now. But I don't care. I'm too content, and they will be gone soon. Besides, Axel seems to want to kiss them every time they're on display.

We sit, watching the last light of sunset descend into the sea. Axel has one foot in the sand with an arm behind his head while his other leg lies happily between mine. His other arm tucks nicely under my neck, snaking around to rest on my side possessively and I love it. And when his fingers lazily skim over my skin without him realizing he's doing it, I melt for him just a little bit more.

After three whole days of Axel's constant fussing over me, I'm mostly healed and swear the salt waters of the sea helped the process. I have been cooked for, bathed, and massaged so much, I don't think I've ever felt so good. Funny thing is, I think Axel enjoys doing everything for me just as much as I am enjoying receiving it.

As the day winds down, we talk hours into the night, stopping only to kiss or touch each other, which leads to exploratory sex and mind-blowing orgasms. Everything is brand new to both of us, which seems kind of silly when I consider all the women Axel has been with over the years. Still, he treats me as if I were the only one. I guess, in a way I am, at least for a time.

I know the soap bubble can pop, reality is going to eventually come crashing down, forcing me to make some major decisions. I put off planning like a champion procrastinator while I'm with Axel. One minute, I'm in a funk, thinking about Ben and trying to figure out what I can do next for money to actually live on, then he is there with his magic hands, pushing any kind of foreboding out of my head. It's a heavenly escape, and I find myself more and more wanting to stay gone.

The only interruption came my second day back at Axel's when Reece came to say he ran a stranger off the beach behind the house. This didn't seem to bother Axel but it made me uneasy and gave me cause to worry. That seems to be my go-to feeling when I have time to think about everything.

Worry is, after all, an old friend of mine.

"What do you want to do tonight?" Axel asks sleepily, pulling me out of my thoughts.

"I need to read over the papers that were sent from Texas A&M. Will you read them with me?"

"Of course, but I meant what did you want to do for dinner?"

I shrug, not caring about food. My mind has been racing with thoughts of my past all day. I want to talk, but I'm also scared to say anything. I don't want to change Axel's image of me just so newly restored, but I want to share with him since he has been so open with me.

Just tell him.

But he has his own tragedies to deal with, he would just try and fix everything.

But there's no fixing me. No fixing Ben.

Chewing my bottom lip nervously, I feel like I'm going to burst if I don't share. But can I expose my raw self to a man I've known barely a month?

He did, and it's time I let someone in.

Being with Axel the last few days has made me feel safe, comfortable, and tonight, I feel like sharing.

Here goes nothing.

"I lied to you," I say almost as if the words were forced from me.

Sitting up, I turn so I can look at him and gauge his reaction. The moon isn't bright enough yet, so I can't see Axel's face as clearly as I'd like to, but it works to my advantage, giving me some measure of disillusion. I don't think I could do this in the bright light of day.

"What about?" Axel asks cautiously, reaching to lay my hand against his chest.

His skin is warm and soothing as the evening chill begins to stir.

"My mom didn't die of cancer," I say in a small voice.

Axel's body tenses, and I can picture his face as he tries to think of how best to respond.

I have to get it out, all of it.

"After my dad died, she fell into a deep depression, like *really* deep. My brother and I, Ben, who is five years younger than me, tried to help her. We kept to our schedules, made sure she ate, bathed, and didn't drown when she'd drink too much. But there was no helping her. She would drink so much her pores seeped alcohol and she smelled of nothing but liquor and vomit. We slowly became the parents and she the child."

My eyes begin to sting at the memories. Axel squeezes my hand in encouragement, but stays quiet, letting me find my words.

"After I got my scholarship, I left him to take care of our mother alone. I worked part-time to help pay for everything, but Ben hid the worsening state mom was falling into after I was gone. I wanted so bad to be normal, but I never could be. I didn't have money to go home much, but Ben and I talked every day." My breath hitches with my rising regrets. "I thought if I could just get through school, then I could help Ben through school when he was old enough. But he was hiding things from me. He quit playing baseball, and after everything happened, I found out he had quit going to school all together."

My voice breaks, and I sit up straighter to breathe deeper as the tears spring forth. My lungs feel like they're failing. Axel rises up with me but still remains silent.

"A police officer came to my apartment. The minute I saw him, I knew something awful had happened to my brother. I didn't even consider my mom. The officer could barely look me in the eyes when he told me my mom had shot Ben, then killed herself."

Shaking with full-blow sobs now, I heave into Axel's chest as he pulls me against him. Pushing back after only seconds, I brush my eyes and shake my head as if arguing a point because I *have* to get this out.

"I never wanted to do adult films, Axel. Never. But Ben didn't die from the gunshot. He's alive and he's mentally disabled." In an effort to calm, I turn my face to the water. Ben's sweet baby face and big blues eyes flash through my memories, causing rips of pain I'm surprised don't kill. "The state took custody of Ben because I couldn't provide for him. He requires all kinds of medical care I can't give him, nor pay for. I did everything to try and keep the house, took out loans and maxed out every credit card to get Ben back home with me. But it wasn't enough. The house went into foreclosure, and I was ordered to vacate the premises. I lost everything, but losing Ben was the worst. He wasn't dead, but he was no longer my baby brother. His mind is like a toddler and there were nights I wished he would have died thinking maybe it would have been better to grieve his death rather than grieve for his life."

Axel tries to sooth me, but guilt rips through my chest so hard, I double over.

"This is all my fault. I left him alone with her knowing she was sick. I'm here with you, and he's in a nursing home with no idea where I am and *it's my fault*. That's why I came out here. I thought maybe if I could make enough money, I could go back and get custody of him. Get a small apartment, get on my feet so I could care for him. Axel, I was so stupid, and I don't deserve your affections or pity." I sob.

Axel takes both of my arms and forces me back to his chest.

"Shhh, Payton, calm down."

But I just cry harder. The loss of my brother is unbearable, the guilt of what I did to him even more so.

"I would do anything to reverse what happened, but I know I can't, so what do I do? Do I just let him live with strangers and go on with my life as if he *were* dead? I can't do that, I just can't."

Axel holds me, rocking gently. It takes ten whole minutes before I'm calm enough my breathing returns to normal. It takes an additional ten for my tears to dry up. All the while, Axel presses his mouth to my hair repeatedly as he squeezes me softly.

"Feel better?" he asks after I settle down a bit.

"A little," I admit.

"I wish I had something wonderful to say to comfort you, Payton, but fuck, that's tough stuff to live through. I don't think there are words big enough to cover it."

Shivering, I wrap my arms around his waist, pressing my face harder against his warmth.

"You always make me feel better, Axel. I'm sorry. I've just been thinking about him today, and I guess I needed to tell you."

"I'm glad you trusted me enough to."

"I'm pretty fucked up, Axel. You already know that. What happens if I do return to school? I can't just forget about Ben."

Axel rubs my arms, resting his cheek in my hair. It makes me feel oddly cherished.

"I don't think you will ever forget, Payton, but you do realize, had you been home, you would have probably died as well? I'm not very philosophical, but maybe things happen for a reason sometimes."

"You think I have some reason to be here with you?"

"Maybe," he says seriously.

He's words stir my emotions, and I recall someone telling me after everything happened, that we as humans needed to feel alive after an emotional upheaval. After all that I just shared, I suddenly feel that need and Axel fulfills it with interest.

My skin tingles from the trail left by his fingers on my arm, and I feel almost weepy, as if I've never been loved before. My dad loved me, I know Ben loved me, and maybe before Katrina happened, my mom loved me, but they are all gone from me now. I want to cling to Axel, knowing he's all I have in the world, but for how long?

Until I go back to school? Will he go back to training girls once I'm gone, or can I believe he really is done with that part of his life? What right do I have to even question that?

"Chinese," I say, breaking the silence.

"What?" Axel chuckles.

"You asked me what I wanted to eat for dinner, I feel like Chinese, and then I think we should take a bubble bath and watch a movie. Have a true chick flick night. Oh!" I rise up excited, "I can pin you down and make you watch 'Steel Magnolias' with me!" I squeal in delight.

Axel sighs, but I can tell he is totally going to give me what I want.

"Chinese and a chick flick. Whatever you want to do," he says, trying to sound defeated, but I can hear the smile in his voice.

Axel wraps a hand around my waist and helps me through the sand and back to the house. My ribs are okay, but my ankle isn't one hundred percent yet. Even if it was, I would still want him to walk with his arm there.

"We can have hot dogs and baseball tomorrow, deal?"

"Now you're talking." Axel lifts to carry me Rhett and Scarlett style, and as if it is the most natural thing in the world, I wrap my arms around his neck, giggling into his scruffy neck.

"But tonight, in the middle of all the chick stuff we are going to do, I am going to give you a killer blow job," I purr, loving the way he feels.

Axel growls and bites my neck playfully, causing another squeal. In three short days, this man has turned me into such a girl.

"Okay, okay! You are giving me whisker burns." I giggle which only makes him rub his chin harder against my jugular.

"Aww, this is so sweet. I wish I had a camera, a real fucking Kodak moment. Boys? Isn't this a picture? Axel Stone and his little *whore*."

Axel's entire body stiffens, and we look to see four men blocking our path into the house. We're still in the sand but mere feet from the back deck. The porch light casts shadows on their faces, but I can make out Travis and the casts that encase his broken hands. The other three are unknown to me, but my stomach flips nervously as I take in their hulking figures. Every nerve in my body screams *DANGER*.

"Time to pay the piper, Axel," Travis says mockingly.

Axel says nothing, but holds me tight, assessing the situation. Deciding on something, he lowers his mouth to my ear, causing my body to tingle with fear.

"I'm going to set you down, and you are going to run. Go to Reece, go anywhere, just run as fast as you can and do not look back."

The soft lighting causes his eyes to glow with what I can only think is acceptance of the situation.

There's no chance of us getting out of this unharmed. Axel and I are doomed, as good as dead.

He gives me a little shake, raising his brows as if saying *got it?* Shaking my head in protest, I feel as if I'm going to be sick. Axel's eyes narrow, and he gives me a stern nod. Slowly, he lowers me to my feet and softly kisses my forehead and whispers so lowly, I have to strain to hear it.

"Run."

As if in slow motion, Axel steps forward to draw the men's attention, and I forget I have a sprained ankle as I sprint harder than I have ever ran ever in my life. All I can think is I have to get to Reece.

Twenty-Three

-

Axel

There's no way out of this, I know before I begin to fight the two men closest to me, that this night is going to end badly. But I'm also convinced I'm going to kill someone before they can kill me. At this moment, I don't care which one of these fuckers it is.

Killing me is the only reason Travis has come with henchmen. He can't fight me with his hands busted up so he brought guys who can do it for him. I suspected he would do something in retaliation, I just didn't expect it so soon.

In a blind rage, I punch and kick at the men just as they punch and kick me. There's no way of knowing if Payton got away, but I'm doing my damnedest to give her enough time to reach Reece at his warehouse post.

A blow lands squarely on my temple, as another man lands a solid kick to my gut. This combination causes my knees to buckle. Struggling to stay on my feet, I pause at a sound that rips through me—Payton screaming somewhere in the dark, and I turn to run in that direction.

That's when one of the guys hits the back of my head with something pretty damn hard, sending me face-first into the sand. My eyes cloud, and a sharp ringing rushes through my ears. White hot pain bursts from my scalp followed by the warm rush of blood. Rough hands pick me up by the arms and carry my limp body over the deck, inside my house, tossing me to the floor with a hard thump to my jaw. My teeth rattle as I land on the hardwood in front of my couches.

Fighting to stay conscious, I have to spit blood from my split lips and squint my eyes to focus. Somewhere in the back of my mind, I'm pissed my nose might be broken, and it fucking hurts. Peeling my face from the floor, I'm met with Travis' weak eyes. Hatred boils through my gut.

"You will breathe your last breath this night," I tell him as blood trickles into my eyes.

Travis laughs as I stagger to my feet, ready to rip his throat out. Two men hold me in place, and I'm too weakened to fight them off. Trying to conserve my energy and give my head time to clear, I look to each man, imagining their deaths.

Travis strides closer, holding up both hands, showing me the hard casts.

"Three different surgeries in two days. I may never have use of them fully again." I try to sneer gleefully, but the pain in my head causes an involuntary sway of the room. "Who do you think you are fucking with coming into my home, taking my property, *again,* then using a hammer to break my fucking hands? Did you think I would just let that shit go?"

"She's not your fucking property," I say, spitting more blood.

My hearing returns in a rush, the pressure so great, my heads falls to the side.

"I *let* you take Beth. I'd already made all I would from her and was finished with her anyway, but Payton? We were just getting to know one another," Travis says conversationally.

As if on cue, the fourth man comes through the glass door holding both of Payton's wrists, pulling her easily to stand in front of Travis. Blood trickles down her chin from her mouth. Standing, trying to fight to get free of the men holding me, my arms are twisted awkwardly and a pop from my shoulder echoes through the room.

I fall to my knees once more as blinding agony takes my breath away. My arm is separated clean out of the socket.

"Aww, here she is." Travis smiles and looks from me to Payton. "If I didn't know you better, I'd think you actually cared for this one. Axel? Could it be that a cold bastard could melt with the right bitch?"

Travis reaches a wrapped hand to Payton's crotch. I twist and fight to get free, but am met with a punch to my left eye. Spots float through my vision, and I fight blackness from taking me.

"Make him stay alert," Travis orders and a hand slaps my face. Payton tries to recoil from Travis. Her face is a mask of terror and repulsion.

"Shhh, settle down, sweet Payton," he coos.

Travis backs away and sits on my couch, tossing his arm on the back as if he were having a pleasant visit.

"Let her go, or I swear, I will fucking kill you," I growl through clenched teeth.

Travis merely smiles at me.

"Axel, you are so *violent*. Let me put your mind at ease. You will be the only one dying tonight, but before you do, I want to give you a show. You need to see your Payton in action, see if all your *training* did her any good."

"No!" I roar as the man holding her has one huge hand gripping both of her wrists while his other hand begins untying her bikini top. His bald head is beaded with sweat and the perspiration runs down his meaty forehead. I use every ounce of strength I have to break free from my captures, but with a couple of fists to my face, I'm easily held in place. I know what's happening, and I can do nothing to stop it.

Even with Payton fighting the man, he easily gets the top tied around her wrists then pushes her forward over the couch directly in front of where Travis sits sneering at me. I scream something foul, but don't understand my own words. One of my capturers pulls my head back by my hair, forcing me to watch what's happening.

The man holding Payton rips down her bottoms and holds her in place, nearly bent double over the back of the couch. She writhes and fights but he slams inside her, raping her viciously.

This isn't happening. Fuck! This isn't happening!
Can't get to her. I can't save her!

Payton's guttural screams slices through me, tearing my soul to shreds. The man pumps and grunts into her body with such force, the couch moves with each thrust.

She goes still when the man orgasms and I watch her body fall limp with helpless resignation.

Please, just be passed out.

"Payton, baby?" I kick and try to head butt my way out from under the hold on my arm, but it's futile.

A small twitch of her hand? She's okay, she's going to be okay.

But there's no other movements. Payton has either passed out or checked out mentally, and I can only watch in horror as the man with Payton pull his pants up with one hand, then with the other, he pulls her by the hair, dragging her to my side, trading places with the man holding me on the left.

Frantically, I search Payton's face for life.

"Payton," I breathe.

Her lids flicker open at my voice, and our eyes meet.

Anguish, repulsion, and death is what stares back at me.

I'm sorry, I should've never brought you back here. This is my fault. I'm going to make this right somehow.

I try to convey anything, *everything* in my eyes before she's pushed to her back and held down so the process can began again.

"Oh Axel, she is a peach." Travis laughs, showing crooked yellow teeth. "I'd clap in a show of support, but you know," he says, holding up his destroyed hands.

In this moment, I regret with all my heart not killing him.

"Soon," I hiss at him.

Much the same as the first, the second man rapes Payton brutally, her face contorting with repulsion while the man pumps with abandon. My body goes limp, my vison blackens just before I'm slapped once again. Opening my eyes wide, I see the second man repeats the same movements as the first, trading places with the one on my right. This time, Payton lies motionless, staring with blank eyes.

Utterly broken. A butterfly stripped of its wings. She's dying, right here, and I can do nothing!

Writhing in agony to reach her, I slip free only to be met with a boot to the kidney, and another to my face before being wrestled back to the floor. My vision clouds from fresh blood at my eyebrow but the sounds are crystal clear.

"You ready for this? Is that ass ready for me?"

The taunts of the man is all I can focus on.

Make it stop, God? Make this stop and let her be alive. I've never asked for anything from you, but I'm begging you to stop this.

But it doesn't. My left eye clears, and I realize I'm crying. The tears flush at the blood and as sight returns, I see the third man push Payton to her stomach. She screams at his entrance, a long animal-like sound as the beast sodomizes her slowly.

The choking sounds I make are not human, and instantly, I'm hoping these fuckers kill me for letting this happen to Payton. For nothing else, I want my throat cut simply because I can't stop any of the horror from occurring.

The man is tearing Payton in two and I can't move!

I begin screaming in agony, trying to provoke a lethal hit to my skull, all the while, Travis sits on the couch laughing. Payton sobs with her face on the floor, and I pray she'll pass out just to stop the pain she's going through. But then I sober, my vison sharpens, and I realize with absolute clarity that I'm going to die, and Payton will be taken to live through this torture time and again.

No, some way, I have got to kill them.

I have to get Payton away from here and kill these men one by one.

The irony of living numb and cut off from feeling for so long is not lost on me as I feel the tears leak from my eyes.

I'm not going to live long enough to kill them, and Payton will be taken to be prostituted because that's what Travis does best. I'm powerless to stop it.

Just as I close my eyes to give in to death, a gunshot echoes through my living room. My eyes fly open and I see the man raping Payton look down at his chest with an almost comical expression on his face. Blood spreads across his t-shirt and after pulling away from Payton and trying to stand, he crumples to the floor dead. The men holding me let go and I fall to the floor as Reece steps inside the back door.

His pistol still smoking, he creeps forward, aiming his gun at each man. I push myself up to crawl to Payton.

"What kind of fucked up shit is going on here?" Reece asks, putting his body between Payton and the retreating men, "First person to move, I will blow your fucking head off."

Travis begins to stutter when the gun swings in his direction.

"Reece," stretching out a hand to my friend, my voice breaks as I plead, "kill 'em Reece, kill 'em all."

Reece's hard frown turns on me, then recognition dawns in his icy blue stare.

"Fucking hell, Axel?"

It's only when I see Reece's shocked expression that I understand my face is beaten so badly, my best friend doesn't even recognize me.

Inching forward, I make my way to Payton. My hand trembles as I reach out to her, but she scurries backward, shaking uncontrollably.

Do I touch her? She might crumble if I do.

"Payton, baby?" I rasp, inching toward her. "It's me. Axel. Nobody is going to hurt you now," I rasp.

She looks like a trapped wild animal as she stares back at me with eyes void of comprehension. Half her face is covered with her matted golden strands, and I can see and smell the blood pool beneath her.

"Payton... Still on my knees, I pause, raising my hands to show I mean no harm. "It's okay now, it's over."

Liar.

This will never be over. She will live with this forever, and I'm responsible.

Reaching out once more, I place a hand gently on her leg, then slowly I untie her wrists.

"It's okay, it's going to be okay." I chant the words like a prayer.

Shaking violently, Payton watches as I work the knots lose with my teeth, freeing her now blue hands. I rub them gently to encourage circulation.

"It's all right now, Payton, everything is going to be all right." My gut feels as if it's being ripped out as finally she lets me hold her. "An ambulance will be here. They'll get you to the hospital. Everything will be okay, I promise."

Payton pushes away from me, shaking her head.

"No. I'm not going."

She's in shock. She must be.

But her eyes are clear, dead serious.

"You have to," I retort gently.

She shakes her head harder.

"They can just claim this was a part of a filming. They have a contract giving them permission to do this, remember? And besides, I won't let them make me a statistic."

She stands and I follow, looking down at her bewildered, not having a fucking clue as to how to handle this. Out of the corner of my eye, I can see Reece still holding his gun ready to shoot anyone who moves.

"Payton, you're bleeding, you need a doc—"

"I said no, Axel! Where are your car keys?" She looks around as if she were not bleeding and naked in the middle of my living room.

"My keys?" I ask, glancing around helplessly

"Yes, your fucking car keys Axel, where are they?"

Don't let her leave, she is too hurt to go anywhere alone.

319

"Okay, I'll drive you."

Payton's hand shoots out before I can get close.

"No, Axel, I'm leaving. *Alone.*"

Streaks of blood and fluids drip to the floor as she moves.

"You are in shock, Payton, please let me help you."

"Look in my eyes, Axel, I am not in shock. I want to get the fuck out of here before anyone sees me."

A movement catches my eye and I turn to see one of the men lunge at Reece. He fires off a round but misses. Travis tries to take advantage of the distraction and runs to the back door, but I tackle him. My shoulder actually snaps back in place as we collide and hit the floor. Pain and relief floods my body with adrenaline, giving me the much needed push to end this once and for all. We wrestle for control as we stand, but unlike Travis, I still have use of my hands and easily overpower him.

Ignoring any resistance my body gives, I shove him into my kitchen, turning his body so we are face to face

I want to see him when I kill him.

The commotion with Reece settles down, but I keep my focus on Travis' fear-filled eyes, backing him to the counter and, without looking, I open the drawer beside my thigh.

Kill this fucker.

He's shaking with fear, and that seems to strengthen me. Gripping the six-inch knife I use to filet large fish, I place the tip just at Travis' pubic bone. His flesh splits easily and I grin as I slowly sink it in deep. Trying to push against me with his beat-to-shit, useless hands, he screams loud and long. In a sawing motion, I begin to move the blade up, slicing through tissue and muscle at his abdomen, chest then neck, ignoring the protest of my bicep.

He takes his last breath well before I reach his chin but I feel I should complete the job, and follow through. Letting Travis' body fall to the floor, I reach blindly for a dish towel to wipe blood from my eyes.

His or mine?

I didn't know, but I'm covered in it.

"That's just fucked up right there," Reece says from behind me.

I turn to see him still holding his gun at the ready, watching me calmly wipe my face and hands off. The guy who lunged at him has a bullet hole through his cheek lying spread eagle at his feet. The last man standing has his hands up in surrender, watching me in horror. "Axel," Reece says my name in warning as I take a step toward him, "think about it. We need his statement."

Ignoring Reece, I wrap my hands around the man's throat and push him to where I just had Travis inside the kitchen. When he tries to move, I break his jaw with my elbow, then bend to retrieve my knife. In one hard upward thrust, I plunge the blade through the center of the man's neck. He falls and lets out one last bloody gurgle.

"Well, shit," Reece breathes.

Pulling myself out of the murderous rage, I turn for Payton only to see her yellow top where I left her. Limping around the house, she's nowhere to be found.

No, no, no.

She's too injured. She wouldn't just leave, would she?

Opening the garage door, all I see is an empty space where my car should be.

"Fuck!" I scream, slamming the door shut.

"Okay, here's what we are going to do—" Reece starts in a conspiratorial tone.

My head swims and a pulsing sensation courses through my scalp. Only vaguely aware of just how badly beaten I am, and only partially able to raise my left arm, I walk to my liquor cabinet and gulp down one fourth of a bottle Jack before throwing bottles against the floor, smashing and spilling their contents.

"Wait, what are you doing?"

"I'm burning the fucking house down." I continue to pour alcohol over bodies, then strip naked to rinse some of the blood from my hands and face, cussing as it burns my open wounds. Reece catches on and begins smashing the wine.

"Okay, we'll burn it down."

"Figure out a way to say they were vandalizing the place. You came in and they jumped you."

"Okay, then what did you do?"

"I was never here. I've been out of town. I'm leaving before they get here. How long do we have?"

Reece turns up his radio.

"I didn't call it in yet. I just came to check after I heard Payton scream, then all hell broke loose."

"Good, then we have a few minutes. You're good with this?"

"I'm good," he assures with a nod. "It's better than going to court to testify for the next thirty years because of these fuckers."

I nod, still naked, wiping myself off at the kitchen sink.

I need to find Payton.

But I have to fix the mess to look good first, otherwise, she'll be living in Hell from the investigation of these fucks for years.

That thought pushes me further, making the intense pain my body is in slide to the back of my mind.

"Okay, let's do this. Hit me, Axel."

Meeting his eyes, I see Reece stand up straighter, bracing himself. Any other time, I would have found this view laughable.

"No," I say incredulous.

"You have to fucking hit me, more than once. Hell, I shot two of them." Reece gives a hard shake to his head as if to clear it. "Christ, I'm glad they're white or I'd probably get sent to the pen. I can say these two must've killed each other and were dead when I chased the other two in here but I need to look banged up *so fucking hit me.*"

Without another thought, I pick up a half-empty bottle of Texas Straight and rear back, hitting Reece's face dead center.

"Aww fuck, my nose!" He staggers back, eyes squeezed shut, fingers pressed against the bridge. "Shit, Axel, I didn't say break my fucking nose."

Just as he stands up, before he knows I'm coming, I hit him again, aiming for his eye. The bottle shatters, slicing Reece's jaw in the process.

"Fucking hell." He stumbles backward, almost falling this time. "That's enough, Christ almighty!"

My vison dims along my left eye and I can feel a throb at the crown of my head growing more persistent.

Get to Peyton, she needs you.

Shaking off the dizziness best I can, I collect clothes from my room, ignoring the stream of fresh blood coming from my scalp, sliding down my neck and chest.

No time, just get out of here.

"I'm calling it in. Get the fuck out of here," Reece barks through my open bedroom door, one hand on his radio.

"Wait," I yell back, shoving my laptop and clothes in a bag then returning to the living room. "Get outside. I'll meet up with you in a few days. I've been out of town," I say in a rush as the thoughts come. Yeah, out of town. "Nobody will question my absence, and I will have an alibi, okay?"

Knowing I can call most any of the girls I've worked with recently, I have no doubt they will swear I was with them if I ask.

Hell, I can even blackmail Barb if it comes to that.

Reece nods in agreement.

"Except I need to get a little smoke in me first, that way I can claim I must've blacked out and that's why I couldn't call it in right away. I'll do it when I know I smell like I was in here fighting them when all hell broke loose." Reece casts his eyes around the carnage assessing his story no doubt as I find a box of matches. When his clear blue eyes land on me once more, I see worry staring back at me. "You are not in good shape, buddy. You need your face and head looked at."

"I'll call Beth, she can get a doctor to patch me up."

"And Payton?" he asks, unable to hide the concern in his voice.

"I'll find her," I swear solemnly, just as I strike a match and drop it onto Travis' body. Flames burst to life instantly. Pausing long enough to make certain the buckets of alcohol feed the flames, I walk naked to my bike, start it up, and drive away.

When I stop a half a mile up the beach to wash off in the ocean, then quickly dress, I hear sirens in the distance.

Please let the fire be strong enough to burn away any of Payton's blood.

Once I'm dressed and my helmet secure, I coast by my home, and bless the dry California weather. In the right setting, a house can burn to the ground in minutes. I love that house, and I hate that house, knowing I'll never be able to return to it after what was done to Payton there.

Not ever.

So, when I see it's gutted down the middle through the living room and kitchen, still burning, I breathe a sigh of relief and keep driving with one purpose.

Payton is out here, hurt, and alone. But where to look?

My only thoughts are to get somewhere and try and locate my car by GPS.

But what happens once I find her?

We heal, together, because I have no intentions of ever letting her go.

Twice, I almost black out on the road as I drive. Pure adrenaline keeps me going, fading then returning with bouts of fresh, searing pain. When the dizziness gets too much, I know for certain I can't help Payton if I'm dead from a bike wreck or blood loss.

Shaking the fog clear from my eyes, I pull into the back of a bar parking lot where I know a rare pay phone sits. Kicking the stand in place, I cut the engine and stay seated as I reach for the receiver, stretching so I won't have to leave my bike and risk falling on my face. After three attempts, I finally get the sequence of numbers right. Just when I begin to think she isn't going to answer, she picks up.

"Hello?"

"Beth, it's Axel, I'm sorry but I need your help."

"I'm listening."

"I need a place to stay for a few days but it can't be traced back to me. Officially, I'm *out of town.*"

"Well, that's not vague at all."

"Beth," my tone brooks no argument. "Can you get me in the hotel unseen? I can stay in a broom closet, I just need to get somewhere with internet access and a phone."

"Are you okay?"

Define okay?

"No, but I can't go into it now. Can you help me or not?"

"Of course, Axel. Use the west rear entrance, the code is 184130, got it?"

"Got it," I repeat typing it in my cell phone. I have to pause to steady myself so I don't fall off the bike.

"There's an older suite we don't use much on the first hall to your right, it'll be open so go in. I'll meet you there."

"Bring a first aid kit."

There's a heartbeat of silence.

"Axel, how bad are you hurt?"

I hang up without responding, then make one more call.

"What?" Barb growls.

"I will fucking kill you," I say without preamble.

"Axel?"

"Did you have anything to do with Travis coming to my house tonight?"

"No," she replies instantly. "Why? What did you do?"

"If I find out you had anything to do with what happened, I will kill you."

"I don't know what's happened. I haven't spoken to Travis since you busted up his hands."

"You won't be speaking to him again," I growl and slam the receiver down on its cradle

Starting the bike, I head toward the hotel.

Get the bleeding under control and find Payton.

Christ, I'm weak and I feel adrenaline draining with every heartbeat. Pain I never imagined possible runs through my shoulder and back, but I ignore it speeding up, flying through the night.

Finally, fifteen minutes later, I reach the rear entrance, park by the dumpster, sling my bag over my throbbing shoulder, and without removing my helmet, I punch the key pad and nearly run to the suite.

The door is propped open with the dead bolt rod. With caution, I push it open slowly. Beth is on the phone with her back to me as I enter and shut the door, locking it. She turns toward me, frowning at my wearing a helmet indoors, then quickly hangs up the phone.

"Axel?"

I take two swaying strides to bathroom, drop my bag and, with great difficulty, I pull my helmet off my head. As the pressure leaves my skull, blackness encroaches.

"Oh, my God, Axel." I hear shock and fear in Beth's voice but can't turn to look at her.

Overwhelmed by nausea, I sink to the floor and begin violently throwing up, barely making the turn to the toilet in time. Somewhere, in between holding onto the side of the toilet and Beth trying to help, the darkness pulls me under.

Twenty-Four

-

Axel

"Payton?" I cry out, feeling blindly at the empty space beside me on the bed.

The room is pitch black and I have no idea where I am.

She's hurt. They hurt her so bad.

"Payton?" I almost sob.

"Shhh, rest Axel."

A small hand presses against my bare chest and a light switches on beside my bed. I'm panicky and feel heavy with drugs.

"Beth?" I try to focus and realize one of my eyes is covered.

"Calm down, Axel, everything is okay."

"What time is it?" I try to sit up, but find it impossible when my body gives a loud *Hell no.*

"It's a little after three in the afternoon," Beth replies softly.

"Fuck. I have to get out of here. I have to get to Payton. She's hurt, Beth, *really* injured."

Those men, their grunts mingled with Payton's scream...

My stomach rolls and I have to swallow the bile from rising at the memory.

"No honey, *you* have been badly injured, you can't go anywhere." And as if my body were made of lead, I sink deeper into the mattress. "Axel, sweetie, you have been unconscious for three days."

"Three days?" I rasp. "No fucking way, Beth. She's been alone all this time? She could die." My heart gallops at the thought.

"You have to stay calm or I'll call the doctor to give you a shot again."

Too drugged to react, I can only blink up at the ceiling as panic consumes me.

"I have to find Payton, Beth. You don't understand."

"You have to recover, or you won't be finding anyone but a mortician."

Beth sits on the bed beside me, ready to push me down if necessary. Aware I have, in fact, been drugged, I lie still trying to let my body wake up.

"Can you tell me what happened? I know your house was destroyed in a fire and four bodies were burned beyond recognition. It's been all over the news. They say they were unable to reach you and your car was found close to the airport."

My stomach lurches.

"My car? The airport?"

Beth nods.

"Fuck. She must've took off."

"Payton? The one that stayed here?"

"Yes."

Beth reaches for a bottle of water and holds it to my lips. Raising my head just those few inches causes pain to tear through my side.

"How about I tell you what's going on with you and while I do that, you can work yourself up to telling me what the hell is going on?"

She went home, had to have.

But she has no place to go, didn't Payton tell me that repeatedly?

With Beth's help with the pillows, I get half-way into a sitting position. Once situated, Beth pulls a chair over to sit next to me.

"Do you remember coming here?" she asks, caution obvious in her voice.

"I have no memory of anything after coming here."

Beth crosses her legs and rests an elbow on a knee.

"You have no clue how badly hurt you are?"

My head is killing me, the light from the lamp a glaring assault against my one uncovered sensitive eye. There's a burning sensation running along my left shoulder and my mouth tastes of blood, but I can think past that. All I can think about is Payton.

"I don't really care. I need to find her."

"Honey, you couldn't help anyone right now, and I'm betting by the time this conversation is over, you are going to be begging for some more pain meds."

Pain slices through my side, and I know she's right.

"You go first then, what happened after I got here?" I demand.

"Once you got in the bathroom and got your helmet off, you started vomiting and that went on a while. Once I saw your scalp laid open, I called a doctor. No way could I have handled that kind of damage."

Absently, I reach to touch my head. It is bandaged, but I can feel what I think might be thick stiches or staples along the top of my scalp to the back.

"Once the doctor got here and tried to figure out what to treat first, he ended up treating the gunshot wound."

I frown then regret it as pain slices through my eye.

"Gunshot wound?"

I wasn't shot, was I?

Reece was the only one with the gun, or so I thought.

"Yeah, Axel, you were shot. The bullet went clean through your side, creasing it, and Dr. Hanover got that bleeding under control and sewed up. Next was your head injuries. Whoever beat on you was trying to kill you."

"Yes, that was the desired end result initially," I say wryly.

"You're lucky to be alive. You have twelve staples in your head, seven stitches in your left eyebrow, your ear was nearly torn off, so there's thirty-seven stitches there. I already told you about the gunshot wound, your ribs are broken but I don't know how many and you most likely have had internal bleeding but not enough for Dr. Hanover to insist you go to a hospital. By the look of your torso, an elephant sat on you." She pauses long enough to look pissed, "Oh and your shoulder was dislocated too. Now, it's your turn."

"I thought it was my arm and it slipped back in place."

"That was probably the other one."

"Where is my laptop? Cell phone? The bag I had when I got here. Payton may have tried to call."

Beth stands, retrieves my back pack from a closet, then sits again unzipping and removing my laptop, setting it beside me.

"Reece disposed of the phone to be cautious. He has been by here but only to check on you. He said you couldn't be found and that," Beth curls her fingers in the air to show she's quoting, "by all things Holy I had to keep you here even if I had to chain you to the bed."

Not bothering to respond, I reach a shaking hand for the computer. After three tries to pick it up, I abandon it all together.

"Did you hear the part about your shoulder was separated from your body?"

Exhausted, I lay my head back against the headboard, cussing from the pain.

"We can check it after you tell me what the hell happened, Axel."

Clearing my throat, my whole body tightens and bucks in pain.

"Fuck that hurts," I grind my teeth as my eyes water. I can't move anything without crippling agony.

"Axel, tell me what's going on. If I'm aiding a criminal, I at least want to know why. The good doctor might do things for cash, but it's going to take a lot more than green to satisfy me. I want details, *all* of them."

Trying hard to calm my protesting muscles and steady my breathing, I have to swallow several times before speaking.

"We were just—"

"We?"

"Me and Payton. We were coming in from the beach. Travis had three guys with him. I told Payton to run but they caught her, or one of them did."

I try not to look at Beth, but I can still see in my periphery a look of horror morphing her otherwise pretty face into something hideous.

"They held me down while they took turns..." I trail off and squeeze my eyes shut. It has been years and years since I've cried, but there is no stopping the tears. Beth sits with a hand over her mouth, silently weeping. The quiet pain that passes between us is oddly comforting to the screaming of my busted-up body.

Is this real? If not, can I please fucking wake up now?

If I'm feeling like this, how does Payton feel?

And she is alone.

"I'm so sorry, Axel. Oh God, that poor girl."

Beth's voice seems to clear my head and anger takes over my emotions.

"Travis sat and watched, laughing even."

Swallowing back the misery, I finally find my voice sounding horse, unrecognizable, and there is a slight whistle if I breathe too deeply.

"By some miracle, Reece had heard Payton scream before they brought her back in and started. He shot the guy that was on Payton, killing him. I got her untied but she wanted to leave. She must've been in shock, kept asking me where my car keys were. I got distracted with the others, then I gutted Travis, literally fucking gutted him, Beth, stabbed another in the throat, and Reece shot the last one in the face."

"The four bodies," Beth breathes in disbelief.

"Yeah. Reece and I put a story together and I burned the place down. Payton left while I was—" My breath catches as my chest heaves with pain. Beth touches me lightly trying to soothe me. Strange, I'm now hyper aware of being touched since Payton has come into my life.

"Shhh, just rest, Axel. We'll find her."

Beth reaches for the water and places a pill at my mouth.

"I can't sleep anymore, Beth, she's out there hurt. Bad. I need to find her."

"You can't do anything until you're strong enough, so take this or it's a shot."

After trying to argue, I give in and take the pill falling asleep somewhere in the middle of Beth speaking rapidly on the phone. One minute, I can hear her talking of swelling, then the next, tunnel vision ending in a sea of black.

Payton screams, but I can't see her.

The sound causes my stomach to clench, and I bolt straight up in the bed, covered in sweat, breathing hard. I look around the room for a clock and find it on a desk in the corner. 4:15 a.m.

A note sits on my bedside table.

If you wake before I'm back, try to drink and eat something. Take your pain pills. You can't heal if you don't rest. – Beth.

Tossing the note back on the table, I try to get out of bed. There's no strength in my left arm and my legs tremble. After twice failing, I finally manage to stand. Every part of me hurts, but I don't want pain pills to keep me asleep. It's ten agonizing steps to the desk where my laptop is charging. Beth must've plugged it in as I slept. Slowly, I lower my body, which is heavy with drugs and pain, into the high-back chair. After typing my password, I log into the remote server connected with my phone's messages and emails, ignoring all except the unknown solitary text.

"I hope you're okay, but don't look for me. I should've listened. – P."

That was it.

Nothing else.

No word on where she is, just nothing.

But why would there be more? Why would I expect more?

My chest feels hollow and dead, exactly like someone has beaten any remaining life out of me and there's no wondering why, I did this to Payton so why would I expect any different?

I let it happen.

My actions with Travis caused him to seek revenge.

I brought all of this on.

Suddenly, I feel dirty, not in the grime of blood and sweat left on my skin, but truly dirty, unkempt, the remains of a well-used city dumpster, down to my worn-out soul, *dirty*. It's as if every loathsome thing I've ever done has risen from the ashes of my past and swallowed me whole, and now I can't stand being wrapped in my own flesh. I want to reach up and yank at my sutures until I'm peeled free of the filth.

Fighting off the undercurrent of the medication, I struggle to stand, and stumble like a zombie to the bathroom. Flipping the light on, I stare in disbelief. Before me, in the reflection, is a man I've never seen before. My chest and stomach are black and blue from collarbone to hip. There's no skin that's not discolored and as I slowly remove the bandage from the gunshot wound on my side, I pause to hiss at the sting. The stiches hold together pink, puffy tissue. It's stretched tight at the seams and I can feel where it slices through to the other side.

Dragging my eyes up, I wince. Both of my eyes are black but the left is swollen shut. The eyebrow is raw and sutured shut. I don't touch the stiches at my ear or staples in my scalp but lightly feel the dried, blood caked in my hair. I look grotesque and disfigured.

I look how I imagine Payton is feeling.

With my remaining strength, I step in the shower and wash the blood from my hair and body, wishing I could bleach the memories from my mind. After the water runs clean, I don't bother drying off or trying to put on clothes with one arm. Inch by agonizing inch, I limp, shuffle and drag myself back to bed, pausing only to drink milk from a jug left in the ice bucket. I don't give the food a glance as my stomach rolls at the thought of eating.

Just lie down and die.

But I have to know Payton is okay before I do that.

Giving into to fog that consumes me, I lie back and sink into oblivion.

Twenty - Six

-

Axel - four weeks later.

"Show me," I say without preamble when I open the hotel door for Reece.

Asshole could've used the card but I think he likes forcing me to get up if only to walk from the bed to the door.

"Hey Reece, how you been? I know you're working your ass off for me around *the fucking clock*, I might add." Reece gives me the stink eye and proceeds to walk inside my messy room, raising a foot, kicking clothes off the chair and literally flopping down in it.

"Show me damn it," I demand once I reach the bed and hold out a hand.

The arm it's attached to is thinner than it was a few weeks ago, just like the rest of me, but other than the lingering pain in my shoulder, I healed for the most part. At least, that's true on the outside. On the inside, I'm still just as raw, just as utterly fucked up from what happened. I make myself eat, knowing I'll never rest until I find Payton and at least know she's alive. I'm at peace with her never wanting to see me again, but I desperately want to see her.

"God damn it, Reece, let me see the fucking pictures." I shake my hand to show my impatience just in case my tone doesn't show it.

Reece lays a manila envelope in my hand and I waste no time in flipping through the contents. Skimming through the details, my heart picks up, hammering hard against my ribs. The report is from a private investigator I paid an arm and a leg for not two weeks prior, but when I see the accompanied photo, I know without a doubt I would've paid the man ten times the amount asked. It's a print from a surveillance camera, and as I take it in, my chest constricts so tightly, my breaths leaves my lungs in one long, relieved gust.

She's alive.

"Can't really say if it's her, can you?"

Ignoring Reece, I lay my fingertips to the photo, tracing the outline of her hair, her elegant neck and shoulders.

"It's her," I finally say, having to clear my throat.

"How can you tell?

"I just can, trust me, okay? *It's her.*" I glare at him, but Reece stares back with a pitying expression. "It's a couple of things," I say, deciding to keep the most obvious to myself. "Firstly, she signed in and used her name. She is the kid's only remaining relative that gives a shit about him."

"Oh yeah," Reece says dryly as if that should have be a given.

"Now I've seen this, I know where she is too, so that sleazy, back woods P.I. is worth every cent."

"How the fuck do you know where she is from that picture? This is the first time she's shown up and we only have a basic grainy screen shot with her face partially obscure by a ball cap."

It's true, that is all I have but Reece is missing a clue I caught onto the second I saw the picture. Closing the file and setting it on the table beside the bed, I stand to leave.

"Take me to see Sue," I say, throwing on a hoodie.

"Now? It's eleven o'clock at night. I know it's been a while but when it turns dark like this," Reece points over his shoulder dramatically, "it means people are in the bed. *Old* people like Sue, anyway."

"I don't care, she'll answer for me, and I've got to talk to her right now."

Not giving him the opportunity to argue, I just put my hood up and exit the room, heading out to the parking lot and Reece's Jeep. Technically, I'm not back from my tour of the Swiss Alps, or the police are under that impression. My alibi is tight as one of the girls I filmed with had long ago married a director who owns a sky cabin in Bern. There's no modern anything in the town, not even cars are allowed, so it is the perfect hiding place.

Reece is quiet, deep in his head while we drive. I can sense he has a million questions but I don't have the answer to any of them. Not all, anyway. I am ninety-nine percent sure I know where Payton is but I need to talk to Sue before I jump on my bike and head east.

As we pull up the narrow drive to the small, two-bedroom house the color of salmon and bark, I breathe a sigh of relief the living room light is still on.

"She's up at least," Reece mutters under his breath and I have to grin at how scared he is of Sue.

A rare mist of rain breezes by as we silently walk to the door. No less than three dogs begin barking at the adjacent house when I lightly knock. Looking around paranoid, I sigh in relief as the door is swung wide. Before I can get out a hello, Sue falls into my arms and to my horror, she begins sobbing.

Her tight, wavy black hair scrapes against my beard as I rest my chin on top of her head, and I look to Reece for help. In all the years I've known this woman, I'd never seen her cry, although I know her as an incredibly stern but kind soul. Sue is the one person I can count on to run the warehouse and see everything is done. But crying when she hasn't seen me for a few weeks? This isn't like her at all.

"Hey, Sue," I say a little bewildered.

"It's about damn time, I thought you was dead. Oh Jesus, I thought you was dead." Before I get my arms completely around the woman's small frame, she rears back and pulls me inside, shutting the door just as Reece steps over the threshold. "I could kill you just for what you put me through."

"I told you he was alive," Reece says from behind me but Sue is once again hugging me, paying him no attention. This time, I get the chance to hug her back.

"I'm sorry I haven't come sooner."

Sue steps away and blots her dark eyes with a wad of Kleenex she pulls from her pocket. Her petite size always makes clothes look big on her, but right now, her pale pink house coat makes her appear dwarf in size. The hem actually touches the floor.

Reece and I wait until she sits in her recliner before we take the couch.

"That one, "she points to Reece like he's the enemy, "only says you're alive and nothing else."

"I'm sorry, I couldn't really say anything else." Reece squirms uncomfortably in his seat as if waiting for the ten lashes the principal has promised at the end of the day for misbehaving.

Sue shakes her head and dismisses him with a wave of her hand.

"So, you've come now, and you're alive. That's all that matters."

Emotion for the woman stirs within my chest, and I clear my throat a little embarrassed.

"I came tonight because I wanted to see you," I pause to clear my throat once more. "But I also wanted to ask if Payton came here a few weeks ago, and before you tell me you don't tell other people's secrets, I'll remind you this is not an ordinary situation for me, Sue. I wouldn't be asking if it didn't mean everything to me."

Christ, it means everything to me.

Sue drops her eyes to the beige worn carpet and when she lifts them again, I can clearly see regret and pain in their depths.

"She came here," she says simply. A long moment passes while Sue takes a drink of water from a large glass on her side table. Once the water is seated back on its wooden coaster, I'm on the verge of screaming for answers, but Sue silences me with a shake of her head. That one small movement speaks of being worried, tired, and burdened.

"She said she found me by your car's GPS. Said her phone was lost so she couldn't call. With the way she looked, I never questioned her, just had her come in and gave her a robe to put on. She was crying and shaking like she was freezing to death, and she wasn't wearing nothing. I thought maybe she was filming and it was just shocking to her, but no. She kept saying you told her this would happen, just said it over and over as if beating up on herself inside." My stomach knots in anguish as Sue wipes her eyes. Reece and I stay perfectly still, perfectly quiet. "She pleaded with me not to tell anyone, especially you, Axel, where she was. I take in the occasional hurt girl off the streets, you know that, but this one was so damaged, I was afraid to leave her alone. She bled from her female parts and there was nasty welts on her arms like somebody had tied her up. When I told her she needed a doctor to look her over, she just said it's all on the outside and nothing was hurt on the inside. I knew that was a lie just looking in her eyes. That girl seen the devil and was messed up from it. I did the best I could, gave her clothes, let her shower and sleep. It was two days before she come out of the bedroom. She said something about moving the car out of a driveway. Next thing I know, a cab is dropping her off and she come back in and goes back to bed. She was as quiet as a church mouse but I got her to come out and eat with me by day five. She didn't say nothing else but she washed the dishes and went back to bed. And that was it. She made a couple of phone calls, and left while I was at the mission one day. There was a note on the counter saying thank you, she loved me and please don't tell Axel she was here. All in all, she was here about a week or a little more. I ain't seen hide nor hair of her since."

The strength keeping me sitting straight leaves my body, and I go limp against the cushions of the couch. So, this piece of the puzzle fit and after seeing the photo from earlier, the rest will too. I have no doubt I have finally found Payton.

Sue and I speak back and forth about the mission, about what I want to do from here. She isn't surprised when I tell her I'm selling my property and leaving the state. Reece, however, looks like I socked him in the jaw. He wastes no time pouncing as we leave Sue's with hugs and promises two hours later. We get as far as the end of the drive way before he speaks.

"You going to tell me where you're going? Or was you just going to take the fuck off and leave me sitting to process this shit all by myself?"

"Your mandatory leave is up soon."

"What the fucks that got to do with anything?" Anger raises in my friend's voice.

"I have disrupted your life enough, Reece, you've had to lie and cover up for me. I am eternally grateful but you should go find nurse Kallie and—"

"Fuck you, Axel, for real. I ain't done this shit for nothing, and you're a fucking asshole to think it's from anything other than brotherly love, so fuck you."

Dumbfounded, I sit silent for several moments, not able to think of a response. If I understand Reece, he is telling me he loves me, *like a brother*. That idea would have been moronic before Payton, but now, I want to grab Reece and bear hug him, would do that very thing if he wasn't driving this very second.

"Kallie's married, so you can drop that shit for good. Nothing ever come out of it except a break in the solitude and a revenge fuck against her old man." Reece shrugs. "She could've told me that's what I was prior to using me like a dildo."

Well, shit. I liked Nurse Kallie. Apparently, Reece did too because his tone is bitter.

"Fuck her," he adds and we both chuckle.

"Payton went to Texas A&M University," I say once the silence gets long.

By the glow of the dash lights, I see Reece's brow furrow.

"How the fuck you get that? Sue said she didn't know."

"The ball cap Payton is wearing in the photo is their logo. Payton and I were talking about her going there right before everything happened. I had already put her in contact with Kelly, and I'm willing to bet Payton followed through with the fall commitment knowing

346

she doesn't have anywhere else to go and nothing to lose."

Nothing to lose.

It stung a bit to say that, knowing I am among that *nothing*. Before I get too far down in my thinking, Reece punches my thigh in what I now recognize as a *brotherly* fashion.

"I've wanted to return to Liberty for a while, or close to it. No matter how old I get, that's still home to me, and the school isn't that far. I just want to make sure she's okay, you know?"

"What the fuck are we waiting for? Let's go get your girl, man. And shit, I fucking love those sorority girls, so I'll have plenty to occupy my time while we're looking."

Shaking my head, I snort in exasperation. As Reece lays out plans of leaving California with me, I turn my head to the dark unknown just beyond my window.

Will Payton run in terror if she sees me?

Will I only be the reminder of what happened to her?

The answers terrify me, and I make the decision to not let her know I'm looking for her.

I have to just see she's okay, then leave her to live her life, without me ruining it even more than I already have.

Twenty-Seven

-

Payton

"Come on, Payton, you need to go. All you do is study, and Christmas break starts tomorrow, so we can live it up this weekend."

"I am not going to a strip club with you, Adeline."

Adeline Stokes, my beautiful, vivacious roommate, drives me crazy. Every week, she thinks up something random to do. I can't blame her, I actually envy her, but it still drives me crazy.

"Have you made plans for break yet?"

I look up from my world religion text book and watch my roomie brush her gloriously long red hair. Adeline makes every guy beg for attention while inadvertently causing every female to feel ugly. Her pale skin and green eyes makes her look angelic. Add the double D's and a tiny waist, you have the Texas native nailed.

"Maybe." I shrug, not caring. "I don't know yet. I may just stay here and try and get ahead on everything."

Like the therapy session I skipped yesterday.

Finally breaking down and speaking with a rape counselor has helped with adjusting to life on my own and processing all that happened with Axel, but it has not healed me completely. It's been four months to the day of the attack, and I exist with very few friends and they're normally always in my study groups. I don't go out, I don't talk on the phone, I do nothing that Adeline feels is "normal." But every day I get up, get dressed, even brush my hair sometimes and go see my counselor then go to class.

Keeping my scholarship has been my biggest priority, and I have rewarded Kelly for her help with a 4.5 GPA. This has given me the Excellence in Academics class scholarship, adding to my Aggie award. This status has enabled me to live without having to work like many of my classmates. This just leads to me studying more, something that sends Adeline in a rant about "being young and in college." I just watch her ramble and smile, loving she's so full of life.

Was I ever like that?

I can't recall a time I wasn't worried about my mom or Ben, then consumed with taking care of my brother, followed by being homeless—which led me to Axel.

Does he think of me?

If he does, it has to be with an "I told you so" thought. How could he not? I was such a stupid girl.

"Good God, you're depressing. It's Christmas for Christ's sake."

I actually laugh out loud, something that has only begun happening the last couple of weeks.

Progress Payton, you are making progress.

I pat myself mentally on the back making note that I need to tell my counselor tomorrow.

"Seriously, though, you're going to be an old maid."

I give Adeline a smile then return to studying Buddhism.

"You are so lame, Payton."

"I know. I'm really sorry, but I'm happy staying in our room. It's quiet, and I like the quiet."

And it's safe.

Adeline huffs out a breath and rolls her eyes.

"Suit yourself. I'm meeting Caleb, so don't look for me tonight."

"Do I ever? We have class in an hour, I assume you're skipping?"

"Yeah." She pulls on a jacket and gives me the familiar, are you crazy look, then hugs me. "If you change your mind, text me? I'll come back for you, or you can always take my car."

I pat Adeline's back, loving her for being the complete opposite of me.

"I won't, but thanks for offering."

Adeline throws me one last sour look and leaves the room. I was skeptical at first about living the roommate life, but after meeting, and ultimately falling in love with, my now best friend, I can't imagine it without her.

After days of being at Sue's lost, hurt, confused and sick to my soul over what happened, I made the ultra-quick decision to go back to school, simply refusing to allow those sick fuckers to ruin what little life I had.

They almost won at one time though, didn't they?

It took me waking up with a pair of sewing sheers gripped in my hand before I realized I couldn't live another day like that. No matter how horrific the crime was, Ben still needed me. That same day, I called Kelly and set everything in motion. She had a plane ticket waiting and picked me up from the airport.

Reece had already told Sue that Axel was alive. He wouldn't give much more details than that, but my heart swelled with relief knowing he would pull through. And although I've confided in a rape counselor, I have never once brought up Axel or the everlasting impact he has made on me. I ache to see him, talk to him, but I can't. I ended up being everything he said I would be, right down to the dead girl on the gurney.

But I survived, I didn't go through with it.

Remnants of the attack remain, and I suppose they always will through my anxiety and nightmares. But still, I won't allow them to pull me under.

My only regret is Axel. I love him. Without a shadow of a doubt, I love him, but from day one, I have been a source of discomfort and regret in his life. That is something I will never get over. To cause someone pain knowing they have had very little happiness is the worst feeling I can imagine. That will continue to haunt me.

Always will.

A car horn blares outside, causing me to jump out of my thoughts. Stretching my neck to look outside the window, I see the same big black Dodge truck I've noticed a few times before. I get the impression whoever drives it must go to school here, and I probably even have classes with them. It's there often when I walk to class, other times, I'd see it parked outside the building.

The truck is huge and the windows so black, I could never glimpse the driver. At first, I was paranoid but after discussing this in therapy, I learned that was normal and how to see past my fears of unknown things. Otherwise, I would stay scared, robbing my mind of sanity a little each day.

Losing interest in the noises outside, I rise from my bed to get ready for class. Not bothering with makeup, I pull on my favorite Aggies hoodie, slick my hair back in a tight ponytail and thread it through my favorite A&M ball cap. It's cool and rainy, but the weather rarely gets under sixty so the hoodie is my constant source of warmth while walking campus.

Stuffing my books in my backpack, I sling it over my shoulder and head to class three blocks away. As I step out onto the damp street, I notice the Dodge truck again. It's parked on the side of the road with the other cars but, unlike to others, it's muddy like the driver takes a back road to get here.

The strange thing is, there aren't any back roads for some distance and there's certainly not any mud holes on campus. A niggling feeling begins creeping up my neck, and I recall all the previous times the truck always had fresh mud on it. Being from Mississippi, I can almost say I'm an expert of the mud variety, and this is why my eyes pick up on the oddity of the truck.

Slowly walking the sidewalk, I pause to take my phone out of my pocket, pretending to text someone but actually taking a picture of the license plate. The unease begins to sink to my bones that something is way off about the truck and its occupant. Now curious about seeing this truck as often as I do, I almost tiptoe closer. As inconspicuous as I can be, I walk and glance at the dark tinted driver's side window as I pass by. Nothing, I can't see anything but can feel there is definitely somebody inside watching me.

They're dead, they're all dead.

It was a crime of opportunity, no one is out to rape you, Payton.

Before total panic can take over, I pick up my pace. Though I have received the best possible counseling available at school to help me cope with not only being raped but what happened with my mother, I still shy away from strangers. I have come to terms with what has happened, having no other choice, but I don't even entertain the idea of dating. I can't for several reason but the main reason is my heart is in California.

I miss Axel so much, it physically hurts sometimes. I checked the news constantly when I first got here, hoping he wouldn't be in it, or the obituaries, or arrested. I finally stopped around Halloween, simply because I couldn't concentrate. I did try, but especially with Christmas being next week, Axel is all I can think about.

Behind me, the truck starts up. I stop long enough to watch it drive by, then quickly send the picture to my friend, Caleb, who happens to be madly in love with my roommate and who happens to work campus security. His dad is also a special victim's detective for the county, so if anyone can run the plate, Caleb can.

Can you or someone you know look up a license plate? Name and address maybe?

I send the text and photo, knowing Caleb will do just about anything to stay in good graces with Adeline, and favors he does for me will win him major points. My phone vibrates just as I take my seat in class.

Give me an hour.

Thx

Our instructor wastes no time diving into Buddhism. I relax and do my best to stay tuned in but my thoughts wander to Axel, as they so often do.

What would he do if I just showed up for Christmas?

Does he hate me and blame me for what happened?

If he doesn't, he should.

Could I even look at him, knowing he witnessed what was done to me?

It's a pipe dream anyway, because I have no clue where he went after his house burned down.

I could call Sue, I need to anyway, and I can casually work the Axel questions in the conversation.

No, I can't. I have to move on.

That's what all these month in therapy have been about, moving on and Axel is in the past.

But I left him so cruelly.

Squeezing my eyes shut, I try to push out the memory of Axel's face as I screamed for his car keys. It surfaces anyway, and all I can see is the blood and his beautiful body broken.

I did that to him.

He warned me about Travis, and I went to him anyway. I caused the trouble. I caused the rape. And I certainly caused Axel's pain.

My phone buzzes and I jump as if someone pinched me. A girl to my right snickers and I give her a smile before sliding open my message from Caleb. My heart flutters wildly as I read.

Axel Stein, thirty-year-old male, owns a horse farm down from Welch Parks.

I couldn't find his employment record but he was born in Liberty. Address coming.

"No fucking way," I say out loud, then clasp a hand over my mouth.

All eyes turn to me.

"Excuse me, emergency." I rise from my seat and nearly run out of the room.

Heart pumping hard, I sprint across campus and back to the road the Dodge was parked on. I scan the area desperately, running up and down the street but he's gone. My phone vibrates and I see an address.

Closing me eyes, I exhale.

Can it really, really be you, Axel?

I reply to the text.

Thank you Caleb. I owe you one, though I don't think you need any help with Adeline because you are the best!

Pressing send, I walk quickly back to my apartment to get Adeline's car keys. She did say she would not be using it and I could take it whenever. I send her a quick text to say I'm borrowing it to visit a friend then sprint to our room.

Friend.

I giggle as I change and prepare myself to see Axel, because come Hell or high water, I am going to see him. I'd fought and hid it long enough. If he hates me, then I can live with that and wouldn't blame him if he does, but I need to see him if only one last time.

Twenty-Eight

Axel

"That's a good girl." I pat my nine-year-old painted horse and her foot gently, then run my hand down the next hind leg to clean out the final hoof. "Let's get you cleaned up for the night, okay?"

Once that one is clear of debris, I switch from the tools to the brush and start rubbing her in circular motions.

"Admit it, Charlie, I'm learning and you're starting to like me."

The horse doesn't respond but I can tell by her body language, I'm growing on her. I finish the sweeping off her coat, then guide her inside the stall to eat. I take my time removing her guide and patting her big, brown spotted jaws.

If anyone would have asked me a year ago what I would be doing this Christmas, being the owner of a horse farm, actually *working* the horses, would not have even been in the top twenty possibilities.

When Reece and I agreed to find Payton together, I gave the realtor the go-ahead to start the bidding on my beach-front stretch. I found the farm the same week, and once I came to view the property, I was sold. I bought the place within the week, closing almost as quickly. The previous owners were retiring and moving to a senior living by the sea community down south. Somerville is not Liberty, but it is Texas. It is home. A place I had not been since I was fifteen.

After catching a glimpse of Payton and seeing she was truly alive, it took me all of a month to get settled, and though only four horses came with the farm, that was enough for me to learn with. I'm awkward but willing. The horses pick up on everything and seem to sense my eagerness to gain their trust.

"Trixie, get," I call for my Labrador to get out of the stall. I don't trust Charlie not to kick her just for spite.

Trixie sulks out, and I pat Charlie one last time before closing her stall door for the night. Pausing to switch on a dim light in the barn as I go, I know it's not so much for the horses, but it makes me feel better for some reason. I follow Trixie outside and secure the door behind me.

The perfect indigo blue night sky of dusk hypnotizes me, and just across the lake, a thin strip of orange stretches wide, casting sparkling colors off the lake water. It's my favorite part of the day. It's also the loneliest.

There are no sounds except that of nature and now the soft pattering of rain. I've lived next to the ebb and flow of the sea so long, I've forgot what a mockingbird sounds like. The first night I stayed in the house, I kept my widow open, listening to their songs. It was the sound of my childhood and it nearly brought me to tears.

Trixie runs to deliver her glow-in-the-dark tennis ball to me and I throw it, laughing as she barks. I take my time wandering back to the two-story, one-hundred-year-old farm house. With Reece back in California to retrieve more of his belongings, it seems extra empty tonight. Bleach white, the house glows against the setting sun light—a beacon to lost ships at sea. I love it and spend most of my time fixing things up.

Right now, I'm actually in the process of building a porch to stretch the length of the house. No idea why, I just want something to do with my time when I'm not taking care of the horses or waiting on the ten minutes I get to see Payton walk from class to her apartment, or from her apartment to class. I know it's a bit stalkerish, but it makes me feel good to know she is all right.

And she is all right.

She doesn't walk with her head down as much as last month, and she even smiled when another girl yelled something across the courtyard.

Payton is all right, or will be.

Stomping up my steps, I pause to throw Trixie the ball again before I kick off my boots by the door, letting them stay where they land. Just as I reach for the screen to open it, a movement in my periphery stops me dead. I jerk my head sideways, anticipating an attack, then slowly, reality takes hold, nearly bringing me to my knees.

Payton is standing with her arms crossed, looking like an angel, and leaning against my unpainted porch rail.

Golden blonde hair frames that angel face with the little nose and bow-shaped upper lip that is slightly bigger at the bottom.

And those golden hazel eyes glinting in the porch light. I don't look down because I've memorized the flair of her hips and curve of her breasts as she walks around her school.

Have I known beauty before this moment?

She doesn't look real to me and I stand still in shock, unable to move, convinced this is a dream, but then she speaks.

"Hey, cowboy," she whispers, almost sounding afraid.

My heart stutters, and finally, I smile. In two strides, I'm in front of her looking down into her hazel eyes which are damp with unshed tears. Silently, I drink her in, searching and waiting for the alarm to wake me up.

Be real.

After getting a whiff of that sweet smell of her shampoo, I know that it is real, because I can't smell her in my dreams.

"Can I hug you?" I croak out.

Payton's eyes dance back and forth between my own, uncertain. Finally, she uncrosses her arms and reaches to wrap them around my neck. I let mine snake around her back, picking her up off the railing while burying my face in her neck. Tears spring to my eyes, and I wonder when I became such a cry baby.

When this female stormed in my life, breaking away all barriers, leaving me raw and exposed.

My chest aches for the girl and I want to stay just like this forever. I do just that for a long time, letting whatever it is between us pulse as our bodies touch.

I've missed you.

I can't think of anything else but you, day or night.

I am so fucking proud of you.

There are so many things I want to say, yet I have no voice, no words. I'm afraid to let go, and I don't think I can handle her running away from me again. Shame sets in when I think of why she could have come tonight.

Maybe she figured out I was watching her and came to tell me to stop?

With great reluctance, I lower her down to stand, keeping my hands at her hips for a moment before she backs away. The movement cuts through me.

"How did you find me?" I ask the first thing my thoughts land on.

Payton tilts her head to the side and gives me a small smile.

"I could ask you the same thing." I don't respond and shove my hands in my pockets. "The mud on your truck stuck out to me this morning. I sent your plate number to a friend, and he gave me your name and address."

I arch an eyebrow, impressed.

"Clever girl," I say smiling. "Will you stay a while? I'll cook something."

She turns her face from the porch light so I can't see, and I fight the urge to grab her, throw her over my shoulder, and carry her into the house. But I don't, I won't force Payton to do anything. If she comes to me freely, not out of need for money or shelter like before, but actually comes to me for me, I will never let her go again. I know that to the marrow of my bones, but I will not guilt her or push her, accepting if she does not want to be with me, I will let her go.

Even though it will probably kill me this time.

Payton turns her face back to mine with a look of uncertainty.

"Sure, I'll stay awhile." She smiles sadly.

Holding the porch door open, letting Trixie led the way, we head to the kitchen, and I suddenly feel nervous, then embarrassed, remembering I'm filthy from the barn.

"If I take a shower, will you be here when I get out? I just put the horses up for the night and need to clean up."

Payton looks around my living room with its pale yellow walls, fire place, and aged wooden floors. It's bare of furniture other than a big brown leather couch I ordered last week.

"I'll be here, Axel," she assures me softly.

The sound of my name coming from her stirs my core with a sweet mix of desire and pain.

Unable to go just yet, I watch her touch the dark leather couch arm, then the mantle above the fireplace, then run her fingers across the old brick wall as if trying to memorize their every groove. I don't want to move, afraid she'll bolt the minute I get under the water, but I have to wash the smell of the horses off.

Taking one last look at her back, I finally turn to enter my bedroom, stripping out of my clothes as I walk, tossing them God knows where. Ten minutes later, I dress in my oldest jeans and a t-shirt, and find Payton sitting at the bar in my kitchen looking over some design ideas I had sketched out for a house I thought about building on the water someday. My gut twists at the realization that Payton is in my home.

She is really here.

"Are you hungry?" I ask, walking to my refrigerator.

I need something to do, keep me occupied.

"I don't want you to fuss, Axel, let's just make sandwiches or something."

Staring back at Payton, still shell-shocked to the core, I can't look away.

I want to squeeze her to my chest, kiss her lips.

Sensing my gaze, Payton looks at me sideways, her pretty lips rising on each side.

"Fine with me." I remove two beers, cheese, mayo, and sandwich meat from the fridge. I sit everything out on the kitchen island, taking the stool next to hers. It feels completely natural to open the beers and sit quietly with Payton as we put together our food. I'm not hungry but for something to do with my shaky hands, I roll cheese inside some ham and take a bite.

"Are you on a low carb diet or something?" Payton giggles, biting into her own three-inch thick sandwich.

"I'm just not that hungry, I guess." I shrug.

My gut is in knots, can't fucking eat if I tried.

She nods and looks at me closely, watching my face.

I want to hold her gaze, I want to hold her body.

"How's school going?" I ask as if the war inside my head is not raging.

"It's fine. I was able to transfer my class credits so I will actually earn my BA next year."

Holy shit, she is all right.

"That's great, Payton, and I'm not surprised."

She nervously picks at some of the bread crust and I drink my beer acting as if I don't notice.

"I meant to thank you for that, Axel. I'm not sure I ever did, but I am grateful."

I shake my head, frowning.

"All I did was call and ask for you. I wasn't the reason you got your scholarship, that's all you. You deserve it."

Plus the world, Payton, you deserve it all.

The corners of her mouth tilt up as she looks at me. She abandons the sandwich and reaches for her beer.

"I don't have anything to drink other than beer, I'm sorry."

"This is fine, thank you."

I rub my eyes, feeling tired now that the shock of Payton actually being in my home has worn down a little.

"Should we go to the living room and talk awhile?" she asks a little hesitantly.

Yes, talk. Anything to keep her here.

"Sure, if that's what you want."

Payton nods and walks to the living room. I follow, taking my time setting a log on the embers of the fire. It comes to life, sending sparks and new energy to the flames within. That now taken care of, I sit on the couch facing Payton. She turns, taking off her shoes and crossing her legs to face me.

Do I say all I'm feeling now that I have her full attention after months of heartache?

But why would I risk it? No way would she ever want me back.

"I suppose I owe you an explanation?" she says without preamble.

Frowning because this is so far off what I'm thinking, I shake my head.

"You don't owe me anything, Payton," I reply sadly, realizing she must have come here with some kind of guilt.

The light from the fire casts us both in a warm glow, and Payton literally takes my breath away. More than once, I have to remember to breathe.

"No, I do. I'll talk, then you talk, okay?"

"Okay." I take a drink of my beer while I wait for her to begin.

Her chest rises and falls in a deep, steading sigh.

"When everything happened, I had one of two choices. I could stay and be subjected to the intrusive rape tests and testimonies or I could get out of there and deal with it." She gives me a shy smile. "If you don't already know, I'm a deal-with-it kind of girl, Axel. The very fact that I came to you to learn the porn business in hopes to make enough money to gain custody of my brother should tell you that."

Stay quiet, just listen.

I just nod, not judging her decision to run, also knowing if I ask the things I want to know, she will most likely shut down and run from me now.

"You had just taken care of me, nursed my minor injuries. I couldn't subject you to further nursing. You have a life, and I didn't want to be cared for. I didn't want to be the *victim*."

"Payton—"

She shuts her eyes a long moment, holding up a hand to silence me.

"No, let me finish, okay? If I stop, I won't be able to start again."

I watch anguish and what I think is shame in her beautiful face.

"I knew if I got out of there, I would be okay. I wouldn't be okay if I stayed. When the—" she casts her eyes around looking for the right word, "when they held me down, all I could think was I should've listened to you. You warned me about Travis and his methods. You told me of his cruelty, and I created the whole situation. You were tortured and beaten because of what I'd done, because of my stupidity."

No. no. no. no.

She can't think this?

Sucking in a breath, I feel like I've just been punched in the chest, but I'm too afraid to interrupt.

"I went to Sue for help," she shrugs as if to say 'no big deal,'"I knew she would either help me or take me somewhere to heal simply basing that on the work she does for the unfortunate. Axel, I couldn't reach out to you. I knew you were hurt, but I also knew how strong you were, then Sue said Reece told her you were not coming to the mission and at least were alive." A single tear escapes the corner of her eye, and she quickly wipes it away. "When I got here, I saw a doctor, made sure I didn't have STD's or anything. After that, I started seeing a counselor, still do, to deal with everything. She has helped tremendously with not just what was done to me but my family, as well."

Anger rises so quickly, I have to make my breath even before speaking.

"Did she tell you to think what happened was somehow your fault?"

Payton's eyes snaps to mine with confusion at my harsh tone.

"No, she's tried to tell me otherwise, but let's face it, Axel, you didn't want me there to start with."

Wincing at those words, I run my fingers roughly through my still-damp hair in frustration.

It's true, I didn't want her there.

But she changed me, completely.

And she sounds like she's taking the blame?

Fuck no.

Payton is broken in every way, and the last person responsible is *Payton*. I sit up on the edge of the couch, placing my elbows on my knees trying to control my anger, my desperation. She gives me time to process everything, but only a second before she is asking me about my injuries. I have to drop my head as if my neck can no longer bear its weight.

"My physical injuries were nothing compared to the injuries to my insides," I answer, sounding dead and for the life of me, I can't speak of any of it. My tongue refuses to move. I finally unglue my jaw enough to say, "If it is all right with you, can we just sit quietly for a while?"

"Sure, Axel, of course," Payton whispers, and I sense she's hurting as she dabs the corners of her eyes.

Hold her, but don't scare her.

Will it repulse her if I reach out?

Desperately, I want to touch her, sooth her fears, but I'm afraid that would be too much. Struggling within, I rub my eyes and lean back against the couch.

Touch her, you fool, this is Payton.

Fuck it, I don't have anything to lose at this point.

As if approaching a caged animal, I cautiously reach out. She doesn't resist but watches me skeptically as I pull her down to lie beside me. Much like our first night in bed together, as if it were the most natural thing in the world to do, I snake both arms around her, one under her neck, the other her waist, cocooning her body with mine. She's tense as I bury my face in her hair.

Warm body against mine, Payton is here.

Heaven.

"It's just this Payton, just let me hold you, okay?"

After a moment of thought, she nods.

The fire crackles and pops as the minutes tick by, and little by little, Payton eases back into me. We lie silent, but a million different things pass between us. Before long, our breaths synchronize, and I have to close my eyes and just listen.

It's midnight before I realize she's fallen asleep. As gently as I can, I pull my arms away and place log in the fire, grab a blanket, and settle back in to watch her sleep by the firelight for hours, finally drifting off myself just before dawn.

Twenty-Nine

-

Axel

Someone knocking on my front door startles me awake. Sitting straight up, rubbing my right eye that refuses to open, I look around with the other.

"What the fuck?" I growl, standing.

Payton giggles and pulls the blanket over her head.

Christ, she stayed with me.

Another knock, this time more persistent.

Payton pulls the blanket down to raise her brows at me.

"Are you going to get that?"

And then she gives me another giggle as I stand and stare down at her. Hair messy, eyes drowsy with sleep, and a secret smile on her face cause funny tingles in my chest, and I chuckle as I reach to see who dares to knock so early in the morning.

Jerking the door open, I'm met with a big, hearty smile.

"Axel," Tom says in greeting.

"Thomas," I grumble and wave him inside the living room.

Payton sits up on the couch, her big hazel eyes watching us where we stand just inside the room.

"Tom, this is Payton, Payton, this is Tom. He runs a special needs program. They come twice a week to exercise the horses for therapy."

Tom walks toward Payton holding his hand out to shake. I watch for hesitation, but Payton smiles and shakes politely.

Better than I thought.

Tom eyes me curiously as he returns to where I stand by the door, clearly not inviting him in for coffee like usual.

"You're here early," I note, crossing my arms.

"Yes, well," Tom looks back at Payton, and I can almost see the wheels of curiosity turning in his head.

I can't introduce Payton as someone in my life because I don't have a label to put on her. Tom will just have to be curious.

"They're calling for heavy rain later, and I didn't think you'd mind if we started early and got out of here before it starts pouring buckets."

"That's fine. Go ahead. Let me know if you need anything."

"Sure thing, Axel, thanks. There's just three of us today, so we will leave Charlie to you, if that's okay?"

"That's fine." I nod again just wanting him to go already.

"Okay, I'll see you later then. Nice to meet you, Payton." Tom nods at her and backs out of the door.

I shut it then flop back down on the couch.

"Special needs?" Payton asks, her curiosity obviously peaked.

"Yeah," I turn to face her on the couch, feeling tired but oddly at peace. Payton looks sleepy, and her hair hangs in tangles. I grin adoringly at her. "You haven't changed much."

She smiles sadly, pulling the blanket up higher while bringing her knees to her chest.

"More than you think, most likely."

"That's probably true for both of us."

"So, Tom?" Payton prods.

"Yeah, Tom's a youth pastor for Calvary Baptist, he kind of came with the house since he was doing this prior to my buying the property. He also works with kids with various disabilities. Some are autistic, mentally, physically, and emotionally challenged, just different needs. He brings different kids out here a couple of times a week to tend to the horses, clean the stalls, or brush them down. He says it's therapeutic, and I can't argue with that because I certainly feel that way. I want to get more horses, maybe a couple of pot belly pigs for them, but that's the gist of it."

I shrug because it's the normal for me now, but Payton looks at me like I've grown a third eye.

"What?" I ask, feeling slightly self-conscious.

"You, Axel. Just you."

What me? What about me?

I'm clueless and wait for an explanation, but Payton stands before I can get one.

"Can I use your bathroom? And then, I need to head back. I didn't mean to crash on you like that."

I stand as well, feeling conflicted because I want her to stay, but can't really tell her to. If she wants to go, I won't stop her.

Maybe she has a boyfriend on campus and she wants to get back to him?

That idea makes me queasy.

"Down the hall. Second door on the left," I grumble, watching her walk away.

Why wouldn't she move on? Her time with me was a nightmare.

But I've never seen her with a guy, ever.

Maybe there is a chance.

When I can no longer see her, I shake off the thoughts I have no right to. I decide to clean the kitchen from last night, and in the process, fix oatmeal. I'm starving, and maybe I can entice Payton to stay with food.

My heartrate picks up and I smile a genuine smile when she joins me by the stove ten minutes later.

"Smells good."

"Don't get excited, it's just oatmeal but not your typical oatmeal. This is Axel's oatmeal."

"Axel's oatmeal?" she challenges, raising an eyebrow.

"Yes, and you need to prepare yourself, it's that good."

I'm rewarded with a smile and a glint of excitement in her eyes.

She's so fucking beautiful, just kiss her Axel, and just get it out of the way. All she can do is push you away, but what if...

When that thought forms, I push the pot off the stove so I don't burn the house down. Payton watches me closely as I slowly close the distance between us. Cautiously, because I'm scared shitless the move can go horribly wrong, I raise my hands, softly placing them on either side of her face.

"Is this okay?" I ask hoarsely.

She presses her lips together, then nods.

Her skin is warm and smooth, and all I can think of is rubbing against it like a cat. I can't judge anything by her eyes, but I can feel a tremor of fear or excitement run through her body as I move closer still. Slowly, very carefully, I lower my face, placing a delicate kiss on her lips. Her lips part, and I have to hide a grin when a soft moan escapes her mouth as we touch and I deepen the kiss further. Payton shocks me, sliding her tongue along my lips, meeting mine hungrily.

Ah God, nothing has changed.

Everything has changed.

I'm instantly on fire and wanting, drowning is lust, confusion, fear, so many things. Breaking the kiss before it goes too far, I wrap my arms around her and try to convey I will not push farther, even though I want nothing more.

Want her so fucking bad.

Her head fits perfectly under my chin, and I stroke her back in a soothing gesture, feeling her relax against me. Landing a kiss on her forehead, I pull back and return to the stove.

"I hope you're hungry, because I'm starving," I say, trying to control the raging need to mount her.

Payton hesitates for moment.

"Um, yeah but, I probably need to go, Axel."

Her words cut me but I act unaffected.

"Your Christmas break starts today, right?"

I stir the milk and began adding sugar and oats.

"Yes, but—"

"Then, why do want to get back?" I give her a quick glance and see the war raging behind her eyes. Taking her hand, I guide her to the stool at the island. "You have to eat, plus, I'm starving, so you might as well keep me company."

I return to my oatmeal, drizzle in honey, then I remove it from the heat, placing the pot on a trivet on the bar, then set two bowls in front of Payton.

"Strawberry, blueberry, apricot, or peach? And before you ask, they're all from the farm. *My* farm," I say proudly.

Now you're resulting to bragging for what? Impress her? What are you, a fucking peacock?

She looks confused but excited, glancing back and forth between me and the jams.

"It's cooling off, so you better hurry and pick one."

She smiles. "Strawberry, please."

"Mmm, good choice."

I spoon oatmeal in a bowl, retrieve the room-temperature strawberry jam and butter, adding heaping tablespoons of both, giving it three stirs, then handing it to Payton. Her eyes light up like a Christmas tree when she takes a bite.

"Oh, my God, Axel, this is amazing."

Giving her a wink and a smile, I stir my own and sit opposite her, just so I can watch her eat.

"Seriously, this is fantastic."

I shrug.

"The previous owners had me stay here while the sale was going through. The woman was very knowledgeable in the kitchen. I picked up a few things."

"So, that's what you have been doing since—"

I look up from my bowl, sensing the coldness sweep through me. She was on the verge of saying since *what*?

"No," I say in a rush. "I stayed a couple of months at the hotel, Beth's hotel."

She nods and I watch as a million questions cross her mind. I take my last bite of oatmeal, pour our coffee, and wait.

"How bad were you injured?"

"Pretty fucking bad," I nod and sip. "I can try and keep that from you, but I don't think it would do either of us any good to be dishonest."

"True," she says sadly. I wait for the next question. "So, you stayed at the hotel while you recovered?"

"Yes."

"I tried to find you before I left, just to make certain you were okay. I didn't know who to ask and Barbara hung up on me when I called her. Sue finally heard from Reece, so I didn't try anymore."

My face crinkles in disgust, but I'm too surprised Payton tried to find me at all to let my thoughts go to Barb.

Payton reaches for her coffee, deep in thought.

"But you sent me a message?"

"I did," she nods. "Once I made my mind up to leave, I didn't want to be found. How did you get by without medical help?"

Might as well get comfortable, we may be here a while.

I settle deeper in my seat, ready to answer her questions.

"Beth is known in the area. She called in a favor with a cardiologist friend. He didn't like it but he treated me anyway. She and Reece wanted to make certain it wasn't found out I was home that night, for the possible trouble I would be in and I knew you didn't want to be involved, so that's what we went with."

"Did you kill them?" she asks in a cold whisper.

Kill them? Slaughtered them but still, it wasn't enough.

My stomach unknots, realizing she didn't witness what I'd done to Travis or the other one.

"Two of them. Reece the other two."

And sometimes, I dream of doing it all over again.

"But, he's a police officer?"

"To Reece, we delivered the fairest kind of justice. Hell, half of it was his idea, and neither of us wanted to be dragged through endless questioning, plus, some might view what I did as murder."

It was murder, justifiably so.

And I'd do it again in a heartbeat.

Thankful Payton doesn't ask me to explain further, I sip coffee waiting on more questions.

"Did you buy this place once you knew I was here?"

That's an odd turn of the questioning.

"I actually put a bid on the property the day it was listed. That was before I knew you were here." I cock my head sideways trying to read her expression. "Would it make a difference either way? I am from Texas. I was coming back here either way."

Eventually, maybe.

Would I have ever done it had things not happened the way they did?

I'll never know but Payton was definitely the reason I had to get out of California.

Payton slowly shakes her head.

"How'd you figure it out? Find me, I mean."

I tap my coffee cup like Morse code and hope she doesn't get spooked from my tracking.

"I had to know if you were okay. I hired a private investigator. Reece was on leave, so he worked it as well. They found surveillance footage from your visit to Ben."

Bless that redneck P.I.. I'd probably still be looking, going out of my mind had it not been for him.

"Why did you look for me, though?"

Why?

How could I not?

I frown at the question, thinking it pretty clear, but maybe it's not as clear as I think it is.

"I wanted to make sure you were alive and okay," I say a little cautiously. Maybe Payton doesn't like the idea of my checking up on her. I suddenly feel like a fool. "I'm sorry, I shouldn't have—"

But my words are cut short by a knock at my door.

"It's open!" I call out over my shoulder, not hiding my annoyance at being interrupted.

Tom comes through the kitchen doorway, pausing to take in the scene of me and Payton as we sit at the bar drinking coffee.

"Cups are in the dishwasher." I nod, knowing he wants some.

"Oh, thanks, I don't want to impose."

"Don't you teach people not to lie? Of course you want to impose. I've never seen you any other way."

Tom chuckles as he retrieves a mug and pours coffee standing opposite me and Payton. I glance at her and she smiles shyly.

"It's wet and cold. Becky is helping the girls finish up. We went ahead and put winter blankets on the three, but Charlie is not being nice so you will have to handle her. We got her to walk around a bit though so she's softening. We will get her to love us soon."

"Good luck. She's just now letting me brush her without wanting to bite me. Trixie in the barn?"

"Yeah, she wasn't going to leave Becky since she brought the snacks."

"Trixie the dog?" Payton asks.

"She's a rescue I adopted a few weeks ago. Best friend I've ever had."

"So, Payton, Axel didn't really give me any clues to who you are. Are you from around here?"

I turn to watch her response, afraid this might annoy her. Instead, she crosses her long legs and seems to relax.

"I'm originally from Hancock, Mississippi. Axel and I knew each other briefly before moving here and I just found out we don't live far from one another." She shrugs. "It's a small world."

I smile in appreciation that she did not say to how we knew each other briefly. I don't want my past known here.

"Where do you live now?" Tom asks, stirring sugar in his coffee.

"I'm a student at A&M. I live in the apartments there, just off campus."

"Oh, nice. What are you studying?"

"Agriculture, communication, and a minor in psychology."

Holy shit!

"Wow, that's pretty impressive stuff."

"I didn't realize what I wanted until I got here. There so much to learn and do with that field of study. It's fascinating." Payton smiles sweetly and I feel like my heart will burst at the sight.

"Tom, I have a question about what you do," Payton says, shifting the focus off herself.

"Give it to me. I'll do my best."

"I have a sixteen-year-old brother that has traumatic brain injury. His mental state is that of a four or five-year-old. His only physical disabilities are a weak left side. Does what you do help kids like my brother?"

Holding my breath, I hide my shock at Payton bringing her brother up in polite conversation.

Maybe counseling really does help.

"Oh, sure. We help a variety of children and young adults with all kinds of needs, some older adults, too. Axel here has been very generous and patient letting us continue to come here. It gives the kids something to look forward to, and it is healing. Some of the kids have suffered horrible abuse because of their disabilities. The horses don't care if they talk funny or look different. The horses only care about the way you make them feel, and the kids want to love and be loved. It's an excellent way for them to just be themselves."

Payton turns to look at me, and I can see the raw emotions for Ben in her beautiful eyes. I reach to lightly squeeze her hand but don't hold it long for fear of making her uncomfortable.

We sit and talk a while longer then walk out to the barn as everyone gets ready to leave. I introduce Becky, Tom's assistant and suspected girlfriend, and she, in turn, introduces the kids. Payton watches them in wonder while they clean up and leave with thank yous and goodbyes. One little girl I have grown to adore even hugs Payton, giving her a toothy grin but not saying a word as she piles inside the van with the others.

"That's Marigold, she was a drug baby and has never spoke a word. She will never be more than nine or ten mentally but she's thriving the best she can. She loves

Trixie but not the horses as much," I explain to Payton when they drive away. The silence grows heavy. "Want to meet Charlie?"

"Sure."

We walk inside the stable and I pet Charlie through her stall window, trying to get her to trust me and get her winter blanket on before the cold and rain comes.

"The others are more sociable, but Charlie is a bit of a challenge. I've ridden her but she still wants to buck sometimes."

Payton inches forward, and I step back.

"Hi Charlie," Payton whispers, raising her hand to pet her. Charlie stills and watches Payton intently. "You're beautiful, Charlie."

Payton pats Charlie's jaw, then shoulder.

"She seems to like you," I say more to Charlie than Payton.

Carefully, I open the stall door. As delicately as I can, I wrap the winter coat around Charlie's neck and body, securing it as she and Payton share a whispered conversation. Charlie never moves. She just tosses her tail, and stares at Payton as she talks.

"That was much easier than usual," I say, a little amazed.

"I like her, too." She smiles at my horse.

The heavens open up, and it pours just as we finish up in the stable. At the open doorway, I look to the hillside and see black clouds rolling in on us.

"We will need to make a run for it. It'll suck but the fire is warm at least," I say loudly over the rain and thunder.

"Axel," Payton places a hand on my arm and I turn to look down in her eyes. They're sorrowful and my heart sinks, "I need to go. I'm glad everything is working out for you. I'm happy for you, but I need to go."

She's running, let her go.

No, I can't...not yet.

"You don't have to go, Payton."

She looks down at the dirt. Rain pours inches from where we stand, causing a damp chill in the air. I try and think of something to keep her here longer, maybe even stay another night but when she looks back up, I see determination set in her delicate features.

Don't say it, Payton, please don't say it.

"You said this was not some love story, you said it would not have a happy ending, no white knights or glass slippers." She smiles sadly but she's not weepy, just resolved. "If I stayed, it would just complicate things further. You can't look at me without seeing the victim wanting to somehow save me either from my past, or current self. I'm not a victim, Axel, and there's no point in you trying to make the reality of what happened easier to live with. It happened, and I've moved on. It took three men and thirty minutes to try and destroy me, but they failed. If anything, I'm stronger."

She steps toward me, stands on her toes and kisses me softly, pulling away before I can return it.

"You're awesome, and I will never forget you, Axel."

She gives me one last smile, one last pat on the chest, and then turns to walk away. I just stand transfixed, like an idiot, and watch her go, taking all the busted pieces of my heart with her.

Thirty

-

Payton

Keep walking, Payton, don't turn around. Don't look back.

The rain is relentless and my clothes are soaked in seconds as I make my way to Adeline's car.

If I turn around, I'll end up in bed with him and the complicated life would begin again with confused feelings and heartbreak.

It isn't going to end anywhere good. Axel never wanted me in his life and I made him keep me there for weeks. I will *not* do that again.

I reach to open the car door and have to fight the sudden wave of nausea as I choke out a strangled sob, nearly doubling over by the loss I feel.

"I was wrong," Axel yells out.

My eyes widen, and I turn to see him sprinting toward me.

"I was wrong, Payton, so fucking wrong, and it makes me sick inside!"

Axel's hair drips with rain and his breath fogs in the cold air. We're both soaked and breathing hard.

Oh God, his dark blazing eyes, his mouth...No! Focus!

"You were not wrong," I say, then question what I'm referring to exactly.

"Yes, I was. I told you this wasn't a love story only because I had no fucking idea what that was. I was wrong about everything, but I know now everything I have done since the day I picked you up from LAX was because I loved you, Payton."

He steps so close, our shirts touch and I can feel his body heat. My knees go weak, but I know Axel is just confused, he has to be.

He has to be.

Did he say loved?

"Axel, you're confused. With everything that happened—" I choke on my words.

"Don't tell me how I fucking feel, Payton. I've never been clearer about anything in my life. If wanting you, every morning and every night, means I love you, then *I love you*. I want your clothes strung all over my room and your pretty smelling shampoo in my shower. I want fucking chick flick nights and everything in between because without a doubt, *I love you*. I want you in my bed, I want a future with you. I love Payton. It may not be enough to become bigger than all the other shit for you, but to me? It's everything."

His eyes search mine.

For what?

My tears mix with rain to blur my vision, and all I can do it stare at Axel's lips while he speaks.

"I should've said that months ago, but I didn't recognize it. I see it now. Tell me you see it, too." Axel doesn't reach for me, but I can sense he's on the verge.

If he touches me, I will crumble.

I drop my head—unable to unwilling to admit my weakness—and I shake it. Axel leans into my body, placing a hand on my face, forcing me to look at him.

"Say you don't see or feel it and I'll never bother you again."

I search his dark eyes through the rain, seeing the feral animal I know I love, but how can I subject him to a life of pity for me?

Too much has happened.

"Stop thinking and just act on it. Whatever has happened, we can get through it together, Payton, but you have got to stop fucking thinking."

He steps closer and a second later, presses his mouth to mine. After a moment he pulls away.

"I love you, now love me back, Payton."

Pressing his warm lips to mine, I finally I stop thinking.

Parting my lips in response, I taste the cold rain and *Axel*. His hands circle me, I respond in kind, placing my arms around his neck, grabbing fistfuls of hair. He picks me up, carrying me just like he did on the beach months ago in the Rhett and Scarlett fashion, never taking his lips off mine. He takes me through the rain and inside the house, kicking the door shut behind him.

Smells so good, tastes so good.

My body is on fire even though I'm soaking wet.

We're in his room in seconds and as soon I'm on the bed, Axel begins pulling off my clothes, peeling my wet blue jeans from my body. I rise up and kiss his stomach as he pulls his shirt off.

He goes absolutely still and looks down at me as if realizing what's happening.

"I love you, and I want to worship you, Payton. So fucking hard, you will never doubt it." He touches my temple with his fingertips, then pushes my wet hair off of my forehead. "Do you want this? We don't have—"

Oh, hell no.

I rise on my knees on top of the bed and end his words with my lips on his. Now, I'm the feral animal, pulling at his jeans to get them down in a frenzied rush.

"Don't talk anymore, Axel, just tell me with your hands," I kiss, "your mouth," then I reach between us, gripping him, "your body."

Axel groans and places an arm around my back as we sink back to the bed. He pulls back to look in my eyes. He's so beautiful, wet, and gentle as he kisses and nips at my neck and ears.

I place my hands on his face, and our eyes meet. Instantly, he stills. Raising my hips to meet his, holding his gaze, he slowly, agonizingly slowly, pushes into me. Tears threaten to spill, and I moan with every inch, every thrust.

His warm mouth encircles my hard nipples, and he sucks, drawing out my cries. Pleasure surges through my body, taking me closer and closer to the edge of sanity. Axel thrusts deep, and I wrap my arms around his neck to hold on for dear life. He raises us up, shifting us both until I'm straddling him, catching me off guard.

The position is so deeply intimate, I have a hard time breathing.

His arms are so strong around me, and his kisses so hungry, I could weep from them.

My body is entangled in his as he holds all of my weight, forcing me to trust he will not hurt or drop me. My breathing turns ragged and crazed, but I hold on as he lifts up and lowers me down, reaching deeper.

"Oh, my God," I breath as Axel places delicious bites along my collarbone. "I love you, Axel. I always have."

And to my horror, I realize I'm crying.

Axel instantly goes still and raises his head to search my eyes. He says nothing, just places his rough hands on my cheeks and rubs gently at my watery eyes. Softly, he lowers me back down to the mattress, and begins deep, slow, burning thrusts that are so consuming, I don't know where he ends and I begin.

He's making love to me.

It's a concept so foreign, I can't wrap my head around it. The slow build of release is agonizing and delicious all at once. The muscles in Axel's back contract and I can sense him nearing orgasm with me, yet he never looks away, only holds my stare as if he's trying to ground me, keep me focused only on the intensity of his gaze.

My breath catches on a particular twist of his hips, and in the next moment, it's pure, bone-shattering pleasure. Sinking my nails in deep at the thick muscles of his ass, Axel quickens the pace, resting his face to mine just as he begins his own release.

"Fuck yes, I fucking love you, Payton."

I love him; he loves me.

Although we are not a traditional love story, we are a story indeed.

Epilogue

-

Axel

"Come here, pay attention." I place my hand on the back of Ben's neck in a brotherly embrace. His eyes dance with excitement. "What is your job today?"

"Walk Payton," he says proudly as his chubby cheeks puff bigger in a smile.

"Yes, walk Payton." I nod and kiss his forehead. "Just walk her to me and then sit down, okay?"

"Okay." He smiles his lopsided smile, the left side not quite as strong as the right.

Ben has now lived with us for four months. He's very much like a toddler, having only short term memory and limited vocabulary, but he's thriving now that he's with Payton full-time and I would like to think because of me, as well. His brain damage has not killed off the gentle nature I see in his sister, as well as other personality traits I'm quickly learning, like their tendency to want the feel everything they come in contact with.

Ben is easy to get along with, eager to help with the horses, and plays endlessly with Trixie, chasing the ducks into the lake. He's a big, goofy kid who will always have a man's body but a child's curious mind, and I love him dearly.

Just like a song on repeat, I remind him every few minutes of his job as we dress in our tuxedoes. Reaching to tie his bow, I watch the interest in his eyes as he looks at me in worshipful fashion.

"Love you, Axel." The proclamation makes my heart swell.

"Love you too, buddy. Now, what's your job today, Ben?"

"Walk Payton."

"Good, it's the most important job, so do your best." He smiles.

"Ben walks Payton good?"

"Yes. Do you know why Ben walks Payton?"

I straighten his shirt, correcting a couple of mismatched buttons.

"Payton loves Axel."

"Yes and we are getting married, remember?"

"Payton marries Axel. Axel is my brother."

"Good." I choke because It never gets old.

"It's time," Tom announces, sticking his head just inside my bedroom.

"Coming." I give Ben one more kiss on the forehead. "Ben walks Payton."

"Most important."

"Yes, most important," I repeat. "Go get Payton, I will be outside."

Ben turns to go find his sister. I look once more in the mirror and notice my hands shaking. I snort and consider what has transpired in my life this past year. It's crazy, but I'm convinced it's all for a reason. Before, I was on a terrible roller coaster ride, then Payton came in and saved me. She would argue that it was I who saved her, but she doesn't get that I was no white knight. We decided to be each other's hero and make the bond more permanent, interlocking our names forever.

I knew long ago I would one day resume my given name of Stein even if it's my drunken father's name, but it's also my war veteran grandfather's name. I am Axel Stein, and even though I wasn't for a while, I never really abandoned that identity. It was taken from me by my parents who put me in an impossible position.

Shaking off the memories, I make my way out to the lake and to where Tom stands, Bible in hand, waiting to marry me to my love.

"You nervous?" Reece leans to whisper as I take my place beside him.

"Hell yes," I whisper back, smiling at my best man.

The small crowd that sits as witnesses consists of a few friends we have collected along the way. Reece and Beth along with Sue and Lenny, were the only ones from my past life present today. Beth winks at me as her husband grins wickedly. They've never seen me in anything but jeans and I'm oddly self-conscious.

The glow of twilight across the lake and the dim lights strung all around have turned my back yard into a fairytale garden. Music begins to play, erasing all thoughts except the one involving Payton. I watch, anticipating her wedding gown, wondering what she chose for the occasion and hope like hell Ben remembers his job.

Adeline steps from the house, bare foot in a simple pale blue lace dress—her red hair darker in the sunset, but no less beautiful. Reece grumbles something under his breath about 'bitches' that I'm suspicious has something to do with their growing disdain for one another. Payton's maid of honor takes her place opposite Reece, purposely looking anywhere but at him and all I can do is wonder what the hell ever went wrong there.

The wedding march begins, and I straighten instantly. I have to clear my throat, feeling like my heart is about to beat clean out of my chest as finally Payton descends the porch steps, escorted by a smiling Ben.

The dress is lace, like Adeline's, but white, with far more detail and fitted to Payton's size. The long train reminds me of what a Spanish bride wears and my eyes grow misty as I look to her swollen belly, smiling at the thought of becoming a husband and a father all in the same year.

A baby was the furthest thing from our minds. Payton was terrified to tell me of her suspicions only weeks after our reuniting.

"What are you so nervous about?" I asked as we showered together.

She kept chewing on her bottom lip and zoning out of our conversations.

"I have something to tell you, and I'm not sure how you're going to take it."

I pushed my head under the water, rinsing, trying to give the impression I was not concerned but actually, I was terrified that maybe she was over me, had changed her mind along with many random thoughts that ended with her leaving me and wanting to move back to her apartment.

"Let's hear it, then," I said, switching places to let her rinse.

I kept my hands on her hips and watched her close her eyes under the stream.

"I didn't keep doing the shots after leaving California."

Okay, that wasn't what I expected. I frowned, not catching on. She raised her head from the water to look at me.

"My birth control? I didn't keep it up."

My frown deepened. "Okay," I said slowly...still the idiot.

Payton reached to turn the water off and grabbed a towel. I watched her, my mind racing as I grabbed my own towel and stood beside her.

"You were afraid to tell me you changed your birth control method?"

She paused to look at me while in the middle of rubbing my hair.

"What?" I asked, truly bewildered.

"I didn't change birth control, Axel. I haven't been on birth control since."

I let the towel fall around my neck and held each side. "Okay?"

I was an idiot who understood nothing. We were both so new at an actual relationship, neither of us really considered consequences when we began again. Payton wrapped her towel around her body and looked up at me with a look of pity.

"What happens when you don't use birth control, Axel?"

She turned to walk to our bedroom, and I stood buck naked, trying to figure out what the hell was going on.

My knowledge on birth control was so limited to the girls I'd been with in the past, and no way in hell I was thinking of that too long.

Frowning deeper, understanding dawned.

"Christ! Payton?" I said in shock, walking into the bedroom. "We're having a baby?"

Payton stood with her arms crossed, looking worried.

"It appears so."

"We're having a baby, me and you?" My lips felt numb.

She slowly nodded her head as if anticipating my passing out. Instead, I picked her up and kissed her hard.

"We are really having a baby, for sure? You're not fucking with me, are you?"

"Yes, I'm sure, but Axel, you're happy about this?" she asked, that look of worry returning to her face.

"That I'm going to be a parent? I'm scared shitless, but having a baby with you? I couldn't be happier. Are you fucking kidding me? Anything that ties me deeper to you, I'm going to want."

The memory dies away as Payton is feet from me now, and I have to resist reaching to grab her just to hurry things up.

"Who giveth this bride away?" Tom says, looking at Ben's smiling face.

"Me."

Payton reaches to hug and kiss him before he takes his seat next to Beth. I wink and mouth *good job*. He beams back at me proudly.

Payton and I stand before God, and our friends, reciting words as old as time, swearing to be the one and only one to each other. I place a platinum ring of diamonds on her swelling fingers, grinning at her condition. She places a band on mine, fighting tears and a shaking voice.

Can life get any better?

Yeah, a yard full of kids is the aim.

As we say *I do* in unison, I'm swept away with emotions at just how we got here. Neither of us planned our lives and the tragedies, but we both decided what makes us happy and chose a different path with each other and that's what matters most.

We will not allow the negative to sweep us under. Together, we will fight to become anything other than our pasts.

No, we are not a traditional love story, but we are a story indeed.

The End

M.C. Webb

About The author

M.C. Webb is a contemporary author of dark romance. First published in high school, the attention shy writer avoided publication for many years, opting to limit her work locally. Her now widely released bibliography includes the suspenseful "The Black Trilogy" a touch of second chance love in "Second String." Born in Chatsworth Georgia, M.C. spent most of her childhood in the Deep South until landing in the place she calls home today, Knoxville Tennessee. She loves interacting with readers and is a huge supporter of film, football, hockey and the Blues.

Contact information

www.mcwebb.net

Facebook_authormcwebb

Email_authormcwebb@gmail.com